Cruise through History

ITINERARY 03

EASTERN MEDITERRANEAN

Greek Islands, Turkey & the Eastern Mediterranean

ISBN: 978-1-942153-10-8 *(Paperback)*
ISBN: 978-1-942153-11-5 *(ePub)*

TABLE OF CONTENTS

PREFACE

Cruise through History© is a collection of short stories grouped by the sequence of many popular cruise itineraries, rather than by country, or period of history. As the stories move from port to port, they randomly move through time. The stories are all true. They introduce the traveler to the history and culture of a port through the story of a long-ago, or not so long-ago, resident, whose exploits left a castle, a palace, or a lovely site that can be explored on a cruise ship shore excursion.

The host character for each port stop is chosen for their inspiring actions and the visible culture left behind. Some names will be familiar, presented in these volumes with depth to their personality. Other characters may become like new friends, too long unrecognized. Either way, the stories offer a new twist to the school-age history of place, drawn together to put travels in a fascinating context for the short-term visitor.

No apology is made for the choice of subjects. They have been chosen in an arbitrary manner on the whim of the author, accumulated from past travels, for your enjoyment. The desire is that the reader will share the fun. No attempt is made to be politically correct, or give a chamber of commerce gloss to the stories evident in the remnants of the past. Knowledge of history can teach us a great deal about ourselves, and the human condition, but only if it is honest and fairly told. No doubt it is the quest for "real" that draws adults to travel as often and for as long as they are able.

The desire to seek knowledge, about distant places and times, fuels international tourism. Many travelers who found history in school to be dull, later in life seek to fill in the gaps in their knowledge, with personal experience. This is the opportunity for the events of one's life to give rich meaning to the human condition and to enjoy stories of fact for which fiction is no rival.

Praise is due to the many historians and other scholars who have delved deeply into source data to ponder the minute details of history for pedagogical pursuits. Such information has been mined here, with attribution, for the lively details, which will heighten the traveler's enjoyment of the past. History is a public good. The more it is found to be enjoyable, the more it will be valued.

Apology is due to those who hoped to foster disciplined scholarship in the author. This is reading for an out-of-the classroom experience. Footnotes are inserted to give due credit to the scholars who have provided valuable information and to remind the reader that these stories are true. The presence of source notes is not to feign an academic appearance. Editorial sidebars and fun bits are in the footnotes.

When there are gaps in the facts, or mysteries remain, they are not supplemented by fiction. Rather, an effort is made to look at the known as a guide to the unknown. The reader can draw their own conclusions, daydream through the gaps, and enjoy the reason that so much popular fiction and movies are drawn from historical facts.

These stories are offered to give historical context to the sites often visited as cruise destinations. In these stories, meet the characters who walked the same streets centuries in the past. Go beyond the castle ruins to envision the people who built them and lived there.

The itineraries in this series have stories at each port that seek to inspire cruise travelers to rise out of their deck chairs and investigate a destination with honesty and irreverence, or the potential traveler to rise from the sofa and embark on a Cruise through History. There is no stigma of a school assignment. Earn an "E" for enjoyment.

Itineraries in the Cruise through History series available and forthcoming-

I. **London to Rome - Coasts of France, Iberia, and Northern Italy - September 2014.**

II. **Rome to Venice – Adriatic, with Sicily, Sardinia, Corsica – November 2014**

III. **Eastern Mediterranean – Greece, Turkey, Cyprus & Israel – December 2019**

Find all the story books through cruisethroughhistory.com.

ACKNOWLEDGEMENTS

Writing travel stories began as therapy from the world of Washington, D.C. Thanks are due to those at Utah State University, Logan, and to the several cruise lines that have given me the opportunity to share stories with their guests and students. Much appreciated are those who helped to produce the series, including:

Digby and Rose, publisher, art director, and publicist; Heather Richmond, editor; and Lisa Lynn Aispuro research assistance. Diana Verkamp, CTH logo. Credit for art of Rhodes Knights is Kirsten Burridge.

These stories would not be possible without the treasure trove of material in libraries and used bookshops. In this increasingly paperless world, bookstores and libraries provide solace and an opportunity to revive our humanity.

Much appreciation is also due to those who apply their skill to preservation and protection of heritage resources in the United States and around the world. The greatest thanks go to my husband, Guy Rouse, who has lugged my camera equipment all over the world for thirty years.

This volume is dedicated to my travel buddies, John and Kathleen Waszolek, who traversed the three continents of the Eastern Mediterranean with us, as we explored Egypt, to the Holy Land and Greek Islands over more years than any of us wish to admit. Since then, on repeat travels to the Eastern Mediterranean, we have met so many wonderful people, too numerous to mention. So many good times, so many photos, have all become the fabric of memory and the inspiration for stories.

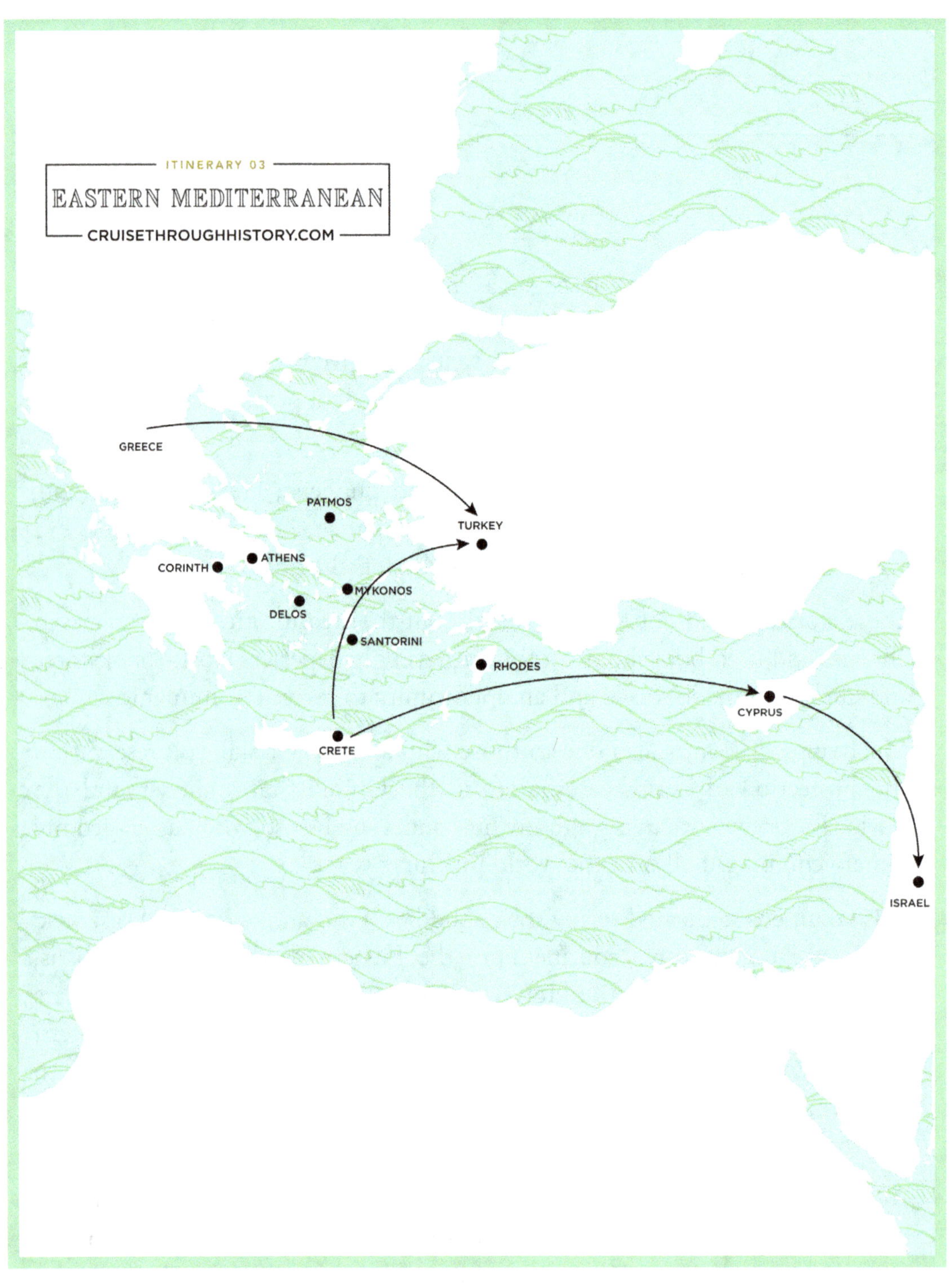
ITINERARY 03
EASTERN MEDITERRANEAN
CRUISETHROUGHHISTORY.COM
GREECE
PATMOS
TURKEY
CORINTH
ATHENS
MYKONOS
DELOS
SANTORINI
RHODES
CYPRUS
CRETE
ISRAEL

Cruise Through History
ITINERARY III

Timeline | cruisethroughhistory.com

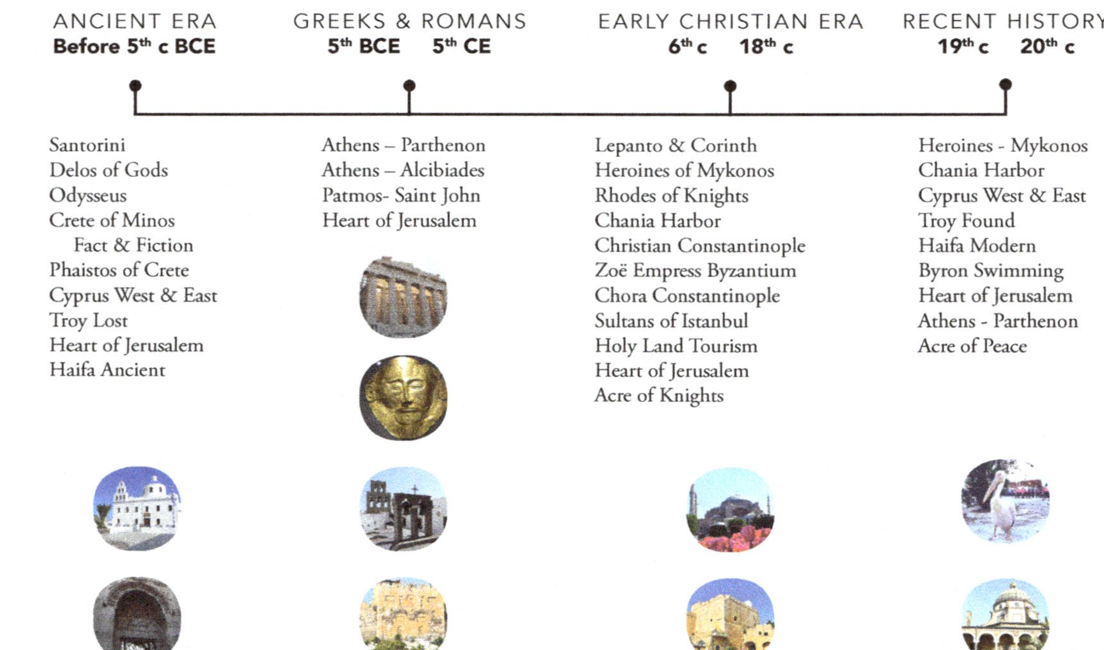

ANCIENT ERA Before 5th c BCE	GREEKS & ROMANS 5th BCE 5th CE	EARLY CHRISTIAN ERA 6th c 18th c	RECENT HISTORY 19th c 20th c
Santorini	Athens – Parthenon	Lepanto & Corinth	Heroines - Mykonos
Delos of Gods	Athens – Alcibiades	Heroines of Mykonos	Chania Harbor
Odysseus	Patmos- Saint John	Rhodes of Knights	Cyprus West & East
Crete of Minos	Heart of Jerusalem	Chania Harbor	Troy Found
Fact & Fiction		Christian Constantinople	Haifa Modern
Phaistos of Crete		Zoë Empress Byzantium	Byron Swimming
Cyprus West & East		Chora Constantinople	Heart of Jerusalem
Troy Lost		Sultans of Istanbul	Athens - Parthenon
Heart of Jerusalem		Holy Land Tourism	Acre of Peace
Haifa Ancient		Heart of Jerusalem	
		Acre of Knights	

INTRODUCTION
LORDS OF THE LAKE

To people of the Eastern Mediterranean from ancient times the great sea was at the center of their world. Homer, the eighth century poet, wrote of Odysseus sailing home from the Trojan War over the *wine dark sea* as the sea became part of the story as much as the hero or the sirens he met along the way. The silk road from the Far East came overland to shores of the Mediterranean. People of Santorini, a speck of an island, had ports from which people sailed north to Greece or south to Egypt. The tiny island was at the center of trade, in the center of the sea, that was the center of their world.

There were no armies on the island of Santorini. People enjoyed commerce, not war. Other civilizations were intent on control of commerce. To do so, they controlled the sea as their lake.

Greeks were early to recognize the advantages of being settled along a peninsula and across a bevy of islands. Trade and communication flowed throughout an empire made possible by the sea. The Greek Empire was so successful that people sailed across the Hellespont into the Black Sea to find farmland from which grain could be shipped home to feed hungry Athenians. Troy, Miletus and Ephesus were made wealthy as trade stations between caravans coming from the east and ships from the west across the Mediterranean Sea. Troy was demolished in 1250 BCE in a war that was either fought to retrieve Helen, the wife of a Spartan general, or to command trade.

Conquest of land around the Mediterranean required more than an army. A navy was required. The great Persian general Xerxes discovered this when he attempted to conquer Greece in 480 BCE, before the current era. Xerxes demolished the shrine of Greeks upon the Parthenon, before he launched his ships. In the Battle of Salamis, the Greeks proved their mastery of the sea. Pericles rebuilt the Parthenon on top the Acropolis, which stood until other aspiring Lords of the Lake, Venetians, Ottomans and British sailors took command of the waterway.

Rome supplanted Athens as the capital of the Eastern Mediterranean, when Roman mastery of rowed galleys made their empire Lords of the Lake. It is ironic that Romans controlled Jerusalem and ordered the crucifixion of Christ, then became a center of the Christian world, home of the pope. The first Christian and Roman emperor, Constantine, established Constantinople, forming the points of the Christian world from his city to Jerusalem and Rome.

In the world of the Mediterranean Sea, city-states with mastery of commerce had power outsized to their small terrestrial base. Venice rose from a small encampment of fishermen, who used their island cluster as a natural defense against aggressors, to become the manufacturing center of ships that made them Lords of the Lake for almost seven centuries, from the tenth to the seventeenth century. Venetian presence on Rhodes and Santorini is seen in their architectural legacy.

Venice built ships to transport crusaders to the Holy Land in the eleventh, twelfth and thirteenth centuries, on which were knights from France, England, Spain and Germany. Their foe was the Ottoman Turkish army, encroaching on and eventually overtaking the Holy Land of Israel and the Christian Byzantine Empire of Constantine in Constantinople. When the Ottoman Turks built their navy, the Eastern Mediterranean became a battle area for control of international commerce. Knights of St. John of Jerusalem and then Rhodes, evolved from caring for pilgrims to mastery at sea, making them competitors with the Ottomans for the title of Lords of the Lake.

Ottoman Turks became Lords of the Lake until their terrestrial empire began to falter in the nineteenth century. In 1805, Napoleon challenged the Ottomans for supremacy of the sea. The Battle of Trafalgar in 1805 occurred just outside the Mediterranean Sea, off the Atlantic coast of Spain, yet it ended French mastery of the sea. Britain became the new Lord of the Lake as the dominant world master of commerce across the sea. The official death of the Ottoman Empire came in resolution of the First World War, when Britain became protector of the Holy Land.

Stories in this volume of Cruise through History run the gamut of human endeavor around the Eastern Mediterranean Sea from ancient times to recent history. They are grouped in four sections: Greece, Cyprus, Turkey and Israel, as a means to move geographically around the sea. Overlapping impacts from events in one area to another are inevitable. History does not happen in one place. Each Cruise through History© itinerary follows a voyage of interrelated ports.

Interaction of personalities in these stories often occur in battles to spread or defend Christianity from the advance from east to west of the growing might of the Muslim Ottoman Empire, though these are not religious wars. The battles of the Cross and the Crescent, at the Battle of Lepanto in 1571, or earlier battles between the Ottomans and Knights of the Vatican, the Knights Templar or Knights of St. John, in Jerusalem or Rhodes, were battles to command commerce as Lords of the Lake. By example, the doge of Venice sacked Constantinople, for which he was excommunicated.

As in all volumes of a Cruise though History©, personalities are key to the story. The goal is to invite visitors to explore homes, palaces, cities and museums of their benefactors as informed guests. There is no shortage of personalities in the history of the Eastern Mediterranean. The challenge attempted here is to select a few, without becoming overwhelmed by all of history.

The stories begin in Athens at the Parthenon, destroyed by Xerxes, rebuilt by Pericles and plundered by an opportunistic Lord Elgin. Heroine of the story is Melina Mercouri, known to many as a movie actress, who in this story is the moving force to open the Parthenon Museum. It is a story of people and an icon of Greek culture.

Less endearing is the story of Alcibiades, who provides a tale of intrigue in Greek diplomacy, at the time Corinth, a center of world trade, was resisting cutting a canal across the Greek isthmus. To its peril, the city took a pass on commanding the sea. Obstinance of the Corinthians was memorialized by the Apostle Paul in his letter, written from Ephesus. The canal was not successfully accomplished until the twentieth century, when the need for the thoroughfare was obsolete. Had there been a Corinth Canal in 1571, during the Battle of Lepanto, the Vatican may not have had its victory. As a side note, Miguel Cervantes lost use of his left arm in the Battle of Lepanto as a sailor for Spain. His return home took almost as long as that of Odysseus return from the Trojan War. For the story of Cervantes, look to Itinerary I. The Odysseus story is here.

Stories of the islands of Greece run across time. Delos is the home of the ancient gods of Greece. The sacred island held the most important Temple of Apollo, as Delos was the place of his birth. Delos was also the sacred international banking center when Greeks were Lords of the Lake.

Santorini's history was thought to have been wiped away by the volcanic eruption at the time Moses led the Israelites from Egypt. A nineteenth century discovery, acted upon in the twentieth century gives a different picture of the vibrant island population, rendering many guidebooks obsolete. On Mykonos, the story is as recent as the lives of its two heroines, one who fought in the Greek independence wars from Turkey and the other who gave the island its prominence as a vacation paradise, Jacqueline Kennedy Onassis.

St, John came to Patmos, where he wrote in the solitude of a cave. Due to heroic efforts of a priest and the resident monks over the centuries, vestiges of early Christian history are preserved on the otherwise inconspicuous island and in its library. Highly conspicuous through time was the port of Rhodes, held for a time by the Knights of Saint John and coveted by the Ottoman Turks as a means to rid the Eastern Mediterranean of their trade competitor. The story of the Knights runs from Acre in Israel to Rhodes and continues in Itinerary V at Malta.

Crete is the home of a trilogy in Greek mythology. Zeus, king of the gods, lived on Crete. King Minos had his palace on Crete, where he kept the Minotaur bull in a labyrinth designed by Daedalus. Theseus, son of the king of Athens, came to Crete to vanquish the bull and liberate Athens from its tribute to Crete of youths of Athens. Imprisoned by Minos for his failure to devise an impenetrable labyrinth, Daedalus and his son, Icarus, flew to the sun on wings of birds. A palace of stone and plaster, identified as the palace of Minos by a museum curator turned archaeologist, Sir Arthur Evans, is the major visitor attraction on Crete today. In Phaistos, the Second City of Crete, the story is one of breaking the code of ancient language using clues left in remains of the ancient city.

That Cyprus is a divided island today is not unusual, given its history of looking east to Turkey and west to Greece, two places with irreconcilable differences. For visitors to Limassol, the popular cruise port, the two stories are that of early Christianity on Crete and the pagan pilgrimage site of the Temple of Apollo. The presence of Aphrodite, rising from the sea on her half-shell, is evident throughout the island.

The earliest stories take place on the western coast of Turkey, where great civilizations that were neither Greek nor Turkish flourished until the Trojan War and the rise of Rome. Valiant queens, who led ships in battle and built monuments to their husbands deserve their fame, as do the builders of Troy and those who battled contemporary politics to rediscover the fabled city.

Constantinople, now Istanbul, began as the ancient city of Byzantium, the port city of Greek grain trade from the sixth century BCE. The story of Christian Constantinople is one of building the city of Constantine. Iconic of city history is the Hagia Sophia, built in the fourth century, burned in a riot in the fifth century in the spillover effect of rivalry between sports fans, and rebuilt to greater glory. The church became a mosque during the period of the Sultans of Istanbul, who built a palace and restored the city, planted heavily with tulips to welcome visitors today.

Outside Constantine's city boundaries, the prime minister to an emperor embellished a church, the Chora, as a monument to its benefactor, in the image of the Hagia Sophia. Eight centuries later, the glitter of the Chora remains, although the niche holding its benefactor is empty. In the Hagia Sophia, the glitter of Empress Zoë, the original lady in gold, still smiles enigmatically from the wall. Before leaving Istanbul, look across the Hellespont, to where Lord Byron swam the channel, in a self-test of his adventurous spirit.

Finally, the traveler arrives in Jerusalem, as Holy Land travelers have been doing for centuries. Follow the travels of two early pilgrims, one who actually visited the city. At the Heart of the Heart of Jerusalem are the Rocks of Ages of the three main monotheistic religions, no less vivid in spirit for the several millennia of reverence. In Haifa follow in the Steps of Jesus around the Galilee and then return to the modern city of recent politics, not yet resolved.

The final Itinerary story of Acre begins with its history as a port built for military purpose and ends with its present-day, self-assigned role as a model city of coexistence. Thus, this itinerary ends on a note of peace. Travelers are distinguished from tourists by the desire to become imbued with the sense of place and not merely the experience of photographing old buildings. Before traveling to the Eastern Mediterranean, travel through the stories in this Itinerary to gain the context of the place and meet fascinating personalities from history. Enjoy!

GREECE

ATHENS – THE PARTHENON: A GREEK TRAGEDY IN THREE ACTS

The Parthenon stands above Athens as the most recognizable of all Greek icons. It has been the center of the Greek world for 2,400 years. The most magnificent of all Greek temples, it was designed and built by those with the justified audacity to know what they were doing. The building was made to last. It was constructed purposely on the Athens Acropolis, visible to all and close to the gods. The best artists adorned the structure with the social history of a people, who were, at the time and to their knowledge, the supreme civilization in the world.

The Parthenon is a stop on all cruise shore excursions in Athens. On any day, the considerable number of steps up the acropolis to the grounds of the temple are crowded with visitors, local and foreign, Greek and non-Greek. Even first-time visitors know what the building will look like. They come to have a first-person experience standing in the presence of one of the most magnificent of

GREECE, ATHENS: Parthenon from Areopagus Hill

human creations. To stand at the temple on an early morning when no one else has yet arrived is to have a memorable interaction with a work of art.

The story of the Parthenon has been told many times and in tremendous detail. The site evokes the intense study of architects and art historians. Custody and transfer rights of the bits of stone from the Parthenon, its marbles, have been the subject of endless legal debates in academia and the press. Tourists receive about fifteen minutes of wisdom from their tour guides, while they wilt in the Athens sun, before being pushed aside by continually arriving adoring masses.

This short story, of a long history, of a loved icon, is told in three parts to give background to an anticipated shore excursion. The first act, construction, is the story of the epitome of what is possible in a time of peace, by a prosperous nobleman, giving thanks to his deities and cultural inheritance for his achievements. The second act, destruction, is set in scenes where the inheritance is either not appreciated or is idolized which such enthusiasm that there is a desire for exclusive control, as though the individual can achieve greatness by association. Act III takes place in recent history, where selfless efforts are expended for the common good. Restoration is the act of reclaiming the culture, through preservation, protection, and restitution.

Act I: Construction

The victorious Greek general of the Persian Wars, Pericles, decided to build edifices in Athens to not only replace what was lost in war but to epitomize his vision of the ultimate Greek city. He did not ponder that his efforts would be known to twentieth-century academics as the classic period in Greek culture. The classic period runs from the victory of Pericles in 479 BCE to the death of Alexander the Great (a Macedonian) in 323 BCE.[1] The classic period of Greek art, literature, philosophy, and theater forms the root of western art and thought from the time of Pericles to today. For Pericles, the pinnacle of Greek achievement would be evident in a temple to Athena, the war goddess, known today as the Parthenon.

---

[1] BCE is before the current, or common, era. Such designation is academic and religiously neutral.

For Pericles, the Parthenon met his expectations of a fitting tribute to the gods. Of the many Greek treasures left to the modern world from the classic period, the Parthenon remains the ultimate icon of Greek culture.[2] It should not be a surprise that any desecration of this icon is a moral affront to the most sensitive core of Greek feelings of heritage.

GREECE, ATHENS: Parthenon

At the center of the temple stood a statue of Athena by Greek sculptor Phidias. The name Parthenon comes from the Temple to Athena Parthenos, the virgin goddess Athena. The forty-foot high statue of the virgin was a goddess of ivory, with a gold gown. She held a spear in one hand and a six-foot victory ornament in the other. She wore a helmet decorated with a sphinx and

---

[2] This story does not ignore the importance of Delphi, adorned by the four horses from Chios about the same time. The four horses traveled to Constantinople in the 4th century of the current era, until the doge of Venice took them to St. Marks in the twelfth century. Delphi was a distant pilgrimage site, sacked by the Celts in 279 BCE, while Athens was the center of Greek life and the acropolis was the center of Athens. See CTH Itinerary II – Venice – The Well-Traveled Horses of Saint Marks, for more on the quadriga. See Cruise through History, Itinerary X for more on the Celts.

gryphon, symbols of power, wisdom, and leadership. Each year a few Greek women had the honor of dressing the statue for festivals.

In the third century BCE, gold was stripped from the statue to pay the cost of yet another war and replaced with copper. In the fifth century CE, the statue disappeared. Romans possibly removed it. The fate of Athena is unknown.

Temple construction took twelve years between 444 to 432 BCE.[3] During the war, Persians destroyed a prior temple that stood on the site. The columns of that temple were left on site, incorporated in the walls and surrounded with another row of columns to build a structure far grander than the predecessor.

The columns of the building support a marble beam to which metopes were attached. The metopes are sculptures carved in place that are visible above the outer row of columns. They were carved deeply into the marble, almost bringing to life the ninety-two scenes depicting mythical battles. There are thirty-two scenes on each side and fourteen across the ends. On the north side are scenes from the Trojan War and on the south side are scenes from battles between Greeks and Centaurs. Olympian gods battle giants on the east side and Greeks battle Amazons on the west side of the temple.

On the ends of the temple, there were high triangles, pediments, which followed the pitch of the roof. Within the triangles were fifty large statutes, fully carved and then hoisted into position. The east pediment statues depicted the birth of Athena and on the west were statues of Athena and Poseidon competing for the rule of Athens. The statues, like the metopes, were painted.

Above the inner row of columns, there was a 525-foot[4] continuous depiction of a procession to the temple for the Panathenaic festival. Some historians believe this inner frieze was positioned such that it would only be seen by those important enough to enter the temple. The carvings are not as deep as those of the metopes.

Upon completion of the temple to Athena, Pericles built the second large building on the Acropolis; the shrine to Erechthion. The namesake of this

---

[3] Historians differ slightly on the dates of construction. The architects were Callicrates and Ictinus, although historians most often mention Phidias, as he was the sculptor.
[4] Some sources measure the friezes at 550 feet.

temple was either a prior king of Athens, or a war hero, or both. The shrine replaced another casualty of war. The new shrine was burned by Romans in the first century BCE and repaired in the first century CE. It became a church in the fourth century and a harem during the occupation of Athens by the Turks beginning in the fifteenth century.

The Erechthion is best known for the six ladies holding up the porch. These graceful figures, also sculpted by Phidias, are known as Caryatids; maidens of Karyatia. The figures seen on the porch today are all reproductions. Lord Elgin carried off one maiden. The remaining ladies were removed to the Old Acropolis Museum in 1979, for their protection from the elements. They now reside in the New Acropolis Museum, except for their sister that is still in the British Museum.

Other smaller structures were built on the acropolis after the Parthenon. In 27 BCE a temple was erected to Roma and Augustus Caesar. Romans built the Roman tribute, in a Greek style, with Greek lettering. The occupiers of Athens evidently wished to mark their presence with deference to the glory of the historic Greek residents of Athens.[5]

Act II: Destruction

In the fourth century, with the spread of Christianity, art and edifices of the classical era were damaged or destroyed as pagan.[6] During the sixth century, the Parthenon was used as a church. Statues on the eastern pediment were taken down, destroyed, or defaced. Crusaders coming to or from the Holy Land in 1204 regarded the Parthenon as a major Catholic cathedral. The temple to the virgin Athena became the church of the Virgin Mary. When the Muslims arrived in the fifteenth century, the Parthenon was given a minaret.

---

[5] About a quarter of the population of Athens at the time was comprised of Greek speaking ethnic Turks. There were large settlements of Turkish speaking Greeks who settled around the Black Sea in 600 BCE. In 1923, Greeks were expelled from Turkey and Turks from Greece. See CTH Itinerary IV – Black Sea – Trabzon.

[6] Alaric the Goth spared Athens before he threatened Rome.

Occupation by pagans, Catholics, and Muslims added layers of evolving use to the Parthenon. Major damage was the result of war and greed. The Ottoman Turks, who used the Parthenon as a mosque, assumed that it was a safe place to store gunpowder. In 1687, during a siege of Athens by Venetians, a stray cannonball hit the building, ignited the arsenal of ammunition, and blew the roof off the Parthenon, as well as resulting in substantial damage to the columns and carvings.

Greece, Athens: Erechthion

The conquering Venetian general decided to remove the statues from the west side pediment. In the process, the statues shattered, and all was lost. The Venetian legacy to Athens was a pile of rubble on the acropolis. Over time, large pieces of marble were repurposed to buildings in Athens. Tourists and locals collected small fragments for generations.

In 1799, Thomas Bruce, the seventh Lord of Elgin, was able to secure an appointment as the British ambassador to the Ottoman Turkish government in Constantinople. He was a fortunate man. Although his personal fortune was modest, he was able to marry a lovely, wealthy woman. The English army and navy were diminishing the strength of Napoleon's forces, making his job as an ambassador to an English ally much easier. In addition, he had access to the artifacts of classical antiquity, with which he could impress his new bride and decorate his homes in England and Scotland. Decorating homes with classical Greek artifacts was the rage in England. Elgin did not need to commission copies. He sought access to real treasures from the Turks.

The document, which the British ambassador received from the Turkish government, for activity in Greece, was written in Italian. The language was ambiguous. For over 200 years, there have been debates concerning what action was authorized by the document. Elgin's agents worked surreptitiously, they bribed guards at the docks and left quickly to avoid detection. The Turks had denied others access to the Parthenon. Elgin's agents had been permitted to dig around the Parthenon and take items that would not damage the building. Their actions on site were restricted. The document gave unhindered access only to "qualche," a term that can mean some or any. Rather than resume prior activities of Venetians or limit collection to the rubble, Elgin's agents began an indiscriminate, sweeping removal of portions of the Parthenon.[7]

Elgin's agents removed half of the frieze, fifteen metopes, seventeen statues left on the pediment, and one of the caryatids. The removal was hastily done, causing much damage to the stones. There were one hundred cases for shipment, amounting to one hundred twenty tons of material.

Elgin's difficulties began when he left his diplomatic post. He was captured by Napoleon's army and held captive from 1803 to 1806. The ship he purchased to transport the cases of marble sunk with its first load. Upon arrival in England, Elgin found that his wife had left him and his finances were precarious. The indiscretions of his youth left him with several diseases, causing him to lose his nose. In Parliament, there was a discussion that supported the legitimacy of the retention of the marbles in England, although Elgin was personally attacked for taking extreme liberties with his position as ambassador to obtain the personal treasure. The well-known bad-boy poet of Britain, Lord Byron,

---

[7] For a detailed analysis of the Elgin controversy, see Jeanette Greenfield, The Return of Cultural Treasures, 3rd ed., Cambridge University Press, Cambridge, 2007.

immortalized Elgin's actions in poetry, accusing the Scott of dismantling the shrine, which had stood for 2,000 years unscathed.

Lord Elgin desired to sell the Parthenon marbles to Britain to recoup his costs and resolve his debts. The purchase discussion in Parliament has added fuel to debates of legitimate receipt and intent of Britain to preserve and protect the marbles in trust for Greece. A bargain price was offered for the purchase, in recognition of the clouded circumstances of collection. Elgin's creditors received all of the proceeds.

A special gallery was built in the British Museum to display the marbles. Twice while in the care of the museum, the marbles received further damage. In 1938, museum workers used wire brushes to scrub colored patina from the statues to whiten them. In 1983, the pieces were again damaged by the use of improper cleaning fluids. Publicity of the care of the marbles while in the museum has increased the volume of requests for a return to Greece, in an ongoing debate that has never abated.

GREECE, ATHENS: Melina Mercouri Foundation

Act III: Restoration

The stones removed from the Parthenon might rightly be called the Mercouri Marbles, such was the dedication of Melina Mercouri to return of purloined bits of Greek art, and her support for all forms of expression of Greek heritage. In all the debates over ownership of the Parthenon Marbles, the name of this Greek patriot is rarely mentioned. A stop at the pink-walled office of the Melina Mercouri Foundation is not likely to be on a tourist itinerary.[8] Knowing something of this remarkable woman is to understand better the passion that Greeks have for their heritage.

Melina Mercouri was a member of the Greek Parliament, better known around the world as a movie actress and political activist. When she was faced with British and American critics, who argued with convincing force that the marbles were best left in London, because they could be better preserved and appreciated, she became the moving force behind the construction of a new museum in Athens to house movable art from the Parthenon. She never doubted rightful ownership lie in Greece. An appropriate museum responded to calls for viewable repose.

Amalia-Maria Mercouri was born in Athens in 1920, to a family that was active in Greek politics. Melina's grandfather was mayor of Athens for thirty years. After college, she went to acting school, performed leading roles in the Greek National Theater, including leading roles as Blanche Dubois in a Streetcar Named Desire and Electra in Mourning Becomes Electra. At age twenty-one, she married a Greek real-estate developer.

As was the custom for intellectuals, of any age, Mercouri went to Paris in the 1950s. She returned to Greece, where she returned to the theater. She also became active in the theater actors' union movement. Three aspects of her life developed, to which she remained devoted: political activism, promotion of all forms of Greek art, and Jules Dassin, her movie director, and eventual husband.

With Dassin as director, Mercouri starred in the movie *Never on Sunday,* for which she received a Best Actress award at the Cannes film festival in

---

[8] MelinaMercouriFoundation.org.gr Last visited 1/9/2015.

1960. The film received five Oscar nominations, including best song, which is memorable to any child of the 60s. Although she would make nineteen movies in her acting career, *Never on Sunday* is the one that brought Greece to theaters worldwide.

In 1967, while Mercouri was in New York, Greek military officers staged a coup. She strongly opposed the tyranny that took hold in Greece. At every opportunity, in the United States and Europe, Mercouri was an outspoken advocate of international support to help return democracy to Greece. The dictatorship seized her property and revoked her Greek citizenship. There were attempts on her life. In response, Mercouri famously stated, *I was born a Greek, I will die a Greek.*

In 1974, democracy and Melina Mercouri returned to Greece. She hosted a television show, *Dialogs*, where she discussed social issues with guests. In 1977, she was elected to Parliament. Still, politically controversial in Greece, her filmed performance as Medea, shown all over Greece, was denied viewing at the Greek Ancient Drama Festival. For this, Mercouri was known as the *exiled Medea.*

The role that best defines Melina Mercouri was her appointment as the first female minister of culture, a post she held from 1981 to 1989, and again from 1993, until her death in 1994. In this role, she promoted all forms of Greek culture. She established a prize for Greek literature, coordinated access to archaeological sites, and established free days for Greek citizens to enjoy their heritage and to support for Greek theater.[9]

In 1992, the United Nations, World Heritage Commission established a Melina Mercouri International Prize for safeguarding and exemplary management of cultural landscapes. The prize was first awarded in 1997, and has recognized such diverse preservation efforts as Borodino Battlefield (Russia, 2007); Elisha's Park (Jericho, 1990); and Park of Koga (Japan, 2003).

For decades the name of Melina Mercouri was synonymous with a call for the return of the Parthenon Marbles to Greece. Most, but not all, of the missing bits of the Parthenon were, in her lifetime, in the British Museum.

---

[9] March 6, is Melina Mercouri Day in Greece, when all museums are open free of charge.

GREECE, ATHENS: Parthenon Museum Entrance

GREECE, ATHENS: Parthenon Marbles in Context

The reticence of the museum to return was defended as support for their purchase of the marbles from Elgin, that the museum was best able to care for the marbles, and that these world treasures could be best viewed by so many of the adoring public in the British institution.

Melina Athena

To Mercouri, Elgin's claim of lawful sale to Britain was dubious. If international law did not exist to resolve the matter, then to her morale law and ethical conduct should apply. The care taken by British curators was not consistent with preservation, although years of civil war and dictatorship in Greece were too recent to assert that Greece was able to better protect its own culture.

As to the removed parts of the Parthenon having a worthy home and being available for view, that was something Mercouri was in a position to resolve. She undertook to establish a new museum of the acropolis. The pieces stored in a small building on the acropolis were replaced with an edifice worthy of its contents. To that end, Mercouri held an international competition for museum design. Her legacy became the museum that opened in Athens fifteen years after her death. She wrote her own epitaph when she said:

> I hope to see the marbles back home before I die,
> but if they come later, I shall be reborn.

GREECE, ATHENS: Parthenon from Inside Parthenon Museum

In 2009, the New Acropolis Museum opened in Athens, to replace the small Old Acropolis Museum on the acropolis.[10] The new museum is built into the city site in such a way as to bring visitors into the Parthenon and engage them in the mastery of the temple, in a way that is lost in the big, enclosed, square room of the British Museum. In Athens, metopes and friezes are mounted in order and in relationship to each other as they were on the Parthenon, just not as high above the floor. The visitor can see the detail of what is present and understand the spaces are preserved for missing pieces. At the end of the row, the wall-to-wall, ceiling to floor windows allow the visitor lookout on the Parthenon. The museum puts the Parthenon art into context, in a true twenty-first-century *museum* experience.

GREECE, ATHENS: Parthenon Marbles await missing pieces

Visitors to Athens are increasing, although the number of viewers does not rival the number of visitors to London. The nineteenth-century notion of a

---

10   The Old Acropolis Museum opened in 1865 and closed in 2007. The contents were moved to the New Acropolis Museum.

museum is still alive in London, where bits of several civilizations co-exist, room-to-room, in a single building at the British Museum. The British Museum is wonderful for what it is, although it reminds us of a provincial antiquarian collecting social order. If there is an excitement that comes with viewing the *real* in context, then the legacy of Melina Mercouri is the best means to visit that which Phidias created.[11]

[11] The next room holds the mausoleum of Mausoleus, without much interpretive signage. In Turkey, there is only a depression in the ground.

Epilogue

In anticipation of the New Museum of the Acropolis, the Vatican and the Heidelberg University Museum of Antiquities in Munich, Germany repatriated to Greece those fragments of the Parthenon in their possession. The British Museum remains intransigent. It does not wish to begin to unwind the ball of string in the process of resolution of historic ownership rights, not knowing where the string will end.

Phidias and Melina Mercouri sought to glorify Athens and Greek heritage. Lord Elgin sought to glorify himself. Lawyers continue to debate whether the common law of ownership of property applies in this instance or generally to cultural property. Common law has its roots in Roman common law, in existence when Elgin and his envoy cajoled the Ottomans out of that which they balked at releasing. Visitors to Athens today thankfully need not become mired in such discussions. They know what entices them to travel long distances. They spend their time visiting Athens to enjoy the beauty in their midst. Visitors can enjoy what is there and see gaps left in the New Acropolis Museum of what could be there, if Melina Mercouri is to be reborn.

GREECE, ATHENS: Parthenon with Erechthion on right

Least Favorite Son of Greece – Alcibiades

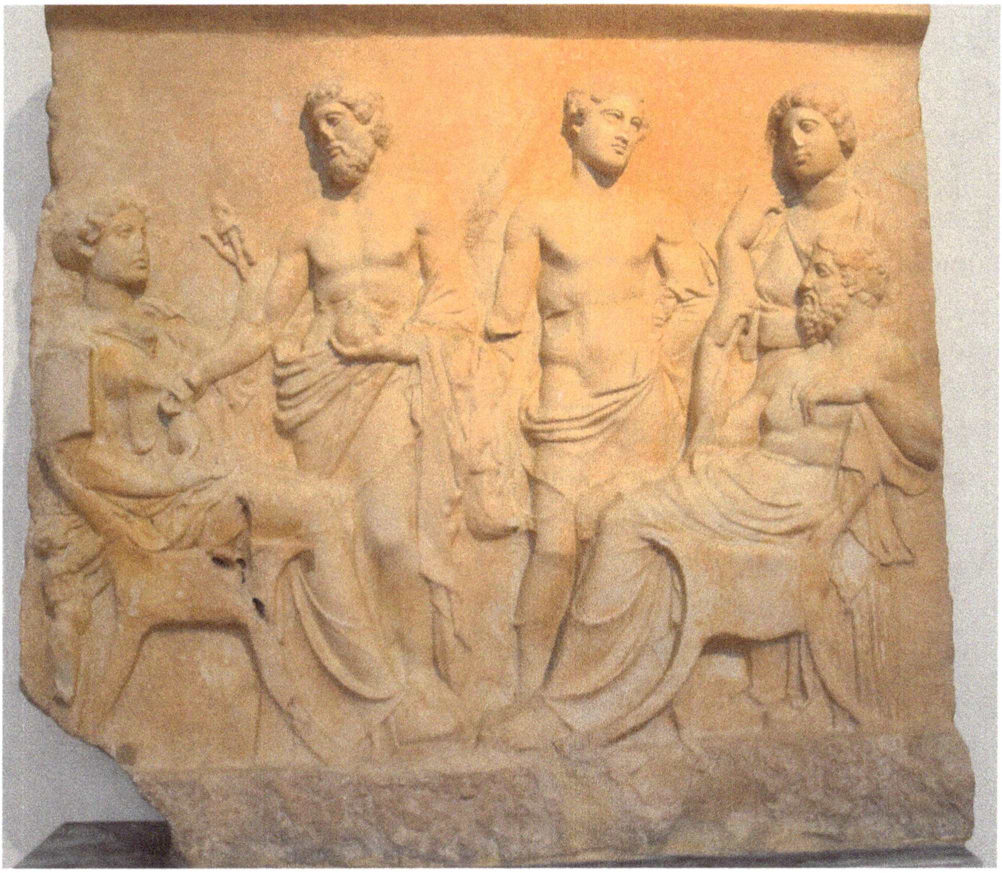

On the "A" list of ancient Greek conquerors were Agamemnon, who carried Greek dominance through Asia and Egypt; Ajax and Achilles of the Battle of Troy; and Macedonian prince Alexander the Great, who commanded the largest force in the world to his time and held more land under one leader in his world until his untimely death. Then there was Alcibiades, of whom few people have heard of today, for a good reason. Greeks no doubt would like to forget this historical figure, although he provides such good material for an entertaining story. Not everyone in Athens can wear a white toga to the Agora and be remembered for their contribution to humanity. In every civilization, there is at least one Alcibiades. This is the story of the original.

The Makings of a Hero: The Early Years

Alcibiades was born in Athens in 450 BC and lived until 404 BC. He fought and lived through several major battles on foreign turf, then died an untimely death, while at home. This future general of Athens had a pedigree worthy of a military leader. Through his mother's family, Alcibiades claimed to be a direct descendant of Ajax, of Trojan War fame. Alcibiades' father was killed in battle on behalf of Athens, when Alcibiades was three years old, leaving him to the guardianship of his father's cousin, Pericles, the brilliant general.

Several exceptional teachers tutored the young Alcibiades, including Socrates. As an eager soldier at age eighteen, Alcibiades rushed into battle, only to have his life saved by Socrates. Ancient writers attribute Alcibiades with returning the life-

GREECE, ALCIBIADES: **Warrior in Battle Chariot in Athens Museum**

saving favor to Socrates later in the teacher's life. The Greek historian and biographer of Alexander, Plutarch, had the opinion that the only person Alcibiades would listen to was Socrates.

Alcibiades was handsome, athletic, rich, and ambitious. He was also a good orator. About all this vision of manhood in ancient Greece lacked were morals. He married a wealthy Athenian woman, Hipparete, who was eternally faithful to him. He rarely returned the sentiment. Together they had two children.

Distinguished Military Career

Alcibiades was a young commander during the war between Athens and Sparta, known as the Peloponnesian War. It was a war fought for control of the lower Greek peninsula.[12] When, after seven years of fighting, a truce was declared, Alcibiades was left out of the negotiations due to his young age. Characteristic of youth, the slight left him pouting.

In what would become the first of many self-serving negotiations to the detriment of his own city, Alcibiades held back-door negotiations with the Spartans, in which he convinced Sparta of insincerity in Athenian diplomats. Alcibiades warned the Spartans that they should recall their diplomatic powers and guard themselves against an agreement with the Athenian assembly. The Spartans did as Alcibiades suggested. Alcibiades then stepped forward at the Athens assembly to denounce Spartans as frauds, something the Athenian negotiators should have seen. The older, experienced, and capable statesmen were publicly embarrassed. Alcibiades was promoted to general. War with Sparta resumed, wherein Alcibiades had a greater part in its leadership.

Alcibiades then traveled through the Greek Peloponnese, soliciting allegiance of small cities. He was able to collect a personal following, the power of which was great enough to force from power Hyperbolos, a long-standing general. Alcibiades aligned himself with General Nicias, whom he had embarrassed at the earlier negotiations with Sparta. Perhaps Nicias felt enemies should be kept close. The allegiance did not last.

By 415 BC, Nicias found himself on opposite sides from Alcibiades as the Athens assembly debated whether to involve itself in defense of the Sicilian

---

[12]   The north-country of Greece, was controlled by Alexander of Macedonia. Modern-day Greeks refer to Macedonia as northern Greece.

city of Segesta from an aggressive Syracuse. Nicias urged caution. To the contrary, Alcibiades excited passions of the assembly. Athens committed itself in Sicily.[13] Alcibiades was made co-general with Nicias and another experienced general, Lamachus, in the attack on Syracuse to conquer Sicily. Alcibiades was thirty-four, young for a general, given his evidenced lack of experience, even in ancient Athens.

Alcibiades was a passionate guy. His liaisons with women were as well known as his desires for battle. He was also known to urge the enslavement of women and children captives, whose husbands and fathers he had slain. Rumors were rampant of children he fathered with young captive women.

The departure of Alcibiades for battle in Sicily was clouded by a bad omen. For good luck, homes in and around Athens kept a statue of Hermes at the front door. During the night several of these house gods were mutilated, the acts of which were attributed to Alcibiades and his intoxicated friends. God mutilation was a capital offense in Athens at the time. Alcibiades did not have the opportunity to clear his name before leaving for Sicily. While he was away, the scandal gained in intensity. Alcibiades did little to add to his community standing while at home. While he was away, antipathy increased.

When Alcibiades arrived in Sicily, there was a ship waiting to bring him back to Athens for trial. He convinced the soldiers to allow him to follow them back to Athens in his own ship. When he was close to shore, Alcibiades rowed to a dark cove and escaped with his crew to the ancient Mediterranean coastal town of Thurii. He was convicted in absentia in Athens, and his property was confiscated.

While Alcibiades dealt with his personal problems, the two remaining generals experienced several victories in the conquest of Sicily. Then they approached Messina, the gate to the straits across to the Italian mainland. Alcibiades planned to take revenge on his Athenian rival generals. He made an alliance with the Syracusans in Messina. By providing Athenian attack plans to their enemies, Alcibiades guaranteed the defeat of Athens at Messina.

---

[13] Read further stories of Segesta and Syracuse in Cruise through History© Itinerary II Rome to Venice.

Next, Alcibiades contacted his former enemies in Sparta. He convinced the Spartans of an Athenian plan to attack Syracuse as a start to take all of Sicily. Acting on his intelligence, in the sense of military secrets, not in terms of high mental function, the Spartans sent a large command to Syracuse in southeast Sicily. Alcibiades also convinced the Spartans to build a large wall that cut the supply road between Athens and croplands that fed Athens. As a final insult to Athens, Alcibiades road through the countryside, inciting revolt in farming communities upon which Athens relied. In this way, Alcibiades attacked his home town on two fronts, by an inability to bring in crops from nearby farms and in the far-away battle for Sicily.

Greece, Alcibiades: Octopus, symbol of cunning from Athens in time of Albicbiades National Archaeological Museum, Athens

While in Sparta, Alcibiades lived as a Spartan. His Spartan existence was tempered by the fact that he was a house guest of the king. His good times in Sparta may have lasted much longer; however, Alcibiades included receiving the favors of the queen as part of his home hospitality. Eventually, the queen gave birth to a son, the child of Alcibiades. The new father seemed genuinely surprised that the king was not willing to make him supreme commander of Spartan troops in Sicily. Instead, on a tip that the king had ordered to accomplish his assassination, Alcibiades left in the night for Persia.

Alcibiades convinced his Persian hosts to give aide to the Spartans in an attack on Athens. Then he warned his old rivals in Athens of the coming attack. Thus warned, the Athenians had the advantage, which they put to good use. Athens scored a big victory over Sparta in a battle in Sicily. Alcibiades was welcomed home as a hero. He was given command of Athenian troops.[14]

Greece, Alcibiades: Artemisian Jockey, from shipwreck 140 BCE
National Archaelogical Museum, Athens

The Prodigal Hero Returns

Alcibiades was able to reenter Athens in 411 BC, at age thirty-nine. He was granted a stay of prosecution, but not absolution of all guilt. To fully regain his prior standing, he needed to perform a heroic act of major impact. Over the next four years, he plotted his grand entrance.

---

[14] Most historians would wince with pain at this brief description of events. In reality, Alcibiades played a much venaler role in inciting leadership of the army to overthrow the democracy of Athens and insert a power scheme comfortable with his style of doing business. After much intrigue, in a complicated plot, the democrats kept the oligarchs in line. It was a true test of Alcibiades' skill in working all sides, that although he supported the oligarchs, the democrats recalled him to Athens as a hero.

An opportunity for Alcibiades to prove his merit to Athens came at a fortuitous moment. Alcibiades had been collecting favors and raising a fleet. He came into the Hellespont[15] at a moment when the Athenian navy required reinforcement. Alcibiades had the opportunity to lend the decisive hand and take credit for the entire victory over the Spartans.[16]

Using his devious nature to military advantage, Alcibiades sent his small squadron of ships out to sea. The Spartan commander gave chase, and the remainder of the Athenian fleet came up from behind to cut off any possibility of Spartan retreat, as they came to aid Alcibiades. As Spartan ships headed to safety on shore, Athenian soldiers were ready to attack. Many of the Spartan ships were captured in usable condition. Alcibiades claimed victory in the episode.

Alcibiades next went in search of his old friends the Persians, who had come to the Hellespont to aid the Spartans. This time the Persians were not fooled by the double-dealing Alcibiades. They refused to join in his exploits.

On the return trip to Athens, Alcibiades went to the north shore town of Selymbria, where he is credited with stealing only enough money to pay his sailors and doing no other harm. He then went on to Byzantium, the future Constantinople, and Istanbul, where he gave effective assistance to the Athenians in a siege on the city. By the time Alcibiades returned to Athens, his former conviction was expunged, and he was greeted in his homecoming with the golden crown of a victor. His property was restored to him. Incredibly, Alcibiades was made supreme commander of the Athenian army and navy.

---

[15] The Hellespont is the narrow waterway that leads from Troy to present day Istanbul. Dangerous currents that shift in the seasons provided the scene for several stories in ancient Greek mythology. No ancient "A" list hero was complete without at least one victory at the Hellespont. See Itinerary IV, Black Sea, for the nineteenth century AD military importance of the Hellespont.

[16] Few historians would give credit to Alcibiades for the Athenian victory at the Hellespont. True, Alcibiades chased Spartan ships to the shore and began to tow them back to sea, where their sinking had a profound effect on Spartan troops. However, most historians point to Thrasybulus, the Athenian general who brought his troops to the aid of Alcibiades, as the critical force to enable overwhelming the Spartans.

Not all was positive for Alcibiades. He arrived in Athens in 407 BC, on the day of the ceremony of Plynteria, the feast day that celebrated cleaning the statue of Athena.[17] Alcibiades did not want to tempt fate and defile another god of Athens. He opted to abstain on ceremony and avoided his drinking buddies. He was forty-three and in good health.

Anxious to seek an additional military victory, Alcibiades set off in 406 BC with one hundred ships. He sailed due east of Athens to the island of Andros and then across the Aegean Sea to Samos. He landed on the western shore of Turkey at Notium, just south of Ephesus. At that point the Spartan army awaited him. Surprise this time was in favor of the Spartans.

By the time Alcibiades saw the avenging army itching to attack him and attempted to turn to his ships seaward, he found that his second in command, Antiochus, had engaged the Spartans in battle. Any ability to leave unscathed was compromised. Alcibiades escaped physically unharmed, with an irreparably damaged reputation. He was relieved of command.[18]

After the battle of Notium, Alcibiades went into self-imposed exile. He went north of the Hellespont to the area of Phrygia. Aristotle wrote of Alcibiades on the mountain of Elaphus. Some historians believe that Alcibiades was about to make yet another plea to the Persians for personal assistance. Others write that Alcibiades escaped to a mountain retreat with his current mistress to assess his options. Political reality in Athens made a return to his home city impossible.

All historians agree that during the night, enemies of Alcibiades set fire to his haven. The assassins may have been Spartans in pursuit, or brothers of a young girl of a prominent family in the area, who had been seduced by Alcibiades. They could have been Athenians, long tired of the strategic gamesmanship of Alcibiades. He had no shortage of enemies and few, if any, friends. The night of the fire, the house was completely engulfed. Armed assassins waited outside.

---

[17]   Donald Kagan, The Fall of the Athenian Empire, Cornell University Press, 1991, p. 290
[18]   Historians mark this battle as the beginning of the end for Athens as a power.

Aristotle and others have written of the death of Alcibiades. His last moments have been the subject of classical paintings.[19] The night of the fire, Alcibiades knew he was surrounded. He came out of the burning house, dagger in hand. Waiting outside the house were assassins with bows drawn and arrows ready. Alcibiades died in 404 BC, at age forty-six, slain in the night.

Much has been written about Alcibiades in the centuries since his death. Historians agree that he was not a sympathetic character. They do not agree on his legacy. Was he an early version of the double or triple dealing spy and a superb strategist? Or was Alcibiades simply a constant opportunist? Certainly, he was talented. He used his beauty, intelligence, and oratorical skills on the ladies more often than in the forum. Artists most often depict Alcibiades in a boudoir, sometimes with Socrates pulling him back to his studies. The only time Alcibiades is recorded as caring for a person, besides himself, is his devotion to Socrates, the ever-patient teacher.

GREECE, ALCIBIADES: National Archaeological Museum Athens

---

[19] Michele de Napoli (1808-1892), Death of Alcibiades, 1839, Naples National Archaeological Museum. Also, Félix Auvray, Alcibiades with the Courtesans, 1833, Museum of Fine Arts of Valencia.

For the casual traveler on a voyage through the Greek islands, Alcibiades is a good story to ponder the last glory days of Athens. Alcibiades need not be taken seriously. Like William Shakespeare's Timon of Athens, there is more satire here than a morality play. The best legacy of Alcibiades maybe his abundant, beautiful, intelligent, talented progeny, unknown by name, portrayed in art.

Note: Historians rely on writings of Plutarch (46 AD – 120) for accounts of Alcibiades, although they may be romanticized. See, Harvard Classics, 1909, Great Books online, http://www.bartley.com/12/4.html. Also, http://penelope.uchicago.edu /Thayer/E/Roman/Texts/Plutarch/Lives/Alcibiades*.html. Plato also wrote a dialog on Alcibiades, as though Alcibiades is having a conversation with his teacher, Socrates, translation by Sanderson Beck, http://www.san.beck.org/Alcibiades.html.

BATTLE OF LEPANTO AND THE CORINTH CANAL

 Ancient Corinth Temple of Apollo

Major events of the ancient and modern world occurred in the area between the Gulf of Patras and the Gulf of Corinth in the Ionian Sea. In this place, great powers of the Eastern Mediterranean brought their navies in quests to take or maintain control of the Mediterranean-dependent world. There on the back-side of the Peloponnese of Greece, far from Turkey and the Holy Land, not yet into the Adriatic Sea and ports of Italy, navies of the ancient and medieval world-traveled far to meet in repeated clashes. Until the Corinth Canal, there was no rear escape.

The critical battle, which set the shape and governance of the modern world, took place in 1571, in the back door to Athens, in the Lepanto Channel. This was the ultimate battle of the Cross and the Crescent; the Holy League versus the ever-expanding and successful Ottoman Empire. There had not been a battle of this magnitude in the Mediterranean world since the Battle of Salamis in 480 BCE, in which a Greek General repulsed the advance of Persian King Xerxes near Athens. Both battles set a demarcation line between Europe and Asia that has never been breached.

The Battle of Lepanto was not the first or last meeting of the Ottoman navy and that of the Holy League of France, Spain and the Knights of the Cross. Venice and the Ottoman navy shot their ship-mounted cannons in battle in 1499, just north of the battle of 1571, giving the Ottomans a victory in the First Battle of Lepanto. The naval victory did not enable entrance to Europe. In 1538, in the same area of sea, the Ottoman navy scored another victory, in the Battle of Preveza.[20] In 1827, the United Kingdom, France, and Russia defeated the Ottoman navy in a battle for the independence of Greece. In each instance, the battle was not of the magnitude of that in 1571.

The naval engagements of the Ionian Sea, in the Corinth Gulf took place far from supply and relief ports. The Ottoman navy faced the battle with no eastern escape from the Corinth Gulf. Not until 1893, was the Corinth Canal able to provide a channel from the Ionian to the Aegean Sea, without going around the Peloponnese peninsula. The channel planned since ancient times had proven too fatal and too expensive to come to fruition. When complete, the best use of the canal has been as a shore excursion into the ancient world of a little otherwise visited area of sea.

This story of the Battle of Lepanto and the Corinth Canal pair two pieces that complete the historical picture of the Eastern Mediterranean. Disparate in time, interdependent in strategic vision, battles gave impetus to the canal. Earlier existence of a canal may have changed the course of battles, if not the history of Europe. This is their story.

---

[20] The Battle of Preveza was fought in the same place as the Battle of Actium in 31 BCE between Caesar Augusta and Mark Anthony and Cleopatra.

GREECE, CORINTH: Corinth Canal

Setting for a Battle and a Canal in Ancient Corinth

The thin strip of land by which the Peloponnese landmass remains attached to the Greek mainland is the Corinth Isthmus, faced on the west side by the Gulf of Corinth and to the east by the Saronic Gulf. The line which may be drawn from gulf to gulf is midway between the Greek power cities of Athens and Sparta. The city which grew on this line was destined by geography to be of significance in the history of the civilized world of Asia and Europe. This city was Corinth.

Human existence in the area of Corinth goes back over eight thousand years. By the eighth century BCE, Corinth was an identifiable city, growing in power by its command of trade routes across land and sea. Corinth controlled ports on its east and west coasts, allowing it to charge for transit overland. Goods from Turkey and Athens came to the port on the Saronic Gulf and were transited by land to the port on the Gulf of Corinth, bound for cities of Italy.

GREECE, CORINTH: Corinth Ancient Center of Trade

GREECE, CORINTH: Remnant Ancient Glory

By the mid-sixth century BCE, Corinth minted its own silver coins. Its theater seated an audience of fifteen thousand. Its Temple of Apollo, built-in 550 BCE had thirty-eight columns, seven of which stand today.

Geography, wealth and likely conceit, placed Corinth too often at war. When leaders of Corinth were not mediating disputes between Athens and Sparta, they were entered into the fray. Corinth aligned with Sparta against Athens and then in 395 BCE, in the Corinthian War, the city aligned with Athens, against Sparta.

When the Romans arrived in Corinth in 146 BCE, they burned the city. They chose to rebuild on the same site. The new Roman city was an ecumenical trading center of Romans, Greeks, and Jews. Archaeology on the site since 1896 has disclosed layers of homes, fountains, and baths. A wealth of statuary from various strata now fills the museum near the ancient city site.

GREECE, CORINTH: Monument to Men & Gods

In 49 CE, the Apostle Paul came to Corinth. He preached in the synagogue and founded a church when he realized the Jews of Corinth preferred to retain their religion and customs. Apostle Paul is deemed to have left Corinth for Ephesus, where he wrote the Epistle to the Corinthians. Today the spot from where he preached is revered and preserved as a sacred remembrance of his visit.

By 1458, Corinth was subsumed into the Ottoman Empire. It served as a land base for operations during the Battle of Lepanto in 1571. When Greece was freed of Ottoman rule in 1830, Corinth was considered as a candidate for capital of independent Greece. It lost the honor to Athens.

GREECE, CORINTH: Remains of Ancient Synogogue

Battle of the Cross and Crescent

From the time the Ottoman Turks left the plains of western Asia in the twelfth century and entered Constantinople in triumph in 1453, the band of horsemen transitioned from a tribe to a military and political empire. The Byzantine Empire, whose capital was Constantinople, had been in decline for centuries. When the Ottoman cannons breached the thousand-year-old walls of Constantine, Byzantium died. Newly named Istanbul became the capital of the Ottoman Empire.

From Istanbul, the Ottoman army swept west to conquer Greece. The next target was Hungary and the bastion of the Holy Roman Empire of central Europe. Italy, with its vast Vatican lands at the center of the peninsula, was in the sites of the Ottoman navy. In 1570, Pope Pius V called together a Holy League to join forces and stand against further Ottoman aggression.

Responding to the plea of the Vatican was Spain, which included Spain's Kingdom of Naples encompassing the lower half of Italy and Sicily; the Hapsburgs of Austria-Hungary; and the Republics of Venice and Genoa, as well as the duchies of Savoy, Urbino, and Tuscany. The Knights Hospitaller of

Malta, having held strong against Ottoman onslaught in 1565, joined with the Papal States to complete the forces of the west. Commander of 206 galleys was Don Juan of Austria.

The Ottoman navy had slight numerical superiority with 222 war galleys, commanded by experienced admiral Ali Pasha. Ali Pasha was prepared to engage based on the success of past tactics. He relied on bowmen and an elite corps of Janissaries. Unfortunately for Ali Pasha, repeated dependency on Janissaries had reduced their number. New wars were outcome dependent upon firepower of ship-mounted cannon and the new muskets, early versions of rifles.

In the fall of 1571, the Holy League sailed from Messina, Sicily, toward the Gulf of Corinth. They anchored at Cephalonia to regroup, resupply, and resolve differences between delegations. The Ottoman fleet was amassed in the Gulf of Corinth. Although neither admiral considered the circumstances optimum, the two navies engaged on October 7, 1571, off the west coast of Greece.

Rowed by galley slaves and tossed by winds, opposing forces were thrust into close contact, which devolved into hand-to-hand combat across the ships. Christian slaves on Ottoman vessels were able to grab arms and fight against their captors, aiding the Holy League effort. Ottoman ships repeatedly ran out of ammunition in a battle of guns. Admirals of both fleets died in the fighting.

The Ottoman navy, sailing west from the gulf, had no retreat option, barred from the Aegean Sea by the thin strip of land at Corinth. Over half their ships were taken, and another fifty were sunk. By the end of the battle, thirty thousand Ottoman causalities bloodied the sea, while the Holy League suffered less than a third of that number.

The battle ended with victory to the Holy League. Absent an admiral, and unable to agree among captains of disparate squadrons, the Holy League was unable to capitalize on the victory and pursue action against Ottoman ports. With the year, the Ottoman navy was rebuilt.

Neither side gained territory by the Battle of Lepanto. The battle is memorable for holding the line on Ottoman expansion. The loss was a great blow to the morale of the previously invincible Ottoman forces. The Holy League broke its streak of fear in facing its eastern foe.

GREECE, CORINTH: Navigating Corinth Canal

The Short Canal that Could Not be Built

Building a canal to make an island of the Peloponnese peninsula and shorten transit times in commerce and war had been contemplated by Greeks from the first century of the Christian era. Ithaca, the island of Odysseus in Cephalonia during the Battle of Troy, was a world away from thriving Athens two millennia after the Trojan hero returned home. Two factors, economic and political, blocked canal construction.

To build a canal, a financial commitment was needed from a nation-state with resolve and resources. Greece was a morass of independent cities until the nineteenth century. Until the middle of the nineteenth century, Greece was occupied and controlled by the Ottoman Empire. Vassal states of the Ottoman Empire served the interests of Istanbul. Facilitating sea traffic for Greece was not of financial benefit to Istanbul. In the absence of large-scale earth-moving equipment, vast amounts of manpower were needed to move the dirt to excavate a channel. For the Ottomans, manpower was best used to either create farm products for trade or populate armies.

Local kings had contemplated a canal in the seventh century BCE. The issue at the time was lack of manpower. Human resources in Greece in the seventh century BCE had the same priorities as in the nineteenth century CE. The seventh-century option was to portage goods over land.

Ancient Greeks were also stymied by superstition and lack of knowledge of the seas. They feared opening a channel would drain existing waterways or flood islands. They knew Hercules parted the pillars of the Mediterranean and waters flowed out to create the Atlantic Ocean. They did not want to tempt the gods again for fear of altering the known world.

The closest any government came to building a canal was the attempt made by Emperor Nero of Rome in the first century CE. Using a workforce of Jewish slaves, a trench was begun across the narrow isthmus at Corinth. The project was abandoned upon the death of Nero. Interestingly, the current canal utilizes the same location as devised eighteen centuries earlier by Nero.

The seafaring trade power with funds and self-interest to undertake a canal project was the Venetians. These early Lords of the Lake had much to benefit by a short-cut across the Peloponnese from the Adriatic to the Aegean seas. No doge was inspired to undertake a project while wealth came easily to Venice. During the crusades of the twelfth century, plundering Constantinople provided immediate gratification, not to be postponed for the digging of a trench. By the seventeenth century, when Venetian traders recognized the value of a canal, their days of mastery of the Mediterranean were too far past to make a commitment economically feasible.

The other prohibition to a canal was voiced by Corinth. Its rise in stature and wealth came from its geographical existence as a double port-side center of overland trade. A canal that would facilitate sea travel might allow the seafaring world to pass it by. Evidently, the idea of controlling transit with a canal tax did not occur to Corinthian leaders. Theirs was an old, established order.

When Greece became independent of the Ottoman Empire in 1830, building a canal became more of a symbol of nationalism than rational planning. Greece was independent, although impoverished, with higher priorities for national spending. A canal could wait.

Once French engineers succeeded in building the Suez Canal in 1869, a Corinth Canal seemed a likely encore to their effort. From Suez, the French team attempted the Panama Canal, which disclosed a lack of engineering knowledge and financial mismanagement. Greece was fortunate to be standing third in line for canal digging. The French debacle was ruinous for investors.

GREECE, CORINTH: Entering Corinth Canal

US President Theodore Roosevelt created the new country of Panama to enable canal completion in the western hemisphere. The US had no financial or military advantage to assert in Greece. If Greece wanted a canal, it needed to raise capital. It turned to a new French entity, created to raise funds and build a canal for Greece. Investors reasoned there were fewer challenges in Greece than Panama. After all, they were not attempting to bridge the Atlantic and Pacific oceans. In Greece, moving the dirt to open a water channel proved to be the least of their problems.

More than a decade and several bankruptcies later, Greece opened the Corinth Canal in 1893. After the ribbon-cutting, there was little to celebrate. In the years since canal planning, commercial ships had grown in capacity, which out grew the width of the tiny Corinth channel. The steep, unreinforced banks were easily eroded, even in the absence of recurrent earthquakes.

Canal builders are not to be faulted for lack of knowledge of ancient earthquakes of 365 and 375 CE, although evidence of quakes can be seen by knowledgeable eyes in the remnants of the early modern city. A massive quake struck Corinth in 856 CE, killing tens of thousands, a significant number, which evidences the size of the city and the magnitude of the quake. The most recent earthquake was in 1858, at which time the city relocated to more stable turf.

Nineteenth-century Corinth Canal engineers were so focused upon digging a channel; they were oblivious to the currents in the two joined seas. Wave action from one opposing force to another increased erosion in the sides of the canal and made consistent transit difficult. Commercial traffic requires consistency of access. Consistency of travel conditions was something Corinth Canal could not provide.

The Corinth Canal was closed for several years, while the channel was widened, the eroded dirt was dredged, and side-walls were stabilized with concrete, at great expense. An anticipated return on investment never materialized. World War II intervened, and a 1941 battle between the Allies and Germany left significant damage to the canal. As a parting shot, the retreating German army did their best to block the canal and deter dreams of restoration.

In 1947, the Corinth Canal became a US Corps of Engineers challenge to reopen by 1948. Once again, the canal opened because willing forces could make it happen, not because they should. The project that had strategic merit in 1571 was without purpose in later centuries.

GREECE, CORINTH: Excitement Over Canal Today

Visiting Corinth Today

The Corinth Canal today is seventy feet wide at the bottom and less than four miles long. There is little interest in expanding the canal to avoid a four-hundred-and-thirty-mile trip around the Peloponnese. The most intriguing engineering marvel at the canal are the submersible bridges that raise to support a road bed and lower to allow the small craft to transit the short distance.

The best and most frequent use of the Corinth Canal today is as a shore excursion for visitors after trekking around the archaeological site of Corinth. Sipping wine and cold drinks on the short cruise nicely completes a hot, dry day. Very seldom do cruise guests avail themselves of the opportunity to bungee jump over the canal. The scenery is not particularly memorable right-side-up or down.

Corinth, the archaeological site of the former town of significance, is memorable. Forearmed with history and augmented by the small, although well-stocked museum, the story of Corinth is a visible experience. The grandeur of early Greece is impressive, made all the more enjoyable without the crowds of Athens.

There are no monuments to the Battle of Lepanto. The event ended westward expansion of an empire, ended the age of rowed galleys and established the boundary of Christian Europe from Muslim Asia. Such a significant battle deserves recognition. Stories such as this must suffice.

Although hailed at the time as the battle of flags of the Cross versus the Crescent, the Battle of Lepanto was not a battle of religious ideology. It was a battle for domination of the sea and international trade. Certainly, the influence of the Vatican was preserved for a few more centuries. Loss of Vatican influence in the east came centuries earlier in the Great Schism, between Catholicism and Orthodoxy. The Battle of Lepanto held firm the ground that divided the world.

In the future, ships of sail and those who owned them dominated the Mediterranean. Urbino, Savoy, Tuscany, Genoa, and Venice, joined temporarily in the 1571 war, returned to petty competition immediately after the major battle. Not quite three hundred years later, they would join to create a nation, in which only the Vatican abstained.

GREECE, CORINTH: Disappearing Bridge Over Corinth Canal

GREECE, SANTORINI: Santorini Fira Harbor Today

Santorini: A History Rewritten in Stone

Santorini is an island of an ancient culture with recent history. Up until the last few decades, the story of Santorini was of a mountain people, whose homes and lives were washed into the sea with the eruption of a volcano in 1500 BCE, that left only the caldera seen today. That there were no relics of culture or bodies of the unfortunate residents found was taken as evidence that all was lost. Due to the talent and persistence of archaeologists, it is now known that the conventional story of the ancients is untrue. The story of Santorini has been recently rewritten as acknowledged from ancient stones.

Rewriting the history of an island whose affluent inhabitants lived, farmed and created art going back 7,000 years, to the times of the Pharaohs in Egypt, has occurred in just the last few decades. It is a story far richer than previously imagined. The ancient culture did not disappear. It was covered in ash, preserved in time, like Pompeii, only 1500 years earlier. For 3,600 years, the ancient culture of Santorini was waiting to be rediscovered, while a new layer of residents enjoyed the island.

After more than a century of geological and archeological investigation, a story has emerged of a highly developed society that lived on the island known as Calliste, the beautiful island. The caldera around which the people lived was a natural harbor. The small island cluster sat at the crossroads of commerce of ancient Egyptians and Greeks.

On Santorini, there developed a unique society that was not purely Minoan like Crete, Hellenistic like Greece, or Egyptian. The people of Santorini prospered as a blend of cultures and talents. Understanding the true history of Santorini has made possible a deeper understanding of the interaction of ancient cultures across the Mediterranean.

The story of ancient Santorini was preserved in mythology, as recorded by early Greek historians. In Greek myths, the island of Santorini is described in shape and the activities of its pre-volcanic eruption inhabitants in a manner that conforms to recent findings of scientists. It is a case of science confirming the myth.

The actual story of Santorini is one of an ancient culture that did not become washed into the sea. Releasing the story from its hiding place is a story of inadvertent discovery that brought French scientists to the island in 1867. A century later, after several wars intervened, a Greek archaeologist led an international force into a scientific investigation that has culminated in a new and fascinating picture of the island.

This is the story of an ancient world and its recent rediscovery. To tell the story requires reliance on geology, mythology, archeology, and a quirk of history. It is also the story of Santorini of the recent past several centuries, which parallels in many ways the lives of the ancients. That two levels of civilization, separated by a millennium in time and layers of ash, could be drawn to the beauty of Santorini to live similar lives, is a fascinating story.

GREECE, SANTORINI: Looking Down Cable Car on Tombs

Santorini in Geological Time

Correcting misunderstandings of the past requires an explanation of the geology of Santorini. Geologists look at the strata of rock visible around the edges of the island today and see the origination of landforms. Volcanic eruptions and earthquakes over millions of years have formed islands in the sea, by depositing layers of lava and rock debris visible above the water, or by upward movement of the earth's crust. Both types of activity have formed Santorini.[21]

GREECE, SANTORINI: Cruise Ships in Caldera

Santorini sits along a line of underwater volcanic activity, responsible for changes in the shape of the island and for appearance and disappearance of neighboring islands and rocks that occurred during times of human occupation. The calm harbor of Santorini is and has always been the caldera of a volcano. Or to be more accurate, the island group is actually the lip of three, concentric caldera. The circle of land was broken at the southwest, in a narrow channel, through which truly ancient mariners could transit the harbor 7,000 years

---

[21]   An apology is due to geologists and students of geology for the simplistic explanation of complex and far more nuanced events.

ago. Whether the channel was created geologically or was assisted by human endeavor, is a matter of continued inquiry by geologists.

In the center of the caldera lake, there were islands. The shape of the islands is unknown, as these were the islands that were blown out of existence more than 1600 years before Christ, enveloping homes, shops, and harbors of ancient people on Santorini in a deep layer of ash. The ash layer was many times deeper than the ash covering Pompeii.

From ancient descriptions and knowledge of island formations in volcano caldera around the world, scientists can make an educated guess that the islands formed by successive expulsions from the volcano of Santorini could have resulted in interior islands, the highpoints of which appeared above the water as concentric rings. These small islands were subject to growing and decreasing with subsequent volcanic activity.

Scientific examination of Santorini in recent decades has resulted in dating the major destructive volcanic eruption at 150 years earlier than the time of 1500 BCE as previously thought. A correction of 150 years is more than minutia to historians. The Minoan culture on Crete fell 1500 years before Christ; about the same time, Moses walked the Israelites out of Egypt. If a cataclysmic eruption on Santorini previously tied to the destruction of a palace on Crete and the plagues that frightened the Pharaohs, actually occurred 150 years earlier, then there were other forces at work to assist Moses in making an impression. Science is a process of refining questions.

The volcanic eruption of 1500 or 1650 BCE, that caused the islands in the middle of the caldera lake in Santorini harbor to disappear, is known as the Minoan Eruption. Minoan is a name given to the highly developed cultures on Crete and Santorini 2000 years before the current era. The name distinguishes the big event from intermittent minor eruptions.

The Minoan eruption not only obliterated the ringed islands in the center of the caldera, but it also caused two rifts in the circle of the outer island, leaving three distinct pieces. The largest remnant of the original ring is Thera; the island commonly referred to as Santorini. The smaller island is Therasia. Therasia last suffered an earthquake in 1956 and is sparsely populated today as a result. The third landform is Aspronsi, a rock covered in pumice from the Minoan eruption.

In comparatively recent history, two islands have been born in the Santorini caldera/harbor. Palea Kameni, meaning old burned island, appeared in 197 BCE. Nea Kameni, the new island, sprang up in 1707 CE. Smaller bouts of volcanic activity have caused these bits of new real estate to grow and change shape.[22] Residents of Santorini watched developments with apprehension. Today these islands are used for grazing sheep.

Scientists predict that volcanic activity in the area of Santorini is not yet quiet. The appearance of new islands north and south of Santorini gives cause to believe that future eruptions and land-forming activity will occur outside of the Santorini Caldera. Like the Hawaiian Islands, formed as a string of successively younger islands, residents of Santorini may someday have new neighbors.

Santorini in Myth and Legend

Now that scientists accept that the shape of Santorini today looks much as it did in antiquity, the ancient myths make geologic sense. Ancient legends describe the creation of Santorini as a time when Zeus, angered by the partially human Titans, reached into the earth and scooped out rock to hurl at the unruly irritants. Zeus created the caldera and left the imprint of his grasping fingers visible in the interior curves of the island.

Greek legends explain the first inhabitants of Santorini. The son of the god of the sea, Poseidon, had several sons and one daughter, Europa. When Zeus became enamored with Europa, the supreme god turned himself into a bull, enticed Europa onto his back, and rode off with her. Poseidon sent his grandsons across the earth in search of their sister. One grandson went to Thera, accompanied by Phoenicians. There they built temples to Poseidon, of which the dolphin sculptures carved in blocks of stone can be seen today.

---

[22] Nea Kameni was occupied with homes until 1866, when an eruption destroyed 50 houses. The island increased in size enveloping Mikra Kameni, also a new landform. There were eruptions and land creation or diminution in 1925 to 1928, 1939 to 1941, and in 1950. Walter Friedrich, Santorini, Acerhus University Press, Denmark, 2009, p, 221.

GREECE, SANTORINI: Fingers of Zeus, with Oia in the distance

Ancient Greeks called the large island of the Santorini group Thera, in honor of a Spartan commander. The island was also known as Calliste, the beautiful island. The name Santorini comes from recent history, in the time of the crusades. Venetian owners of the island at the beginning of the thirteenth century called the place Sant Erini, in honor of Saint Irene. Sailors shorted the expression to Santorini.

The most notable legend with which Santorini is associated is that of the mythical city of Atlantis. There are scientists who refuse to give time to the consideration of a factual basis for the existence of Atlantis, while other scientists spend much time debating its location. Candidates for Atlantis include Santorini, Crete, southwest Spain, and Uppsala, Sweden.[23] All discussions of Atlantis start with Plato.

---

[23]   Yes, Uppsala. See CTH, Itinerary I – London to Rome – At Sea, Atlantis, for the story of the scientists, politicians, and armchair explorers who examined Plato's story to devise their own conclusion.

Plato lived in Athens from 427 to 347 BCE. He often wrote dialogs as a means to pose philosophical questions of the day. In Plato's dialog of *Critias and Timaeus*, Critias relays a story told by his grandfather, who heard it from a traveling salesman recently returned from the Nile Delta. The story was recorded by Egyptian priests as reported by arrivals from Santorini at the time of a catastrophic event. Adding up years, and allowing for differences in counting between Egyptians and Greeks, the catastrophic event occurred 1500 BCE.

The story described by Plato told of an ancient city of wealthy mortals, whose extravagance angered the gods. In punishment for their overly lavish life, the entire city was cast beneath the sea during the night. Poseidon shook the island city until it was covered in stone. The city had consisted of rings, connected by bridges, leading to palaces of magnificent wealth. Then it was gone.

Connecting ancient legend to scientifically known facts of the time led to placing Atlantis in the center of the Santorini caldera, despite the detail in Plato's story, which placed the event outside the Pillars of Hercules, in the Atlantic. There is no question that the inner island of the Santorini caldera disappeared in the Minoan eruption of 1650 BCE. Thera was shaken by earthquakes and then covered in ash and stone.

Five hundred years later, Greeks came to Santorini and established settlements. Descendants of Alexander the Great utilized Santorini as a military port strategically located in the middle of the Mediterranean.[24] By the fourth century of the current era, a church was erected to house the Bishop of Thera.

In 1204 CE, Venetians set off in the crusades to conquer lands, even if they were already in control of Christians. Five generations of a noble Venetian family-controlled Thera, the island they called Santorini. For centuries Santorini passed between control of Greek kings and Venetian princes, until the Turks arrived in 1579, as part of the Ottoman domination of the eastern Mediterranean. Ottoman Turks held Santorini until 1821 when Greek independence arrived to bind the islands with the mainland in a democratic nation.

---

[24] Christos Doumas, Santorini, Ekdotike Athenon Publication, 2002, p. 12.

Greece, Santorini: Venetian Santorini in Fira Town

Santorini 1867

In 1859, French promoters and engineers were busily building the Suez Canal. Construction required an endless supply of cement. To secure the ash to mix with lime to make cement in sufficient quantities, the builders looked to Santorini. The island was close to the construction site and offered mountains of ash at the edge of the sea, where it could be easily loaded onto cargo ships. By 1867, massive ash removal on Santorini began.

French geologist, petrologist, and volcanologist, Ferdinand Fouqué was 39, in the prime of his academic career, when he received a distress call from colleagues urging him to come to Santorini at once. The shovels had easily dug through volcanic pumice until they hit rock. The rocks appeared to be cut blocks in a wall. There was something unknown that lay dozens of yards below ash.

Fouqué was intrigued. If there were an earlier civilization, buried beneath the ash on Santorini, then all of the existing scientific records were in error.

From the French School of Archeology in Athens, Fouqué began excavations that consumed the remainder of his professional life. His published papers formed the basis of a new history of Santorini and informed investigations of archaeologists who resumed his efforts a century later.

GREECE, SANTORINI: Akrotiri street restored

In the newly exposed caldera walls of Thera, Fouqué saw elaborately carved entrances to ancient tombs. Only people living on the island prior to the Minoan Eruption could have constructed the tombs. On the southern shores of Thera, French archaeologists excavated a settlement known as Akrotiri. The site has been dated for habitation that began between 5500 and 3300 BCE, the beginning of the Bronze Age. The city flourished between 2000 and the seventeenth century BCE, the time of the Minoan Eruption.

GREECE, SANTORINI: Cracked stairway steps evidence of eruption warning

GREECE, SANTORINI: Akrotiri storage jars

GREECE, SANTORINI: Homes in Akrotiri

In Akrotiri, Fouqué and his team found jars of almonds stored in the sand to keep them fresh. They found jars of fava seeds for drying in the sun and grinding in millstone, as residents of Santorini do today, to create flour. There were jars of olives, figs, chickpeas, and lentils. From a large number of man-size jars found in close proximity, Fouqué concluded that Akrotiri was a major port for commerce in the twentieth to seventeenth centuries BCE.

In his excavations, Fouqué uncovered multistory buildings with lovely painted frescos on walls of upper floors. The frescos were important for stories told in pictures, as well as for the level of technique displayed. Frescos displayed birds, flowers, and decorated pleasure boats. They evidenced a culture more dedicated to pleasure festivals than a celebration of war. They displayed a culture connected to trading partners of the Nile Delta.

Fouqué wondered whether colors in the frescos; the blue, red, green and black were fabricated from imported supplies. He explored the island looking for answers. In caves and crevices in walls of the caldera, he found iron ore used to make red pigment, copper used in blue and green pigment, and manganese that produces black pigment. White paint made from talc was used on walls and to decorate jars. There was an abundance of talc on the island. Fouqué concluded that though the artists may have come from across the sea, they were able to mix their paints on site.

Greece, Santorini: Lady of the house fresco

Greece, Santorini: Fish Seller Fresco

GREECE, SANTORINI: Papyrus fresco

Conspicuous by absence were human remains of the seventeenth century and gold and other precious objects of great value. There were harbors without ships. All that Fouqué could conclude was that the volcanic eruption was not a surprise when it occurred. There must have been ample warning in which residents could pack their ships and travel south to Egypt, or north to Greece, depopulating the island.

Fouqué created a stir in the archaeological world when he presented his paper on Santorini Eruptions in 1879. He called Santorini the new Pompeii. The find on Santorini was much more dramatic as it was older than Pompeii and the site of activity that could reveal much about commerce in the Mediterranean if the site were more fully excavated.

Greece, Santorini: Ancient tombs cliffside

Greece, Santorini: Oia pre-eruption residence reclaimed

Santorini 1967

Two world wars, minor wars, and several economic crises intervened from the time Fouqué left Santorini to the century later when a new group of archeologists were able to devote their skills to unearthing the story of pre-Minoan Eruption Santorini. In the interim, Greek archaeologist Spyros Marinotos kept the scientific community from forgetting opportunities waiting on Santorini. In 1939, Marinotos connected the Minoan Eruption on Thera to the decline of the Minoan civilization on Crete. He spurred academic discussions on what caused the decline of Crete; a discussion that continues today.

Perplexing scientists was pottery on Crete dated to be more recent than that unearthed on Santorini. The difference has been explained to some extent. The ash from the volcanic eruption and the resulting tsunami which ended civilization on Santorini did not fatally impact the civilization on Crete. Certainly, these events caused much damage to Crete. The sky was dark for days. The final and later blow to Crete was political, not geological.[25]

In 1922, a New Age Clairvoyant, Edward Cayce, predicted that Atlantis would be discovered in 1967. Although scientists were not impressed with Cayce, donors may have been. Leading up to 1967, there was a flurry of renewed interest in Santorini.

In 1967, Marinotos and teams of Greek and international archaeologists worked continually on Santorini, focused in large part on Akrotiri.[26] Thousands of tons of pumice were removed from the city revealing streets of multi-story buildings. As in Pompeii, before removal of solidified ash, plaster was poured into negative space to reveal objects that had decayed over time. Rather than human forms as found in Pompeii, the negative space amid ash in Santorini revealed wooden furniture of delicate shape and intricate detail. Wood beams between stone walls and supporting windows dissipated over time.

---

[25] Jan Driessen and Colin F. MacDonald, The Troubled Island, Univcrsité de Liège, Belgium, 1997.

[26] In 1974 Marinotos was killed in an accident while working on the site. There is a memorial plaque to his accomplishments on the site, which is now a museum.

Archaeologists used information gathered to reconstruct a city from fallen blocks. They placed new wood support beams in the same shape as the original beams. Slowly, an accurate picture of Bronze Age Santorini began to appear.

Santorini of 3000 to 1650 BCE was a place of great affluence. Wealth came from international trade. The civilization was unique in the Mediterranean as it was a blend of Greek, North African, and Egyptian cultures. People of Santorini were among the first in the Aegean to use the Phoenician alphabet to write Greek words.

People of pre-Minoan eruption Akrotiri left a record of their lifestyle in frescos painted on walls of their homes. The first floor of the buildings often had unfinished walls. The living areas had stuccoed walls. Upper stories had large windows through which frescos on walls could be seen from the street. People displayed their affluence.

GREECE, SANTORINI: Orthodox Church Oia

Many impressive frescos from Akrotiri are in the National Museum in Athens. The much-studied *Ships Fresco* can be seen in the Prehistoric Museum in Fira when visiting Santorini. The small fresco is rich in detail. Houses are painted in blue. People are seen sitting at home, walking to the harbor and sailing in ships decorated with flowers and hung with drapery, in a festival procession.

There are frescos of papyrus plants, blue monkeys and a fisherman with a daily catch on a line. There are pictures of beautiful women. The women wear gowns, large earrings, and hold elegant dishes. They may be portraits of the lady of the house.

With all that has been learned about Santorini in the last decades, based on the surprise discovery of 1867, it must be remembered that as of 2010, the site of Akrotiri was estimated to be thirty times the area of the excavated portion. There is still much information buried beneath the ash.

GREECE, SANTORINI: Oia shopping street

Santorini Today

Today cable cars bring visitors up from the dock to the streets of Fira. From the cable car house, it is a short walk to the Museum of Prehistoric Thera that opened in 2000, the old Archaeological Museum with historical objects, restaurants overlooking the caldera and shops. Amid the shops, there are eighteenth-century mansions. At the city, the highpoint is the Venetian castle vestige from days of the crusades, when Venice controlled the island.

Excursions take visitors to the highest point on the island, the Monastery of Prophet Elias, founded in 1711. The sanctuary is small, although beautifully preserved. From the patio, there is a view of the south of the island, with its vineyards and farms. Santorini does not grow many food crops given the short rainy season. It is an island known for having more wine than water. At the foot of the Prophet Elias Mountain are remnants of fortresses built by Venetians to protect the island from pirates.

GREECE, SANTORINI: View into Caldera from Oia

The south of the island holds popular sites for visitors. The archaeological site at Akrotiri reopened to visitors after closure in 2005, when the protective roof gave way. Although many of the frescos have been removed to museums, the site allows visitors to walk streets that are 5,000 years old. To the southeast are sites of Ancient Thira and the ninth century Spartan community of Mesa Vouno, where life on Santorini began after the Minoan Eruption. There remains a pre-eruption site cut into the rock to honor Artemidoros admiral of the Greek fleet. It displays a relief of the admiral, as well as a porpoise and eagle, which are signs of Poseidon and Apollo.

Santorini is proof that some lifeways never change. From the time of the Pharaohs to today, Santorini has been a favored vacation destination. Today homes that sit above the caldera replicate the shape and structure of ancient dwellings. People drink wine from barrels and eat dates, olives, and lentils, as they did 5,000 years ago. The sun and the flowers have never abandoned Santorini. It is no surprise that all year round there are cruise ships tied to buoys in the bay.

Further reading on Santorini:

Christos Doumas, Santorini, Ekdotike Athenon, Athens, 2002.

Jan Driessen and Colin F. MacDonald, The Troubled Island, Université de Liège, Belgium, 1997.

Walter Friedrich, Santorini, Acerhus University Press, Denmark, 2009.

Nigel McGilchrist, I. Santorini, Genius Loci Pub. London, 2010.

Nanno Marinatos, Santorini, Athens, 1997.

Papers of the International Scientific Congress, Santorini, Greece, 1978, 1980, 1990.

GREECE, MYKONOS: Ancient Harbor

Two Heroines of Mykonos

Mykonos, a small Greek Island so popular with cruise guests today, was for most of its history a quiet stopover, while the great events in human history swirled around it in the Aegean and Mediterranean. Ancient Greeks stopped by for supplies on their way to all-important Delos. Romans conquered the island, as they conquered all in their path. It was not until the Greek revolt from Ottoman control in the nineteenth century that Mykonos became of consequence.

Mykonos is a non-strategic island of the Greek Cyclades. Of the Cyclades, Naxos and Tinos are larger. Andros and Syros are closer to Athens. Thira, or Santorini, has been in the cross-currents of trade for thousands of years, before the eruption of its volcanic islands, and since.

There are no natural resources on Mykonos, other than the clear water and warm sunshine common to other islands of the Aegean. Most important to Greeks of the nineteenth century was that which they did not have, and that was independence from the Ottoman Empire. Greeks are culturally and politically Greek.

On Mykonos, a heroine appeared in the person of a young, wealthy woman, who need not have been troubled by political matters. Manto Mavrogenous of Mykonos gave all she had; personally, emotionally and financially, to the cause of Greek independence. The people of Mykonos carry her memory as a talisman of freedom.

Mykonos was always a small fishing village. Beautiful, but forgotten, major development and commerce passed it by. Until, in the twentieth century, with its population barely surviving, a real-life angel was drawn to the island for reasons that most mariners passed on it. Jacqueline Kennedy Onassis found on Mykonos quiet seclusion that evaded her outsize personality in the well-known venues of the famous. She found Mykonos to be a healing spirit, and the island found a benefactor.

Little known outside of Mykonos, and well-known to every resident, is how the woman, known as the style maven of the world, discretely displayed her generous side on Mykonos. Jackie O, as the world knew her, kept residents going through a difficult period, by direct generosity. Then she left the island with the *Jackie O* effect. Those who wished to emulate Jacqueline Onassis, share her idea of Aegean beauty, or simply regarded her choice of place, were forever drawn to Mykonos. Since the 1960s, the island has consistently been a vacation haven.

This is the short story of Mykonos and its two heroines; one who placed it on the map of cruise guests and the one who made that map Greek national blue.

GREECE, MYKONOS: **Street in old Mykonos**

Manto Mavrogenous:
Heroine of Greek National Independence

Born into a wealthy family, in 1796, in Austrian-controlled Trieste, Manto Mavrogenous was set for a carefree life in anonymity. She studied French, Italian, and Turkish language, although it was with Greek philosophy and history that she was enthralled. Hers was an ancient family from the Greek island of Paros, one of the Cyclades. When Manto was thirteen, her family returned to Paros, inspiring her passion for Greek dreams of an independent nation.

After the assassination of her father, Manto took up the cause of Greek independence. As a woman of twenty-two, with independent means, she spent her funds and time commandeering a ship, which set out from Mykonos to defend against threats to life on her favorite island, either from pirates, or marauding Ottoman Turks, the Greece overlords. Manto became an enthusiastic member of a growing number of young Greeks responding to Ottoman rule with violent acts of insurrection, where their parents had struggled with diplomatic efforts, or left the country. In the paradigm of fight or flight, her compatriots chose to fight.

The period from 1818 to 1822, was a time when Greek nationalistic passions were rising. In 1821, Greek forces, in which Manto was not involved, set siege on the Ottoman administrative center in the Peloponnese city of Tripoli. In the battle, the Ottoman forces were overcome, giving the Greek nationalistic forces their first military victory in the war of independence. By 1822, Greece was in a full-scale war for independence.

The taking of Tripoli exposed a rift in Greek military and political leadership. Military leaders in the taking of Tripoli entered the city and slew the occupants, Muslim, Christian, and Jewish; military and civilians; men, women and children. Estimates of slain civilians go as high as ten thousand. Although the action was a success in dislodging Ottoman rule from the Peloponnese, indiscriminate massacre offended most Greeks, including the intellectual core of the nationalistic Greek independence movement of which Manto was a part. The Tripolitsa Massacre set back Greek support from Europe, so necessary in funding nationalist military efforts.

Manto dug deeply into her inheritance and sold her jewelry to fund ships and fighters across mainland Greece and the Greek islands. She impressed her European friends with the need to support Greek intellectual leaders, fighting a military battle for independence, not a war of retribution. Writing in French and Italian, Manto begged Europeans to support Greece in independence, or at the least, not support the Ottoman regime.

Manto was popular among the young intellectuals of Paris, who admired her beauty and spunk. They idealized her efforts as the spirit of freedom. While her fund-raising travels in France may not have raised significant funds, Manto ameliorated the barbarous image of freedom fighters and popularized the movement in Europe. She became the poster child of Greek independence.

In her personal life, Manto experienced as much turbulence as she faced in national struggles. Her mother disapproved of active involvement of the young woman in the war, even if she approved of the goals. European in dress and independent in leading ships in battle, Manto shared an apartment with the man whom she loved, Prince Dimitrios Ypsilantis. He is known in the United States as Dimitri Ypsilanti, particularly in Michigan, which honors the man. In turn, Dimitri was known to refer to Manto as the love of his life.

The tale of the two lovers in war-time Greece has all the drama and tragedy of Greek theater. She was a beautiful woman in her mid-twenties, and he was a few years older. Their living together was frowned upon by early nineteenth-century society, all the more because Manto was educated and enjoyed non-traditional roles for a woman. Greece would never forgive her for her brave and independent acts, regardless of her contribution to the cause of Greek independence.

Dimitri came from a powerful family, with royal connections. His title as a prince had historical legitimacy. Born in 1793, to a family of statesmen in the Ottoman regime, Dimitri was educated in France and served as an officer in the Imperial Russian army. It was not unusual for Tsar Alexander I of Russia to have a multi-national corps of royalty in his army.[27]

---

[27] See, Cruise through History Itinerary XI, Port of Helsinki, Defense of Helsinki, for another story of an officer for Imperial Russia, who became a national hero and president of Finland.

Young Dimitri belonged to a cadre of Greek patriots, living in Odessa, then in Russia, known as the Society of Friends, or in Greek as the *Filiki Eteria.* The group functioned as a Greek underground until the war of independence became open and declared. Dimitri led a successful rebellion mission in 1821, at the time Manto was arming ships and supporting fighters on land.

The two lovers became the power couple of Greek independence efforts. Theirs was a passion amid a revolution. Besides the ladies of Greek society, who did not appreciate Manto visiting Dimitri in his battle tent, the lovers had a powerful, jealous, vindictive adversary in Ioannis Kolettis.

Kolettis was a Greek physician with political ambitions. He successfully maneuvered himself to a position of leadership in the military during the war for independence, although his goal was to be acknowledged as the political leader of an independent Greece. At least one man who stood in his way of becoming prime minister of Greece died under suspicious circumstances in which Kolettis was implicated.

When knowledge of Dimitri's proposal of marriage to Manto came to Kolettis, he was livid. The thought of two attractive, popular, young people of powerful families joining was a threat to his political ambitions. As the leader of the Greek independence military, in 1828, Kolettis appointed Dimitri to be the commander of troops in the front lines.

If Kolettis hoped that the brave warrior Dimitri would be killed in action, he was disappointed. Dimitri led Greek troops in the decisive Battle of Petra in 1829, in which Greeks prevailed. It was the final battle of the war for independence. Dimitri became a war hero. Greece achieved independence in 1830.

While Dimitri was engaged in battle operations, Manto was forbidden to join him in his tent. Her home was burned, and her remaining assets were stolen. Kolettis convinced colleagues of Dimitri that it was necessary to kidnap Manto and take her to Mykonos, far from her lover. They did so, although they later confessed their action to the aggrieved Dimitri. He forgave his friends. Kolettis did not relent.

Greece, Mykonos: Balconies

Kolettis informed Manto that Dimitri was ill and would never marry her. The villainous doctor then told Dimitri that Manto had been unfaithful. The two lovers never reconciled. By 1832, Dimitri died of an illness, alone and without speaking to Manto. She came to his funeral in black.

In the celebrations of independence, Manto celebrated quietly on Mykonos. The locals regarded her as a true Greek hero. She received no recognition from the independent Greek government led by Kolettis. In a hiatus in leadership from Kolettis, the first popularly elected head of state, Ioannis Kapodistrias gave a house and title to Manto in 1830, in recognition of her service to Greece. In 1831, Kapodistrias was assassinated.

Until her death in 1840 of typhoid, Manto petitioned the government to award her more than a widow's pension. He argument was that she fought as a soldier, not as the wife of a veteran. Never married, deprived of a personal relationship, and having given her personal assets to the Greek independence movement, she requested recognition given to men of lesser service.

Mykonos remembers Manto fondly, with a statue in her honor on the central city square. Other Greek heroes of the independence movement have statues in Athens. Ypsilanti is remembered in the city of that name in Michigan. They are remembered as soldiers. Manto is notable for selfless devotion to country.

Jacqueline Kennedy Onassis: Heroine of the Quiet Jewel in the Aegean

When Jacqueline Kennedy Onassis first arrived in Mykonos in 1961, as the first lady, the island had become a sleepy fishing island once the war of independence resolved. The island was well known to archaeologists as the meeting point to organize expeditions to Delos. Mykonos was the place to find provisions for teams of scientists uncovering the past on the famous island of the gods. The biggest celebrity encountered by Jackie Kennedy in Chora, the harbor town, was Petros, the pelican. The celebrity of Petros has been preternatural. No one knows how many intervening pelicans have succeeded Jackie's pelican. Chora would not be Mykonos without its pelican.

In the first half of the twentieth century, there were insufficient scientific expeditions and visitors from Athens, who had insider knowledge of the great beaches on Mykonos, to keep locals supported by tourism. As a fishing island, Mykonos was surpassed by larger suppliers to the mainland. Locals survived by working in Athens and returning home on a seasonable basis. Life on Mykonos was little more than survival.

Jackie Kennedy did more than just vacation on Mykonos in 1961, when she arrived with her sister Lee Radziwill to stay at the Theoxenia Hotel, a simple, hidden beach hotel at the time. She fell in love with the island. Islanders reciprocated the sentiment. They had little else to offer.

When Jackie returned to Mykonos as Jackie O, the wife of Aristotle Onassis, her visits were more frequent. Onassis owned the nearby Cycladic island of Skorpios, secluded and remote, without restaurants or the opportunity to engage with others, except as house guests. Jackie O developed a sincere concern for the well-being of her island neighbors. Aging islanders can still recall her gifts of food sustaining families when the Greek economy was at its worst.

It was the *Jackie O* effect that saved Mykonos from depleting the population in search of sustaining employment in Athens. Her visits to the Mykonos beaches were followed by Grace Kelly, Brigitte Bardot, and Sophia Loren. Each glamour lady of Hollywood had a retinue and followers. Lovely people required lovely hotels. Beautiful hotels lured more vacationers.

In 1973, Pierro, the first gay bar, opened in Chora. Mykonos became known for late-night parties and yachts crowding the tiny harbor. The island was discovered. Bars, restaurants, and shops were joined by jewelers and quality retail. Almost fifty years later, the party continues, with a Jackie O beach club.

GREECE, MYKONOS: Longtime resident mascot Mykonos

Visiting Mykonos Today

Only mythical birds live forever. The pelican that delighted Jackie Onassis was saved by a fisherman in 1958, to become the island mascot. It is believed that the original Petros expired in 1985. Jackie had sent a mate for Petros that outlived him. The Hamburg Zoo sent Petros II to Mykonos. If anyone knows how many birds have walked the alleys of Mykonos as Petros replacements, no one is talking. Visitors who encounter a pelican in the tiny plazas are too delighted to ask questions. They pose for photos with the local feathered celebrity.

In response to its growing popularity with cruise travelers and the increasing size of cruise ships, Mykonos built a dock capable of giving space to several mega-ships at the same time. Guests are driven to the bus stop near Chora, the harbor town. Small ships still anchor in the ancient harbor and tender in their guests. In high season there is scarcely room to roam in the narrow winding streets, which open to the windmills and town plaza. Even the familiar pelicans feel pressed.

GREECE, MYKONOS: 16th Century Windmills

To find the Mykonos of the two heroines, take a bus or taxi to the inland city of Ano Mera, or a private beach resort at Platys Gialos. Mykonos natives, who appreciate the economic boon from all the attention, migrate away from the harbor for quiet. Fortunately, the building frenzy of small hotels and condos is centered by the new cruise terminal and away from the historic harbor. Large hotels are not an option in this fragile environment. Jackie O would appreciate the success of her island, as long as its character is preserved. Cruise visitors will agree with her, as they appreciate the legacy of the heroines of Mykonos.

Delos – Home of Gods and Bankers

Delos, the center of world-wide commerce, powerful bankers, political thought and religious ceremony of the sixth century BCE, is today a sidelight to a port stop in colorful Mykonos. Looking at the ruins of life on the tiny island today, it is hard to visualize all that it has been. Add the story of island history to fill in the visual picture, and Delos can come alive again.

The inauspicious start to residents of Delos, the cast-offs from Crete for over a millennium, took a royal turn in the eighth century BCE. At that time the minor goddess Leto had a dalliance with Zeus and came to Delos to hide her pregnancy from Hera, the powerful and vengeful wife of Zeus. Dates are approximate; such is the nature of mythology and Greek gods.

Greece, Delos: Lions of Naxos

Leto gave birth to Apollo on Delos. Apollo was a twin and second in birth order. Leto first gave birth to Artemis, a girl, on the transit to Delos. Apollo became one of the most highly venerated of Greeks gods. Therefore, the place of his birth was instantly imbued with special meaning.

Goddesses attending to the birth, and Greek priests desirous of building temples, founded temples to Apollo, Leto, and Artemis on Delos. The minor island of the Cyclades group of Greek islands became the focal point of pilgrimage from near-by Mykonos, Naxos and Paros, the source of building materials. Delos was never self-supporting, requiring that all food be imported. The caché of the island made it the go-to place of the Aegean and soon all of the Mediterranean.

Delos was unique in islands of the ancient world, dominated by Greece, in that it was maintained as an independent port, not owned by any king. As such, neutrality translated into a commercial safe harbor. The island flourished. Bankers outnumbered priests in the many temples to Apollo.

Merchants of the Mediterranean world came to Delos to build warehouses from which goods were redistributed. Royals and wealthy merchants developed the port city by financing buildings, which were dedicated monuments to self, in the guise of donations in the name of Apollo, or other gods. Delos developed in three sections: temples of the Sacred Way, the commercial port, and lavish residences on the road leading to the theatre. These sections are discernible today.

As a neutral port and international sanctuary to Apollo, Delos needed only international regard rather than walls for protection from attack. Occasionally, Athens raided the Delian treasury, never damaging the sacred sanctuary. When Rome rose over Greece as the power capital of the ancient world, Rome deferred to Athens regarding Delos. The nod to neutrality was not sufficient to protect Delos from enemies of Rome. Destruction came to Delos in 68 BCE.

The devastation to eight centuries of building on Delos in the first century BCE did not end life on the island. Residency persisted into the Christian era, although to a lesser-known extent. Seeking the story of Delos began in 1872, by French and Greek archaeologists. The effort is ongoing.

This is a short story of the grand and sacred island, to help begin the mental picture that will develop on a visit to Delos. Preserved from modern development, which covered many cities of the ancient world, Delos enjoyed lack of attention for centuries, which kept its remnants preserved for pilgrimages today.

GREECE, DELOS: Avenue of the Sacred Way

Life on the Island of Gods and Bankers

Apollo is the god of light. He is also a vengeful god. When priests at the temples on Delos could not decide which mood of the god to follow, they consulted the Oracle at Delphi. Oracles of Delphi were a cadre of fifty-five-year-old virgins, chosen for life within the temple. There they breathed radon gas that expelled from the mountain top through the floor of their temple. Temple priests at Delphi communicated to temple priests of Delos the mood of the time in garbled messages, ostensibly the wisdom of the Oracle.

Priests at Delos were indeed fortunate to have the Oracle decree success in the battle for kings and smooth sailing for merchants. In return, grateful royals and merchants endowed infrastructure on Delos to rival any city of the time. Roads were paved in granite and marble. Huge cisterns collected water, which was filtered as it entered houses. Great villas were built, with floors of inlaid mosaics. Numerous temples crowded the island. Two ports, a theater, several gymnasiums, and bathhouses were constructed. All of the infrastructure necessary to a proper Hellenic city, although far from Athens, was constructed without taxing the locals.

GREECE, DELOS: House of Merchant

There were no locals to tax. When the goddess Leto came to Delos, attended by goddess midwives, and shortly after temple priests came to herald the event and direct temple building, there were few people on the island. Those permanent residents were either exiles of King Minos of Crete, or deposited by pirates of the Aegean.

The Athenian priests deemed occupants to be below standard in their vision of the pure island of Apollo. They called in buyers and sold the locals off as slaves. Then the island was purified, that is, dispossessed of burials. All burials that could be located were opened, the contents boxed and transported for reburial to the neighboring island of Rheneia. No one consulted the Rheneians. That larger and less prosperous island produced food for its nearest neighbor and best customer.

To keep Delos pure, the priests decreed that no one was allowed to die, or be born, on Delos. The only recognized birth was that of Apollo. It is unknown how this was enforced, or what the punishment could be for an infraction. No executions were tolerated on Delos.

There was no army, no enforcers, and no property owners on Delos. Delos was land of Apollo. When large homes and warehouses were built, tribute was appropriately paid to Apollo.

Since not even an emperor or general could own Delos, it held the coveted neutral status of an island of praise to gods and commerce. Port fees and tributes to Apollo went into the treasury. The treasury grew outsized to the population. With no emperors to support and no armies to pay, there were few draws on income.

GREECE, DELOS: Delos Theatre

In the sixth to fifth century BCE, there were festivals to Apollo on Delos. The two ports; people transport dock, and merchant docks, were filled with visitors. Artisans were kept busy all year-round building temples, long corridors of display buildings, restaurants, and conference spaces, as well as creating statues, dedication inscriptions in stone, and interior decoration in stone and delicate mosaic, or painted surfaces of walls and floors.

Merchants built large warehouses for grain and non-perishable goods, such as wine, on Delos, where it could be safely held until times of festival, or sent to buyers in other ports. Merchants built grand villas for their residence. They were patrons of temples, roads and public spaces.

Imagine walking down a long, shaded portico, with columns, where there is a succession of small shops. Shops sold such fine goods as locally made perfume, wine and copperware. Other shops sold goods imported from the reaches of the Greek, Roman and Egyptian world. On Delos there were several choices of places to shop. There was a shopping plaza in the commercial area, near the cargo port, as well as near the conference center and restaurant, in the temple complex. Shops were also incorporated into the exterior walls of villas in the residential area, particularly on the main road to the theater. Sixth to fifth century Delos was cosmopolitan and lively.

In the sixth century, Delos began to mint its own coins. So much commerce and safe-haven storage of currency drew bankers to Delos. Over the centuries, the devotional purpose of Delos became diluted by the addition of temples to foreign gods. Apollo became just one of several major gods with active temples on Delos. There was even a temple to Hera, the wife of Zeus, from whom Leto fled to Delos. No doubt, the patron of that temple was hedging all bets. Godly devotion became secondary to commercial pursuits. Bankers proliferated on Delos as the number of priests diminished.

Emperor of Athens, Pericles, the victorious general of the Battle of Salamis fought in 480 BCE to deflect an incursion of Persians, celebrated his accomplishment by rebuilding the Parthenon on the Acropolis in Athens. When he ran short of cash, he tapped the treasury on Delos. After all, Athens was the protector of Delos. Independence had its limits.

Greece, Delos: Inner courtyard of wealthy resident

Greece, Delos: Cleopatra and her spouse at home Delos

Alexander the Great of Macedonia conquered much of the civilized world in the fourth century. Upon his death, his generals divided the empire and established their own dynasties. Delos prospered under Macedonian emperors. New temples and public spaces were built and old places still popular were repaired, including the baths, gymnasium, and theatre.

Greece, Delos: Mount Cynthus

In 168 BCE, the last of the Macedonian emperors, Perseus, was defeated by the Romans. Rome inherited protection of Delos, in which it deferred to Athens. Rome was pleased to see Delos compete in commerce with Rhodes, which had taken the wrong side in Roman politics. Athens took the opportunity to make another substantial withdrawal from the banks of Delos.

By the first century BCE, the festival of Delos drew few spectators and then ceased. Poor Athenians came to the island to farm, where once flowers were grown to create perfume. A mélange of migrants; Syrian, Jewish, Italian, and Egyptian came seeking release from oppression.

Although less vibrant than its height as a commercial power port, Delos was still a formidable location at the beginning of the first century BCE. Vestiges

GREECE, DELOS: Monument to Man & Gods

of greatness could still be seen in structures needing repair. It was still possible to walk around the island for a lesson in history.

Visitors arrive at the passenger harbor of Delos today, as they did in the sixth through first century BCE. The open plaza, paved in stone was and is perfectly drained. To the left began the Sacred Way, an open street, flanked by long stoa, that is, covered passageways, lined with columns. Amid the Sacred Way were the temple to Apollo and other temples.

The Sacred Way ended at the sanctuary, a complex of temples, conference spaces, restaurants, and an open courtyard. The courtyard had an oversize, copper palm tree, the gift of an Athenian general in 417 BCE. Near the palm tree stood the Colossus of the Naxians, a giant statue of Apollo, dedicated by people of Naxos in the seventh century BCE. When the palm tree fell in a wind storm, it knocked over the Apollo statue of Naxian marble, which broke into irretrievable pieces.

Beyond the Sanctuary is the road to the commercial port. On the road is the Sacred Lake, revered on Delos where water was precious. The lake is considered the actual birth site of Apollo. Overlooking the lake are the Lions of Naxos. Naxos island is known to have contributed the marble from which somewhere between nine and fifteen lions were sculpted. Five lions survive today, four in the Delos museum, and one carried away to Venice, where it sits outside the armory building, with some other lion's head tacked to its headless body.[28] The outside lions today are copies.

The commercial port sits on Fournoi Bay, on the west shore of Delos. It was an area thick with warehouses and shipbuilding activity for several centuries. So many merchants far afield of Athens transacted business in Delos that it is not unusual that the main agora, that is open business area, was the Agora of Italians, so named for its benefactors, known by inscriptions in stone. By example, one benefactor was Philostratos of Askalon in Phoenicia,[29] who built a long arcade offering shade to business meetings.

---

[28] The larger lion in Venice, next to the Delos lion, was spirited away from the Port of Piraeus, in twelfth century crusades.

[29] Phoenicia is the area stretching across Syria, Lebanon and part of Israel today.

Notably, the largest building in Delos was not a temple. The largest single structure in Delos was the merchant warehouse of Gaius Ofellius Ferus of Champagne.[30] The structure is well identified as Ferus commissioned an oversize statue of himself to fit in a niche in a high traffic area.

After the festivals ceased, and fewer people came to Delos, and with the loss of caché associated with Apollo, merchants found other vibrant ports in which to do business. Buildings fell into disrepair. Building materials were repurposed by farmers inland to the east. Amid farmland was the House of Fournoi, the headquarters of a religious society, active in the glory days of Delos.[31]

From the passenger port, there is the option to turn right, toward the sacred mountain of Delos, Mount Cynthus. It is revered as the only mountain on Delos. Water captured on Mount Cynthus flows into the only stream on Delos and the Sacred Lake. Mythology regards the stream as emanating from the Nile. No doubt the mythology began when Egyptians began frequenting Delos and built the Temple of Isis.

GREECE, DELOS: Residential street with a view

---

[30] Champagne refers to a large community in ancient times, 45 miles south of Rome.
[31] Much material for this story was gleaned from repeated trips to Delos and from materials sold on site, including the book by Dr. Fotini Zaphiropoulou, Delos: Monuments and Museum, Krene Editions, Athens, 2016.

The oldest residential section, with its haphazard streets, flows downward from the base of Mount Cynthus. It is the area with the highest density of opulent residences of wealthy residents. The uphill streets end at the theatre.

Houses of wealthy merchants and bankers were built on allowed lots, to the extent of space allowed. Residents could not own real estate, yet they invested great amounts in construction and decoration of villas. Houses were constructed of granite, with fascia of gneiss, giving a natural striped effect in compressed rock. Walls were often plastered and painted to look like marble, or decorated in bright colors. Interior design often associated with the better-preserved Pompeii actually originated as a style trend in Delos several centuries earlier.

Houses were built without exterior windows. All light came in through the interior courtyard, around which were columns supporting interior beams of the roof. The exterior side of the roof was supported by the exterior wall. Many houses had a second level, with an interior corridor, overlooking the courtyard. Floors were inlaid with mosaics, the most elaborate found in the courtyard.

Over centuries, corners inside homes were decorated with intricately carved corniches, with frequent use of copper. Copper was the design feature of choice for wealthy residents. Copper legs on couches and tables were a sign of business success.

Today, homes in Delos are identified by unique features that survived ravages of time. One house is known for the cache of gold jewelry hidden in the floor. The house of sealings is thought to be the home of a banker, who collected them. Sealings, cast in clay, impressed with a stamp of the sender, held the string, which enclosed a document of parchment. Sealings in the house, about fifteen thousand of them, baked into discs during a fire, otherwise survived the fire.

Houses in Delos were blessed with good spirits and warded off bad spirits by symbols etched into exterior walls. A popular symbol was the winged phallus. The phallus was the symbol of strength and fertility, in other words, success and abundance. Colossus phallus statues sit on columns at the entrance to the theatre and other important gathering places in Delos.

In Delos, everyone enjoyed the theatre. The semi-circle Greek designed theatre on Delos was begun in the fourth century BCE, and was completed over a seventy-five-year period. After that, it was repaired and embellished over time of continuous use. It could seat 6,500 patrons.

Beyond entertainment, the theatre had a practical use. In an island of scarce water resources, the theatre acted as a water capture sleeve, with a cistern at the low point. This cistern held water for public use. Water entering houses of the district had filters before water entered private tanks.

GREECE, DELOS: Public Water system

Politics of Destruction 68 BCE

Delos needed no walls to protect its residents. The shrine of Apollo was a powerful talisman of protection. During wars of the ancient world, Delos remained neutral, where otherwise waring kingdoms could send their merchants to transact business and purchase grain.

In the first century BCE, an enemy of Rome seethed with growing contempt. The future Mithridates VI repulsed Roman-backed aggression in his empire of Pontus, present-day Turkey. Mithridates was not the man to irritate. Born in Sinope, northern Turkey on the Black Sea coast, his mother preferred his brother as successor to his father. When he became of age, Mithridates imprisoned his mother and brother. He took control of the kingdom and enjoyed victory in battle over the Romans. Then he annihilated about 80,000 Romans living in his kingdom in 87 BCE.[32]

There were two reprisals of war between Rome and Pontus. In the third war, Mithridates brought his vengeance to Delos. Unprotected by walls, and never having needed an army, Delos, the outpost of Rome in the most meager way, was still a Roman protectorate. By obliterating the most successful island in the known world in 68 BCE, Mithridates took a poke at Rome.

The destruction of Delos was not a strategic military maneuver. It was senseless destruction of a non-political island of 25,000 residents, of which Mithridates was responsible for the death of 20,000. The island had diminished in importance in trade before the raid. The festival had long ceased. Sons of Mithridates rose against him. In 63 BCE he died by poison.

The rubble of Delos became pickings for scavengers. Copper decorations were salvaged and carted away on ships. Marble statues were ground into powder for the lime from which to make cement in growing communities on other islands. Athens tried to sell the island. There were no interested buyers.

---

[32] Mithridates was a consummate politician. Sinope was a Greek city. Much of the southern coast of the Black Sea was settled by Greeks as early as the sixth century BCE, from where they sent grain to Rome. Mithridates considered himself Greek and Persian, whichever he needed to be to gain allies against Rome.

Surviving in the Christian Era

Life persisted on Delos 500 years into the Christian era, or perhaps due to the Christian era. On Delos there was no resistance to new communities of the new faith. Christian basilicas rose from the ruins of pagan temples, with repurposed building materials on site.[33] Communities built slowly, living on produce grown in small fields, watered from the Sacred Lake and stream.

Little is known of life on Delos in the Christian era. The visible traces of life to the sixth century CE were scraped aside, to tell the story of ancient Delos. In 1872, the French Archaeological School, based in Athens, came to Delos to excavate the story of past glory days. It is known that by the late sixth century CE, the island was almost abandoned.

Venice had mastery of the Mediterranean in the thirteenth century. Venetians who came to Delos held the island. They could never decide what to do with it. In 1329 the Knights of St. John came to Delos. They surveyed the harbor for its use as a base from which to harass ships of the Ottoman Turks and decided to move on to Rhodes. After the siege of Rhodes, by the Ottomans, who forced the Knights to become homeless and then move to Malta, the Ottoman naval commanders came to Delos. They found the place lacking in strategic merit.

Delos became a little-visited backwater of the Mediterranean. The lack of attention to the island made it an attractive home for pirates, looking for a safe haven. There were no entertaining diversions on Delos to interest even these scavengers of the sea. Delos became abandoned.

Reviving the Story of Delos Today

Since 1960, the Greek Archaeological Service has been active on Delos conserving walls and mosaics. The amount of material excavated, still possessing historical context with which to tell the story of ancient Delos is amazing,

---

[33] Christian communities rose from ruins of pagan cities on islands of the Mediterranean. It was a recurring theme, as seen on Cyprus in this Itinerary.

given the centuries of exposure to scavenging visitors since 68 BCE. Statues and personal goods are on display in the Delos Museum, on-site, and the Greek National Museum in Athens. Museum collections evidence opulence and majesty of a glory period in the pagan era.

The ferry to Delos is a short trip from Mykonos today. Mykonos was a small fishing village whose inhabitants lived a modest life until Jackie Kennedy Onassis discovered its beaches in the 1960s. She literally fed a starving population, until wealth came to the island in its iteration as a retreat for the glitterati of the world. On Mykonos, Jackie O is revered as a goddess. Rightfully so, but that is another story.

Greece, Rhodes: Primary and Secondary defensive walls

Greece, Rhodes: Entrance to Mandraki Harbor

The Knights of St. John in Rhodes

Mention of the Knights of St. John evokes visions of heroism in medieval times. They were a gallant order of knights, with their chain mail, banners and closed society. The knights were also central to the development of trade between nations in the Eastern Mediterranean. Often conjoined with histories of other orders of knights, the Knights of St. John has a singular history and fascinating story in war and peace.

It is descriptive of the centuries-old order to know its full name – The Sovereign Military Hospitaller Order of St. John of Jerusalem and later with Rhodes and then Malta added to the title. The Order, as it can be referred to, in brief, began as a Vatican-sanctioned organization to aid pilgrims to the Holy Land. The Order rapidly evolved to a military order of pilgrim protection and then to protection of Christendom, in all its domestic and commercial affairs in the Eastern Mediterranean.

When the Knights of St. John took up residence in Rhodes, they imposed on an ancient city the sovereign government of a fraternal organization. It was a unique arrangement. The story of Rhodes and its most famous resident are inseparable.

Ancient Rhodes

Rhodes is the largest of a group of Greek islands, known as the Dodecanese, so far east of Greece that they almost touch on Turkey. Rhodes is only forty-five miles long and twenty miles at its widest point. Since the fifth century, BCE Rhodes has provided a home to mariners with its freshwater streams, cool breezes, and natural ports.

The ancient Greeks who first settled Rhodes named it for the rockroses that grew on the hills. They planted grapevines, olive trees, and grain. The timber-covered island provided ample material for shipbuilding. From Rhodes, seventh century Greeks traded with Syria to the east, the Nile Delta to the south, and its Greek neighbors to the north and west. Residents became wealthy from exporting wine to Greek ports on the Black Sea. Travelers from Rhodes settled the southern Sicilian town of Gela, now an archaeological site. Rhodes received settlers from Crete. From the inception of civilization, Rhodes was a prosperous port.

Upon the death of Alexander the Great in 323 BCE, the warring factions of his former generals threw the vast Greek Empire into tumult. For a year from 305 to 304 BCE, Rhodes was under siege, due to its neutral stance amid those who would use its resources to mount an attack on Egypt, a valuable trading partner. The strong walls of Rhodes resisted the siege, adding to prominence of the city.

After the siege, residents of Rhodes emerged from the walls, sold the siege equipment, and used the funds from the sale to build the Colossus of Rhodes. This marvel of the ancient world was a monument to the strength of the city, dedicated to the Greek sun-god Helios. The Colossus stood 110 feet high, perched on a fifty-foot pedestal. It did not span the harbor entrance as so often portrayed. The statue was constructed out of bronze plates attached to an iron frame, much like the copper-onto-steel construction of the Statue of Liberty.

In 227 BCE, Rhodes was the epicenter of an earthquake that brought down the Colossus and damaged city walls. So high was regard for the Colossus throughout the Greek world that financial aid came to Rhodes from Greeks and from trading partners who wanted to assist in rebuilding the city. The city fathers gratefully utilized the funds to repair city walls and build an even greater city within.

When it came to rebuilding the statue, the patriarchs of Rhodes chose instead to use the remaining donated funds to enhance their fleet. To appease critics, the city fathers reported that they had consulted an oracle, which advised that rebuilding the Colossus could bring harm to the city. The statue went to a scrap heap, and the city did indeed experience a century of peace and prosperity. A millennium later, ruins of the Colossus were sold to Arab traders, who required nine hundred camels to carry away remains of the bronze god.

Leaders of Rhodes were better builders and merchants than politicians. In 201 BCE, they sided with Rome against Philip V of Macedonia. As a Roman ally, Rhodes was required to aid the unpopular war to destroy Carthage, a trading partner, in 146 BCE. When Rhodes supported Perseus of Macedonia against Rome, Rome retaliated by making neighboring island Lykia a free port, which reduced the trading revenues of Rhodes by 85%. Rhodes supported Pompey against Caesar, then held back support for Cassius in 42 BCE. Cassius responded by bleeding Rhodes of ships, art and finances.

Rhodes entered the Christian era after a visit by Apostle Paul in 57. A century later, a series of earthquakes devastated the once independent city. It became a vassal outpost of Rome, then to Venetian and Genoese traders, and finally of the Byzantine Empire. In 1306, the governor of Rhodes declared independence from the Byzantines of Constantinople to avoid high taxes levied on its trade. Pope Clement V authorized the conquest of Rhodes by any Christian nation in good standing with the Vatican. The timing was fortuitous for the Order of St. John of Jerusalem, which had just been ousted from their Holy Land home and was adrift in exile in Cyprus.

GREECE, RHODES: Emblem of the French Tongue of the Knights

The Order of St. John of Jerusalem

The Order of St. John, the Knights Hospitaller, was formed in 1085, comprised of a volunteer group of monks whose mission it was to nurse pilgrims on their way to the Holy Land. Muslims seized Jerusalem in 1071, from the Byzantium Christian domain with its capital in Constantinople. The Byzantine emperor reached out to Pope Urban II for help to restore Christian control. The pope envisioned that a crusade to the Holy Land, endorsed by the Vatican, could be a path to reuniting all of Christianity under Rome and mending the Schism of 1054 with Eastern Orthodoxy.

The first crusade was known as the Peoples' Crusade. The crusaders were a motley group of pilgrims fleeing life as feudal serfs. When hungry crusaders reached Jerusalem, brother Gerard, a Christian monk who remained in the city, threw loaves of bread over the wall to feed them. When they entered the city, the monk found shelter for the pilgrims in his hospice, which became known as a crusaders' hospital, a place of rest and nourishment.

Christian pilgrims made a visit to brother Gerard their favored Jerusalem destination. Grateful pilgrims with ample means made dying bequests to the group of monks. The order of Hospitaller monks became an institution.

In 1097, the Vatican launched the Princes' Crusade. The cadre of armed nobility, hungry for loot, enjoyed military victories as they roamed from Nicaea to Antioch, before entering Jerusalem to loot and slaughter even peaceful Muslims and Jews. The Muslims practiced religious toleration. The crusaders were interested only in easily obtained spoils. Out of a sense of religious mission, to atone for unchristian acts, these crusaders made donations to the monks, which made Hospitaller monks wealthy.

By 1113, the monks had sufficient funds to attract the attention of the pope. The little volunteer band became the Vatican ordained Order of St. John Hospitaller. At the time of Gerard's death in 1120, the Order had hostels along the route of Holy Land pilgrims in Marseilles, Bari and Messina.

Gerard's successor, Raymond de Puy, quickly caused the Order to evolve from tending to the sick, to protecting the pilgrims from infidel aggressors that may prey upon them. The peaceful order of brothers became militant. The mission of servants of the poor, sick and hungry, was expanded before the end of the twelfth century to be soldiers of Christ. The Order of St. John became Knights of St. John.

There was a precedent for a military/religious order in the Knights Templar. This older order of knights was a purely military organization. They wore a red cross of religious war on a field of white. For contrast, the Knights of St. John adopted a white cross on a red background, symbolizing a priority for peace.[34]

The Order of the Knights of St. John enjoyed immediate success and outlived other medieval orders, due in large part to their string of able leaders and dedication to an efficient organization. The Knights of St. John covered the Christian political map, grouped into eight sections, called Tongues. Tongues lived separately by group, had separate duties to avoid competition in daily affairs, were supported by their nobility at home and owed unquestioned loyalty to the Order.

Tongues were those of Auvergne, Provence, France, England, Castile, Aragon, Italy, Germany, and England. Over the centuries of nationalization of Italy, France, and Spain, the Order kept their separate Tongues. England withdrew its Tongue when Henry VIII had a spat with the pope, just after Henry had generously funded sagging coffers of the Order.[35]

The governing council of the Order was made up of the head of each Tongue, a Bishop as the religious leader, a Prior of the properties, a Bailiff of the Convent home to young knights, and the senior Knights of the Grand Cross. The Knights of Justice, a senior group from whom key leaders were usually selected, were required to have proof of noble lineage. The Grand Master was

---

[34] Teutonic Knights wore a black cross on white. Formed after the other orders of knights, and comprised of Germanic knights, they returned from Jerusalem to Christianize Prussia by force. They ended with defeat in 1410, in battle with King Ladislaus of Poland. See Cruise through History© Itinerary XI Ports of the Baltic Sea for the port of Riga in Tales of Black Knights, Blackheads and Black Cats.

[35] Queen Victoria revived the English Tongue in 1888, although England was a Protestant country. The Queen appointed her son Edward VII Prior of the English Order. In 1960, the English Order sponsored a branch of the Knights of St. John in the United States. Today the Order is a peaceful service organization.

Greece, Rhodes: **Warning or Tribute**

the top of the leadership structure. Three-quarters of all Grand Masters were from a French Tongue. All had served time at sea and had a minimum of thirteen years of prior leadership experience.

By the mid-thirteenth century, the Ottoman Turks swept through the Eastern Mediterranean and down to Egypt, bringing all in their path under their control. Increasingly, the Ottoman Empire chipped away at the Byzantine Empire, although the newcomer Muslims would not vanquish the Christian capital until 1453. In 1291, when the Ottomans captured Jerusalem, the Knights of St. John fled to Cyprus.

GREECE, RHODES: Gate to the City of Knights

For the next two decades, the Order was adrift. Wherever they had a presence, the Order reverted to their core mission of maintaining hospitals to heal the sick and feed the poor. Although homeless, the Order was still wealthy. Their estates in Europe, as well as land in Cyprus and other islands, kept the coffers refilled. When King Philip of France attempted to use the fifteenth century Inquisition to indict the Knights Templar, in order to discredit the order and claim their wealth in Spain and Portugal, the pope acted quickly with a papal bull transferring all of the lands of the Knights Templar in Spain and Portugal to the Knights of St. John. Philip's frustration fueled the fortunes of the Hospitaller Order.

The Order Takes Residence in Rhodes: 1310 – 1522

The military Hospitaller order became a sovereign when they began residence in Rhodes in 1310. Locals disputed the sovereign moniker. They had welcomed freedom from one foreign over-seer and were not interested in a new foreign ruler. To obtain tax relief, Rhodes declared itself independent of Byzantium in 1306. That naïve action left the island with no protectors in a literal sea of hungry suitors.

Even with the backing of the pope, and alliance with a crafty sea pirate, it took two years for the Order to conquer Rhodes. A Venetian moneylender financed their effort. Finally, to slip into the heavily fortified city, the Knights donned sheep's skin and entered in the early morning as sheep were being led out of the city to pasture.

GREECE, RHODES: Inside hospital of the Knights of Saint John

Rhodes became the first permanent home of the Order in 1310. Their initial action was to build a hospital in acknowledgment of their mission. They improved water and sanitation systems in the city. After that, the knights established Rhodes as the greatest fortified town in the Mediterranean. With the introduction of gunpowder as a weapon of war, city walls needed to be thick. The Palace of the Grand Masters was built low and thick as well. Leading to the palace, the Knights built a street of homes reserved for the Tongues. Again, the architecture is low, with thick walls, few windows and heavy doors. For two hundred years, Rhodes was home.

GREECE, RHODES: Street of the Knights

The Knights were good for Rhodes, and location in the city was a defining moment for the Knights. The Knights of St. John were quick to recognize that their military skills, combined with local master seamen, could result in a navy in command of trade in the Eastern Mediterranean. Instead of a ground war with Muslims, the Order planned to benefit their treasury in the name of their lord by harassing Ottoman ships laden with trade goods. For almost two thousand years, Rhodes grew wealthy in sea trade from the Black Sea to Egypt and from Greece to the ancient trade routes of Syria and the Holy Land. That tradition was their inheritance. The Knights sought to continue the tradition.

An opportunity to establish mastery at sea came in 1312. Turks had a fleet of ships at Amorgós, a Greek island north and west of Rhodes. While not an immediate threat to Rhodes, any such incursion was a statement of future intent. In the brief sea battle, the Order obtained a quick victory and a notable reputation.

GREECE, RHODES: City walls

The importance of a Christian outpost in the otherwise Ottoman Lake that was the Mediterranean Sea was not lost on the Vatican. Often tempted to allow the Order to be vanquished in battle and absorb their valuable assets, popes utilized the tactical position and skills of the Order to support future crusades. For the Knights of St. John, focused upon income from the sea to finance good works, the crusades were rarely to their benefit. Still, they never failed to follow orders of a pope.

In 1365, the pope sanctioned a crusade to Alexandria. European nobles amassed 165 ships, with help from the Knights, to further their ambitions of quick wealth under the guise of Christian purpose. Once in the old city, the crusaders looted all homes and killed Christians, Jews, and Muslims. Venice lost a valuable trading partner. The Knights of St. John of Jerusalem and Rhodes lost a period of peace. Retribution from the Ottomans was quick, but not particularly strong. Division within Ottoman ranks and their focus upon taking the Danube spared Rhodes.

The Order lost heavily in 1396 in service to a crusade against the Turks east of the Danube. The Knights were ill-prepared to wage a siege war against superior strength of the Turkish army. The Order preferred a negotiated truce in 1403, which allowed trade and a consulate inside Jerusalem. The truce ended in 1440, when Pope Eugenius IV ordered a crusade. European nobles were not interested, so the Order used its naval forces against Egypt. They were victorious over the Egyptians, weakening the country and enabling an easy takeover of Egypt by the Ottomans.

In 1453, the Eastern Orthodox Christian capital of Constantinople fell to the Ottoman Turks. The Muslim Turkish wave was at the height of its power. Turkish Sultan Mehmet II established himself in his new capital, renamed Istanbul. He then looked west at Hungary and south to Rhodes for his next conquests.

GREECE, RHODES: Back Gate to the harbor,
low walls where atackers tried to swim ashore

GREECE, RHODES: Reinforced Amboise Gate

Siege of Rhodes 1480 and 1522

Frenchman Pierre d'Aubusson joined the Auvergne Tongue of the Knights of St. John in 1445, about the time news of the spread of the Ottoman Turks was filtering through Europe. He was twenty-two when he joined the Order and immediately went to Rhodes. Rhodes and the Order were home and family for d'Aubusson for the next fifty-eight years of his life. He dedicated his life to fighting Ottoman Turks and building a strongly fortified Rhodes. As an engineer, d'Aubusson personally directed work on fortifications. Seasoned as a soldier, sensitive and intelligent, d'Aubusson was elected Grand Master of the Order in 1476, when he was a strong fifty-three years old. In 1480, his leadership was tested when the Turks arrived to lay siege to Rhodes.

The siege of 1480 pitted the cross and the crescent with its epicenter at Rhodes. The Turks had a force of 70,000 to face 600 knights aided by about 2,000 paid troops and locals who feared the Turks more than they had disdain for the knights. The Turks also had cannons, the war tool that enabled them to blow through the walls of Constantine, which had guarded Constantinople for over a thousand years. Each cannon could be fired once an hour to allow the metal cannon sleeve to cool between firings.

Greece, Rhodes: Tower of St. Nikolas, guardian of the dual harbor

Rhodes had and still has dual harbors, guarded at the tip by the Tower of St. Nickolas. The Turks made the tower their first target. As the siege began, relief boats came into the harbor at night to deliver newly arrived knights and supplies. Older and non-military members of the Order worked tirelessly at the hospital to avoid the scourge of medieval warfare, death from infection in otherwise minor wounds. Injured knights returned to fight repeatedly during the siege.

When the Turks positioned their boats close enough to walls for swimmers to advance, guns from the walls blew up the ships within range and repelled the swimmers. When the elite, fighting core of Turkish Janissaries built pontoons to mount a night attack, the Knights set the pontoons on fire. When cannons blew a hole into the fortress, d'Aubusson led hand-to-hand combat into the breach.

Although the Turks came within reach of victory when fighting in the narrow corridor blown through the wall of the city, the Turkish advance brigade of "new soldiers," illiterate conscripted fighters, were superstitious. The sight of men in metal armor, waving flags, put them into a panic. They tried to turn back as the Janissaries pushed them forward. Turk fought Turk in the tunnel of the wall in the crush of hordes of men pushing back and forth.

Five thousand Turkish soldiers died in one day of battle. Nine thousand Turks died before the Turkish generals headed to their boats and left the harbor. Casualties among the Knights were comparatively light. The Grand Master was injured three times and recovered well. He became a hero all through Christian Europe.

Sultan Mehmet II had not been part of the siege party. He was otherwise engaged in military actions toward Hungary. He was incensed when he learned of the defeat of his army. Mehmet vowed that he would personally return the next year to defeat the Christians. Had he done so, the knights would have been hard-pressed to resist, not being able to complete repairs to the walls in a short period of time. During repairs, Rhodes suffered another earthquake. In 1481, while on his way to Rhodes, the sultan died of dysentery. Thoughts of a new siege died with him.

For the next forty years, the Order enjoyed a period of peace and prosperity on Rhodes. Financial gifts poured in from nobility of Europe in gratitude for holding back spread of the Ottomans in their threat to advance westward to Italy and France. One of the heirs of the Sultan paid an annual tribute to d'Aubusson to keep watch over his brother so that the Christians did not enlist him to mount an insurrection in Istanbul. In recognition of the tribute, the pope made d'Aubusson a Cardinal and gave him autonomy in affairs of the Order.

In his final years, the Grand Master focused on improving internal business affairs and instilling a strong work ethic in young knights. He received a mixed reaction to his expulsion of Jews from Rhodes, in consort with the Christian led Inquisition in Spain. Pierre d'Aubusson died in 1503 at the age of eighty. He left the Order in firm control of finances and secure at home in Rhodes.

GREECE, RHODES: Ancient Mandraki Harbor entrance with Venetian colunnade

In the decade following the death of d'Aubusson, not all was quiet in the Mediterranean. By 1510, the Order was proving its prowess at sea in skirmishes with Turkish ships. Each side considered the other to be a pirate in raids on transports of goods in commerce. The Order had new technology in smaller, faster ships under sail, that could outmaneuver the older rowed galleys of the Ottoman navy, dependent upon slaves to power awkward vessels.

In 1522, Suleiman was a young sultan intent on proving his ability to rid the sea of Christians. He set out to lay siege to Rhodes on July 28, with 200,000 men on seven hundred ships. The Knights of St. John called out to the crowns of Europe for help. There was no response. France and Spain were at war with each other. Henry VIII had a spat with the pope over his marriage. European sovereigns looked forward to absorbing assets of the Order upon its demise.

Suleiman was denied his quick victory. For months the Order held their city. From the outside, the Knights looked invincible. Inside the walls the story was not as bright.

Two Knights had competed for the position of Grand Master. The loser never lost his disappointment. After several months of siege, the angry knight was discovered to have been sending messages to the Turks, encouraging their continued battle. Amid the battle, the Knight was tried, convicted and executed. That a Knight would betray his Order was bad for morale.

Still, the Knights fought bravely. The Turks tunneled under the city to set explosives. The Knights dug countermines. Turkish miners became trapped in rubble. The stout walls of the city held despite continued cannon fire.

By the end of December 1522, it was apparent to the Grand Master that the numbers were not in their favor. He negotiated a peaceful surrender to Suleiman. The Knights left Rhodes with their sacred relics: the hand of St. John in its jeweled case and the precious piece of the True Cross. Once again, the Order was homeless.

GREECE, RHODES: Habor windmills, post conquest
Mosque & Walls of the Knight's City

On to Malta and a Future for the Knights

When the Knights of St. John decamped from Rhodes they went into a period of exile in Cyprus. Among them was a young knight, Jean Parisot de la Valette, who had not yet been recognized as having the potential of a great leader. In the future, Suleiman and Valette would have another chance to meet in battle.

Europe had little to offer the homeless Knights of St. John. Martin Luther was threatening the papacy. Henry VIII gave relief funds to the Order and then seized their real estate in England. Eventually, a benevolent monarch, Charles V of Spain, granted the Order a new home on Malta. That chapter of the Knights is the beginning of a new story.[36]

Rhodes became a vassal of the powerful Ottoman Empire, which had conquered Constantinople a century earlier. The Ottomans brought a period of peace as they enabled the port of Rhodes to trade throughout the Eastern Mediterranean, all of which was within Ottoman control. In the eighteenth century, as the Ottoman dynasties lost their grip on far-flung possessions, domains such as Rhodes pursued independence. The Italians returned to dominate trade at the ports. The history of Rhodes came full circle, always maintaining its role as a critical link in maritime trade. From 1912 to 1945, Italians controlled Rhodes as part of the Fascist regime.

GREECE, RHODES: Inner court of the Palace of the Grand Master

---

36   See Cruise through History, Itinerary V – Arabia to the Atlantic, Port: Malta, for the rest of the story of the Knights of St. John.

GREECE, RHODES: Tribute to Italian king

Today in Rhodes

The Ottoman Turks held Rhodes for three centuries, during which time they made very few changes. During the restoration of historic Rhodes in the twentieth century, latticework was removed from windows and minarets from churches, leaving the island much as it had been during the time of the Knights of St. John. The Gate of Liberty was opened in the wall in 1924, to allow for traffic flow. In 1948, Rhodes became part of the Greek nation.

Just inside the city walls, the Street of Knights still runs from the hospital to the Palace of the Grand Master. The lodges of the Tongues can be identified by coats of arms above doors and windows. The Turks used the Palace as a prison. It was restored in 1940 to opulence beyond that known to the Grand Masters, when the Palace was offered as a residence to the president of Italy, Victor Emmanuel, and then to Dictator Benito Mussolini. Visitors to the Palace of the Grand Master today will walk through rooms, as Mussolini would have done, had he stayed there. The famous second century BCE statue from Rhodes known as the Laokoön, a man caught in serpents sent by Apollo, is a copy. The original is in the Vatican Museum.

GREECE, RHODES: House of Tongue on Street of the Knights

GREECE, RHODES: Signature of the Grand Master Architect of the Walls

The Museum Library today was an arsenal for the Knights. It may be the oldest structure on the island from the era of the Knights, dating from 1355. On the next square, the Hospital of the Knights of St. John is still open as it has been since 1440. Opposite the Hospital is the Lodge of the Tongue of England, as it was rebuilt in 1919. Today it houses the Archaeological Museum. On the next square is a fifteenth-century mansion that was the Palace of the Admirals. It overlooks the Square of Jewish Martyrs, a reminder of the late fifteenth century Inquisition.

Around the harbor are three windmills, rebuilt to represent thirteen windmills in existence during the siege of 1522. The Gate of the Mills still bears the coat of arms of d'Aubusson, responsible for fortifying the gate after the Siege of 1480.

Bronze deer sit on columns at the entrance to Mandraki Harbor. Not present is the Colossus. The bronze god, Helios, never straddled the harbor entrance. He is remembered in second-century coins and twenty-first-century souvenirs. It is fitting that cruise ships arrive in Rhodes today as ships have done for 2500 years and will into the future.

GREECE, RHODES: Auto entrance to the old city today

Patmos – Fortress Monastery of the Cave of St. John

 Popular Patmos on the Bay of Skala

which was a fishing and farming area. For Arab sailors of the Near East in the seventh century, enslaved people were the currency. By the eleventh century, the islands were depopulated.

In 1088, the Byzantine Emperor in Constantinople gave the vacant island of Patmos to a cleric, who had shown a talent for administrative strength, as well as leadership in matters of faith. Hosios Christodoulos left his parish in Kos, in the south of Turkey, and came to Patmos to establish a monastery. Kos was a well-settled center of Christendom. Patmos was a desert.

GREECE, PATMOS: Monastery Fortress

For a Patriarch, a far-flung piece of the realm of the Orthodox Church such as Patmos was a small assignment for a cleric to hold as a position of high esteem. The island is only thirteen square miles, mostly of intermittent coastal plains, with few trees or natural terrestrial resources. It could not be and has not been, self-supporting. Hosios decided that, no matter how insignificant the island on its own merit, it was the place of refuge chosen by Saint John. Therefore, as curator of the place of the cave of the Saint, Hosios had a special mission.

Hosios claimed the highest point on Patmos for his new church, which would be the centerpiece of a monastery. His small church displaced the existent pagan temple. Later, followers of Hosios built a larger church and expanded the monastery. The setting of the monastery, its design and internal structure, were all established by Hosios before his flight from pirates in 1093.

The Holy Monastery of Saint John, the Theologian on Patmos, has a design unique among monasteries of the Christian world, even among those of the Eastern Orthodox Church. Hosios had the foresight, before arrival of the first pirates, to assume that for this monastery to effectively protect the memory and spiritual legacy of Saint John, it must be built as a fortress. That the monastery has survived for an unbroken nine hundred years, is testimony to the wisdom of its founder.

This story is a brief tribute to the monastery-protectorate of the refuge of Saint John, as the safe harbor of relics of ecclesiastical time kept there, and to its paternal care of the community of Patmos, drawn to the island by the Holy Monastery of Saint John. Patmos and its monastery are interdependent small jewels preserved to delight visitors, even for a short stay.

900 Years of Devotion

In the first century of the Christian era, Patmos was an insignificant island off the coast of Turkey, not far from Ephesus. Ephesus was the major city, where the Apostle John came with the Virgin Mary, at the direction of Christ. It was in Ephesus that John wrote his biblical text and preached to the masses. The ancient Basilica of St. John is preserved outside of the city of Ephesus today.

In 95 CE, Roman Emperor Domitian exiled John from Ephesus. He sailed for a safe haven to the quiet little island of Patmos. There he lived in a cave, half-way up the mountain, overlooking the bay of Skala, where cruise ships dock today. It was while in quiet contemplation in the cave that John recorded his vision of the revelations of Christ. The Book of Revelations became the final book of the Bible. John returned to Ephesus in 96 CE, where he died and was buried, in 101 CE.

As word of Revelations to John on Patmos spread, people came on pilgrimage to his cave. By the fourth century, the Cave of the Apocalypse, as the cave of St. John was known, was an established pilgrimage site. Small churches dotted the island of Patmos.

Before the visit of John, residents of Patmos were devoted to the Greek god Artemis, god of the hunt. There was a temple to the pantheon of gods on top the hill, the highest point on the island, uphill from the Cave of the Apocalypse. Amidst the statues to Greek gods, people established a place of Christian worship. Later, monks of the monastery held the ancient statues in protective storage. They became relics of life in a continuum. The hill-top site became a church.

The history of faith and population on Patmos went into a period of darkness from about the seventh to eleventh century. Open to the seas and vulnerable, people of Patmos were easily captured by pirates, generally regarded by Christian historians as Saracens, able seafarers from the area of Syria. There were few people left on Patmos eking out a meager life during this time.

In 1088, the Byzantine Emperor in Constantinople, Alexios I Komnenos, looked out on his expanding empire and saw potential in small islands of the Aegean. From the island of Kos, the emperor plucked an able cleric to establish Byzantine dominance on vacant Patmos. To Hosios Christodoulos, the chosen cleric, the assignment was not a career-enhancing position.

Kos, a Greek island closer to the beaches of Turkey than other Greek soil, was a fortified city from the time of Alexander the Great in the fourth century BCE. It was rumored to be the place where Queen Cleopatra hid her jewelry after the death of Caesar. In Kos there were extensive monuments to the declining pagan world and birth of Christian faith. The Bishop of Kos attended the First

Council of Nicaea in 325 CE, convened by Roman Emperor Constantine, and held a seat of authority equal to the bishop of Rhodes. In 1088, Patmos was a modest goat pasture. However, it held the supreme natural treasure of the Cave of the Apocalypse. Patmos had sacred virtue.

Hosios threw himself into his assignment like a soldier of faith. He designed a monastery in the style of a crusader castle. Looking uphill at the stone fortress rising from the midst of white-washed modest houses clustered at the base of the monastery today, the sight of armed knights would seem more likely than robed monks emerging from prayer.

Hosios chose his building site with safety and sacristy in mind. The top of the highest peak on Patmos had centuries of history as a site of reverence. On this spot, Hosios commanded that a larger church be built. He designed the monastery cloisters, with the church and living quarters at the center, to be surrounded by an imposing wall, with a strong gate, topped with battlement towers. The walls were made impervious to breach.

GREECE, PATMOS: Monastery lookout for pirates

Pirates came to Patmos before Hosios could enclose his monastery behind a wall. He escaped from the island in 1093, never to return. The plans he began were sufficiently detailed that returning monks carried forth to complete the monastery as begun by its founder.

Besides bequeathing the monastery with an architecture of protection, Hosios made two additional contributions, which have sustained the monastery for a millennium. Hosios was an able statesman, who negotiated political advantage for the monastery. He also brought a library, which became the basis for a collection of manuscripts kept safe for the life of the monastery.

Monasteries, like churches across the European continent, depended for their support on vassal estates and relief from onerous taxation by secular lords. When the Byzantine emperor sent Hosios to Patmos, he endowed the monastery with ownership, control and command of the entire island of Patmos, the small islets surrounding Patmos, as well as estates on Rhodes, Naxos, Crete and Thera, which is Santorini. Rent from the estates and a duty of tariff to the monastery, paid out of religious contrition by faithful farmers, sustained one hundred and fifty monks in the Monastery of Saint John, devoted to prayer. To a large extent, it still does.

GREECE, PATMOS: Patmos Harbor Today

Throughout the Orthodox world, taxes were paid to the emperor in Constantinople, the capital of Byzantium. The Monastery of Saint John of Patmos was relieved of such taxes. Its estates were taxable only to the monastery. In 1453, when the Ottoman Turks invaded Byzantium, causing its downfall and replacing governance of the capital city with Caliphs of the Turkish regime, who renamed it Istanbul, the Monastery of Saint John received a letter from Istanbul continuing its tax-exempt status. The letter is a prized item in the library collection today.

Hosios arrived on Patmos with scrolls and texts of religious treatises of great value in their time as relics of Christendom. The material became the beginning of a substantial library of over a thousand books, plus hundreds of scrolls, codices, icons and treasured relics of Orthodox and early Christian knowledge. Value of the library to world knowledge of Byzantine thought became even more important in 1453, when Ottoman Turks invaded Constantinople and

GREECE, PATMOS: Library of Treasures

ended the Orthodox empire.[37] To preserve important works, escapees from the Ottoman army sought shelter in islands of Greece. The fortress Monastery of St. John afforded safe sanctuary.

Among the treasured library possessions are thirty-three parchment leaves of the Gospel of Saint Mark. The so-called Purple Codex, for the dyed purple pages to denote their majesty, dates to the sixth century. From these pages, the King James Bible was written. Other leaves of the Purple Codex are in possession of the Library of St. Petersburg, Russia; the Vatican Library holds six pages, and the Byzantine Museum of Athens has possession of one page.

GREECE, PATMOS: Monastery Frescos above the Trapeza

---

[37] See The Humble Work of Sister Anthousa, Hermits of Patmos and Heritages, translated by Kallippi Prokes, 1998. Ecclesia.gr last accessed Nov. 12, 2018. See generally: Archimandrite Antipas Nikitaras, Guide to the Holy Monastery of Saint John the Theologian, Patmos, 2014.

The monastery library also holds a ninth-century copy of the Book of Job and other books of the pre and post-Byzantine period. Hosios may have been thinking of his library when he designed the fortress-monastery. Since 1454, the library has kept safe and preserved the original document signed by Mohammed the Conqueror of Constantinople, granting relief from taxation and control during pendency of the Ottoman Empire. The guarantee was effective for five hundred years.

From the eleventh to the seventeenth century, monarchs of the Orthodox faith sent gifts to the Monastery of St. John, in tribute to its mission of safeguarding the Cave of the Apocalypse and the devotion of its monks to prayer and education of all who came to the island seeking knowledge. Among the treasures is a painting by Domenico Theotokopoulos, also known simply as El Greco, "The Greek," and a cross, inlaid with precious stones, a gift of Catherine the Great of Russia.

GREECE, PATMOS: Monastery frescos lining the courtyard entry to the church

Secular Life of Patmos

In addition to being the spiritual and administrative leader of the monastery, the Patriarch of Patmos is the law of the island. Since the land of Patmos belongs to the monastery, all residents have the monastery as a landlord. Regardless of whether they are Orthodox, they are under the jurisdiction of the Patriarch. Parish priests are chosen by and report to the Patriarch of Patmos.

In matters of divorce, civil law, inheritance, and deeds to property, the code of law is that administered by the Patriarch under the Orthodox system. The Patriarch is judge, administrator, and keeper of the island record. Patmos is an island of Greece, subordinate to the Parliament in Athens, although on this island the church is the state. Social services are overseen by the Patriarch. The monks have duties to families well beyond what Hosios could foresee.

In the long history of the Monastery of Saint John, there have been attempts at island conquest. Venetians came to the island in 1659, although there was little commerce in the port and thus little to interest them. The Knights of Saint John took a look at Patmos before they settled on Rhodes. The Knights made Rhodes their base, from which they attempted to tax Patmos. The monks did not appreciate being taxed and certainly did not appreciate a tax imposed by knights of the Vatican. The monks must have resisted payment, and the knights did not push the matter.

When Ottoman and Venetian forces battled on Crete in 1668, those fleeing the battles came to Patmos. The monastery regretted the loss of income from estates on Crete. They were otherwise not affected by the war.

In the twentieth century, Italy controlled Patmos, until it came under the control of Nazi Germany. The best defense Patmos had to protect itself among aggressors of the day, was its insignificance. Germans, like the Italians, Venetians, and Ottomans before them, found little about Patmos to be worthy of the effort to control. In 1948, Patmos was united with Greece. In 1999, stable and accessible Patmos was honored by recognition of the Monastery of Saint John and the Cave of the Apocalypse as a World Heritage Site.

Visiting Patmos Today

Monks invite guests into the Cave of the Apocalypse and the Monastery of Saint John today. They wish guests to know that they are entering continuous functioning places of worship. These are not museums. The idea of a museum connotes something of the past. The lives of the monks are of the present, imbued with tradition of the past, which they will carry into the future.

A portion of the bright, newly remodeled library, is filled with glass cases and displays of gifts to the monastery and relics of the faith collected over the last nine centuries. There is an entrance fee charged for access to the museum, although the rooms should not be construed as a *museum* in the sense of discarded objects of a past practice. Rather, the monks actively conserve the heritage of constant reverence. In rooms where centuries past monks meticulously copied sacred text, today monks are trained as highly skilled conservators of aging items of culture.

The day in the life of monks in the Monastery of Saint John has not changed in routine over the centuries. They rise at 2:30 in the early morning and are at prayer by 3. The twelfth-century sanctuary of the church is the most sacred place within the walls. It is covered by frescos, which have suffered over time from moisture. Constant efforts are made to maintain the restored original environment.

Twice a day, monks pause in the Trapeza, the outer porch of the church, lined with seats. Prayer inside the church is undertaken standing. There are no internal pews. In the Trapeza, monks confer, beneath sixteenth-century frescos of the travails of Saint John and the Apostles, as they have for centuries. Today, they are joined in the open plaza by hundreds of guests.

Today, Patmos is home to less than three thousand permanent residents, of whom one hundred-seventy are monks of the Monastery of Saint John, found either in the main monastery or in small, single monk dwelling Hermitages around the island. Living as a hermit is a tradition as old as the visit of Apostle John, patron saint of Patmos. Some visitors are drawn to the cave; others come for study at the school run by the monks, while others come for the pristine beaches and quiet seaside life of Skala. All are welcome on Patmos.

GREECE, PATMOS: Shopping in Skala Today

Travel Homeward with Odysseus

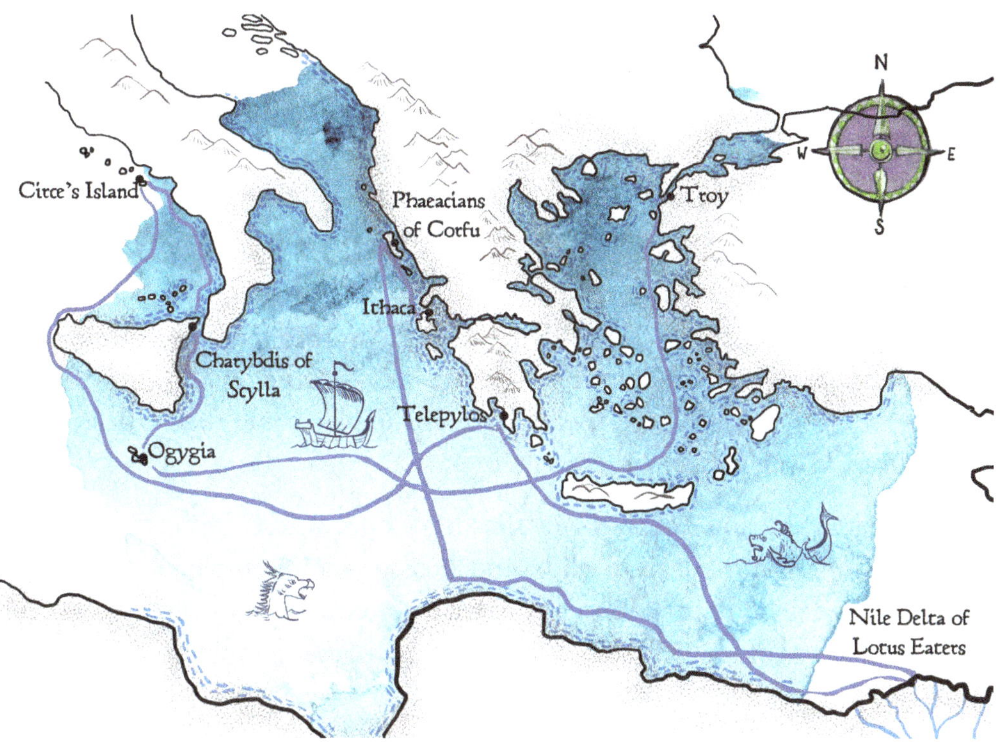

Greece: Travels of Odysseus

Odysseus was a man with the stature of a god. He fought at Troy with Achilles. They argued. Achilles died; the result of an arrow driven where he was most vulnerable, into his exposed heel.

Odysseus was a complex character. He was an orator, a skilled soldier, and sailor, but most of all, he was cunning. It was Odysseus who contrived the idea of a wooden horse, in which the army of Agamemnon would hide. The horse ruse turned the advantage in battle. Troy was obliterated. Odysseus headed home.

The battle of Troy takes place in the forty-two days chronicled by the Greek poet Homer in his eighth-century epic poem, the *Iliad*. Later in life, Homer wrote of the homeward journey of Odysseus in the *Odyssey*. It is in the *Odyssey* that the tale of the wooden horse is told. The *Iliad* is a story of heroes in battle. The *Odyssey* is the epic of one man, who has spent ten years away from home in battle and then must spend ten more years in his quest to return home.

Like Shakespeare, twenty-five centuries later, classical scholars disagree whether Homer wrote both poems. Each line of the twelve-thousand-line poem has been analyzed for historical context and consistency. Such inquiry has led to some agreement about the identity of Homer, the function of epic poetry and its construction. There is still some debate over whether Homer was literate, since he wrote, or spoke, at a time the advent of Greek writing was at its inception.

Regardless of whether a scribe functioned to record the poetry of Homer, the *Odyssey* was performed repeatedly to appreciative audiences. It was a spell-binding masterwork of Greek theatre. The entire play could not be performed at one time. It was performed in installments.

In his ten years of homeward travel, Odysseus encountered female gods, who wished to detain him, dead or alive, and trips to the underworld, thick with ghosts, that encircled him. Homer inspired the centuries later works of Dante, in his description of Hell in the *Inferno*. What is not discernable from the words of Homer is the actual itinerary of Odysseus. He traveled a mysterious route, before reaching his home in Ithaca. Once home, Odysseus faced competition, deception and further tests of his god-like wisdom and strength.

There are scholars who have devoted a lifetime to the study of Homer and his epic poems. For the benefit of the modern traveler from Troy to Ithaca, this story applies a lighter brush to follow a possible homeward route. The traveler today need not encounter Calypso, Circe, or the Sirens in a cruise through the eastern Mediterranean to have a memorable experience.

GREECE: Odys and Penelope

About Homer and Eighth Century BCE

The flower of ancient Greek culture opened in the eighth century BCE. In this time, the Greeks rediscovered written language.[38] Poetry proliferated as an art form and a means of spreading news. Great Greek theatres began construction in the Greek mainland and Ionia, the western area of today's Turkey. Each city of any merit had a theatre capable of seating most of their population.

In the second half of the eighth century, around 750 BCE, Greeks modified the Phoenician alphabet, by adding a few vowels, and written language as we know Greek today was born. Early Greek was written in all capital letters, without punctuation. Punctuation came later. Words filled the page from right to left and then left to right in a continuous running expression. Deciphering ancient written Greek was limited to scholars at the time, and now.

The rediscovery of the written word in the eighth century accompanied new technology in writing instruments. No longer were words chiseled on rock or clay tablets. Greek scribes wrote books on leather, papyrus, or sheets of velum, that is, treated animal hide. Inks to dye velum could be washed away and the velum reused. Pages were more valuable than the written word. Books on papyrus were kept as scrolls. Flat sheets, bound on one side, came much later than Homer.

In the eleventh through the eighth centuries, culturally Greek people could be found living throughout that which is mainland Greece today, the islands of the Aegean and the western coast of Turkey. After the fall of Troy and its sister cities in the middle of the thirteenth century BCE, Greek seafarers traveled the eastern Mediterranean. Eventually, they sailed through the Bosporus to the Black Sea, to populate the north coast of Turkey. Travel was spurred by the need to find new lands to farm. The success of Greek society created a large population to feed.[39]

---

[38] With the fall of Troy, the loss of the Minoans and Mycenaean cities, of Crete, Turkey and elsewhere in the eastern Mediterranean, around the twelfth century BCE, ancient language was lost. Before Homer, poetry was oral.

[39] Greeks lived on the south coast of the Black Sea from the eighth century BCE to 1923.

Homer lived in western Turkey, possibly Smyrna, in the eighth century BCE.[40] He is regarded as a blind poet, knowledgeable of the old stories and descriptions of travelers from distant ports of the Greek world. His existence is confirmed by poets of the sixth and later centuries, who quoted Homer and wrote of his life. Greek historian of fifth century BCE, Herodotus, the great traveler, tells us of Homer. Homer, poet and his poetry, became part of continuing stories of bards.

Greek poets following Homer wrote that Homer traveled to the site of the battle of Troy, to walk the battlefield, to better have a sense of the action as it took place. It was as if he measured the scene of the action, to enable his ability to tell the story of the battle with credible accuracy. In a metaphysical sense, the great poet was communing with dead spirits inhabiting the battlefield.[41]

The battle of Troy was a real event. Before Homer, the battle was well known as a massive, bloody affair. In the battle, the elite of Greek warriors met their end. The cities of Troy and Miletus were destroyed, and Ephesus was impacted. These cities of western Turkey before the battle were centers of trade and wealth. After the battle, only Ephesus continued to prosper.

Homer's Epic Poetry

For eighth-century poets and performers of poetry, it was all about the meter. Drama was conveyed in short sentences, even when the speech was lengthy. Of the many translations of Homer, which exist today, the verbiage changes slightly to attempt literal, or meaning of the time, adjusted to vocabulary of today. It is the form of poetry translators seek to sustain in modern efforts. To keep the action going, the speaker moved through thoughts with a tempo, often accompanied by a drum beating the rhythm. Homer was a master of meter. His poetry was the height of form.[42]

---

[40] Smyrna, on the central west coast of Turkey has been known as Izmir since 1930.

[41] Alexander the Great came to the site of the Battle of Troy in the fourth century. The story goes that he ran three times around the grave of Achilles. As a great warrior himself, Alexander wished to make a pilgrimage to his gods.

[42] Of the many English translations of Homer, available over the last two centuries this story relies most upon, Robert Fagles, Homer, The Odyssey, Penguin Classics, translation 1996; introduction and commentary.

For Homer, who lived at a critical time in the evolution of language and the written word, to have completed a lengthy opus of folk tales of his time, in twelve thousand lines of poetry, regarding the greatest battle of the ages; and to have done so in a display of mastery of written words in the meter of spoken performance, is too great a feat for many scholars of ancient texts to accept as the work of one man. In the same vein as critical analysis of Shakespeare, there have been lengthy treatises espousing that poetry attributed to Homer was written by more than one poet.

Homeric studies are a genre of study of the structure, language and content of the two known poems of Homer, the *Iliad*, and the *Odyssey*; the stories of the Trojan War and the return home from war of the hero Odysseus. In these two epic poems, two of the greatest in the period of Greek epic poetic performance, Homer brings to life a "great company of imagined persons." Homer's characters loom as real in our knowledge of gods, heroes and heroines of ancient Greece.[43] Homer had the story of Jason and the Argonauts as model for his work. From Homer forward, his work has been the standard for modern knowledge of the classical Greek world.[44]

Scholars have spent entire careers, since the fifteenth century, dissecting Homer, looking for inconsistency, or a break in form, which would signal work of two or more authors. None have been found. The conclusion that we are left with is, that a highly creative and talented poet, well aware of a legacy of story and form in Greek spoken theater, was skillfully able to put the story into an organized format, which has achieved immortality, just as the gods, whom he has given personality, were launched into popular knowledge by the poet we know as Homer.

Zeus, the all-powerful God, who enjoyed his dalliances with many women, is known in the *Iliad* for deferring to his wife, Hera, in her desire to destroy Troy. Goddesses Hera the powerful, Athena victorious in battle and Aphrodite the embodiment of beauty toyed with the vain, superficial and gullible Paris, son

---

[43] Fagles at p. 493.

[44] The era of classical Greece is a narrow period, usually regarded as the time from the defeat of Persia in the Battle of Salamis in 480 BCE, when victorious Greek general Pericles rebuilt the Acropolis with the Parthenon, to the death of Alexander the Great in 323 BCE.

of the King of Troy, by tempting him with a choice between power, victory in battle and a beautiful woman. Paris chose Helen, the most beautiful woman of the time, the wife of Menelaus, king of Sparta and brother of the great general Agamemnon. Helen left home with Paris for Troy. Generals of Greece launched their ships for Troy to bring Helen home.

The first of Homer's epic poems, the *Iliad*, takes place during the final ten months of the battle of Troy. By the end of the poem, ten years of effort have resulted in the fall of Troy and the total destruction of a magnificent city of trade. All inhabitants of Troy, the super-heroes, including reluctant warrior Achilles, and the defenders of Troy, have perished. The Greek generals, including Agamemnon, Menelaus, and Odysseus go home. Menelaus goes home to Sparta with Helen. Agamemnon arrives home safe, then becomes victim to his wife's desire for another man.

In the second of the great poems of Homer, written later in his life, Odysseus leaves Troy to begin a ten-year, adventure-filled *Odyssey*, across the wine *dark sea*.[45] Odysseus is a mortal, with the strength and cunning of a god. He is tested by Zeus and Poseidon in the many episodes that take him from islands off the coast of Turkey, around the Mediterranean, to finally reach Ithaca, his home. Along the way, Odysseus is reunited with his son, Telemachus. Father and son overcome fifty-two suiters of Penelope, the wife of Odysseus, who has been faithful for twenty years, while she mourned for Odysseus, whom she thought was lost in battle, or at sea.

While she awaited return of Odysseus, Penelope fended off suitors by knitting a shroud for her father-in-law, Laertes, the king. The shroud ruse lost credibility when it became unduly long, and Laertes did not die. The old king is distraught. He has lost his wife, his son and heir, and possibly his grandson, who has gone off in search of Odysseus. Laertes cares not to live.

When Odysseus arrived home in Ithaca, he adopted a disguise, the better to gauge the reception he will receive. Dressed in rags, Odysseus is given refuge by the faithful goatherd, who protected property of Odysseus from suiters of his wife, who became costly guests of the estate. Penelope's maid recognized Odysseus from a scar on his leg. Penelope devised a test for the beggar to prove his identity.

---

[45]   *Wine dark sea* is Homer's description of the water of the Mediterranean.

In Homer's story, Penelope announced to all suiters that she will marry the man who can string the bow of Odysseus and shoot an arrow through a row of axes. Though several men try, none are successful. The beggar waited to be the final contestant. He set the cat-gut bow, like a man familiar with the shaft. He shot the arrow straight through the row of axes.

The suiters quickly realized they were in the company of the great warrior, Odysseus. For the remainder of book twenty-two, Odysseus, Telemachus and their loyal warriors kill the suiters, their serving men and bodyguards. The scene is as thrilling read today as it was 2,800 years ago.

Tests, disguise and deception continue when Penelope tests Odysseus with the riddle of their marriage bed. She states the bed will be removed, knowing only Odysseus would know the bed is made of a tree, still rooted to the earth. He passed the test. Husband and wife are reunited.

Next Odysseus seeks out his father. He goads the old man to renew his self-esteem before ending the disguise. Father and son are reunited. The last book of the poem is the book of peace.

Performances of the *Iliad* and *Odyssey* enchanted audiences in the time of Homer. Vases have been found, dating from 670 BCE, with scenes from the *Odyssey*, like souvenirs of a performance. Inspiration from Homer for plots of disguise and mistaken identity can be seen in Shakespeare's Two Gentlemen of Verona, All's Well That Ends Well, Comedy of Errors and Twelfth Night.

Where did Odysseus Travel?

In the *Iliad*, Homer displayed his ability to describe battles in lurid detail. The *Iliad* is a tale of super-heroes in the battle of gods and men, in which everyone loses. There is no wooden horse in the *Iliad*. Achilles raged through warriors, battle axes flying, as he destroyed all in reach. He slew brave Hector, son of the king of Troy. Acting in the heat of the moment, in his least noble display, Achilles dragged the body of Hector around the burning palace of Troy. That night, when passion cooled, Achilles invited the king to retrieve the body of his son for a proper burial.[46]

---

[46] Unburied bodies leave the being in limbo, the inspiration for purgatory in Dante's *Inferno*.

Homer is not to be denied credit for the *Odyssey* when later in life, he has evolved as a poet. Odysseus is still the god-like hero, this time a flawed human, whose duplicity, cunning and deceit are survival skills. In the *Odyssey*, the gods challenge Odysseus to find the means to stay alive. Even when Odysseus decides to die, the gods thwart his desire, by sending him to the underworld on a ship with the black sails of death. When Odysseus meets Achilles in the dark world, Achilles tells him that he would rather be a man's servant on earth, than live among breathless souls. The ghosts of the dead, and not yet buried, surround Odysseus as if to smother him in their cries. The scene is daunting. Odysseus chooses to live.

In the *Odyssey*, Homer displays his skill as a poet/playwright. Typical Greek theatre of his time placed a muse in front of the audience, who began the story at the beginning and proceeded through chronological events. In the *Odyssey*, Homer begins with Telemachus searching for his father. When Telemachus reaches the home of Helen and Menelaus in Sparta, the gracious hosts tell him stories of his brave and honorable father. Menelaus introduces the blind poet, Demodocus, and begs the poet to entertain guests with the story of Odysseus and the wooden horse.

The poet obliges with the story of how Odysseus disguised himself as a beggar to enter Troy and assess their military strength. He credits Odysseus with the idea of a wooden horse in which warriors would hide until the horse was brought within the palace at Troy. The battle plan turned the tide for the Greeks. Troy was breached. The war ended. The warriors came home.

When, after seven or eight years, Odysseus landed at a friendly harbor, he enchanted his hosts at a banquet in his honor, with tales of his travels since leaving Troy. In this manner, the audience hears of the perils and adventures with cyclops, cannibals, and bewitching women, who tried to detain him. The audience already knows what Odysseus does not, and that is Penelope waits for him, pressed by suitors who wish to murder their son and take the kingdom.

The mystery that persists today is where Odysseus traveled during his ten-year odyssey. Brilliant classical scholars have tried to put the pieces together from fragments of descriptions offered by Homer. Maps of known Greek ports of the eighth century are of little use. Homer wrote of what he knew.

For the *Iliad*, Homer walked the actual field of battle. In the *Odyssey* he wrote of ports imagined. The cyclops live on an island so fertile no seed need to be sown to live off the land. The cave of the cyclops locked shut with a boulder, could be anywhere.

Ogygia, the island of Calypso, who held Odysseus for seven of his ten years of travel, is somewhere in the middle of the sea. It has been identified as Gozo, the northern of the three islands of Malta. Odysseus was blown from the center of the sea into harms' way as he traversed Charybdis, the whirlpool that fed mythical beast Scylla the torn remnants of sailors. Charybdis is often identified as the whirlpool which existed in the straits of Messina, between Sicily and the toe of the boot of Italy. An earthquake in the nineteenth century dislodged the subsurface stones, which had for so long created havoc for sailors. If these places were on the unintended itinerary of Odysseus, then arrival at the island of Circe, in Aeaea, would not be out of place in the bay of Naples. Circe enchanted Odysseus, wishing to hold him as her prince in the underworld.

Odysseus was blown east and west in the great *wine dark sea* that is known as the Mediterranean. The gods took their wrath out on Odysseus when they blew him to Telepylus, the land of Laestrygonians, who were cannibals. Today, the lightly populated town of Mezapos self-identifies as the location of Telepylus. It is in a likely place, the edge of the sea, in the middle prong of the trident that is the southern coast of the Greek Peloponnese. A ship sailing to Ithaca could stop there. There are two large caves in the area that are candidates for homes of Laestrygonians.

Odysseus was held captive in the Land of the Lotus Eaters. The location is most often construed as the mouth of the Nile. If Odysseus could sail to Gozo, it was not much farther to Egypt.

Finally, Odysseus found safe harbor with the Phaeacians. From their obliging kingdom, Odysseus was deposited on his home turf of Ithaca. The best guess identity of Phaeacia is Corfu. Corfu is a lovely island, with a long history of peaceful people, near Ithaca in the Adriatic Sea. Of course, all of the assumptions of places in the itinerary of Odysseus are guesses. Homer never traveled far from home in the west of Turkey. All places he described were either imagined, or described by sailors at the docks of Smyrna, and fed into the rubric of poetry.

Following the Route of Odysseus Today

The places that Odysseus did not go were those places with which Homer would have had greater real knowledge. Crete, Cyprus, Phoenicia and Sicily, were ports known to Smyrna sailors in the eighth century BCE. Homer well describes these places through the tales Odysseus tells when he is in disguise and wishes to conceal the actual places of his travels. For the route of actual travels, to lands of strange sorceresses, monsters, and cannibals, the traveler is left to wander the *wine dark sea,* to view Homer's *rose-red Dawn* from distant shores.

It is known that Odysseus left from Troy and ended at home in Ithaca, off the west coast of Greece in the Adriatic. To follow the route of Odysseus as Homer may have wished, take a wonderful, readable translation of Homer to a comfortable deck chair, on a balmy cruise through any ports of the Aegean Sea. Enjoy the Greek ports along the way, noticing renditions of Zeus, Poseidon, and Hera on souvenirs. Think of the cunning Odysseus and know that when given a choice between life and death, regardless of the troubles facing him, he chose to live and sail the *wine dark sea*, wherever it might take him.

CRETE, CHANIA: Harbor & Turkish Legacy

CRETE

THE HISTORY OF CRETE VIEWED FROM CHANIA HARBOR

Crete has a history that spans five thousand years. Much of it was turbulent. The best vantage point from which to contemplate the long and violent history of this Greek outpost is in a comfortable chair, in one of the harbor-side restaurants, which ring the Venetian Harbor of Chania, on the north coast of Crete. This is the place where friends and aggressors entered Crete, from sea and air, in waves of colonizers and conquerors over several millennia.

Chania is considered to have one of the prettiest harbors in Crete. Although tourism has swelled on the island, employing almost half the workforce, and turning popular sites such as Knossos Palace into an ant-hill of visitors, the ring-side seat in Chania harbor affords an unspoiled, and most of the time, uncrowded view of the history of Crete. The spot is evidence of continuous life on the island. It is not a reconstructed museum piece.

Crete is the birthplace of the father of the gods, Zeus. Zeus is central to Greek cosmology. The Minoan people built a prior civilization on Crete from 3000 BCE, two thousand years before the Greeks arrived in Crete, around 1100 BCE. While Jason sailed into the Black Sea looking for the Golden Fleece, and the Trojan War decimated kingdoms in western Turkey, Minoans lived lavishly on Crete. Notably, Minoans lived peacefully for fifteen centuries.

Who were the Minoans and where and why did they go, are questions which dominated international symposiums of scholars for most of the twentieth century. Such is the importance of Crete in the landscape of ancient world history among academics. Few questions have been answered. None of them conclusively. Study on Crete continues.

When the mythological Zeus turned himself into a bull to carry off the daughter of Poseidon, Europa, he brought her to Crete, instigating the first battle of the gods on the island. Ever since Zeus, Crete has been marked as the center of real-life struggles. Early Greek culture focused inwardly on regional disputes, then united briefly in the first century BCE to unsuccessfully hold back arrival of the Romans.

On Crete, people felt the effects of the Roman empire falling under its own weight in the fourth century CE. Transition to Christianity on Crete was spurred by the arrival of Apostle Paul in 63 CE. Crete was part of the Byzantine Empire, until Venetian Christians sacked Eastern Orthodox Christians in 1204, leaving Crete, and the remnants of the Byzantine Empire, exposed to Arab and Ottoman conquests. The Ottomans came to Crete in 1645, after more than two hundred years of Arab, Venetian and Byzantine shifting control.

Ottoman Turks began their occupation of Crete by landing in Chania. Cretans were never quiet supplicants. Opposition to foreign overlords turned into rebellion. The recent history of Crete is filled with violent clashes with Turks, in an effort to maintain Cretan identity, Greek culture, and Christian religion, despite overlords.

Early twentieth-century independence for Crete was a time of almost continuous civil war. When the world erupted into the Second World War, the Battle for Crete in 1941 became one of the bloodiest battles of the war. Civilians fought the Germans and suffered reprisals. Hitler remarked that he could not afford another victory as he had in Crete.

Post-war Crete suffered along with mainland Greece through military coups and social upheaval. Greece is at the center of struggles in the European Union. It is examining its place in world affairs, as it absorbs new arrivals, resulting in rapid growth in a multicultural population, one hundred years after the 1923 population exchange in which Turkey sent ethnic Greek Christians to Greece after 2,600 years of living on the Black Sea coast and Greece responded sending ethnic Turkish Muslims to Turkey, after two hundred years of Ottoman Turk control of Greece.

The traveler to Crete today is served the best of its history without the turbulence. Ottoman and Venetian era buildings still ring the harbor. The marketplace of Chania is Arabic in feeling; European in design. Old-world narrow streets are a maze of modern shops. To soak in the aura as a casual visitor, sit in a harbor-side café and contemplate history in the authentic setting.

Becoming and Being Greek – Bronze Age to 1204 – Downfall of Byzantium

The first inhabitants of Crete were Stone Age people who worshiped a female fertility goddess. They occupied caves, such as the first caveman recognized by the Greeks, Zeus, who descended from Mount Ida in the middle of Crete. In 3000 BCE, people arrived from north Africa or western Turkey. They came on rafts, which they perfected to be ships worthy of sailing the Mediterranean. This great civilization of early Crete is known as the Minoan.

Minoan culture flourished on Crete from 3000 to 1450 BCE. They built towns, clustered near major palaces. Palaces were built from 2000 BCE to store grain and other goods for shipment. Palaces became the power centers and homes of ruling families of the island.

Then in 1700 BCE, a major earthquake shook the entire island. Multistory palaces fell. The people quickly recovered. New and larger palaces were built. On the open-air plazas, there was entertainment for the masses; that is, those who had the time to enjoy boxing matches and acrobatic performances of bull-riders. In the lower level of the palaces grain, olive oil and wine were stored. The rulers controlled critical commodity distribution.

From Turkey, the Minoans either received or brought with them clay tablets using the Linear A form of writing. The language of the hundreds of tablets recovered from Minoan palaces in the nineteenth and twentieth centuries has yet to be deciphered. Late in their time on Crete, the Minoans engaged in trade with the people of the mainland Greek city of Mycenae. From them the Minoans received business documents on clay tablets now known as Linear B. In 1952 CE, a British architect, with a passion for ancient language, deciphered the language of Linear B. It is now recognized as an early form of Greek from Mycenae.

In 1550 BCE, a volcanic eruption on the nearby island of Santorini sent clouds of dust to darken the skies of the Egyptian Pharaoh. He felt so cursed by the God of the Hebrews that he released them from slavery and sent them wandering off into the desert. On Crete, the effects of the Santorini blast were felt in their economy and destabilized their previously peaceful society. In 1450 BCE, there was a riot throughout land of Minoans in Crete. Palaces were smashed and burned. The Minoan people disappeared as a civilization. Where they went remains a mystery. Decades later, opportunistic Mycenae arrived.

The Mycenae people were the new lords of the Mediterranean. They absorbed remaining Minoans on the mainland of Greece, forming the beginning of the Greek world. Crete was joined with Libya as an outpost. Cretans identified with evolving Greek culture, while they fought local turf battles that kept them divided.

In 1100 BCE, Dorian people from Macedonia swept through Greece. A warrior people, they did not stop to build cities as had the Mycenae in Corinth. As the Mycenae rebuffed the Dorians, the Dorians came south to Crete. From 1100 to 700 BCE, Dorians dominated Crete. Peaceful Mycenae fled to the hills of Crete or decamped for Turkey.

Dorian destruction was followed by four centuries of dark ages on Crete. The Dorians did not disappear. Rather they melded with the remnants of the Mycenae, evolving into classical Greek society on the mainland. Society on Crete lagged mainland development. The Greek capital on Crete was Gortyna, Gortys today.[47] Ancient Kydonia, known as Chania today, was a seaport.

The Greek backwater of Crete had no king or major ruling representative. Cretans resumed squabbling among themselves. They were prey to pirates of the Mediterranean. When Alexander the Great went off to the east to conquer Persia, the Romans saw their opportunity to attack Crete. The Romans caused the Cretans to come together, twenty-six thousand strong, to oppose them. Nothing raises the ire of a Cretan more than foreign domination, then or now.

---

[47] Spelling of place names is confusing on Crete. Chania is Hania and ancient Kydonia. The spelling differences arise from ancient and modern spelling originating from Greek or Latin. Guide books drop silent vowels. Heraklion is Iraklion. Gortyna is Gortys. Phaestos is Phaistos.

At Chania, Romans landed, and battle ensued. Well organized Romans took over Crete, where they built roads, as Romans were accustomed to doing. Zeus and his god-family became melded with Roman gods. Crete was joined with Libya as part of the Roman district of Cyrene. The capital remained at Gortys. Cretans were subjugated, but they had peace. Apostle Paul arrived in 63 CE and preached to calm multitudes.

The calm of the first century of the new era was followed by a millennium of political storms. During that time the Christian world became divided between Rome and Eastern Orthodox Byzantium in Constantinople. Crete was tossed between Arabs to their east and south and Christians to their west and north. Powerful cities of the Mediterranean Sea; Genoa, and Venice vied with Arabs and Orthodox Christians for control of Crete.

When Cretans built Orthodox churches, the Genoese and Venetians preferred them to be Catholic churches. Arabs preferred Mosques. United by opposition to whoever was their overlord, Cretans identified with Greece.

CRETE, CHANIA: Venetian Fortress

Venetian and Ottoman Harbor – Venetian 1204 to 1645 and Ottoman 1645 to 1895

The two forces that brought down the Byzantine Empire had a great impact on Crete. That impact can be seen today in the Chania Venetian harbor, ringed with Venetian and Ottoman Turkish buildings. Though Turks were expelled from Crete in 1923, and Arabs are returning, Crete remains a special arm of Greece, with its Italian/Turkish mix.

In 1204, the French requested the pope to grant them a fourth crusade to the Holy Land. For transport, they convinced the Doge of Venice to commit all his shipbuilding activity for the year to satisfy their need for ships. Venice agreed to supply ships if France would guarantee compensation to Venice for the year of lost income from trade.

When the ships were delivered by Venice as promised, the French found that their crusade was undersubscribed. Landowners of wealth had run out of expendable sons, funds, and desire to participate in a crusade. Those who turned up at the docks were old men, adventurous women, and generally impoverished souls looking for relief from destitute feudal life. France could not cover its debt to Venice, so the doge decided he must devise a plan to cover costs and lost income.

Crete, Chania: From Venetian Fortress looking across time into Chania Harbor

The Venetians sent their ships of French knights and Venetian adventurers across the Adriatic to loot the Christian city of Zadar for supplies. Then they sailed for the capital of Byzantium, the city of Constantine, Constantinople. There they sacked the city, weakening the center of Orthodox Christianity. Even the pope was embarrassed. Edifices of Saint Marks Square in Venice are today studded with loot from Constantinople.

Orthodox leaders on Crete lost their support from Constantinople. In 1217, Crete was sold to Venice. Venetian families who controlled Crete in the thirteenth through fifteenth centuries also controlled Santorini and other islands. Venice was king of the Mediterranean, Lord of the Lake.

To support trade activities, Chania became the Venetian capital of Crete. The harbor was improved. Buildings of Chania and the harbor reflect Venetian architecture today. Wealthy families of Venice moved to Crete and became feudal overlords to Cretans.

Life was not peaceful on Crete during the Venetian period. Rival Genoese came to contest control. Arabs from north Africa made forays to test Venetian strength. For a few years, Byzantines reasserted themselves. Byzantine aspirations ended abruptly in 1453, when Ottoman Turks used their new war machine, the cannon, to blow holes in walls Constantine built a millennium earlier. Ottoman Turks conquered the Byzantine Empire and began their sweep of Europe.

Cretans organized their resistance to Venetian overlords within Orthodox monasteries. The monks grew olives, made wine and olive oil, and fomented rebellion. Venetian reprisal to local uprisings was brutal. Mortality of Orthodox priests was high.

In the Mediterranean, Ottoman Turks were supplanting Venice to turn the sea into an Ottoman lake. In 1665, the centennial year of the Great Siege of Malta, where the Ottoman Turks attempted to remove the Knights of St. John from their bastion, the Ottomans lay siege to Chania. The battle lasted two months, primarily centered on the Chania harbor.

By 1669, Crete was the property of the Ottoman Turkish Empire. Turks exploited Crete, as had the Venetians, and the Cretans rebelled. There were

Crete, Chania: Greek-Turkish-Venetian Architectural Heritage

minor rebellions where the population of a village was sacrificed in Turkish reprisal. A major rebellion was planned in 1770, with promised aid from Russia. The aid never arrived, and the two thousand Cretan fighters became martyrs to independence.

For most of the nineteenth century, Crete was engulfed in a war for independence from Turkey. After a major battle for independence in 1821, Turks massacred Orthodox clergy. When mainland Greece achieved independence in 1830, Crete hoped to be united with Greece. Instead, Crete was gifted by Turkey to Egypt, a Turkish ally during the war.

Crete became a pawn of world events. In 1840, after a war with Syria, Egypt gave Crete back to the Ottomans. The Cretans responded with a slogan of Union or Death. First came death. Civilians were slaughtered. While the Turks were distracted by war with Russia in 1877, Crete pushed again for union with Greece. As a concession to end the bloodshed, the Turks allowed Cretans to use Greek as their official language.

Emboldened by their independence, and supported by Britain, Greece fought a war with Turkey in 1896. The Ottoman Turkish Empire, powerful since the twelfth century, came to an end. The nineteenth century ended with a British supervised transfer of Crete to an international commission. As the Turks made their exit from Crete, there was a last slaughter of Cretans, for which the British hung Turks. Crete was a step closer to unity with mainland Greece.

Twentieth Century Independence, Unification with Greece and Civil War

Crete's hero of independence from foreign control and pursuit of union with Greece was Eleftherios Venizelos. Born in Chania in 1864, a capable civic administrator, charismatic, and unifying leader focused on Greek ethnic unity of the parts of Greece, the mainland and Crete, Venizelos served terms as Prime Minister of Greece, through tumultuous periods. Tumult and Crete had become synonymous through history.

Crete, Chania: Greek Independence Monument

In 1905, Venizelos flew the Greek flag in opposition to the coalition government of the Great Powers: Britain, France, Italy and Russia. Greece was sympathetic to Crete, but could not seat ministers from Crete in the Greek parliament for fear of antagonizing Turkey, engendering further war. War came in 1912, despite the efforts of Greece.

 Burial monument to Eleftherios Venizelos

The Balkan War barely preceded the First World War. In it, Greece, Serbia and Bulgaria joined in pushing the last vestige of the Ottomans into Turkey, from which a modern Turkey was born. By the Treaty of Bucharest in 1913, Crete achieved unity with Greece. Enjoying their first experience with peace since the Minoans, Greece remained neutral in World War I, until 1917, when they joined with the Allies.

Venizelos capitalized on the post-war fervor and weakness of Turkey to lead Greek forces into Turkey. He almost reached the Turkish capital of Ankara, before he was repelled. This is the war that catapulted Mustafa Kemal into leadership of modern Turkey as Ataturk. General Kemal pushed Greek forces back to Crete by 1921. Greeks in Turkey were then slaughtered in reprisal for the incursion.

As the world watched Greeks and Turks battle each other, international leaders stepped in to resolve the centuries' old hostility with a severe act. By the Treaty of Lausanne, in July 1923, there was a mass population exchange. Over 1.5 million ethnic Greeks, some of whose families began life on the Black Sea coast in 600 BCE, were transported from Turkey to Greece. Over 400,000 ethnic Turks in Greece, 30,000 from Crete, some of whose families lived in Greece for centuries, were transported from Greece to Turkey. The move was abrupt. There were no support systems awaiting transferees. Many died in transit. Cultural cleansing of the two countries did not resolve historic animosities.

A united, one hundred percent Orthodox Christian Greece, was not a peaceful place. Having accomplished independence and unity, Greeks focused inward on dissension. This time the controversy was over the form of government as a republic or monarchy. In the decade of civil war, from 1924 to 1935, there were military coups and counter-coups. Dictatorships were times of repression and imprisonment of political opponents. Venizelos died in Paris in 1936. His last efforts were to leave Greek as a republic, neutral amidst growing world events, which would erupt into World War II.

Crete, Chania: WWII War Graves Memorial

Crete 1941

In 1941, the forces of Nazi Germany invaded Greece. The Greek government went into exile on Crete. Crete looked to Britain for defense. The Allies wanted to help, but they were stretched thin. Allied troops hastily exiting Greece, were told to leave their weapons behind. Once in Crete, they found no weapons cache waiting for them. On May 1, there were thirty-five Royal Air Force planes on Crete. By May 19, bombardment by the Nazis reduced the number to seven. The seven planes were sent to Egypt to aid British forces there.[48]

Hitler made the conquest of Crete a priority. It was to become his center of operations for the battle for North Africa. He assumed that his forces would be welcomed by locals when they landed on Crete. Obviously, Hitler was not a student of history.

On May 20, 1941, the elite corps of Nazi parachutists rained down on Chania. Parachute and glider battalions landed near Rethymno and Irakleio, along Crete's north coast.[49] They were greeted by old men, women, and children, armed with farm implements, who hacked them to death. Some gliders and parachutists landed among British forces, including ANZAC battalions. Casualties were high on all sides, military and civilian.

The Nazi objective at Chania was to control the Malene airfield, enabling landing carriers of troops and supplies. There were forty-one thousand Allied troops on Crete, including ten thousand Greek forces. They met an incursion force of eight thousand Germans, accompanied by considerable air support.

In retrospect, the British Commander Bernard Freyberg, a veteran of Gallipoli, the Allied disaster in Turkey, has been criticized for not aggressively pushing an offensive, before Germans took the airfield. Battalions of Scottish Hussars, New Zealand Maori and Australians, had high spirits and sustained an ability to move forward, despite living on half-rations, poorly supplied with

---

[48] Nigel Cawthorne, History's Greatest Battles, Arcturus Publications, London, 2012, pp. 260-269.

[49] Rethymno and Irakleio are harbor towns going west from Chania. The fourth harbor is Agios Nikolas, to the east. All four are cruise ports today. The major highway of Crete connects them.

ammunition and lacking effective air support. When German troops took a hill on Crete to overpower anti-aircraft guns, they found the guns to be dummies. With three weeks to prepare, the Allies were resourceful.

The Battle for Crete has become one of the best examples of why war is the worst means to resolve conflict. Hitler achieved his objective on Crete at such cost that he canceled plans to invade Malta and Cyprus. He never again utilized paratroopers in offensives.

On May 27, the British called in its navy for an evacuation. The Royal Navy had sunk the first flotilla of German ships headed for Crete. Under fire from German Stukas, the British lost two cruisers, four destroyers, and sustained debilitating damage to two battleships.

In the dark of night, fewer than seventeen thousand Allied forces were rescued at the southern Crete port of Chora Sfakion, directly south of Chania. Greek government officials walked through the Samaria Gorge, now an attractive tourist hiking venue, to end their nightmare by transport to Egypt. Almost twelve thousand Allied troops became German prisoners on Crete. There were additional casualties when the relief transport ships encountered airborne fire at sea.

The remainder of the forces were left on their own to survive in the hills of Crete. There are many stories of endurance, survival, rescue and imprisonment.[50] Civilians suspected of hiding Allied soldiers were executed. Fortunate soldiers found anything that would float and headed to sea, carried by the winds until they landed on the coast of Egypt. Others perished, exposed in the Crete hills during the winter, or were shot on sight by Germans.

In 1944, civilian Cretan resistance fighters captured the German Commander Kreipe and sent him to Egypt on a boat. The victory left little to celebrate. Germans in reprisal shot their Cretan captives. In 1945, Germans preferred to surrender Crete to the British, rather than face Cretans.

---

[50] See: Alan Clark, The Fall of Crete, Efstathiadis Group, Athens, 2004.

CRETE, CHANIA: Chania harbor cafe

CRETE, CHANIA: Market

CRETE, CHANIA: Relaxing Today Harborside

Chania Today

In the post-World War II period, the British backed King George II to lead Greece. Civil war resumed, led by the Communist party. On Crete, British efforts to rebuild kept them in favor. Cretans did not take part in the Greek mainland civil war. In 1974, sixty-nine percent of Greeks voted for a Greek republic, that was neither royalist nor communist.

The 2004 Athens Olympics brought investment in Greek infrastructure. Financial advancement could not be sustained amid the worldwide recession, decades of Socialist leadership with increased public benefits, and repeated financial scandals of politicians.

On Crete, Cretans looked at the United States military base at Souda Bay as another foreign incursion to their lives, although the base brought economic benefits. Cretans prefer the benefits of international tourism. On Crete, visitors enjoy Greek culture in a natural landscape, with preserved edifices of history. Today cruise ships dock at Souda Bay, to enjoy Chania, while Iraklion and Agios Nikolaos are the gateways to central and eastern Crete, home to the best-preserved Minoan palaces.

Sitting in a comfortable chair, enjoying Greek cuisine, at a table just feet from the edge of the water in the Venetian Harbor of Chania, several millennia of history can be easily seen. Reaching the harbor along the pedestrian walk-way from the tour bus drop-off requires walking through the Ottoman market, also known as the Roman agora, and then walking the same stone streets of Venetians and Ottoman Turks, whose palaces and mosques ring the harbor. The Byzantine Church commands a major square just off Chania harbor.

Looking over the top of the harbor-side mosque of Turkish Janissaries is a hill, built up from years of Minoan life in the ancient city. It is now an archaeological site, promising a future interpretive center of another Minoan palace. On the waterside of the site are Venetian boat houses, renewed to house small craft shops of locals. Everywhere there are shops and eateries, as there have been for thousands of years. All that is missing is turbulence. Chania invites visitors to relax and enjoy the climate, the food and Greek heritage in a tranquil environment.

Crete, Minos: Palace Reconstruction

King Minos in Fact
–Minoans of Crete

Minoans landed on Crete in 3000 BCE. They soon created an advanced civilization known by monumental palaces throughout the island. They dominated sea commerce in the Mediterranean, long before Greeks and Romans entered the landscape of history. Much is known about how Minoans lived. What is not known is where they came from, what this Bronze-Age culture called themselves, and where they abruptly went in 1450 BCE. There are many theories, supported by many years of study, and few answers.

In 500 BCE, the Greek historian, Homer, reflected upon the ninety Minoan cities of Crete. Much of the lore surrounding Crete derives from Greek mythology. Zeus, the god at the top of the Greek hierarchy, was born on Mount Ida in Crete. Greeks identify Zeus as the first cave dweller on the island. Greek myths supply stories for populating Crete and the relationship between Crete and Athens, as though the two places co-existed in time. While Greek gods supply creation stories for the birth of Greek culture, Homer's ninety cities of Minoan Crete have been supported in fact, by scientific excavation over time.

The name Minoan is a creation of Sir Arthur Evans,[51] a museum curator at the Ashmolean Museum at Oxford. Trained in the classics, like all his fellow British academics in 1900, Evans assigned the name for all Bronze Age people of Crete as though they were all descendants following King Minos of Greek myth. After that, Evans excavated his carefully chosen site in Crete, seeking to support myth with reality. In so doing he is credited with discovery of the greatest of Minoan palaces, Knossos, which he *reconstituted*, his word, to display to the world a real-life home of mythological royals.[52]

---

[51] Sir Arthur Evans, 1851 to 1941. Given knighthood in 1911 for discovery of Knossos.
[52] J.D.S. Pendleburg, Palace of Minos, MacDonald, London, 1954, forward by Sir. Arthur Evans.

Due credit must be given to Evans for the attention of the scientific community, which focused substantial resources on Crete in 1900. As though seeking to discover all of Homer's ninety cities, excavations were staked out across the island, where British, Italian, German and Greek archaeologists sought to earn their equivalent knighthood. The names of the palaces and Minoan sites discovered were assigned in Evan's tradition of looking to Greek mythology. Trained in the classics of Homer, these adventurers contributed not only to knowledge of ancient Crete but to techniques of archaeology.

As archaeological investigation rose in academia to true science, Minoan scientists convened periodically to ponder the critical questions of the Minoan world. Among themselves they asked from where did these people come? On this point, they agreed upon two possibilities. They asked, what social circumstances resulted in the style of palaces left on Crete, which are unique in the ancient world? On this point, there is an increasing number of answers spawning continuing study and questions left to be answered.

The history of Minoans on Crete can be traced in a time-line on which there is a consensus. From 3000 to 1900 BCE, Minoans lived simply, in what is termed the early phase. From 1900 BCE to the great earthquake of 1700 BCE, Minoans of the middle phase built palaces and cities, evidencing a peaceful, advanced culture. The late phase began in 1700 BCE, in a rebuilding effort across the island, resulting in grand structures and additional cities.

Scientists agree that the Minoan civilization ended in 1450 BCE. They do not agree on why. There are no arguable theories as to where Minoans went. Over the twentieth century, periodic scientific symposiums were held to bring great minds to share recently obtained knowledge to address the question of why did it all end, island-wide, at about the same time, except for the one palace at Knossos. Attention was focused for decades on the eruption on Santorini, so long assumed to have been the critical event, such that Santorini was relegated to academic importance only to the extent it could shed light on the demise of Minoans.

Coming at a time and in a place between the lesser-known ancient world and the better-known civilizations that gave birth to Greek society, Minoans remain fascinating. They exist in a space between myth and reality. Minoans left clues to their world in the Cretan landscape, which visitors can enjoy today. Walk through their palaces today to enjoy a story without an ending.[53]

CRETE, MINOS: Palace of Minos in Crete

Minoans: Who Were They?

Minoans were great sailors who landed on Crete in 3000 BCE. They came from either Anatolia, the area of northwestern Turkey, or from Egypt. Centrally located in the Mediterranean, peaceful, and able traders, Minoans traded with people around the Mediterranean. They traded with Egypt and western Turkey, by flowing with the winds from Crete. As their sailing skills improved, they enjoyed a wider scope of travel around the Mediterranean. Their storehouses were filled with wine, olive oil and grain. They exported pottery and perfume. Crete was a forested paradise.

---

[53] There is also disagreement on spelling, arising from pronunciation in multiple languages of ancient and modern city and palace names. Heraklion is also known as Irakleio. Chania is Hania and Kydonia. Knosos is also Knossos. Phaistos is also Phaestos. Minos is always Minos.

CRETE, MINOS: Famous Frescos of Minos

The Minoans enjoyed a long tenure on their home in Crete of fifteen centuries. Theirs was a peaceful existence. Only in lengthy times of peace could such large cities be built, without walls. The only evidence of spears is found at the end of their era, when invaders began to arrive from the mainland of Greece. The Minoans wore tunics, not armor.

The Minoans, that is, the Bronze-age people who predated Greeks in Greece and the Greek Islands, also lived on mainland Greece. They were builders of ancient Corinth. On the mainland, Minoans built walled palaces for defense. There was no need to build such walls in Crete. Historians hypothesize that there was no incentive for invaders to come to Crete, nor were the Minoans of Crete desirous of conquering other kingdoms.

Minoans enjoyed entertainment. Most popular were bull-riders. Performers were lithe youth, who would grab the bull by the horns and catapult themselves across the back of the bull, to land behind the beast. Bulls were part of the act. There were no bullfights or taunting of the animals.[54] It was all peaceful and graceful. Bulls were prized.

Women were integral to Cretan society. Minoan deities were female goddesses of bountiful harvests. There were female bull riders. Royal women wore gold jewelry and were seen in public. There is emerging thought on Minoans that the throne room in the lower level at Knossos, a sight on every visitor itinerary to the palace, was the throne not of the king, who would sit in a large reception room on an upper floor, but that it was the throne of the goddess of the harvest.[55] Sacrifices made in the chamber were offered to increase the yield, encourage healthy births, and continue the good life.

Minoans were sufficiently at peace with their trading partners and their environment that they did not feel a need to build large self-effacing monuments to the gods. Minoans placed small altars in their homes, where they acknowledged gratitude to their deities. The palace at Knossos is known as the House of the Labyrinth, the name given by Evans and taken from

---

[54]   James Walter Graham, The Palaces of Crete, Princeton University Press, Princeton, 1962, 1972, p. 75.
[55]   Graham, p. 31.

labrys, the crossed ax symbol found throughout the palace and on small altars. The goddess of Knossos was regarded as Our Lady of the Labyrinth.

Minoans left such an impression on Greeks, that Homer reflected upon them in his writings as a great culture, in the same manner that he wrote poetry heralding the major battle in the fall of Troy. Greeks anointed the first caveman of Crete as Zeus, the father of the gods. Athens looked to Crete as the beginning place of civilization.

Complex palace structures on Crete, such as Knossos, still evident to the Greeks in the time of Homer, were like a maze with rows of storerooms. The maze of the House of the Labyrinth became to the Greeks the labyrinth of the bull, prized by Minos. Minos demanded annual tribute from Athens of seven youths and seven maidens, as compensation for the death of his son in their city. In perpetrating myths, Greeks created greater time-depth to their culture.

CRETE, MINOS: Palace corridors

Late in life, Sir Arthur Evans acknowledged that his labeling the culture as Minoan caused some misconceptions in the division between fact and myth. He did not instigate the confusion. The Greeks created their deities from stories informed by events on Crete a millennium before Homer wrote of the cities of Minos, and Plato wrote of a playful culture of Atlantis that disappeared in one night. When Zeus turned himself into the bull, who kidnapped the daughter of Poseidon, Europa, he took her to Crete.[56]

Crete, Minos: 19th vision of palace view

[56] To enjoy mythology, read Mary Renault, The King Must Die (1958); and The Bull from the Sea (1962), chronicles of the life of Theseus, who killed the bull and lived to escape the labyrinth and flee with Ariadne, daughter of Minos, who gave him the helpful twine (her clew).

Minoans: What Did They Build and Why?

There is general agreement in the scholarship regarding Crete that palaces arose from former modest dwellings. These were the palaces of the royalty of Crete from 1900 BCE to 1700 BCE, prior to the major earthquake. It is difficult to know the appearance of these palaces. The tremendous earthquake that shook Crete in 1700 BCE destroyed all the structures.

In 1700 BCE, Minoan civilization was resilient. They rebuilt their homes as stronger, more opulent palaces. They built new cities. The middle period ushered in by the quakes was a high period for Minoans. Of the old, pre-quake palaces, excavators found a "fragment of a fragment" in their excavations, to quote Sir Arthur Evans.

The uniqueness of Minoan palace architecture fuels arguments of cultural origination. The new palaces have some resemblance to Egyptian palaces, although travel and not heritage could account for this. The Minoan middle period to late-period palaces are entered off a large open area with sweeping staircases at the entrance. Royal reception and private living areas were filled with air and light, made possible by windows and air shafts. The buildings are multi-level, with the more important rooms on upper levels.

CRETE, MINOS: Interior Palace Frescos

The lower level rooms are smaller and more numerous. Many of these were storerooms. The small chambers, with more numerous dividing walls, give support to larger rooms on upper levels. Remnants of old palaces, repurposed into new palaces, with irregular joining passageways, give the effect of a maze of rooms, hence, the labyrinth of myth.

Minoan palaces have in common large reception halls, elegant staircases, with pillars, creating impressive entries from open areas, which are more than courtyards of later Greek and Roman grand homes. Courtyards in Greek and Roman dwellings brought light and air to surrounding rooms. In Minoan palaces, airshafts kept homes fresh throughout and large rectangular windows brought in light. Window shutters kept out dust. The courtyards of Minoan palaces were large enough to stage events and invite a crowd.

Grand homes in Crete were decorated with frescos, the art of painting on wet plaster, a number of which have survived. The paintings depict Minoan life, such as bull games and boxing matches. They record Minoan people as light-skinned, with dark hair, and trim bodies, with tiny waists. Women wore gowns and jewelry. For the wealthy, life was good.

Some Minoan palaces had doors, enclosing the interior from the entry area. In others, including Knossos, there were balustrades, of the type found on a balcony, only they are at entry plaza level, a few feet from the main structure. The answer to the riddle of the design was confirmed at the palace at Phaestos, second largest of the Minoan palaces.

Typical of construction of palaces on Crete, Phaestos was built between 2000 and 1700 BCE, then rebuilt after 1700 BCE. It was excavated in 1900, by Frederico Halbherr.[57] The palace at Phaestos yielded fewer frescos than Knossos, and is less-visited, but has been highly informative for research. Phaestos palace has doors on ground floor openings. There is also a balustrade between the building and the open area of the large plaza. Coins recovered near Phaestos illustrate bull-riding.

---

[57] Frederico Halbherr, 1867 to 1930. His hometown was in Italy at his birth, then became part of Austria.

A highly-studied fresco from Knossos shows a crowd of spectators enjoying a show of bull-riders. Since there are no coliseums in Crete, the conclusion is that these shows occurred in the open area in front of the palace entrance. The balustrade protected spectators from bulls. Doors were closed to the palace to keep wandering bulls from entering the halls.

Other significant Minoan palaces excavated in 1900 are Malia, Zakros and Galatas. Eventually, German, Swiss and American archaeologists entered the scene on Crete, each seeking a new palace in which to lead an excavation. In the 1960s, spurred by additional information coming from Santorini, and informative scientific work by Greek archaeologists on the Minoans and later cultures in Greece, more work was funded on Crete. In the 1960s, American and Swiss archaeologists uncovered a previously unknown Minoan palace in the center of old-town Chania, in northwestern Crete. Prior to the find, all Minoan palaces were thought to exist only east of Mount Ida.

CRETE, MINOS: Throne Room

The later findings are sobering reminders that the study of ancient cultures, Minoans included, relies on that which is known of that which is left behind. The large palaces, the burials, and possessions of royals, religious leaders, and wealthy occupants of a city, receive the greatest attention from excavators, as they are significant finds of a wealth of material. Recreating history from significant material remains causes lesser attention, or none, to be given to the common folk, slaves, and those whose dwellings did not survive time and whose possessions were few.

In 1900, when leaders of excavations across the landscape on Crete sought out Minoan sites, they hoped to locate the next Knossos. Although no excavation has brought to the surface a palace larger than the find of Evans, the effort resulted in discovery and recording of more than the palaces of royals. Archaeologists have located sprawling cities and several ports. Under examination, continuing today, are lives of common folk. Books on Minoans are still being written. The effort attempts a full picture of Minoan life.

Minoans: Where Did They Go?

Minoan experts agree that the culture ended abruptly on Crete in 1450. Palaces were smashed and burned. Only Knossos survived the cultural cataclysm. On mainland Greece, the Minoan culture fell at the same time. Survivors were absorbed into the rising Mycenaean people. The prevailing thought is that the Mycenaean people subsumed the Minoans and came to Crete by 1400, not as aggressors, but as opportunists in the void left by Minoans. Peaceful Minoan society simply fell apart in a wave of internal dissension. Whether dissension was spawned by famine or other natural event is a matter of continuing study.

For a while after 1450, Knossos remained a cultural center. Then it too became dormant. Chania rebounded quickly as a major port. It was refounded as a Mycenaean city.

In an effort to find a reason for the abrupt demise of a long-standing culture, scientists looked to events of the time on Santorini. It was first thought that the volcanic eruption on Santorini wiped the settlements off the land and the resulting tidal waves destroyed Minoan Crete. Additional work by French and Greek archaeologists on Santorini have proved that the eruption, though major, covered Santorini with volcanic dust, preserving cities long thought lost. Santorini is enjoying renewed scientific study of its seaport.

The Santorini eruption occurred around 1550 BCE, the time Moses led the Israelites from Egypt. The volcanic dust would have covered the Egyptian sun, sent plagues of locusts in advance of the clouds, and the falling iron oxide dust would have turned Egyptian streams into blood-red currents. The resulting tsunami would have parted waters.[58]

CRETE, MINOS: Stone & beam architecture

---

[58] Additional studies of Santorini place the eruption a century earlier, giving Moses little help from the volcano and suggesting that divine assistance aided the cause for Egyptians to release the Israelites. Most scientists ascribe to the 1550 BCE date for the major eruption on Santorini. Meanwhile, Biblical historians place the Exodus at a later time, around 1250 BCE.

The prevailing academic explanation for the demise of Minoan culture is that the eruption on Santorini impacted life on Crete, causing destabilization of social systems. Impact on crops affected the fortunes of leading families and reduced food available for common folk. If palaces were storehouses of the rich, not distribution centers for the masses, then smashing and burning palaces for loot to sustain life on a widespread basis ended society as it was known for fifteen hundred years. Survivors wandered into the oblivion of time.

Visiting Minoan Palaces Today

Today the most popular Minoan site for visitors is at Knossos, which is a short drive from the cruise dock at Heraklion. Evans has been criticized for "reconstituting" the palace. Some of his interpretations of the site have been contradicted by subsequent study. Still, had Evans not put the pieces together, there would be little to see at Knossos other than rubble. Academically correct or not, the palace is a wonder for visitors to experience Minoan culture in a way Evans, who was a museum curator, can appreciate.

The popularity of Knossos renders it crowded much of the year. For those avoiding crowds, there are other Minoan palaces off the main highway to the east at Malia, and south at Phaestos. To see the best of Minoan treasures, including gold jewelry and the Phaistos Disk, the Heraklion Archaeological Museum is a must-see. Although all the questions have not been answered, such as where the Minoans went, a good deal is known about how they lived. Be amazed by the grandeur of society 3500 years ago.

King Minos in Myth – Of Gods and Bulls

Zeus, the king of all Greek gods, was born on Crete. He lived in a cave on Mount Ida, in the center of the island. When he was lonely, Zeus turned himself into a bull and enticed Europa, the daughter of the god of the sea, Poseidon, to jump on his back. Then Zeus carried Europa to Crete.

Zeus and Europa had a son named Minos. Minos married the mortal human Pasiphae. Poseidon took his revenge on Zeus when he sent Minos a white bull to sacrifice. As Poseidon well knew, Minos prized the bull and could not kill it. Poseidon caused Pasiphae to fall in love with the bull. The off-spring of the bull and Pasiphae was the half-bull, half-man, the Minotaur.

Thus, begins creation stories of the ancient Greeks. Zeus had other frolics. He had other wives. His children became gods at the top of the Greek lineage: Hermes, Persephone, Dionysus, Heracles, Helen of Troy and the Nine Muses, who were the sources of poetry, literature and the arts. The Muses told family stories, which became the basis of Greek mythology.

Among the stories at the heart of Greek mythology is the Athens creation story. In this story, the king of Athens, Aegeus, reunites with his long-lost son, Theseus. Theseus undertakes, at his considerable risk, to resolve a grievance between King Minos of Crete and his father, King Aegeus. The problem arose from the death of the son of Minos, while in Athens. To end the tribute paid in the lives of the youth of Athens to King Minos, Theseus must travel to Crete.

In Crete, King Minos employed master architect Daedalus to build a labyrinth to contain the Minotaur. If he is to slay the Minotaur, Theseus must defeat not only the beast; he must also survive the labyrinth. The story of Crete will not end with Theseus and the Minotaur.

King Minos became so enraged by the outcome of Theseus and the Minotaur, that he imprisoned Daedalus and his son Icarus. Daedalus solved another feat of engineering to be free. The story of Daedalus ends the Cretan trilogy in Greek mythology. The story of King Minos continues for a final reprisal of grief and vengeance.

Greeks enjoyed attending theater and hearing lengthy poems of feats of gods and other heroes. They knew their creation stories and follies of the gods. The joint cultural heritage of mainland Greeks and Cretans runs deep into ancient times. Pottery from the sixth and fifth century BCE, found in Crete and elsewhere in Greece, depicts the trilogy of stories of Theseus and Aegeus, Theseus and the Minotaur, and Daedalus and Icarus. These stories are basic reading before a trip to Crete, or a visit to the home of King Minos, not far from the port of Heraklion.

Theseus and Aegeus

The story of Theseus and his father Aegeus introduces a god, born to mortal parents, with a little help from a god. Aegeus was the king of Athens, in competition with his four siblings. He had no children, despite two marriages. One of his brothers had fifty sons, waiting for an opportunity to become king. Anxious for a male heir, Aegeus visited an oracle.

Oracles were known for giving perplexing prophecies. To help sort out the meaning of life, Aegeus went to visit a neighboring king. The king offered his daughter to Aegeus for the evening. Just to be safe in securing her pregnancy, the young woman also spent the night with the god Poseidon.

Before leaving the home of his obliging king, Aegeus left instructions with the young woman to have their son identify himself in Athens by the sword, shield and sandal Aegeus left behind. Aegeus left the items under a large rock. Only a strong young man could lift such a rock.

Back in Athens, Aegeus married Medea. She had recently left Jason, of Jason and the Argonauts. She and Jason met when he came to Georgia, on the Black Sea, in search of the golden fleece. That is another story. It was always rumored in Athens that the son born during Medea's marriage to Aegeus, was Jason's child.[59] That son grew up with dreams fostered by his mother that he would succeed Aegeus as king.

Years later, a handsome, strong young man came to Athens looking for Aegeus. The young man was preceded by tales that he had dispatched five thieves along the road, through cunning and skill in boxing, rather than brute force. The young man was Theseus, son of Aegeus, or/and Poseidon, although his identity was not yet disclosed. Medea proposed that Theseus be sent to kill the bull, which Hercules brought to Athens from Crete. The bull was a menace to locals.

This was no ordinary bull. This was the legendary Marathon Bull, which tested the strength of Hercules. The bull had killed another young man sent to vanquish it. That young man was Androgeus, the son of King Minos of Crete. Undaunted, Theseus took off his red cape and used it to distract the bull, while he set the bull's hind legs into a noose. The bull was subdued and led back to Athens for ritual butchering to feed the poor.

Medea prepared a victory dinner to which Theseus was invited. She gave him a chalice of wine, laced with poison. At the fateful moment, Theseus disclosed the sword, shield and sandal of Aegeus. Father and son were united. Joyful moments do not often occur in Greek myths.

Aegeus banished Medea and her son from his kingdom. Theseus quickly became adored by the people of Athens. Aegeus no longer had nightmares featuring his brother and the fifty nephews.

Theseus and the Minotaur

Theseus soon learned that Athens was not a happy place. King Minos of Crete held King Aegeus responsible for the death of his son, Androgeus. Androgeus came to Athens in good spirit to compete in the Greek games. Victorious in several games, Androgeus was given the task of taming or killing the Marathon

---

[59] If the child of Medea's was Jason's son, that would mean that Aegeus was with four women, none of whom had his child. No wonder the Greeks look to Theseus, the virile god, as the founding king of Athens.

Crete: Theseus & Minotaur

Bull. When the task proved fatal, Minos accused Aegeus of intentionally causing the demise of his son in spite of the young Cretan's athletic superiority.

To atone for the death of his son, and heir, Minos required Athens to send seven maidens and seven young men to Crete, every nine years, to be fed to the Minotaur. The youths were chosen by lot. When they arrived in Crete, there was a festival in which the youths were led to the labyrinth and locked inside. They wandered the interior of the labyrinth, from which no one ever emerged.

Soon after Theseus was untied with his father, it was again time to select youths for the trip to Crete. Theseus insisted that he be one of the males, despite not having been selected by lot. Aegeus gave a white sail to Theseus. If Theseus returned alive, he was to remove the black sail of the ship and hoist the white sail as a message to his father that all went well. Theseus agreed.

On the trip to Crete, it became obvious to Minos that Theseus was calming the youths and making them brave. Minos tested Theseus by throwing a gold ring into the sea. Theseus jumped from the ship to retrieve the ring. Aided by porpoises and goddesses of the sea, Theseus not only retrieved the ring, he was able to swim up to the ship and rejoin as it sailed quickly toward Crete.

Waiting in Crete for the ship to arrive was Ariadne, the beautiful daughter of Minos. She spotted Theseus and instantly felt love for him. Ariadne sent her nurse with a gift and a message for Theseus. She sent a ball of string, known in mythology as her "clew." The message given to Theseus was to use the string to find his way back out of the labyrinth. When he achieved his freedom, princess Ariadne would be waiting to flee with him from Crete.

The thirteen scared young Athenians and brave Theseus were led to the labyrinth, where the gates were closed behind them. Theseus told the others to wait near the entrance, while he alone dealt with the beast. As Theseus wandered through dark passages of the labyrinth, he carefully unwound the string. It was impossible to note his direction in the dark, narrow halls.

No one really knows what happened next. Theseus was not the sort of fellow to brag about his conquests. The paintings of Theseus and the Minotaur all show Theseus armed with a weapon, although he was allowed no weapon when he entered the labyrinth. Ariadne furnished string, not a sword. Of course, the gods could intervene. If so, none of them told any tales.

Most likely, Theseus used cunning to wrestle the beast into its own demise. Then Theseus followed the string back to the entrance, where he was greeted by thankful youths. The fourteen Athenians crept back to the boat, joined by Ariadne, and sailed for home.

On the return from Crete to Athens, the boat landed on the island of Naxos. Here the story has several alternate events. Either Ariadne died while on Naxos and the god of wine, Dionysus, raised her to heaven as his wife, or Theseus abandoned her, while she slept. Other versions of the myth put Ariadne as previously married to Dionysus and Theseus left Ariadne on Naxos to be claimed by Dionysus. Athenians prefer to consider their city founder as a gentleman.

Theseus was so consumed by the events of his travels that he forgot his promise to his father. As the ship sailed into the harbor at Athens, the black sail was still in place. Aegeus saw the ship approach with the black sail. He committed suicide by throwing himself into the sea. The sea was named Aegean in his honor. Theseus became the great king of the new city of Athens.

Theseus spent his life as a great king of Athens. He defeated each of his fifty cousins in a battle to maintain his throne. Then he went with Hercules to fight the Amazons, from which he returned victorious. The people lived across the land on farms, so Theseus brought them into the city in times of terror, where they were safe within city walls. During times of peace, people went out to farm. When there was trouble, the people of Athens had Theseus to protect them. They still do.

Daedalus and Icarus

Back in Crete, King Minos was furious. He had now lost a son and a daughter, due to actions of Athenians. Angry at Daedalus for not building a better bull-trap, Minos put Daedalus and his son Icarus in a locked courtyard, from which there was no escape but skyward. Daedalus thought about the situation and devised a solution.

Daedalus collected wings of birds that fell into their prison. Then he glued the wings to frames so that he and his son could fly like birds over the walls of their prison. Away they flew.

CRETE: Daedalus & Icarus

Daedalus flew until he landed in Sicily. Icarus was young and impetuous. Thrilled with his ability to fly, he tested the limits of his wings. When he flew too near the sun, the wax melted, the feathers drifted away, and Icarus fell into the sea. Where he fell, the sea is named for him.

Minos was still an angry man. He searched for Daedalus. When he reached Sicily, he proposed a riddle, which only Daedalus could answer. The local king heard the riddle and knew the man Minos sought. Minos asked how a string could pass through a conch shell. Of course, Daedalus knew that a string tied to an ant could be pulled through to the small exit. He was disclosed.

The king of Sicily promised to make Daedalus the prisoner of Minos the next day. That night, Minos was a guest of the king and was treated to a nice bath. As occasionally happened to kings and generals in ancient times, Minos drowned in his bath. Daedalus was a free man.

Mythology in Life

Caves have been found on Crete, which wind for miles. One group of natural tunnels, near Gortyn, about twenty miles from Knossos Palace, has been dubbed the Labyrinth Caves. They could be the source of myth. There are other caves, higher in central mountains, which have been attributed to early cave dwellers. One of the first cavemen of the island is referred to as Zeus.

Daedalus, the mythical labyrinth builder, was an architect and engineer. As such, his designs for palaces on Crete, prior to Greek history, in the time of the Minoans, may inform tales of labyrinths. In fact, Minoan palaces had numerous storage rooms, which were rebuilt after earthquakes, leaving a meandering mess of hallways.

Mythology developed as entertainment; a means to educate people about their history and to answer questions that resound in the environment when fact and science are not available. Myths, like Biblical stories, do not require factual corroboration to be accepted as a social reality. Minos in myth lives on in art, derivative literature and great theater; Greek and contemporary.

PHAISTOS – SECOND CITY OF CRETE

Crete sits at the top of the celestial hierarchy of Greek gods as the home of Zeus. When Zeus enticed Europa to go for a ride on his back, he brought her to Crete. Of their three sons, Minos, Aiakos, and Rhadamanthys, Minos graced Crete with cities. Cities with great palaces were built two thousand years before Christ. Almost four thousand years later, European archaeologists excavated the cities, to renew fame of the heritage of Crete. They named cities for Minos and his family of rulers and heroes.

CRETE, PHAISTOS: View from the Upper Plaza

In the classical period of Greece, that is the era between the eighth century and third century BCE, stories of Minos and his clan were well-known across the Greek world, which included the Peloponnese peninsula of the mainland, islands of the Aegean, eastern Sicily, southeastern Italy, Black Sea coast of Turkey and Crete. Poets of prior centuries, Homer and Hesiod, recorded stories of gods, their escapades and accomplishments. Homer wrote of cities in Crete that sent soldiers to the battle of heroes in Troy in 1250 BCE. By that time, palaces of Minos had been built, rebuilt and salvaged after calamitous earthquakes that rocked Crete in 1650 BCE and 1450 BCE.

King Minos kept the largest of the palatial estates on Crete for himself. Homer tells us that. In 1900 CE, a British museum curator, engaging in archaeology in Crete, Sir Arthur Evans, named the site of his find Knossos, the palace of King Minos. He intended no slight on Homer by choice of name. Despite a bevy of archaeologists who descended on Crete, from around the world, in 1900 and the years after, hoping to find a larger palace than that located by Evans, Knossos remains the largest and the first of the known ancient cities of Crete.

The second city of Crete is Phaistos. Minos either gave Phaistos to his brother, Rhadamanthys or delegated to him the city to administer, under the auspices of Minos. Regardless of the basis of city leadership, there was no apparent sibling rivalry, rising to war between the brothers. Homer writes that at some point Minos sent Rhadamanthys to the islands to settle administrative matters abroad. Rhadamanthys was popular with locals and appreciated for his scholarly skills. Trade kept flowing to Crete and made the family wealthy.

Homer and Hesiod have differing stories on how Phaistos was named. Neither historian could anticipate that an archaeological find in 1908 would give notoriety to Phaistos that continues today. An inauspicious storeroom, off to the side of the royal apartments, yielded a round, terracotta disk, with still-to-be-deciphered inscriptions. Known as the Phaistos Disk, the spectacular find could unlock secrets known only to Minos and his brothers. This is their story.

Mythical Phaistos

The brothers Minos, Rhadamanthys and Aiakos, were known as law-givers. They all ended up as judges in Hades, the underworld. Evidently, being relegated to Hades as a judge was not a remark on terrestrial bad habits. There was much work to be done in Hades. Rhadamanthys was also known as the inventor of laughter.[60] He was a popular fellow in Crete.

The origination of Phaistos in mythology is complicated. There are several versions of his parentage. This is not surprising considering the devilish pranks of Greek gods, the repetitious use of names and the curious sense of time attributed to immortals.

In one version of the life of Phaistos, he was the son of Heracles (Hercules), who came to Crete on the advice of an oracle. Phaistos liked the weather in Crete, so he stayed. His fame as a hero in the Trojan War preceded him to Crete, which caused a great reception to be given on his arrival. Naming a city for Phaistos, particularly a grand city, with a foremost palace, was a due honor.

Greek historians also wrote that Rhadamanthys was a stepfather to Heracles and had been his teacher. If so, Phaistos was a grandson to Rhadamanthys, of sorts. Rhadamanthys honored his grandson in giving the town he administered for his brother the name of his grandson the hero.

If Rhadamanthys was the grandfather of Phaistos, then Minos was his granduncle. To be fathered by Heracles made Phaistos a god. In the mortal vein, Minos had a half-brother Kres, who had a son Talos. Talos had a son named Phaistos. That would make Minos the grand-uncle of a mortal Phaistos. Phaistos, the city of a god/hero, had much more caché. Minos appreciated caché.

As a side note on naming cities in Crete, founded in mythology, Europa gave birth to her boys with Zeus in the area of Gortyn. Rhadamanthys had a son Gortys, who valiantly fought a battle in the area. The town that grew near the

---

[60]   A sense of humor is a valuable asset for a judge. Minos has his own story.

site of the battle was named in his honor as Gortyn. In the second century BCE, the travel writer Strabo came to Crete and noted that Gortyn defeated Phaistos and raised it to the ground. Gortyn became the Roman capital on Crete. Phaistos declined as a center of grandeur and power. However, in this story, Phaistos has the final glory.

Crete, Phaistos: Theatre & west court

Phaistos the Second City of Crete

There are four major palaces from the Minoan era in Crete. In order, they are Knossos, Phaistos, Malia, and Zakros.[61] All were excavated early in the twentieth century in the wave of enthusiasm for Minoan study instigated by the find of Sir Arthur Evans at Knossos. Knossos is the only one of the palaces to be partially reconstructed, per the vision of Evans. While he can be faulted for over-exuberance in some of his ideas, he is due credit for opening the island to study. Knossos also receives the highest number of visitors each year. Knossos put Heraklion on the cruise port map. As a result, other sites enjoy visitors, who are intrigued to learn more about Minoan culture. Phaistos is also reached as a shore excursion from the port at Heraklion.

---

[61] See: Costis Davaras, Phaistos, Hannibal Publishing House, Athens, 2016.

The four major palaces are described as early palaces, that is, prior to the first earthquake, which occurred in 1650 BCE. The early period is 1900 to 1650 BCE. When pyramid tombs were being built in Egypt, Minoans were building palaces, with grain storage rooms, large plazas for entertainment and columned boudoirs. The second palace phase is between earthquakes, a period of 1600 to 1300 BCE. The lifestyle of Minoans declined after the second earthquake until their society vanished from history. Their golden age was prior to the first quake.

Minoan palaces were not pre-planned complexes with dramatic entries, such as those seen in Roman agoras, with dramatic temples, well-placed and festooned with rows of columns. Minoan palaces grew in an organic fashion, from the inside out, to accommodate growing needs. The outer walls seen on arrival at Minoan places were solid, blank, imposing masses. Beauty was found inside, at the plaza level.

To understand the layout of a Minoan palace, it is helpful to know its purpose. The palace was a center of administration in society, which may have had several cooperating kings, or one main king and several vassal kingdoms. There was no evidence of wars between Minoan kingdoms. The cities did not sit behind walls. Protection from theft was afforded by doors and storerooms. There were guards on the premises, not large separate fortresses. Palaces were trade complexes.

The Minoan palace was the residence of the king, the administration center for the collection of taxes and dispensing justice, and storehouses of goods to be traded and to be distributed to the people. Taxes were paid in goods. Coins were minted in the late period, although it was grain that held value in trade. Manufacturing occurred within the palace complex, including pottery, household and ceremonial items. Weights from looms found in some palaces provide evidence of making cloth and clothing four thousand years ago.[62]

Palaces were centers of religious practice and ceremony. The palaces included altars for god worship, oracles, and shrines, where the supplicant could leave gifts to the gods in thanks, or in hopes of fulfilling wishes. Central to each

---

[62] See generally: Dr. Antonis Vasilakis, Phaistos, V. Kouvidis – V. Manouras OE, Heraklion, undated. Dr. Vasilakis was born in the area of Phaistos and made Minoan study his life's work.

CRETE, PHAISTOS: Palace Storage

Minoan palace were large plazas, in the middle of the complex, where the population could stage festivals and ceremonies. There were also theaters. The Minoan theaters had a row of deep stair style seats, in a straight line, with a plaza in front. These were not like the curved Greek or Roman stages, built a thousand years later, with back walls for a chorus, or scenery. Minoan performance was open on all sides. Seating was uniform.

Phaistos was excavated in 1900, by leading archaeologists Frederico Halbert and Luigi Pernier of the Italian School of Archaeology. They determined that true to Minoan culture, Phaistos was first built between 1900 and 1650, in stages as the needs increased. After the first earthquake, some of the older sites were filled in, and the new area was built, smaller and on top, or incorporating the new into the older site. The plazas from the first palace were retained.

After the second earthquake, Phaistos was replaced in importance by another city. It remained a temple site. People in the valley below built a simple village site. Phaistos, on the hill, was a place of reverence. It no longer was a place of festival with bull-leaping. Royals moved elsewhere.

CRETE, PHAISTOS: Monumental Staircase

At Phaistos, archaeologists found three plazas. Upon entering the site from the visitor center, there is an upper plaza. It dates to the first palace phase. There are no surrounding buildings. The next plaza is reached by a short flight of stairs, leading down to the theatre plaza. This open plaza has seating on one side. The back of the seating area has a high wall that forms the retaining wall for the upper plaza. The builders of Phaistos used the three hills of the site to terrace the palace complex.

Slightly downhill from the theatre are rooms from the first palace phase. They are covered for protection. Visitors are not allowed. To the opposite side of the theatre are later buildings to accommodate residents in the last days of palace use. Their shrines are next to the theatre.

From the theatre plaza level, there is a grand staircase leading up to the central plaza and the royal apartments. The large central plaza had columns on the sides and buildings for storage and some manufacture. One area is considered a place of stamps, such as those used in Linear B, to make tablets. Stamps are evidence of trade records.

CRETE, PHAISTOS: Queen's Boudior

On the far side of the plaza are modest buildings. It is believed that bulls were kept in stalls in this area, away from the royal apartments, and close to the entry to the plaza for the festival. Bull riding was a great spectator sport. Coins found of the era of Phaistos show a bull rider. Spectators could stand around the plaza, behind balustrades, to protect them from wandering animals. The surrounding apartments were two stories high. Verandas on the second, or third level, provided a privileged view of the festival, without fear of encountering a beast.

At one end of the plaza are grand gates to the royal apartments. The room known as the Queen's Room is spacious and has interior columns. This was the area of the palace where records were kept. Palace guards lived nearby.

Although no longer a city of importance, Phaistos was a functioning city until 180 BCE, long after Minoans disappeared as a society. In the void of the loss of Minoan society, Mycenaean culture moved into Crete, becoming the Greek society of 800 BCE to 800 CE. They were overcome by the Byzantines. The Byzantine Empire ruled from Constantinople, which was the center of Eastern Orthodox Christianity, the dominant religion of Crete today. Churches constructed in the Byzantine era stand in Heraklion today.

Down the hill from Phaistos are the ruins of Chalara, the city that formed in the demise of Phaistos. Looking down on Chalara from the central plaza of Phaistos, it is easy to see how Phaistos was initially formed as a grouping of rectangular dwellings, so close together. There is no large central plaza in Chalara. It was never a center of administrative power. People of Chalara could climb up to Phaistos to the shrines, long revered after other purposes ceased.

After the earthquake of 1450 BCE, palaces of Minoan Crete, including Phaistos, were abandoned. Only Knossos survived. In 1100 BCE, Chalara began as a village site. In Chalara there is a temple to Leto, the mother of Apollo. Greek culture was well ensconced in Crete.

Linear A, Linear B, and the Phaistos Disk

History is a product of written record. Cultures without written record are regarded by historians as prehistoric. Egyptians of 5,000 years ago had hieroglyphics. Minoans had Linear A. Linear A is a form of writing found in ancient Anatolia, Turkey today. That hundreds of clay tablets containing Linear A writing have been found in palaces in Crete, notably Knossos and more recently in a find in the palace at Chania, supports

the argument that Minoans arrived in Crete from Turkey. They actively traded with Asian groups. The tablets could reveal much information about Minoan life and culture. They could answer many questions, except the last chapter on the end of Minoan culture on Crete. Linear A has not been deciphered. It remains a mystery.

At the palace of Knossos, in a lower chamber, near storage vaults, Evans located tablets containing Linear B writing. The tablets have been dated to near the end of the late period of Minoan life, that is around the fifteenth century BCE. Linear B has been identified as an early form of Greek. It has been deciphered. Decoding the language of Linear B is a compelling mystery story.[63]

Sir Arthur Evans was so enthralled with his find at Knossos, that in 1901 he commissioned, from personal funds, the creation of typeset of the symbols, to use in decoding the script. Just before she died in 1950, the classically trained American, Alice Kober,[64] was on the verge of understanding the meaning of those symbols. Her work was completed by a dedicated British architect, Michael Ventris, who was fascinated by the symbols since childhood. He unraveled the code in 1956, at the age of 34. He died soon after that. His death has spawned a wave of new mysteries.[65]

The Linear B tablets found near storerooms in Knossos palace by Evans contained letters and numbers, comprising an accounting of trade goods. They were written in the language of the Mycenaean people, of mainland Greece. The Mycenaean culture eventually absorbed the Minoans of mainland Michael Ventris, 1922 to 1956. He died at the age of 34 in an auto accident, just weeks prior to publication of his book, Documents in Mycenaean Greek. Greece and arrived as the dominant group on Crete by 1400 BCE. Existence of the tablets is evidence of trade between the Cretan Minoans and mainland Mycenaean merchants before the demise of Minoans on Crete.

At the palace of Phaistos, sometimes spelled Phaestos, in 1908, archaeologists located a clay disk, hidden or stored below floor tile. The find was momentous. Unlike other disks containing symbols, the Phaistos Disk is a circle, with writing on both sides. The symbols are composed of stamps, used repeatedly, like stamp technology used on Linear B tablets. However, the language of the Phaistos Disk is neither Linear A, nor Linear B. The message, written in a spiral, center to the outer edge, or reverse, remains a mystery.[66]

---

63   See: Margalit Fox, The Riddle of the Labyrinth, Harper Collins, New York, 2013.
64   Alice Kober, 1906 to 1950. PhD 1932 in classical language. In 1946 Kober received a fellowship from the Guggenheim Foundation to study Linear B. A chain smoker, she died of lung cancer.
65   Michael Ventris, 1922 to 1956. He died at the age of 34 in an auto accident, just weeks prior to publication of his book, Documents in Mycenaean Greek.
66   On exhibit in the Heraklion Archaeological Museum.

On the Disk, there are lines forming a spiral. Between the long lines are 242 signs, of forty-five different characters. There are cross lines, dividing the characters into sixty-one boxes. Each box contains two to seven characters.

The sides of the Disk are not identical. There are obvious corrections made. No stamps have been found. They may have been of gold, long since melted down. The forty-five characters on the Disk could be words or syllables. The symbols are unlike any other tablets.

With the mystery Disk was a Linear A Tablet. In the room where they were located, there was a series of chests, with mud-brick partitions, similar to chests used to store temple repositories. So many people left valuables at a shrine, as part of devotions or wishes, that shrine keepers would periodically clear the items to a storage area. The room of the find was close to the shrine complex and near the royal apartments. One of the small rooms, in the same row of rooms, was used to store pottery. Pottery in the room has been dated 1650 to 1600 BCE, prior to the first earthquake.

Attempts to decipher the Phaistos Disk exemplify the dangers in decoding by guess. Kober's attempts at Linear B began by determining whether the symbols were pictograms, letters, or parts of phrases, when combined, resulted in language. On the Phaistos Disk, a circle with seven dots inside appears multiple time prior to, or after, a head with an unusual hairstyle, or a row of short plumes on a helmet. Some stamps are easily identified as a boat, a woman, or a bird. Others are shapes of unknown items.

The Phaistos Disk has been surmised to be the greeting of a Minoan king to the survivors of the earthquake; a poem of sexual desire, filled with imagery of plowing a field; and a curse on anyone who attempts to enter a shrine, where the Disk may have been posted. The message may also be religious. Whether the Disk is a poem, greeting, or warning, remains unknown.

Complicating the mystery of the Phaistos Disk, is the earthquake, or earthquakes, which occurred after it was made. There was originally an upper floor to the rooms where the Disk was found. It may have been on the upper level, having nothing to do with shrine items on the lower floor. The upper rooms were used as a residence by palace guards. After the first earthquake, the section of rooms was used by those involved in rebuilding the palace. If the Disk was placed in the storeroom for safekeeping, it became part of mixed debris after the second earthquake.

The detailed work of archaeologists, to excavate slowly in a grid pattern, discloses not only items but also the context of the item as it was used or displayed. The story of purpose or use lies in understanding context. In Minoan sites, where 3,500 years and two earthquakes intervened from the time of use of the room at Phaistos and discovery of the Disk, context can be muddled. That the Phaistos Disk is one of a kind, leaves the task of deciphering a vexing mystery.

Visiting Phaistos Today

CRETE, PHAISTOS: Chalara settlement

Visiting these sites will put into perspective how great a contribution will be made to history by those who break the code of Linear A and determine the message on the Phaistos Disk. So long ago, people lived in multi-purpose complexes, of work, play, residence and shopping, in much the same manner as they do today. They did so then, to conserve scarce resources in a sparsely wooded landscape, with little water. The Minoans were a highly developed, successful, large population. How they lived is known. The written messages will tell us what they thought.

In the Mesara valley below Phaistos, people farm today as they have for thousands of years. Their produce and grain no longer go to storage magazines in the palace complex at the top of the hill. Trucks take farm products to regional markets. Visitors go to the top of the hill in buses, by the thousands each year. They easily walk the site, made meaningful by local guides.

Knossos was reconstructed at the direction of Sir Arthur Evans to provide an understanding of the past in a walkable afternoon visit. Some of his interpretations have come into question. At Phaistos, the site has been stabilized, not reconstructed. Analysis and study are ongoing, without presumptions made in interpretive new building. To gain an understanding of what can be known of Minoan culture, an ideal visit would be to walk the first and second cities of Minoan Crete. Visit Knossos for one man's view, then visit Phaistos for an open look, using your mind's eye to fill in the story.

When the code is broken on the Phaistos Disk, it may provide some insight on Minoans. It may also be a singular piece of artwork, with a song, poem, greeting, or warning. Visit the site to enjoy the fun of a mystery seeking a solution.

Crete, Phaistos: Venetian Fortress Heraklion Harbor

CYPRUS, LIMASSOL: Center of World Trade

CYPRUS

CYPRUS FACING WEST AND EAST

Situated in the eastern Mediterranean, under the imposing landmass of Turkey, ancient Anatolia, yet facing west, to Greece, Cyprus has, since it was populated by Mycenaean Greeks, faced west and east. Populated by early Greeks 3,500 years ago, the history of Cyprus includes frequent subjugation to Persia, Egypt, Turkey and multiple invasions by Arab bands. Romans followed Greeks, adding population and culture to Cyprus. Invaders kept coming from the east. Today, in a replay of history, Cyprus is divided: west-facing Greece and east-facing Turkey.

Cyprus is also divided by faith. Today, the west looks to the Greek Orthodox church, and the east is predominantly Muslim. Historically, Cyprus has been an island where pagan deities Apollo and Aphrodite loomed large, while at the same time Saint Barnabas, a Cyprus native, traversed the island leading his guests, the Apostles Paul and Mark. In recognition of its bi-facial cultural history, the Cyprus tourism bureau promotes two tourism routes: The Byzantine trail leading to Orthodox churches and monasteries, which as a group are a recognized World Heritage Site, and the footsteps of Aphrodite, who was born in the surf on the shores of Cyprus and carried to land on a seashell.

Since 1974, Cypriots are enjoying the first period of peace in the long history of the island. It is an uneasy peace. Orthodox Greeks and Muslim Turks continue to spark religious and political divisions. Cyprus sits on the schism line of west and east today, as precarious a spot as was its location in 365 CE, when Cyprus was the epicenter of the great earthquake, that violently and abruptly brought down the ancient pagan world and enabled Christianity to build from the rubble.

Emblematic of pagan and Christian life in Cyprus is the city of Kourion. The ancient Greek city held an enviable position, high on a hill overlooking the sea. It was an active place when it became the epicenter of the great earthquake. Extensively excavated, and welcoming visitors today, Kourion is an apt vehicle for telling the pagan to the Christian story of Cyprus.

From the popular cruise port of Limassol, it is possible to visit pagan and religious sites of Cyprus. Imagine medieval king Richard the Lion Heart walking his bride down the shopping stalls of Limassol and ancient pilgrims walking to the shrine of Apollo at Kourion. Enjoy now the peace that has settled on Cyprus.

Pagan Cyprus

CYPRUS: Birthplace of Aphrodite

Aphrodite, Venus to the Romans, was born in the seafoam off the coast of Cyprus, near Paphos today. A large, standing rock, just off the beach marks the site. This goddess of beauty, love and procreation was carried to land on a scallop half-shell by an equally mythological zephyr.[67]

The origination of a goddess such as Aphrodite may have been the land of Canaan to the east. By the sixth century BCE, she was simply the Lady of Paphos, the godly embodiment of beauty and fertility. Temples to the goddess no longer exist on Cyprus, although veneration of her shrines continued into the Christian era.

Temples to Aphrodite greeted pilgrims until the Great Earthquake of 365 CE. After the quake, Byzantine emperor Theodosius issued an edict from Constantinople outlawing reverence to the goddess. By that time, the cult of Aphrodite enjoyed lascivious parties not palatable to the Christian emperor. Today, the route of Aphrodite winds past natural springs and windy peaks.

Apollo was the other deity of note on Cyprus. The largest shrine to Apollo on Cyprus, and the most important site in the ancient world on the island, was the shrine closely positioned to the ancient city of Kourion, today conveniently located on the road from Limassol to Paphos. The shrine dates from the eighth century BCE and shows signs of use up to the earthquake of 365 CE.

The Greek historian and geographer, who traveled the eastern edges of the Greek empire and chronicled his travels, was Strabo, who spent considerable time on Cyprus.[68] He tells us that the deer, sacred to Apollo, swam to Cyprus in tribute to the god. Strabo visited the shrine at Kourion and admonished anyone who would touch the shrine should be expected to be flung into the sea.

Pillars of the Apollo shrine stand today, high above remains of the sanctuary site. At the entrance to the sanctuary were rooms for visitors to cleanse themselves in hot and cold-water baths, before robing to enter the temple.

---

[67] The imagery of Aphrodite is most memorably captured by the Sandro Botticelli painting in the Uffizi in Florence, of Venus Rising. In the painting, Venus is Simonetta Vespucci, the most beautiful woman of Florence.

[68] Strabo lived in Turkey from 63 BCE to 23 CE. His opus work is *Geography*.

CYPRUS: Temple of Apollo

In a pit near the temple, hundreds of small terra cotta figurines have been found. No doubt these were the less-elegant tributes left at the base of the statue to Apollo, which was cleared to a pit, to make room for more extravagant gifts. Valuable offerings were kept in the treasury. In its day, the shrine was well funded.

In the ancient, that is pre-Christian era; there were seven kingdoms on Cyprus. The bastion of a powerful king was Kourion, high above the sea. Kourion had little water and great breezes. There was no natural harbor, although Kourion had all the other components of a Greek city.

Kourion has a theatre, where, since the second century BCE, dramatic plays by Sophocles and comedies of Aristophanes could be enjoyed. It was remodeled in 50 CE, during the time of Roman emperor Nero, to accommodate spectacles of strength by gladiators who faced wild beasts. Fifty years later, the theatre was enlarged to return a larger audience to plays, with a chorus. Today, live theatre is performed in the Kourion theatre, to another era of appreciative audiences. While the seats may not be comfortable, the acoustics are wonderful.

Cyprus, Kourion: Theatre

During the Roman era in Kourion, there was a stadium for sports, built in the first century of the Christian era, public baths, with heated floors, and an agora, that was the main center of commerce. The city was resplendent with columns, gardens and statues. There were grand homes, known today by the mosaics that have survived on floors.

The house of gladiators was a private residence of a gladiator enthusiast, who used the theme to decorate his floors with imagery of favorite contestants. The house of Achilles, which stood at the entrance to the city, likely housed visiting dignitaries. The floor tile has a scene from the life of Achilles when his mother disguised him as a woman to keep him from going to the Trojan war. The guise was undone when Achilles heard the sound of a war trumpet and jumped from his woman's' wear to join the superheroes on their mission to Troy.

CYPRUS, KOURION: House of Gladiators

The king of Kourion in the eleventh century BCE held a scepter with a double eagle on the top.[69] It is a fitting symbol for a king who kept one eye looking west to Greece and Rome, and the other eye looking east to the kingdoms of Assyria, Egypt and Persia. In 709 BCE, the king of Kourion was required to pay homage to King Sargon II of Assyria. The tax was paid to stall invasion.

In 569 BCE, all of Cyprus was a vassal of the pharaoh in Egypt. A few decades later, Persia became the ruling empire of the eastern Mediterranean. In the major revolt against Persian rule in 499 BCE, most of the kings of Cyprus joined with the Greeks. Stasanor, the powerful king of Kourion joined with the Persians, in a fateful betrayal of his homeland. He enabled victory for Persia.

Christian Cyprus

Cyprus, Kourion: Christian Kourion the Basilica

---

[69]   The scepter is in the Cyprus Museum in Nicosia.

Christian and pagan observance cohabitated on Cyprus from the Edict of Milan in 313 CE, which formulated approved Christian church cosmology, to the Great Quake of 365 CE. By the early fourth century, the ancient Roman empire was in such decline, that its hold was broken, in part, by the geological cataclysm that was the earthquake, which had its epicenter on Cyprus.[70] A generation after the quake, when life began to rebuild on Cyprus, around 385 CE, the newly built town housed a Christian civilization. Paganism became a remnant practice.

Before the Great Quake, a magnificent palace was built in Kourion. The House of Eustolios may have seen fifty years of opulent use before the quake. From multiple house levels, there were glorious ocean views. Floors were decorated in early Christian motifs of pheasant, falcon and fish, early symbols of Christ. Early Christianity had not yet reached the stage of human iconography.

In mosaics of stone and glass, in the floors of thirty rooms of the House of Eustolios, are tributes to Christianity. The owner notes that, where Apollo has given protection in the past, this house has a new protector. One mosaic inscription reads, "this house is girt by the much-venerated signs of Christ."[71] Another inscription reads, "the sisters' Reverence, Prudence, Piety tend the platform and fragrant hall." Incense and votive lights transcended into Christian practice, although the focus changed from reference to gods to virtues of Christian life.

The House of Eustolios had a section of baths, including cold, tepid and hot water basins. After the death of Eustolios, his home became a public facility for gatherings. The baths and reception halls were open to public use.

In 365 CE, all life on Cyprus was disrupted. Kourion, so close to the epicenter of the quake, ended life as it had existed for almost fourteen centuries. The modest population in Kourion at the time of the quake was that of early Christians, eking a life from remnants of Rome. It is known that many died instantly when stone walls were thrown several feet, like blown leaves. It is not

---

[70] The concept of looking at Kourion as a window into early Christian life in the Roman world, was explored by the lead archaeologist in several years of field study: David Soren and Jamie James, Kourion, Anchor Press, New York, 1988.

[71] See Dr. Demos Christou, Kourion, 8th ed. Filokipros publication, Nicosia, 2007, at 26.

known how many survived. It took several decades for signs of new residents to become apparent.

By the end of the fourth century, a Christian community grew at Kourion, sufficient to support a basilica, with an adjoining baptistery and palace of the bishop. Like homes of the former city, which grew from the rubble, reusing building materials left askew from the quake, the basilica and adjoining buildings repurposed columns from the Roman agora to the interior of the church. Walls of the basilica were embellished with a mosaic of glass and pearl. Fund-raising for the basilica can be seen in the entry mosaic, which reads: "Vow and pay to the Lord your God."

Ancient Kourion, prior to the Great Earthquake, had extensive public baths. Evidence of the size of the baths can be seen today by the number of piled-stone pillars, which held the floor above heated water. After the quake, some of the bath rubble was repurposed to crude homes on the same spot of the baths. Evidently, Christians did not enjoy large scale, nude, social bathing.

There may have been numerous statues and embellished fountains, with the shell symbol, a nod to Aphrodite. After the quake, such statues were no longer in style. In the eighth century CE, a massive kiln was built opposite the baths. Archaeologists suggest the kiln was used to break down bits of statues for reuse as lime in mortar. Early Christians were practical people, with few resources. Representations of Apollo and Aphrodite were no longer sacred.

There was a minor earthquake in Kourion in 77 CE, centuries before the Great Quake. The area of the agora was cleared each time, allowing the road to lead from the early basilica to the nymphaeum, a large complex of swimming pools. The several pools are massive and have depth.

Archaeologists and historians of early Christianity believe that the connection from the basilica to the relaxation and athletic use of the nymphaeum was not coincidental. The pools were damaged in the first century, repaired, and then heavily damaged in the quake of 365 CE. They were repaired for frequent use between 370 CE and 650 CE, as places of mass baptism for adults.[72] Once the adult population had been baptized, baptism of infants was performed in the

---

[72] Soren and James, at 42.

small fount of the baptistery adjoining the basilica. The nymphaeum returned to relaxing pursuits.

Obvious wealth in the basilica, sitting high above the ocean, became a tempting target for pirates and bands of Arabs in the seventh century CE. There were no protective walls around Kourion. Walls had never been necessary. Walled cities rose in the eighth to twelfth centuries, the height of the Byzantine Christian era, prior to the conquest of the east, including Greece, by Ottoman Turks. By that time, Kourion was abandoned. The bishop moved up the road to Episkopi.

Reconciling West and East on Cyprus: Enosis and Partition

In 678, Arabs raided Salamis, the capital of Cyprus. Over the next three hundred years, there were long periods where the emperor of Orthodox Christian Byzantium in Constantinople and the Muslim Umayyad Caliph both claimed tribute was due to them by residents of Cyprus.[73] Thus, continued the island history of being pulled west and east.

Early Muslim presence in Cyprus can be seen in Hala Sultan Tekkesi Mosque, built over the grave and shrine of Umm Haran, a maternal aunt to the Prophet Muhammed. The lady died while traversing Cyprus on a donkey in 698. The mosque was built by the Turkish government in 1816.

During the late nineteenth and early twentieth century, as the Ottoman Empire went into decline, and Greece struggled for independence, Cyprus desired independence from the Ottoman Empire and unification with Greece, known as *enosis*. Instead, Cyprus came under British administration. From 1878 to 1975, Cyprus was in a state of periodic armed conflict.

---

[73] In 1453, Ottoman Turks entered Constantinople, breaking down the walls of Constantine, which had stood for a millennium, changed the name to Istanbul, and completed the conquest of Byzantium. All of Greece was under Turkish rule.

Cyprus: Kolossi Castle of the Knights of St. John

Britain took control of Cyprus under the auspices of protecting the island from control by Russia. Cypriots accepted the premise of protection until control became onerous and Greek heritage of Cyprus was marginalized. In 1955, Cypriot freedom actions turned violent. Bombs exploded.

In 1957, Greek demands for enosis were met by Turkish demands for *taksim*, that is, partition. Violence was halted in 1959, by the British-drafted constitution for an independent Cyprus, where enosis and taksim would be absent. The terms of the constitution required in part that the president of the new country be a Greek Cypriot and the vice-president be a Turkish Cypriot, both of whom would have veto power over any legislation.

Cyprus became an independent nation and a member of the United Nations on August 16, 1960. Almost immediately, the country was thrust into civil war. UN peace-keeping forces were deployed to Cyprus.

CYPRUS: Looking East Limassol

The crisis on Cyprus came to a crescendo in 1974, when Turkish forces invaded the island. Turkish Cypriots fled to the north of the island and Greek Cypriots fled to the south. In 1983, Turkish Cypriots occupying the north declared that part of Cyprus to be the Turkish Republic of Northern Cyprus. The independent nation of Cyprus does not recognize the Turkish Republic. During this impasse, UN forces maintain peace from a buffer zone on the north-south border.

Cyprus became a member of the European Union in 2004. In 2014, leaders of Cyprus and the Turkish north agreed to open discussions toward unification. Talks are ongoing.

Visiting Cyprus Today

In the environment of peace and relaxing of cross-border traffic, it is now possible for visitors to enjoy Cyprus in full. Cruise ships port at Limassol, where there is easy transit to the city historical and cultural attractions. Just beyond the city are archaeological sites, ready for prime time, to tell the story of Cyprus as an ancient island of Aphrodite and Apollo, which became an early home to Christianity.

At Kourion, the city site opens to visitors at the point of the House of Eustolios, as though the wealthy host is continuing to welcome visitors to his home. Objects from the site are now in the British Museum, the museum at the University of Pennsylvania, which owns part of the site, and in the Kourion Museum, housed in the two-story home of George McFadden, a former excavator of the city.

There is an interesting side-story to the collection of artifacts from Kourion, one that tells the tale of nineteenth-century relic collectors, more than the story of Kourion. It is a cautionary tale. In 1865, General Emmanuele Pietro Paolo Maria Luigi Palma de Cesnola came to Kourion. He claimed to have excavated three rooms, in which a treasure of gold objects was found. The objects were offered for sale to top museums of the world, which were willing to pay a high price to accession the notable collection. The collection went to the Metropolitan Museum in New York City, where, for the next thirty years, Luigi Palma de Cesnola was the museum director. Do not expect the Met to offer the objects today as the material culture of Kourion. The so-called *Treasure of Curium* is a hoax. Holes were dug at Kourion, and the General brought home gold objects. The matter remains a cautionary tale for museums on verification of provenance.

CYPRUS: St. Barnabas Cathedral Limassol

TURKEY
KINGDOMS AND QUEENDOMS OF EARLY WESTERN TURKEY

Long before modern-day Turks, Byzantine Christians who preceded them, and the stretch of the Roman Empire, that spanned the coming of the Christian era, highly developed civilizations thrived along the coast of western Turkey, in an area known as Asia Minor. Pre-Greek people spoke languages derived from Aramaic, as were Hebrew and Arabic. Three thousand years ago, these cities grew into trading centers that traded by sea with Greece and the islands of the Aegean to their west, and by land with Persians to their east.

Tribes of people known as Lydia, Caria and Lycia became distinct societies that preferred trade to war. Their kings and queens preferred gold ornaments to bronze objects of battle. They resisted conquest by Persian kings, although

TURKEY, WEST TURKEY: Castle of the Knights of Saint John overlooking Marmaris bay

their independent un-fortified cities made them quick conquests by aggressive military civilizations.

By the time of Christ, a road that ran southward along the coast, then eastward to Syria, connected the coastal cities of Asia Minor. The northernmost Lydian cities of Ephesus and Miletus; the Carian cities of Bodrum (ancient Halicarnassus) and Marmaris (ancient Physkos); and the Lycian cities of Fethiye (ancient Telmessos) and Kaş (ancient Kyaneai), competed for trade. Royals visited among the cities. In the larger scope of history, these cities shared a similar fate. Locally, each royal domain has a history of individual personalities and fates from the time of the Greeks, or the Persians, to the present day.

This is the story of kingdoms, and inclusively queendoms, of Asia Minor, as they moved through Greek to Roman, to the Christian and Muslim eras. Of the group, Ephesus was the largest and had the longest continuous habitation. Miletus was the wealthiest. Bodrum had inspiring individuals of note. All are destination ports of cruise ships today for many of the same reasons that enchanted their early rulers. Enjoy their stories to understand why.

The Larger Scope of History

The end is not apparent from the very outset.
– Herodotus, about 420 BCE.

Herodotus was born in ancient Halicarnassus, Bodrum today, around 490 BCE. He was a young boy when his Queen Artemisia I of Caria left home to join ranks with the great Persian king Xerxes in Persia's quest to conquer Greece. As seen in his recollections of his hometown, Herodotus adored his queen. He did not have the same regard for her successors. Exiled for taking the losing side in an uprising around 430 BCE, Herodotus traveled the Greek world, recording his observations. The resulting opus work of Herodotus, *The Histories*, became, from its inception to today, a basic text of the ancient world of the Eastern Mediterranean.

TURKEY, WEST TURKEY: Herodotus in Halicarnassus

TURKEY, WEST TURKEY: Bodrum Castle

Historians, theologians, and archaeologists study *The Histories* to confirm or dislodge the writing of Herodotus. Seeking to emulate Homer's lengthy poem on the Trojan War, Herodotus put into prose local history, gossip and views of the world. Cicero called Herodotus the Father of History. Others regarded him as a teller of lies, or at best, pandering to the Greeks, who paid him a fortune for his entertaining recitals. Regardless, Herodotus is a wonderful source for this story.

According to Herodotus, Caria people, as well as the Lycia tribe, originated on the islands and moved to the coastal mainland known as Asia Minor. Caria people disputed this origination story, preferring to assert that they had always lived on the land. They did not dispute the close connection to King Minos of Crete,[74] having sent ships for his fleet in tribute, which they claim not to be the tax of a vassal domain.

As the hometown of Herodotus, Halicarnassus receives much attention in *The Histories* and maps informed by the work, as if it was in existence from the beginning of time. Other Caria and Lycia cities came later to prominence. The northern cities of Ephesus and Miletus pre-existed their southern neighbors.

Turkey, West Turkey: Theater of the Once Grand City of Miletus

---

[74]   King Minos of Crete was the son of Zeus and Europa. He maintained the famous bull of the labyrinth, which is the subject of its own story.

Coastal cities of Asia Minor were in an ideal position to thrive from trade in the ancient world. Being neither Persian nor Greek, they transferred goods from the Persian world in the East to the growing world of the Peloponnese and islands of the Mediterranean to the West. As the Greek population grew, and expanded their land to the grain-growing region around the Black Sea in 800 to 600 BCE, the merchant kings of Asia Minor grew in wealth.

When knowledge of the wealth of the coastal cities of Asia Minor grew, they became the envy of first the Persian kings to their East and then the great Greek king Alexander from the West. Persian conquest came quickly in 540 BCE. The trading centers were not interested in warfare. They paid tribute to their overlords to be left alone. When the Persians pressed for more control, the cities of Asia Minor, Crete and northern Greece pushed back in what became known as the Ionian Revolt, that lasted from 499 to 493 BCE.

The great Persian king Darius united his people and led armies from the area of present-day Iran through Turkey to put down the revolt. He enjoyed a quick and decisive victory in subjugating those cities that had led the revolt. The wealthiest of the cities and chief belligerent, Miletus received the harshest attention. Darius razed the once beautiful and thriving Miletus, from which retribution it never fully recovered. Darius moved on to Greece. He was stopped by a defeat at the Battle of Marathon in 490 BCE and went home, where he died four years later.

The son of Darius, Xerxes, wanted to prove his capabilities by returning to the site of his father's defeat at Marathon. He pushed his great army to make the famous crossing at the Hellespont. Since they were soldiers, not sailors, Xerxes entered Greece by land in 481 BCE, from the north. In the Battle of Thermopylae, in 480 BCE, 1,000,000 Persian soldiers defeated the united Greek force of 7,000. Xerxes paraded into Athens, where he burned the Greek temple on the Parthenon.

The conquest of all of Greece, to include the Peloponnese, required a naval engagement. Three months after Thermopylae, in the Battle of Salamis, off the coast of present-day Port of Piraeus, outside of Athens, Xerxes commanded a consolidated force of Persian, Phoenician, Egyptian, Cypriot, Carian and other kingdoms of diverse languages, which were part of, or friendly to, the Persian Empire. The Persian navy included 1327 triremes, large ships with three rows of oarsmen to engage 310 such ships in the united Greek navy.

Turkey, West Turkey: 6 faces of Lycia

The prelude to the Battle of Salamis was an omen for Xerxes. In a series of storms, the Persian fleet lost half its ships. Problems were compounded for Xerxes by his need to supply forces two thousand miles from home.

Eager for a Greek traitor to give Persians a tactical advantage, Xerxes accepted the message from a Greek slave, which was actually a trap. The Persians rushed into an engagement, thinking the Greeks were in disarray and were leaving Salamis when the bulk of the Greek fleet came out of a cove on the island of Salamis to decimate the Persian fleet. Xerxes left a small force in northern Greece and went home.[75]

Alexander the Great left home in Macedonia at age twenty to conquer the Persian Empire one hundred fifty years after the Greek defeat of Xerxes. Alexander's empire was far greater than that of the Persians, stretching to the Far East and Egypt. Revered as a god, the young leader succumbed to either a mosquito bite or the poison of his tutor, Aristotle. Influence of Alexander in Asia Minor served to reinforce connection of coastal cities to the West.

In the breakup of the post-Alexander empire, former Alexander general Seleucus ruled small kingdoms of western Turkey. The warrior was not an administrator. He left most commercial affairs to the locals. Caria kingdoms enjoyed freedom until the arrival of the Romans around 129 CE. In 330 CE, Roman General Constantine I became the first Christian emperor and founder of the Christian Byzantine Empire, with its capital in Constantinople. Ancient trade roads to Syria through Asia Minor became the route of pilgrims to Jerusalem.

In 1299, the Byzantine Empire went into decline as the Ottoman Empire rose. Upon the decline of the Ottoman Empire in the nineteenth century, coastal cities of western Turkey transitioned to cities of modern Turkey. Churches became mosques, or museums, as the layers of conquest were left as architectural remnants on the landscape for visitors today.

---

[75] Greek General Pericles rebuilt the Parthenon, which begins another story.

Long-Lived Ephesus

TURKEY, WEST TURKEY: Ephesus Library of Celsus

The history of Ephesus runs from the tenth century BCE to the fifteenth century CE, although the site of the city provides evidence of habitation by Caria people centuries earlier. Ionians, a civilization of pre-Greeks, who were attracted to the harbor, founded the present city. The road from the amphitheater ran to the harbor, now silted over, leaving an abrupt end. Residents adapted the city to the silting harbor over time, leaving irregular pockets of development, which has confounded archaeologists in their effort to interpret life in Ephesus in any single era.

Citizens of Ephesus rebelled against an increase in taxes levied by Darius, which led to the Ionian Revolt. In 498 BCE, Persian and Ionian forces engaged in the Battle of Ephesus just outside the city. Ephesus was defeated, but not destroyed.

Daily life in Ephesus was quite cosmopolitan. Newcomers of any background were welcome in the city, where people lived in areas by economic status. Men and women were educated. Women headed households and were artists. As wars between Greece and Persia altered governing affairs to the East and West, the people of Ephesus focused upon trade, the arts, and education.

In the breakup of the empire of Alexander the Great, Seleucus ruled Ephesus. In 263 BCE, his progeny lost in battle to the heirs of Ptolemy, the post-Alexander general who took Egypt. For less than a century, Ephesus became part of the Egyptian Empire, until it was conquered by Rome.

TURKEY, WEST TURKEY: Ephesus

Initially, the Romans plundered Ephesus to supply art to Rome. Then in 27 BCE, during the reign of Emperor Augustus, Ephesus was given status second only to Rome. The Romans were great builders in Ephesus. Notable are the terrace homes of wealthy residents, excavated in the last twenty years, the large theater that runs down to the harbor, and the elaborate Temple of Hadrian. In the theater, twenty-five thousand spectators could watch Roman gladiators fight to the death.

TURKEY, WEST TURKEY: Ephesus Theatre

It is a testament to the importance of Ephesus as a center of culture and trade that when Rome gave way to Constantinople as the capital of Christianity, Ephesus remained second to that city in the attention of the rulers and population. For a thousand years of the Byzantine Empire, from the late fourth century to the early fourteenth century, Ephesus remained a key city, despite Arab attacks in the seventh century.

The decline in the power of the Byzantines and silting of its harbor led to an eventual decline in Ephesus. Ottomans looted the city and built a Turkish town focused upon a new harbor. The city was abandoned in the fifteenth century until archaeological work began in the nineteenth and twentieth centuries. That work continues.

Visitors to Ephesus may appreciate its importance in the birth of Christianity. Apostle Paul lived in the city from 52 to 54. Apostle John brought Virgin Mary to a home outside of Ephesus. The site of that house rivals the ancient city of Ephesus in the number of visitors.

Loss of Wealthy Miletus

Miletus was founded more than a millennium before the birth of Christ. The earliest settlers likely came from the Hittite Empire of the interior of Turkey. Homer tells us that Miletus was an ally of Troy at the time of the Trojan War. If so, the city may have felt the bond of close associations between neighbors. Absent the wife-stealing actions of Paris, the son of the king of Troy, who absconded with Helen, the wife of the Spartan king Menelaus, launching the thousand ships of the Trojan War, ending in the total destruction of Troy, Miletus was on good terms with Greek cities. Typical associations were more closely aligned with Crete and western cultures than with interior cities of Turkey.

By 550 BCE, Miletus was the wealthiest city on the western coast of present-day Turkey. Income was derived from its central location as a port between Persian traders from the East and the Far East, and goods going east from all points on the Mediterranean. Miletus is credited with founding Olbia, Odessa, and Sinope, as well as other cities on the Black Sea, as collection points for merchandise from interior Black Sea cities and the amber region of the North Sea.[76]

When the king of Miletus balked at paying high taxes to Darius, king of Persia, Darius sacked the city. There is some evidence that when Alexander the

---

[76]   See Cruise through History, Itinerary IV. Ports of the Black Sea.

TURKEY, WEST TURKEY: End of the Ephesus Harbor

TURKEY, WEST TURKEY: Blessings at the House of Mary outside Ephesus

TURKEY, WEST TURKEY: View from covered seats in Miletus Roman Theatre

TURKEY, WEST TURKEY: Lion of the Baths in Miletus

Great reestablished Miletus as a trading partner with Greek ports, city fortunes rose again. Miletus is mentioned in the New Testament as a place where the Apostle Paul met with church leaders. Biblical scholars ponder whether the visit was in the year 57 or 66, but regardless, Miletus was a notable city at the time of Christ.

Ottoman Turks were interested in the port of Miletus, not in the revitalization of the city. When the port became blocked by silt in the fourteenth century, the city and port were abandoned. Archaeologists rediscovered Miletus in the nineteenth century. In the twentieth century, tourists returned. While not as impressive as Ephesus, Miletus is a fascinating place to visit.

Queens of Caria

Herodotus was enamored of Queens who led armies. He was the first to write of Queen Tomyris, who is credited with vanquishing Persian king Cyrus in 580 BCE, to put an end to a war. There is no doubt that his favorite was

TURKEY, WEST TURKEY: Artemisia II monument to Mausoleus Today

Queen Artemisia I of Caria. He was a young boy in 480 BCE when Artemisia led five ships in the Battle of Salamis, sent by his hometown of Halicarnassus. His fondness for his queen never wavered. Little known today, his queen was worthy of admiration.

Herodotus recorded a description of his queen for *The Histories* as shrewd, intelligent and charming. Her parents chose an apt name for the future queen. Artemis is the Greek god of the hunt. Artemisia would be the female huntress, powerful as Artemis, like the warrior goddess Athena, yet seductive as Aphrodite. Artemisia was also a tactful politician, as ambitious as Hera, the wife of Zeus.

Artemisia was illustrative of her times and her city. Her father was of a long-standing Carian family of Halicarnassus. Her mother was from Crete, the city with which Halicarnassus conducted much trade and the place from which many residents claimed association.

Halicarnassus was a small outpost of the Persian kingdom when Artemisia took the throne. She ascended to control after her husband was killed in one of the Greco-Persian Wars. It would not be fair to say that she became ruler as regent for her son. At the time Artemisia assumed leadership of Halicarnassus, her son was of age to rule in his own right. When she went into battle, her son followed. History does not record if the son became king upon the death of Artemisia, or whether she stepped back. The date and cause of her death are unknown.

As queen, Artemisia needed to conduct business with Greek traders and negotiate with Persian generals, neither of which were accustomed to female leaders in their home cultures. To advantage Halicarnassus in both arenas, she needed to be as educated in Greek and the terms of trade, as she was in battle strategy. She was savvy enough to realize that minor leaders need major leaders as mentors if they are to succeed. It is no wonder that she sought the friendship of Xerxes, the self-proclaimed "king of kings," as her protector and she as his confidant.

By the time of the Battle of Salamis in 480 BCE, the relationship of Artemisia and Xerxes was well established. She was the only non-Persian and non-male in his close council of advisors. Her out-size role for a minor royal was well known to the Greeks. The Persians accepted that Xerxes relied on a woman for critical advice. That her status enraged Greeks was seen when they engaged in battle.

In the days following Xerxes burning of Athens, he gathered his advisors on the shore, not far from present-day Piraeus. Artemisia was among them. Xerxes had battle-hardened, but weary, troops on the ground, and more than 1300 ships in the water nearby. Artemisia was in command of five of those ships. Xerxes was astute enough to know that to control the Greeks he must cripple their navy. He asked his advisors if the place and time for that battle had arrived.

The generals were anxious for a final victory. The naval commanders wanted that victory to be theirs to claim. With great bravado, all the council members voted for the battle to begin immediately, except one. Only Artemisia advised against the location as the place for battle. Her reasons were tactical, pragmatic and honest. She was concerned about engaging an enemy in their waters, without knowing their position. She praised Xerxes as a general in land war. Battle at sea, when so many ships had already been lost in storms, required mastery of the new locale.

Xerxes had often enhanced his position in battle by bribing locals or engaging spies. On this occasion, a fortuitous spy appeared. Based on information that the Greek navy was disorganized and some Greek cities were withdrawing their ships to safer positions, Xerxes plunged into battle. The result was disastrous for the Persians.

Despite being averse to the engagement, Artemisia led her fleet from the deck of one of her ships. She fought bravely and displayed considerable skill. Her loyalty to Xerxes was unquestioned.

During the battle, one of the Greek commanders realized that he was engaging ships of Artemisia. He pursued her ship with fervor to eliminate the female commander in their midst. To escape and evade capture, Artemisia utilized the confusion of battle to ram a friendly vessel. In doing so, she led her pursuer to think the ship he chased was part of the Greek alliance. He ended his chase. Artemisia only wished Xerxes to believe her actions were appropriate in the crush of battle.

As the Persians regrouped in the aftermath of the Battle of Salamis, Xerxes called Artemisia to his tent. He awarded her a full set of battle armor as he praised her leadership and her wise counsel. He acknowledged that if he had followed her advice, he might have been king of Greece, instead of headed home without his prize.

Xerxes gave the head of his navy a wooden wool spindle, the accouterment of peasant women. According to Herodotus, Xerxes proclaimed that his women were men and his men were women. It was high praise for Artemisia.

Artemisia sailed for home entrusted with the children of Xerxes, whom she delivered to his family in Ephesus. Salamis was her last known naval battle. Although the campaign was a loss for Persia, the status of Persia was not of concern to the queen of Halicarnassus. By her actions, she secured the status of her city. It would not be necessary for her subjects to live in a fortified castle. The natural harbor of Halicarnassus continued to receive ships of many nations, as the city became known as Bodrum and continued to perform a lucrative part in world trade.

Queen Artemisia I should not be confused with Queen Artemisia II of Caria, who ruled a century later as a regent for her young son, at the death of her husband. Artemisia II outlived her husband by three years. In that time, she built the memorial to her husband, Mausoleus. This Artemisia was demure, unlike her namesake ancestor.

Artemisia II was known as more interested in plants than governance. She is depicted in art as the epitome of devotion to her husband. Paintings by seventeenth-century Dutch Masters and Rembrandt depict her dissolving ashes of Mausoleus in wine, which she drank out of grief and devotion.

Today the memorial built by Artemisia II in Halicarnassus, modern Bodrum, is an archaeological site, damaged in an earthquake in 1404. Architectural remnants of the mausoleum were removed to the British Museum. Signage in the museum makes no mention of devotion of the one who commissioned the structure to her husband. Design of the mausoleum informed the work of twentieth-century architects, among them John Russell Pope, who built the Masonic House of the Temple of the Scottish Rite in Washington, DC, in 1911, in the style of the Mausoleus monument.

From the time of Artemisia II, Halicarnassus was closely aligned with Rhodes. In the fifteenth century, when the Knights of St. John were the sovereigns of Rhodes, they fortified the castle at Halicarnassus, now Bodrum, in part by using stones from the mausoleum complex. The Knights repurposed works of art on the site to Bodrum Castle. The tombs of Artemisia and Mausoleus were looted before the Knights arrived; thus, those treasures are lost to history.

Marmaris at the Intersection of the Cross-and Crescent

Marmaris, previously known as Physkos, was a Carian settlement that developed later than its northern neighbors. Although Herodotus wrote that the site was occupied in ancient times, there is little evidence to sustain the gracious compliment by the traveling historian. His reference may be to Nimara Cave, off the coast of Marmaris, where ancient ceremonial rites were conducted. When Alexander the Great arrived, there was a castle, which he appropriated for his use.

TURKEY, WEST TURKEY: Marmaris Bistro

The Marmaris Castle, open to visitors today, was built more than a millennium after Alexander decamped the area. The castle is still impressive. Built quickly by Ottoman Turks for use as a basecamp in their assault on the Knights of Saint John in Rhodes in 1522, it has stood strong for five hundred years. Ottomans graced the castle with a garden of tulips, in honor of the mother of conquering sultan Suleiman. Suleiman was a tulip aficionado. Hardy tulips grow there today.

Beautiful Beaches of Lycia

TURKEY, WEST TURKEY: Tombs of Xanthos

Turkey, West Turkey: Viewing Chamber Tombs in Kas

Cities of Lycia are much appreciated today for their beaches, natural beauty and climate. In 547 BCE, Fethiye, ancient Telmessos, and Kaş, ancient Kyaneai, were among cities conquered by Persians. Telmessos was home to an oracle in a temple to Apollo. Alexander enjoyed visiting oracles, so he no doubt paid tribute when he arrived in 334 BCE after he conquered the city.

In the fall of the Greek Empire, about 200 CE, Fethiye was abandoned. There is nothing of the age of the Romans there. The city had a resurgence as a Christian settlement, part of the Byzantine Empire. Fortifications attest to battles between Byzantines and Arabs in the rise of Muslim influence, until Ottoman Turks conquered the city in 1424, as they advanced on Constantinople.

In 1923, cultural Greeks of Telmessos were resettled to Greece as part of the larger resettlement effort. The city was named Fethiye in 1934, in honor of a Turkish pilot killed in action. Today the modern harbor and beautiful beaches welcome an international array of visitors.

TURKEY, WEST TURKEY: Shopping Kas with ancient tomb at the end of the street

Just west of the major city of Antalya is the resort city of Kaş. Settled since the Stone Age, when it was known as Habesos; long a Greek settlement and one of the coastal cities of Lycia, known as the seaport for Phellus; enjoyed by the Romans as a seaport; and adopted by the Arabs as Kyaneai, Kaş has always been desired for its natural resources, clear water and climate.

Early in the nineteenth century, the port was deserted. In the 1923 resettlement, remaining Greek inhabitants of the area were removed, leaving the old city deserted. Archaeologists have kept ancient history alive with excavations. Cruise visitors paddle boats in shallow water to view ancient tombs in canyon walls. A shopping district has grown around a several millennium old tomb, sitting incongruously at the end of a street. Beaches and natural underwater habitat attract twenty-first-century visitors as the area has for several millennia.

Visiting Coastal Turkey Today

Western Turkey boasts of having more well-preserved Greek and Roman ruins today than in either Greece or Italy. While the western kingdoms of Turkey were not founded and ruled individually by Greeks or Romans, the Greek period of influence, like that of the Roman Empire, left remarkable vestiges of culture on the landscape. Later Ottoman Turk and modern Turkish rulers have been good stewards of heritage. For visitors today, a cruise along the turquoise waters of the western coast of Turkey, with excursions at its ports, provides immersion into deep history, an opportunity to enjoy beaches and vistas and to experience shopping in the same streets where people have been shopping for thousands of years.

TURKEY, WEST TURKEY: Turquoise Coast Today

Troy Lost: 1250 BCE

The battle for Troy in 1250 BCE may be the most famous in history. Ironically, the event is known for the *Trojan Horse*, a fabled contrivance that made its first confirmed appearance hundreds of years after the fall of Troy. The battle is well known as its ballad was sung over time until set to popular poetry by Homer, five hundred years after the battle, in the *Iliad*. Homer never mentions a wooden horse in the *Iliad*.[77]

---

[77] First mention of a Trojan Horse is in the description of the valor of Odysseus in Homer's Odyssey.

The Trojan War deserves its prominence history. It was the First World War. Of this, most historians and archaeologists agree. Some historians believe that the war had nothing to do with the powerful and famous of the thirteenth century BCE. The inglorious explanation points to the manipulation of grain futures markets in Athens, by the powerful kings of northwestern Turkey, who controlled the entrance to the Black Sea. Whether the growing population of Athens was fed by Greek farming settlements of the Black Sea at such an early date is speculation. Future discovery of clay tablets on which thirteenth-century business was recorded may give credence to this theory. Until then, the tale of love and glory will take precedence over an economic reality tale.

The story of Troy lost begins with a beauty contest. Then it builds momentum with an ungrateful houseguest. The story comes to a crescendo when the gods interfere in a battle of the superheroes. Troy lost is the story of the destruction of superheroes and the civilized world.

Judgment of Paris

In 1300 BCE, the civilized world was sufficiently stable to allow powerful kings to amass large fortunes, build sturdy palaces and travel the known world. There was frequent trade between Egyptians, Hittites, who controlled central Turkey, and Achaeans, who would become known as Greek. The upstart kingdom of Babylonia, Assyria, was rising in world prominence, further to the east. In the geographic middle of ancient world, powers were Mycenaean kings of western Turkey. These were dynasties of Miletus, Ephesus, and Troy. The royalty of all thirteenth century BCE kingdoms visited between each other, on vacations, or when banished from home.

There were occasional wars, such as in the thirteenth century when Greeks conquered Miletus in southwest Turkey. These were limited affairs, in which the Hittites showed great statesmanship. They developed treaties to exploit trade without draining resources in expensive wars. Some of these treaties and letter writing diplomacy practiced by Hittites are preserved on clay tablets, the stationary of the day. However, when the gods intervened in the affairs of mortal kingdoms, diplomacy was of no use.

Zeus has always been undisputed king of the gods, feared by all mortals. Within the domestic household of Zeus, this was not the case. In his life at home in the Mount Ida region of northwestern Turkey, Zeus was just another husband ineptly mediating family squabbles. His wife Hera and his girlfriends, Athena and Aphrodite, were frequently at odds. As a trio, these goddesses were a formidable force and constant headache for Zeus.

During the wedding party of Peleus and his bride, Thetis, parents of Achilles, the goddesses were ensnarled in a tiff over who was the fairest goddess of the universe. Was it Hera, the powerful queen, Athena the goddess of wisdom, or Aphrodite, the goddess of love? Zeus wisely determined that the better part of discretion was to duck the question.

Then playful minor god, Eros, threw down a golden apple to be awarded to the winner of the first Miss Universe contest. Young, handsome, and evidently not too bright, Paris, the second son of King Priam's fifty sons, and heir to the house of Troy, picked up the apple and agreed to be the contest judge. Hera offered Paris wealth and power, which meant nothing to the heir of a large estate. Athena offered Paris victory at war and wisdom, but he was not bright enough to realize the value of such assets. Finally, Aphrodite offered Paris the most beautiful woman in the world in exchange for the apple. That was a meaningful offer to the young man. Paris eagerly gave the golden apple to Aphrodite.

The undisputed most beautiful mortal woman in the world was Helen. Unfortunately for Paris, Helen was already married to Menelaus of Sparta, the richest of the Greek kings. Spurred by the protection of Aphrodite, lust, and a lack of intelligence or scruples, Paris paid a visit to the home of Menelaus.

Paris was a guest in the home of Menelaus for ten days. During this time, he charmed and was charmed by Helen. Paris had two things going for him. First, Menelaus was gone from home on a business trip during the visit. Second, Helen was a woman who was young and desirous of some excitement. After all, she married in her teens a man twice her age. Her home in Sparta was rather Spartan. A trip to Troy seemed a wonderful adventure. Whether Helen was abducted or left Sparta willingly has always been an open question in the tales of Troy.

When Menelaus returned to an empty home, he was predictably angry. He called upon his brother Agamemnon, the most powerful king in Greece, for assistance. Agamemnon mustered the one hundred and sixty-four kings of Greece to join in pursuit of Paris and Helen. They were then joined by kings of other lands in the civilized world. The Hittites were not among them.

Hittites considered the pursuit of a wife stealer as not a matter of much interest. Their attention was focused to the east where the Assyrians were a growing threat. When the armada rallied on the shores of the island of Lesbos, off the coast of western Turkey, there is no one to dispute the legends that one thousand ships launched to reclaim Helen. It was possible.

Meanwhile, life in Troy for Helen and Paris was not all fun and amorous games. The residents of Troy were unaccustomed to being the object of military attention. Troy was the home of a monarch of a large empire built on trade, not conquest. Behind the well-built walls, there were few soldiers and even fewer supporters of Helen. Five hundred years later, the poet Homer wrote to tell us of Helen's thoughts at the time: "Slut that I am (why)…did this ever happen?"[78]

There Was No Wooden Horse in Troy

The Trojan War was fought over a ten year period from 1260 to 1250 BCE. The leader of the Greek troops was Agamemnon. His family was from western Turkey. Through successful marriages, the brothers rose to control Greece. Agamemnon was married to Helen's sister, Clytemnestra. Clytemnestra was not quite as beautiful as Helen, nor did she have Helen's romantic disposition.[79] In the Agamemnon household, Clytemnestra was the more politically astute, responsible for the rise in power of the family. Agamemnon ruled the north of Greece, while Menelaus ruled in the south from Sparta.

---

[78] Caroline Alexander, *The War That Killed Achilles,* Penguin Books, New York, 2009, p. 53. Alexander notes that Paris and Helen may have sat out the war in Egypt, while 1,186 ships, under 44 leaders, commanded 60,000 men in pursuit of Helen. p. 43.

[79] After the war, Agamemnon eventually returned home, where he was brutally murdered by his wife. She had joined in a conspiracy with his enemies in Greece.

TURKEY, TROY: Trojan Horse in Movies

The Trojan expedition began badly. In 1260, 1,186 ships amassed for the war on the island of Lesbos, not far from Turkish shores. Under the leadership of Agamemnon, they attacked the southern coastal town of Mysis by mistake, thinking it was Troy.[80] The Greek army was beaten back by the angry Mysisians. Agamemnon was devastated. He returned home for eight years to regroup.

As the second campaign for Troy began, Agamemnon wished to guarantee favorable winds and a successful landing. To achieve his ends, prior to leaving for battle, he sacrificed his youngest daughter, Iphiannassa, to the gods. The

---

[80] Michael Wood, *In Search of the Trojan War*, University of California Press, Berkeley, 1998, p. 22. Note: the 1998 edition is updated from the 1985 edition to include information from recent finds in the archaeology of Troy.

ships landed safely. Then the troops set up a siege around Troy that lasted for two years. By 1250, the Greek ships lay rotting in the harbor outside Troy. The battle was in a stalemate. Agamemnon's army had lost all confidence in their leader.

Homer's epic poem, the *Iliad*, opens in the tenth year of the effort to take Troy.[81] It chronicles the deciding battle on the plains below the fortified city. The geography and the city are described in great detail. The specificity of the poem rendered the *Iliad* a definitive guide for all those who used Homer as a guide to Troy, including Alexander the Great in the fourth century BCE. As a historical account, the Iliad is regarded as the beginning of European literature.

Homer lived not far from Troy in Smyrna, or Chios. He walked the site of the battle as he envisioned the story. Greeks understood the significance of the battle at Troy from the time it occurred. Since the site was continuously inhabited by a remaining Greek population from the time of the battle to well into the time of Homer in 730 BCE, it is easy to picture tour guides at the site telling Trojan stories to visitors for centuries before Homer. Homer's task was to compose the ultimate epic national story of Greek heroes in all its detail.

Given the impetus of his task, Homer showed great restraint. His details of the scene of battle, the city, the Greek encampment, over the hill from Troy, between the harbor and a lagoon, have served as accurate scenes of the battle through time. Description of heroes in battle dress and brutal events have been substantiated in the archaeological record three thousand years later.

The *Iliad* describes the battle in gory detail, not for sensationalism, but for realism. Homer wished to depict the agony and futility of war. Although mischievous gods at play filter through the story, Homer tells his listeners that this is not fantasy or mythology. The *Iliad* is a serious lesson in history.

More than 2,250 years after the battle, and 1,750 years after Homer, a tenth-century CE manuscript was crafted in Constantinople. An *Iliad* dating to 860 CE is in the collection of St. Mark's Cathedral in Venice. There are two hundred surviving texts of the *Iliad* dating to the fourteenth to fifteenth centuries CE, a tribute to the reverence held for the pagan poem by Byzantine

---

[81]   Iliad comes from Ilios or Ilion, names for Troy in ancient texts, referred to in Hittite tablets of the thirteenth century BCE.

scholars.[82] To have survived, clerics must have gone to great lengths to protect the *Iliad*.

In the fourteenth century CE, the Italian poet Petrarch was given a gift of the *Iliad* by the Byzantine Emperor. Petrarch undertook the study of Greek so that he could read the text. In 1360, Latin scholars attempted a Latin version. Copies were still popular at the time of the printing press. Today the *Iliad* and its companion, the *Odyssey* of Ulysses' twenty-year homeward travels, form the cornerstone of a classical education.

As the *Iliad* opens, the failure of Agamemnon as a military leader is apparent to all. Unable to penetrate Troy, the Greeks spend their time terrorizing and looting surrounding villages. Achilles, who was not born at the time Helen left with Paris, is the one to whom the troops turn for leadership. Achilles is portrayed as a reluctant leader. This is not a war he desires. There is no military objective. He leaves the field of the battle, ready to go home.

The leader of King Priam's troops in Troy is his eldest son, Hector. Homer depicts Hector as an admirer of Achilles. Hector is the wise and respected heir to the kingdom. He is happily married, with an infant son. He sees no reason to risk his life and have his wife and son become slaves after his death. There is great animosity between Hector and his younger brother Paris, as Paris has risked ending their lives and the lives of occupants of Troy, for the sake of a lustful romp.

The *Iliad* ends with a confrontation between Achilles and Hector. The end of the poem is not the end of the battle. Homer leaves it to others to chronicle the death of Achilles and the sack of Troy. There is no wooden horse in Homer's Troy.

War of the Super Heroes

The ancient Greeks gave homage to their gods, but they immortalized their super-human mortal heroes such as Hercules, Ajax, and Achilles. The *Iliad* takes place at the height of the age of superheroes. The battle for Troy was the ultimate war of superheroes.

---

[82]   Wood, at 123.

At the beginning of the decisive battle in the tenth year of the siege of Troy, Achilles leaves the field to pout that there is no military objective deserving of glory for a superhero. Agamemnon leaves the field to pout that his popularity with the troops is below that of the younger Achilles. Hector decides that there is no reason to risk lives needlessly due to irrational acts of his brother, Paris. Hector decides that the matter of who leaves with Helen should be decided by a duel between her husband, Menelaus and her lover, Paris. The troops on both sides applaud Hector.

Menelaus agrees to fight with Paris. He is twice the age of Paris, but he is smart and focused. Paris avoids the confrontation, so his father, King Priam, agrees to the duel, committing Paris. The two men prepare to fight. The troops prepare to return home.

If there were no back-story to this battle, if the gods stayed at Mount Ida, Homer would have had no poem. Zeus knows that for Agamemnon to appreciate Achilles, there must be a war. Queen of the goddesses, Hera, hates the Trojans. Aphrodite prefers toying with Paris and his affection for Helen. Zeus decides not to interfere in the goddess intervention in the events of mortals. Homer will have his poem.

The two-man, winner-take-Helen, begins well. Menelaus and Paris exchange sword thrusts warded off by their shields. They each throw their swords, and again they each defend with their shields. They fall into a hand-to-hand brawl. Menelaus is clearly the stronger of the two. As Menelaus strikes to land a solid punch, his fist goes through the air. Aphrodite has intervened and spirited Paris away to his bedroom, where Helen awaits. Menelaus is confused. He wanders around the battlefield calling out to Paris.

In the bedroom, Helen refuses to be beguiled by Paris. Aphrodite threatens to make Helen unattractive should she refuse the charms of Paris. Helen contemplates for a moment what it would be like to be unattractive in a hostile city. She relents to Paris.

Hector enters the castle and comes looking for Paris. He finds him and drags him back to the battle to finish the matter. As he is leaving his home, probably for the last time, Hector stops to have a tender moment with his wife and son.

Out on the battlefield, the goddess Athena jumps into the fray. She throws an arrow at Menelaus, which draws blood. Agamemnon is enraged. When the Trojans send out a truce party, Agamemnon kills them. The soldiers erupt into battle, hungry for plunder.

At this point in the *Iliad*, Homer describes the brutality and agony of war. Greeks did not know what part the internal organs played in the body, but they knew their placement and gave them names. Homer describes spears piercing organs, releasing bile and blood. There are screams, grunts and the crush of metal upon bone.

The Greeks fight well, but neither side moves to an advantage. Agamemnon acts as Zeus predicted. He puts aside pride and calls Achilles into battle. Achilles arrives on the field in a battle chariot. He is swinging a huge sword in each hand. As Achilles moves across the field, he leaves a wide swath of dead Trojans in his wake. Eventually, Achilles reaches the walls of Troy. Hector and Achilles come face to face. These two men, who only hours before were the voice of reason, and who wanted to live; these two who considered each other with admiration, faced off in mortal combat. Achilles chases Hector around the walls of Troy three times, angry that Hector killed a young friend of Achilles.

Finally, Achilles runs a spear through Hector's neck, killing him. Achilles then ties the limp body of the future king of Troy to the back of his chariot and races through the field of battle, back to his camp. That night, King Priam arrives to ransom the body. Achilles has calmed down. He washes the body of Hector and wraps him in cloth so the king will not see the desecration of the dead. Achilles and the king of Troy share a meal. Achilles remembers his manners and asks the king how long he would like for the funeral of Hector. The king requests ten days. Achilles grants a ten-day reprieve in the battle to allow for a proper funeral ceremony for Hector.

The *Iliad* ends with the funeral of Hector. Allowing for the funeral is a gracious act of a superhero. The later acts of the plunder of Troy are not the sort of conduct to memorialize in a national epic of civilized people.

In the Aftermath of War, the End of the World

Achilles was correct in his assessment that there was no military objective in sailing for Troy. However, the consequence of the battle was not without military and historical significance. In the events following the *Iliad*, all surviving superheroes met their end. By 1170 BCE, the age of heroes ended. Ionian Greece fell to Dorians from the north, and all of Greece settled into a dark age. The plains of western Turkey were inhabited by bands of subsistence settlements, hardly reflective of their glorious past civilizations.

Achilles died on the field of battle at Troy when Paris shot his arrow. The arrow, aided by the gods, struck the only vulnerable part of Achilles' anatomy, his heel. Paris died in the battle soon after that. Menelaus and Odysseus either hid in a wooden subterfuge or commandeered a battering ram to penetrate the walls of Troy, depending on whether mythology or archaeology is the basis of the story. In either event, Priam and his family perished in the battle. Hector's wife became a slave, and his son was thrown from the walls of Troy and crushed on the rocks below.

Menelaus ran through the streets of Troy looking for Helen. The songs relate that he was so angry he looked for Helen intending to kill her. However, at the moment Menelaus entered Helen's boudoir, she was so startled that she dropped her gown. Menelaus was overtaken with her beauty, grown more voluptuous over their ten years apart. He professed his undying love and desire. Helen now older and wiser, as well as more beautiful, decided that life in Sparta would be better than being a homeless, ex-lover to Paris. Menelaus and Helen returned home and lived happily ever after in Sparta.[83]

---

[83] Alexander, at 219.

Troy Found – Then Lost and Found Again

No other event in history has been the subject of such long-standing constant interest as the battle for Troy. Troy fell in 1250 BCE. The site became an instant tourist attraction. The battle occurred in the age of Hercules and Ajax. It pitted reluctant adversaries Agamemnon and Hector in a death sequence. This was the battle in which Achilles died. Helen and the fabled horse became side notes to the story of superheroes and the gold of King Priam of Troy.

This is the story of Troy found. The quests to find Troy have created new myths, built careers, and shattered lives. Once found, the treasures of Troy were lost and found again. The story of Troy is not only ancient history. It is continually building layers to the present.

TURKEY, TROY: Myceane Cup

Early Tourists

Archaeologists believe that the site of Troy was continually inhabited by a remnant population. They must have been a tenacious group as earthquakes shook remaining city walls. Homer walked the site of the battle in preparation for composing his *Iliad* in about 730 BCE.

In 480 BCE, the commander from the east, Xerxes, stopped at Troy to pay homage to Priam. He then crossed the Hellespont on his way into Greece, where he terrorized the Greek population in memory of Priam's tragedy. In 334 BCE, Alexander of Macedonia, also known as Alexander the Great, came across the Hellespont in the opposite direction. He was on his way to Afghanistan to avenge an earlier defeat of his father. Alexander believed that he was a descendant of Achilles. His visit was an apology for the war that should not have ended a civilization.

There are stories of Alexander running around the funeral pile of Achilles three times in the nude, in memory of Achilles' pursuit of Hector around the walls of Troy. Alexander then laid his golden garland upon the site. He is reputed to have said that Achilles was fortunate to have Homer write of his deeds. Who, he asked, would write about him?

By the time Julius Caesar arrived in 38 BCE, the plains of Troy were covered in mud and overgrowth. He was frustrated that he could not have a visual connection to the great events of the past. Roman emperor Caracalla was able to locate the tomb of Achilles during his visit in 215 CE. Its location was documented as visible until 355 CE. The apostles of Christ likely walked the area now known as Troy Level IX.[84]

Emperor Constantine came to Troy to found his great city of Byzantine Christianity at the end of the first millennium of the Common Era. He was unable to locate a suitable port, so he went up the coast and founded it at Byzantium or Constantinopolis, now known as Istanbul. After Sultan Mehmet II conquered Constantinople in 1453, and then Athens in 1456, he stopped by the site of Priam's Troy in 1462 to pay his respects.

---

[84] Michael Wood, *In Search of the Trojan War,* University of Cal. Press, Berkeley, 1998, p. 14.

In 1580, Queen Elizabeth I opened modern trade with Turkey. Relationships between the two countries have been continuous. British tourists and those with academic interests in Troy have been arriving in cruise ships along the coast for over four hundred years. In their quest to find Troy, several sites were identified using Homer as a guide, even though not all the landscape fit descriptions given by the Athenian poet.

The magnetism of Troy has sustained for visitors over two and half millennia. Perhaps Troy was closer to gods on Mount Ida than can be presently understood. Whatever the reason, it is certain that Troy is a special place.

The Odd Couple: Calvert and Schliemann

The British believe that the tutor for the eldest of King Priam's sons, Hector, was a man named Brutus. Brutus left Troy before the big battle. He eventually founded London. Thus, the descendants of Brutus are known as Britain's.[85] At least this is what British schoolboys are told is the reason that their *classic* education must include an intense study of Homer and his *Iliad*.

Frank Calvert and Heinrich Schliemann had little in common except that each carried a prize copy of the *Iliad* and both made finding Troy their life's ambition. Their meeting in 1868, began a series of events that resulted in finding bits of Troy. That which can be known of Troy today, or is unable to be known, is a result of their relationship.

Born in 1828, Frank Calvert dreamed of finding Troy as a young British schoolboy. The Calverts were a family of gentlemen, lacking independent wealth. The family lived in northwest Turkey, where the eldest brother, Frederick, was British counsel in 1847. Another brother, James, was the agent for the United States. The brothers made their income collecting fees from ships passing through the Dardanelles. During the Crimean War, traffic was heavy. The family had sufficient means to live a respectable life, although far from London society.

---

[85] Susan Heuch Allen, *Finding the Walls of Troy: Frank Calvert and Heinrich Schliemann at Hisarlik,* University of California Press, Berkeley, 1999, p. 39. The more credible version of Britain comes from Brittany.

The family lived in a waterfront mansion. The family members were elegant hosts for British dignitaries and royals passing through Istanbul. Fred was an entrepreneur. He purchased land on the plains of Troy for future English settlers. He also built a three thousand bed hospital for those recuperating from the Crimean War. Fred hoped to establish himself as landed gentry.

Frank was the reclusive, studious, younger brother. While his brothers planned business deals and his sisters planned social events, he hosted scholars at his farm. Over his years of living in the Troad, as the area of northwest Turkey is known, Frank dug in ancient sites in methodical fashion, collecting information about early people while recording precise information about the context of his finds. Although he did not have a college degree or academic connections, Frank's accumulated artifacts and field notes put him at the top of that which passed for archaeology in British scientific circles of the time. He purchased land at the site of Hisarlik, where he was certain ancient Troy could be located. Frank's home became a de *facto* center of Trojan studies.

By 1860, Frank was an honorary member of the Royal Archaeological Institute of Great Britain, housed in London. He published articles in which he credibly dated sites, successfully refuting academics who were distinguished armchair archaeologists. His drawings of artifacts were relied upon by others to identify and date sites. When an official letter arrived from Rome, conferring certified membership in a highly regarded antiquarian society, it mistakenly was issued in the name of his brother. This was not the last time attribution for accomplishments of Frank was bestowed upon others.[86]

In 1863, Frank's world fell apart. His brother Fred came out at the short end of one of his own schemes. Fred went to prison. Frank went to work to support the family. His excavations at Hisarlik were put on hold. This came at a bad

---

[86] The mistake in recognizing which Calvert brother had made finds near Troy was understandable. All six brothers had interests in ancient sites. Henry was regarded as a scholar of Mycenae history, Edmund was an expert in Oriental and Egyptian artifacts, Charles corresponded regularly with the British museum on statues of the area, James had been excavating on the shores of the Dardanelles and was the first to come into contact with Schliemann, Frederick dug on the family farm, although it was not a passion for him. Frank made his first noteworthy finds just yards from the family porch. Allen, at 54.

time as Frank had dug a trench at Hisarlik which exposed the altar site of an ancient god. He was certain that he was at the cusp of finding Troy. Less than a decade later, Frank learned how right he was.

Frank offered artifacts out of the site at Hisarlik to the British Museum, requesting in exchange funding for an excavation. They turned him down. His article on the site at Ilium Novum, which turned out to be Troy, was edited in London to misidentify the site as Cebrene. Frank was literally sitting on the greatest find of the modern world, and he could do nothing. By 1868, Frank went to work to help support the family.

Johann Ludwig Heinrich Julius Schliemann was born in 1822, to a German family that lived from day-to-day. Family life offered him no opportunities. His mother died when he was nine. His father was a Lutheran pastor, who was dismissed from his job when he had an affair with the woman who cleaned the church. Unable to pay tuition, Schliemann left academic school for trade school. At age fourteen he was a grocer's apprentice.

Schliemann learned about Troy by listening to a drunk recite Homer in the street. Later, in his diaries, he wrote that he was inspired by a picture in a children's storybook and knew he needed to learn Greek. Regardless of which story was true, his passion for finding Troy was real. The dream sustained him while he stacked groceries.

A crushing blow to his arm from falling stacked groceries liberated Schliemann from his apprenticeship. At age nineteen he became a cabin boy. The ship sank in a storm, and only Schliemann and the captain survived. He sailed to Amsterdam where he learned all the languages he could: English, French, Dutch, Spanish, Italian, Portuguese and Russian. At twenty-four he was a bookkeeper for a trade agent in St. Petersburg, Russia.

By 1846, at the age of twenty-four, Schliemann was an entrepreneur. He opened up a commodities trade business, independent of his employer. He took vacations from St. Petersburg, to travel to the British Museum to admire their Egyptian collection. When his brother died in California, Schliemann traveled to a gold rush town to resolve his brother's estate. Unable to tell between his brother and a partner, who was stealing from whom, Schliemann stayed on in San Francisco to become a gold agent for the Rothschild Company.

When a dispute arose between the company and the miners as to where shortages in weighed gold occurred, Schliemann left California, having cleared several hundred thousand dollars profit in his dealings.[87] He traveled back to St. Petersburg, to resume his commodities business, which enabled him to clear $1 million profit by cornering the market in indigo during the Crimean War.[88] Schliemann perfected his Greek to deal with Greeks regarding supplies for the Crimea.

The year 1863 was a pivotal year for Schliemann. He interrupted his grand tour of Sweden, Denmark, Italy, Egypt, and the Holy Land, to profiteer in the American Civil War. He left a wife and three children, while he completed his world tour of the Far East. He brought home to his son a piece of the Great Wall of China. His son was not impressed. Schliemann was entranced by collectible antiquities.

The study and collection of objects of antiquity was the rage in 1863. That was the year that Sir John Lubbock published the bestseller, *Prehistoric Times.* Party conversation included discussion of Neolithic and Paleolithic people.

By 1868, while Frank Calvert was shelving his academic dreams to support his family, Schliemann was enrolled at the Sorbonne, in Paris, to obtain his classical education. Schliemann decided to find Troy that year. He traveled to the Troad and excavated at a place called Pinarbasi, thinking it was Troy. Upon discovering his error, he booked the next steamer to Constantinople. During his waiting time, he took the advice of a friend in Athens and made a social call on the Calvert family.

Frank Calvert was a font of knowledge for Schliemann. Calvert was willing to share, hoping that the wealthy collector would fund his dig at Hisarlik. As soon as Calvert mentioned Troy, Schliemann was captivated.

Schliemann went into high gear on Troy. In one month, while Calvert was distracted by family matters, Schliemann wrote a book on his excavations at Troy. He double-dated his meticulous, and later infamous, diaries, to indicate

---

[87]   Allen at 112. Schliemann cleared $243,000 while working for Rothschild for a short time.

[88]   Robert Payne, *The Gold of Troy, Funk & Wagnall's, 1959, at 69.* The book is informed by Schliemann's diary.

that he always knew the site of Troy. After excavating at two sites, for two days each, Schliemann had a book on Troy published and earned himself the title of Dokter in German and Greek academic societies.

Schliemann came to the United States to avail himself of its divorce laws. He divorced his Russian wife and made plans to marry the daughter of a Greek business associate. They wed after she passed an exam on Homer, which Schliemann wrote for his bride.

Schliemann did not have permission to dig at Hisarlik, beyond the small section owned by Frank. He did not possess any artifacts from Priam's fabled gold treasure, nor did he have conclusive evidence that his brief time in the field was at Troy. He was a wealthy man. He held a position of title and respect. Facts were merely incidental details. Frank Calvert was rarely mentioned in Schliemann's publications. To Schliemann, Calvert was a usable and disposable commodity.

TURKEY, TROY: Schliemann claimed this to be the death mask of Agamemnon and part of Priam's Treasure

The next decade was a fruitful one for Schliemann. What he lacked in scientific methodology, or patience to meticulously record all data, he made up for in natural instinct. Unencumbered by scruples or scientific technique, he rapidly dug where he thought logically gold should be. As he dug throughout western Turkey and Greece, much of the time he was right. He was assisted in the field by his field captain and wife, Sophia.

Once Schliemann's finds were safely in Greece or Germany, he announced them to the world. The items were typically attributed to famous ancient kings or warriors by the most general of associations. The Dokter, as he referred to himself, built a reputation associated with Troy.

On August 4, 1872, Troy was found, according to Schliemann. Calvert had been excavating slowly and meticulously on his land at Hisarlik. He came as far as finding walls and the floor of the Temple of Athena. Schliemann went in full tilt with a crew and accidentally went over the line into the land of Turkish neighbors. At night, he dismissed his crews early. He and Sophia finished burrowing into a place near a wall. It was there that Schliemann found gold jewelry, which he quickly proclaimed to be Priam's treasure, the fabled gold of Troy.

Schliemann still needed help from Calvert. There were stone tools found at levels above bronze age tools. The strata at Troy confused him. Schliemann had his gold, but he did not have conclusive scientific evidence of the civilization at the site. Calvert was mortified by Schliemann's actions, which compromised Calvert's credibility with the scientific societies in London and with his Turkish neighbors in the Troad. Finding Troy was Calvert's life's work. He wanted to salvage what he could. Schliemann had Calvert over a barrel. Calvert did not have the funds or time to excavate on his own. Meanwhile, idle workers at the site pillaged it for the well-cut stone that could be used in their homes.

In exchange for Calvert's expertise, Calvert negotiated with Schliemann to purchase the Calvert collection from the site and fund the remaining excavation. Schliemann agreed. Then Schliemann discredited Calvert to the Turkish authorities, as a member of a family with the head of the family in prison for fraud. Schliemann took control of the site and undervalued the collection he obtained. Calvert submitted articles for publication discrediting

Schliemann. Schliemann responded with his own articles, taking credit for finding the Temple of Athena, and discrediting the Calvert household.

In 1874, the Ottoman government of Turkey sued Schliemann, in his home city of Athens, for removal of patrimonial objects of antiquity from Turkey. Schliemann sought to influence the Greek courts by openly promising the items to Greece for a museum, even as he secretly negotiated sales in London and Paris. The suit was settled by a £2000 payment by Schliemann to the Turks from whose land he removed the items. Schliemann kept the collection.[89]

In 1878, Schliemann made another trip to Hisarlik, where he found more gold treasure. This time he employed 150 workers and some professional archaeologists. He installed his treasure in his home on the Boulevard de l' Université in Athens.[90]

By 1880, the Schliemann collections from Troy and Mycenae were on display at the British Museum. Schliemann wrote a best-selling book, built on the organization of the collection by the professional curators at the museum. Some at scientific societies in London scoffed at the finds. Schliemann was accused of having fabricated some perfectly preserved golden items, such as death masks, one proclaimed to be the death mask of Agamemnon. Schliemann was a media darling as he deflected all accusations. The British Museum display was a success with the public.

Calvert turned to his association with the Archaeological Institute of America. He worked lawfully through the Turkish government to bring artifacts to the Boston Museum of Fine Arts. In 1883, the Boston Museum recognized Frank Calvert for his efforts and contribution to archaeology.

In the 1880s, the Turkish government passed strong laws on the export of antiquities. They began efforts to establish their own museum. Schliemann turned his attention to Crete. However, the government stalled progress on his plans there based on his history at Troy. In 1886, Schliemann opted to dig at the Nile, but officials there were not impressed by his credentials.

---

[89]   Allen, at 177.

[90]   The home is now the Neumanistic Society of Athens museum and offices.

Schliemann established the first International Congress on Trojan Antiquities in 1889. In 1890, at the time of the second congress, he traveled to the foot of Mount Ida and looked at Troy one last time, according to his diary. Suffering from pain in both ears, he went to a clinic for surgery in November 1890. On Christmas day, he collapsed in the street and was carried to a hotel, where he died. He was sixty-eight. He is buried in Athens.

Frank Calvert remained on his farm in the Troad to his death in 1908. He is buried in the small family cemetery overlooking the Dardanelles, in Çanakkale, Turkey. Although never recognized in England for his work, obituaries of Frank Calvert in Turkey and Germany recognized his success in locating Troy and in advancing Trojan scholarship.

Archaeologists at Troy

After Schliemann left the sites of his trench digs, it took years for archaeologists to remediate damage done to the archaeological record. Much history has been learned from careful examination in strata that remained. Some pieces of the record will never be known. Artifacts without context tell only part of the story.

Following Schliemann, archaeologist Wilhelm Dörpfield worked at the site of Troy for a year in 1893. American archaeologist, Carl Blegan, worked there from 1932 until 1938. Then world war erupted and efforts stalled. In 1988, archaeologist Manfred Korfmann, funded by Daimler-Benz, cleared away Schliemann's ramp and trench. He restored city walls, to the extent that stone remained at the site. Korfmann was able to disclose a Roman street plan well after the battle at Troy.[91]

As a result of meticulous study, more is known about events at Troy, than is seen in a few gold artifacts. Troy was not a major city. It was a walled palace. The city was much closer to the shoreline than it is today as the deposition of sand has extended the land.

---

[91]   Michael Wood, *In Search of the Trojan War,* University of California Press, Berkeley, 1998, p. 260.

TURKEY, TROY: Schliemann home in Athens

In over one hundred years of archaeological research, it has been determined that Homer remains an accurate authority on Troy. Homer noted that the Greek encampment was by a cemetery at the seashore. That has now been determined to be Besika Bay, at Besik Tepe. The *Iliad* describes the site of a freshwater lagoon and the rise of land between the lagoon and the city of Troy. Standing on that rise, both the city and the Greek encampment could be seen, but otherwise, each was hidden from the other. Archaeologists have located the underground spring mentioned in the *Iliad*, which flowed from Mount Ida and fed the Scamander River. They have also determined that Bronze Age Warriors spoke Greek, the language of Homer.

Archaeologists have found no wooden horses at Troy. This is corroborated by Homer. It is known that Assyrians came to power after the fall of Troy. It is also established that they used *wooden horses*, to break down city walls during their conquests. These may have been manned contrivances or battering rams of wood propelled by men. It seems that as legends build over time, the later stories merged with those of Troy. The battle for Troy is a great story. It has not been diminished by a little embellishment.

Troy Lost Again and Found Again

TURKEY, TROY: Schleimann recovered statue of unknown location

The "Jewels of Helen," as Schliemann called his find at Troy, laid in the site for over three thousand years, before they traveled from Turkey to Greece and then to Britain. Between 1870 and 1890, Schliemann moved his treasures to Berlin. Although Schliemann remade himself as an American, Greek and Russian citizen over his life, in the end, he remained German in national spirit. The Berlin Museum of Pre-History is the ultimate beneficiary of his collection.

TURKEY, TROY: Schleimann home now a museum

In the closing days of the war, in 1945, Schliemann's treasure was hidden in the Berlin Zoo. When the Soviet army entered Berlin, many objects were taken to Moscow. Some of the bronze statues recovered by Schliemann went to St. Petersburg, which seems natural given Schliemann's resume. During the Soviet Socialist era, the world lost touch with Troy.

For over fifty years, gold treasures of Troy were thought to be lost. In 1991, newspapers ran stories of Troy found, again. A descendant of Schliemann made a trip to the Soviet Union to discuss permission to exhibit the collection. Since the Soviets had not acknowledged having the collection, the trip served only to fuel speculation.[92]

It is now known that in 1945, the Schliemann collection went to the Pushkin Museum in Moscow, where it was in continued care. In 2001, the museum opened an exhibition to the public.[93] Parts of the collection have toured the world.

The battle for Troy has not yet ended. The battleground has shifted from the plains of Troy to museums and governments of several nations. At issue is ownership of Schliemann's collection. In 1906, heirs of Frank Calvert questioned whether Calvert had a claim to items taken from their land without permission. The Turkish government has acknowledged unauthorized methods of Schliemann. The German museum regards the collection held by the Russian Museum as a gift from Schliemann to Germany, taken as war booty. Mixed in with claims of right and title are assertions that some of the collection was manufactured by Schliemann and that it did not originate in any archaeological site.

Ongoing controversies will keep the story of Troy alive for future generations. Travelers may still make a pilgrimage to the site that is now known to be Troy. Those with a sense of history will regard the site as more than a deep hole with a silly wooden horse in the parking lot. They may regard Troy as it was known to Homer.

---

[92] Jeanette Greenfield, *The Return of Cultural Treasures,* third edition, Cambridge University Press, Cambridge, 2009, p. 197.

[93] Greenfield, at 200.

CHRISTIAN CONSTANTINOPLE: 330 – 1453

TURKEY, CONSTANTINOPLE: Constantine Door to Hagia Sophia showing Constantine on right with city & Justinian on left with Hagia Sophia

For so many culturally resplendent reasons, Istanbul is a popular cruise ship port stop on any itinerary that includes ports of the Black Sea, or the Eastern Mediterranean. This city of 14.2 million is the fifth-largest city in the world by population.[94] It sits part in Asia and partly in Europe. Most notable for cruise ship travelers, just a short walk from the cruise ship dock there are famous

---

[94] Based on 2014 statistics.

buildings and familiar sites from storybooks and travel catalogs that are more amazing when seen in person.

There are few places in the world where a visitor can stand in the middle of a city park and look to their right or left and see two distinct eras of history, preserved in place. Look one direction and see the imposing Blue Mosque, built by the sultans to make known their dominance of the center of the world after 1453. Look the opposite direction and see the red Hagia Sophia, more than one thousand years younger, just as imposing, and made mystical by the ability to stand as dominant cultures of the city evolved.

Constantine the Great, the Serbian born, Roman general, who expanded the world the Greek Alexander the Great conquered six centuries before, took the city of Byzantium and made it his new capital, Constantinople. Constantine may not have had cartographers to tell him his choice spanned Europe and Asia. He made a strategic decision to put his capital at the center of his world. It was as defensible as it would be profitable for trade. All of the old roads led to Rome. From 330 CE forward, the hub of world land and sea traffic would be Constantine's capital city. It was the new Rome.[95]

The decades between 330 and 380 CE are recognized as the time of the fall of the Roman Empire. Historians debate the various reasons for the fall of the great society. They blame overspending on Roman military, overreliance upon slaves and mercenaries to populate the military and a corrupt government. In addition to internal decay, there were threats from Huns, the roving marauders that eventually sacked Rome. Diocletian, the emperor who preceded Constantine, decided in 285, to split the unwieldy empire into east and west divisions. Diocletian then retired to Split on the Adriatic Sea, and Constantine opted to become the supreme ruler of both sections with his capital in the eastern empire.[96]

If Constantine was looking for new real estate upon which to stamp his identity, with a new political, social and architectural infrastructure, he needed

---

[95] Byzantium was at the time a Roman city founded and occupied by Greeks.
[96] See Cruise through History, Itinerary II. Rome to Venice, Port Split - Diocletian's Retirement Home.

to look far from Rome. He found a suitable place at the entrance to the Black Sea, the grain port that fed Athens for almost a thousand years: Byzantium. To fund the new city, Constantine heavily taxed the Romans. The transfer of wealth contributed to the breaking point for Rome, apart from war, invasion and overextension of resources.

Constantine ruled from 306 to 337 CE. By any ancient or modern standards, three decades of rule was a long time. The stability of his leadership enabled him to build a great city. Since the great man was not too proud to listen to his mother, Helen, and since Helen was a devout Christian, Constantine too became Christian.[97] In him, religion and leadership converged to result in building great monuments in Constantinople to himself and Christianity.

Constantine commissioned the first Bible, although the content is unknown. He then convened the Council of Nicaea, to resolve the definition of Christianity. At issue was whether the Son of God was subordinate to the father, or whether the son was part of the Holy Trinity. The former thought, of Arias, was dominant when Constantine was baptized. Later emperors declared Arians to be heretics. Emperor Heraclius separated the Orthodox Greek-speaking church from the Roman Latin church early in the seventh century, opening the way for Eastern Orthodox and Roman Catholic churches to formally split in 1054.

Division of the Christian Church and development of separate liturgy began three hundred years after the death of Constantine. His remaining lifetime was spent building magnificent churches as peaceful symbols of reverence. Without established church doctrine to guide him, he was open to designs of churches, new and distinct from Roman temples.

There remain buildings of the Christian era of Constantinople, built between 330 and 1453, which greet visitors to Istanbul today. They are revered today as still grand. To imagine how these structures appeared to people living in the times of their construction is to understand their importance as commanding symbols of Christianity.

---

[97]   Constantine issued the Edict of Milan in 313, making Christianity lawful.

Turkey, Constantinople: Hagia Irene

Constantine repurposed temple sites to the foundations of his churches. He fused the might of his kingdom with churches for the people. His palace may have been of diminished importance, had it survived. Constantine was a military leader and an innovator of a new society, where deadly sport in an arena was banned and prayer was legitimized. For him, buildings serve as more than grand places. They were the first icons of a new world order.

Constantine dedicated several churches, two of which stand in Istanbul today. The first church was the Hagia Irene, followed by the Hagia Sophia. He also dedicated a massive Church of the Holy Apostles, which may have been his most impressive work, and the place where he was likely entombed. The church was in ruin by 1453. Like many other relics of the Christian era, it did not survive conquest.

Constantine protected his city with massive walls, interrupted at strategic points with gates suitable for suggesting entry into a great city. The great city required a massive system of aqueducts and cisterns to deliver water and baths for the enjoyment of a plague-free population. The baths are gone. Portions of the aqueducts remain. The cistern of the palace remains, although the palace of Constantine does not.

TURKEY, CONSTANTINOPLE: Obelisk in Hippodrome of Constantine

Turkey, Constantinople: Serpent Column of Constantine

The Hippodrome where so many residents of Constantine's time enjoyed chariot races is now a public square, dotted with a few relics of the original Hippodrome. These remaining columns were prizes brought to Constantinople from faraway places by Constantine, that were left behind by Dandolo, the doge of Venice, when he sacked Constantinople in 1204, in the debacle of the Fourth Crusade. Dandolo's crusaders accidentally set fire to a building, then left the entire city in ruin.

Toward the end of the Christian era, private nobles dedicated smaller, but still elegant churches and palaces. No structure could match the size of those dedicated by Constantine, in the fusion of religious dedication and political strength. This story is a visit to the Christian era in Constantinople.

Devine Hagia Sisters: Irene (Peace), Sophia (Wisdom) and Dynamis (Force)

To distinguish pagan practice from Christian places of prayer, churches could look nothing like Roman temples. Constantine built two Roman temples in his new capital. He recognized that forty thousand builders and artisans were not yet baptized and needed their places of worship.[98]

For the architectural concept of a church, Constantine looked to the democratic Roman structure of a basilica. A basilica was a meeting hall; a place for the commodities exchange market and law courts. It was an oblong building with a center aisle leading to an apse, the raised area. On the raised area, there were chairs in a semicircle, where speakers could discuss matters and be open to those seated or standing along the aisles. The bishop's throne was not a democratic concept, so it was not found in a Roman style basilica. It came later.

Constantine wanted a narthex, that is a vestibule, in his churches, near the entrance, where the unbaptized could be welcome to listen to the word of god.

---

[98]   Christianity was lawful, not mandatory. Emperor Theodosius, the ruler from 379 to 395, decreed Christianity as the mandatory religion of the realm.

TURKEY, CONSTANTINOPLE: Angel of Hagia Sophia

TURKEY, CONSTANTINOPLE: Constantine Doorway

Next to the entrance, there were side vestibules for baptism. Over the next century, the form of a church developed into a cross, retaining the center aisle lined with columns, with side vestibules. The shape of a Catholic cross became standard in Roman Catholic churches and a center cross in Eastern Orthodox churches after the Great Schism of 1054.

Since there was no church doctrine to dictate his choices, Constantine dedicated his churches to the virtues of divine peace, wisdom and force, also referred to as divine power. Hagia Irene was dedicated to peace, Hagia Sophia to wisdom and Hagia Dynamis to force. There is no Hagia Dynamis in Istanbul. A church of that name exists in Greece. Whether Constantine actually built all three sanctuaries in Istanbul is unknown. He built numerous monuments in Rome and throughout the empire.[99]

Hagia Irene is the large brick church most often seen and ignored by tourists as they walk through the garden on the path to the Topkapi Palace. It was Constantine's first shrine, built on the foundations of the temple of Aphrodite before the Hagia Sophia was begun. After 360, the Hagia Irene was upstaged by the grandeur of the Hagia Sophia.

Hagia Irene, like Constantine's other churches, was first built of wood and stone. It was burned in the Nika Riots of 532, in which much of the city was burned. By 548, Emperor Justinian, who was responsible for igniting the riot, repaired the Hagia Irene to its present configuration. An earthquake in the eighth century caused damage to the building. Once repaired, the Hagia Irene stood as it stands today.

The timing of the earthquake and repair resulted in Hagia Irene having an interior very different than Hagia Sophia. When it came time to redecorate the interior, Constantine V was in charge. He was an iconoclast of the mid-eighth century, that is, he believed, as did the Jews and Muslims, that the figure of Christ and saints should not appear in a church. It was heresy to do so.

---

[99] For a guide to Rome in the time of Constantine see www.pilgrimstorome.org.uk, last visited January 19, 2015.

Hagia Irene received lavish gold decoration using geometric design motifs, popular in the time, rather than the portraits of Christ, saints, and church benefactors immortalized on the walls in frescoes and tiles of other early Byzantine churches. The practice of decorating churches with Christ, saints, and scenes from the Christian era resumed in the Byzantine Renaissance later in the millennium. Until then, Hagia Irene was allowed only a large cross, still seen in the dome, visible above the heads of the faithful.

Hagia Irene was the central church until completion of the Hagia Sophia. Although it lagged in importance, it remained in use until 1453. The sultans chose to build their palace on the tip of the peninsula, enclosing it and the Hagia Irene behind a wall. At that time Hagia Irene became a storage depot for arms and treasure.

By 1703, old armaments were displayed in the Hagia Irene, so it evolved into a weapons museum. It remained a museum until 1978 when it was turned over to the Turkish Ministry of Culture. Today the perfect acoustics of Hagia Irene makes it an ideal venue for classical music concerts.

Hagia Sophia the Beautiful

Constantine placed the Hagia Sophia in a commanding spot in his new city. Completion of the church was left to his son Constantine II, who dedicated the new home of the Orthodox patriarch in 360. The commanding structure that stuns visitors today was the result of the effort of Emperor Justinian, completed in 537, after two former structures burned. The first church burned in 415, and the Nika Riot claimed the second structure, along with most of Constantinople in 532.

Perhaps Justinian put so much effort into the Hagia Sophia because he wished to overcome the effect of the Nika Riots. He may have wished to place his own mark on the capital city of a realm that he enlarged and reconquered during the early years of his reign. Whatever the motivation, Justinian succeeded in building a church that was the largest house of prayer for the next millennium.[100]

---

[100] The next church to compete with the Hagia Sophia in size was the Seville Cathedral completed in 1520.

Its golden dome inspired the faithful, converts and visitors, who could swear that the sun came down to kiss the gold lid of the church.

Turkey, Constantinople: Interior Hagia Sophia

Justinian retained the Constantine model for the church. He enlarged the proportions and succeeded in building the large dome with a diameter of 101 feet and a height at the center of 160 feet. Unfortunately, the dome imploded during an earthquake and was replaced just before the end of Justinian's rule, in 562. The final dome kept the same diameter with a higher center soaring to 182 feet.

The Hagia Sophia was built to be at the center of the Byzantine world. Justinian brought the interior green marble from Thessaly, black stone from the Bosporus, and yellow stone from Syria. Columns were transported from the Temple of Artemis at Ephesus.

Justinian II added decorative and figurative mosaics to the walls. Unfortunately, during the iconoclastic period in Eastern Orthodoxy, the period from 726 to 843, the figurative mosaics were destroyed. The mosaics seen today were created from the late ninth century. Christ, the saints and church fathers are amply represented, as are Justinian and Theodora. Later monarchs Constantine IX and Zoë flank Christ, surrounded in gold tile. Some mosaics were lost in an earthquake in 1894. These have been replaced in part with paintings.

When the doge of Venice came to Constantinople in the Fourth Crusade, relics held and displayed in the Hagia Sophia were taken. Upon the reconquest in 1261, a stone marker was placed in the floor of the repaired Hagia Sophia, as though it was the tomb of Enrico Dandolo, the doge in command of the sacking. It was a popular place to stand, in a dark corner, for personal relief. Locals discretely and humorously paid their respects to the doge. Archaeological investigation in the nineteenth century revealed that the tomb was more symbolic than actual. Truly a barb to the destructive doge.

TURKEY, CONSTANTINOPLE: Disparaging monument to the doge of Venice Dandolo, who raided Constantinopal 1204

In 1453, the Hagia Sophia became the Ayasofya Mosque. The new owners were good caretakers. Under the Turkish regime, the building received much-needed repair. The technology of reinforcing buildings to withstand earthquakes had advanced and was employed to strengthen the walls.

The mosaics of Justinian II and later emperors were placed under plaster when the church became a mosque. A minaret was added and then replaced with a taller tower and two additional minarets. Spectacular candles from the conquest of Hungary were brought in the sixteenth century, as were alabaster urns from Pergamum in western Turkey. Mausoleums of sultans Murad III and Mehmet III were built into the complex at that time.

TURKEY, CONSTANTINOPLE: 5th Century Byzantine Mosaic

Over the eighteenth and nineteenth centuries, the church-turned-mosque received maintenance, and the interior was cleaned and polished. Old candle chandeliers were replaced with oil pendant lamps. Medallions of sayings of the Prophet Mohamed were hung from the walls. After a substantial restoration in 1849, Justinian would have been pleased to see his building, even though it was not a church.

In 1935, the Turkish president of the Muslim republic opened the Hagia Sophia/Ayasofya Mosque as a museum. The carpets were removed, bringing Justinian's floor into view. The covered-yet-preserved mosaics were uncovered in a careful restoration effort.

Today the Hagia Sophia remains one of the greatest surviving examples of Byzantine architecture. If it looks like a mosque and resembles the Blue Mosque across the park, it is because the design was the inspiration for great buildings in the East. When Justinian first entered the church, even without the stunning mosaics that followed, he is reported to have fallen to his knees and cried, "Solomon, I have outdone thee!"

The Hagia Sophia exceeded the expectations and created awe in a man who expanded the territory of the Byzantine world at the height of its power. To people of the sixth century, the building was fitting for an all-powerful deity. For visitors today, the Hagia Sophia still evokes awe. To stand in the open hall and know that the building has been a place of prayer for over fifteen hundred years is a travel experience that is never forgotten.

Public Works: Walls, Aqueducts, and Cisterns

The Romans were masters of building civic infrastructure, so Constantinople received the best technology of the time. Aqueducts that brought water to the city in the fourth century can still be seen in sections that cross modern city streets and where remnants cross fields. Water was stored in the city below ground in cisterns, the largest of which was under the palace. Although the palace has not survived, the cistern greets visitors today to its fantasy of eternal cool, nocturnal quiet, beneath the city streets.

The Walls of Constantine were intended to encompass a city four times the size as the former Byzantium. Later, Theodosius extended the walls to include fields that had become neighborhoods. The walls repelled all invasions until 1453 when a small breach allowed the invading Turkish army to enter and take control of Constantinople. By that time, the capital city of the empire of Constantine was a fraction of the size that it had been at the turn of the millennium.

TURKEY, CONSTANTINOPLE: Roman Aquaduct

In the nineteenth century, large portions of the walls were removed to allow the city to expand. Still visible today are the walls that abut the Golden Horn and cruise ship docks on the Bosporus. Of the remaining fortifications, some of the impressive gates of Constantine remain. The Gate of Charisius stands. At that gate, the last Byzantine emperor, Constantine XI, tried in vain to halt Sultan Mehmed II's entry to take the city.

Sports Fans Riot

The Nika Riot of 532 had nothing to do with pagans versus Christians. It is mentioned in this story only because the riot resulted in the burning of so much of the early building efforts of Constantine. The riot was the result of fan rivalry in a sporting event that spilled beyond the arena to encompass the city.

In the spirit of Christianity, Constantine outlawed deadly gladiator games. Instead, chariot races became the emperor-approved sport of the Constantine era. The people enjoyed watching the excitement of a dangerous sport. They attended the races with the same fervor of competition that they had brought to the Coliseum. At the end of the day, the chariot races were only slightly less deadly than the gladiator contests had been.

TURKEY, CONSTANTINOPLE: Walls of Constantine

Chariot races were held in the Hippodrome on a long and narrow oval track. At the center of the track in Constantinople were a line of stone columns and statues collected by Constantine from across the realm. Three Constantine souvenirs remain in place today, on the open mall that is the site of the former Hippodrome.

As the charioteers raced around the track, those on the outer edge would try to drive the racers on the inside into the stone columns, where they would be crushed, or severely injured. Sometimes spectators threw obstacles onto the track to cause racers to swerve to avoid the item and cause a crash. The crowd did not come to see the winner so much as the survivor. There were no rules, no referees, and sportsmanship was not a term equated with fair play.

In Rome, charioteers were on one of two teams. They were either on the Blue or the Green team. Team alliances were in full force in Constantinople. Some historians speculate that the teams were divided on class, political, or religious lines. There seems to be no basis for believing that the teams were any more than long-standing alliances that held deeper loyalties than political factions, or social status. Although Cheese Heads in Constantinople were unlikely, it is not unreasonable to think that people attended games wearing face-paint of their team color.

People typically attended games with a heightened sense of excitement. On the fateful game day in 532, there was additional tension surrounding the games brought about by a recent riot over two dozen new taxes to pay for a series of successful, but expensive wars. Emperor Justinian had rounded up and hung the ringleaders of the riot. The rope broke sparing two condemned men. One man was a Blue, and the other was a Green. Crowds cheering their racers turned to direct their cheers to the emperor. They shouted, "Nika, Nika," which means win, win, or conquer. They wanted the emperor to spare the men.

Empress Theodora was a notorious Blue supporter, after Green supporters disappointed her earlier in her life. Emperor Justinian was a former Blue supporter, who created a rift with the Blues when he instigated new taxes. On game day in 532, Greens were angry that the royal family did not show them greater support. Blues were angry with the emperor for his recent withdrawal of support. Cheers for the racers became taunts at the emperor and his tax ministers.

The royals sensed the crowd boiling with anger. They left the arena through their private exit. The crowd poured into the street. In their anger, they lit fires.

After three days of riots in which most of the city was in flames, the crowd demanded the termination of the chief tax officer. Emperor Justinian complied. The concession was too late. The crowd was invigorated as they continued to rage. They called for a new emperor.

Justinian felt the better part of discretion was to pack up and leave quickly. Theodora had a cool head. She famously told Justinian that he would regret leaving. She stayed. She saw the power in the purple; the ability to lead like a royal.

Justinian called in his generals. They came to the city in full armor with their Goth mercenaries. The trained soldiers went into the Hippodrome with axes and swords slashing unarmed citizens. By the end of the fifth day, all was quiet. An estimated thirty thousand people lay dead in the city of three hundred thousand.

At the time of the riot, Justinian had only been an emperor for five years. He continued to rule for another thirty-three years. Once the riot was over, the tax minister was reinstated. Games at the Hippodrome continued with fewer and subdued fans.

Visiting Constantinople Today

TURKEY, CONSTANTINOPLE: Theodosius and spectators in Theodosius Obelisk 390CE

There may have been a marketplace in Constantinople, where the Grand Bazaar sits today. In any tour of Istanbul, guides will end their tour at the Bazaar for some shopping before returning to the ship. At the entrance to the Bazaar, typically unnoticed by travelers, and hard to notice over the covered walkway leading to the Bazaar is a fragment of Constantine's most important moment in Constantinople. To mark the day in 330 when he dedicated the royal city, Constantine erected a column to his achievement.

The original column still stands, charred from several fires, devoid of the statue of Constantine that stood at the top, and held together with metal bands, that give it an odd appearance. The column does not evoke the feeling of a photographic moment. The column is the cornerstone of Christian Constantinople. That it still stands is a credit to Constantine, who assumed that his capital would live forever.

On any tour of Istanbul that winds through the streets look for the gates to the wall of Constantine. The Gate of Spring, Golden Gate, Selymbria Gate and Belgrade Gate, also known as the Xylokerkos Gate, are still stone and block reminders of the power of an emperor expressed in his battle victories, his city structures and the institutions and styles of life that he pioneered. Constantine's Constantinople is still present in modern Istanbul.

Zoë - Golden Woman of the Hagia Sophia: A Byzantine Soap Opera

Turkey, Zoe: Detail of Zoe mosaic in Hagia Sophia

The Byzantine era has so often been portrayed as the Dark Ages that the understanding of history for so many people runs to the fall of the Roman Empire in the fourth century and skips to the Renaissance in the fifteenth century, as though nothing much happened in the interim. Actually, many interesting and important events occurred between the fall of the Roman Empire and 1450, the approximate time of the Renaissance in Europe and domination of the Christian East by sultans of Asia Minor, that we know today as Turkey. This in-between period in the Christian world is known as the Byzantine era.

The name Byzantine comes from the Roman city of Byzantium, located in present-day Turkey at the entrance to the Black Sea. Constantine, who was born in Serbia, was the great Roman general, who became an emperor of Rome. He was the first Roman emperor to become a Christian and make it the official religion of the Roman domain, which was considerable. He established as his capital the city of Byzantium, which he renamed Constantinople.[101] Eastern Christians of the early era retained the moniker of Byzantines, for the Byzantine eastern empire controlled by the city.

Another important contribution of Constantine to world history generally, and specifically to this story, is the establishment of dynastic succession. Instead of a triumvirate of senators, or the most powerful general taking the helm at the death of an emperor, leadership was kept in the family. The family member ascending to the throne did not need qualifications other than royal birth. In Constantinople, daughters were eligible rulers. Rome would never accept female rulers.

War and plague decimated populations of once-great cities, such as Rome and Constantinople. After Venice raided and burned Constantinople in 1204, in a vicious crusade, the rising Ottoman Empire nibbled at the fringes of Byzantium, until the Christian empire became a small area around its capital city. In 1453, an Ottoman Sultan breached the walls of Constantine's city and brought Byzantium to an end. At the same time, the Renaissance began. The spring time of art and culture occurred in Florence, a city not invested in war.

During the middle period in Constantinople, between Constantine building a new Christian city in the fourth century and its fall in 1453, there were vicious battles, also deadly, not played out with armies. They occurred in the palace. Another reason for teachers to avoid the Byzantine era in the curriculum is that young students may not be ready for stories that expose palace intrigue. The

---

[101] Constantine named everything and everyone associated with him with some form of his name. His daughter was Constantina, his sons Contantius and Constans. Most of the men in this story are named Constantine. Constantine issued the Edict of Milan in 313 to end persecution of Christians.

true-life stories of Byzantine rulers have more plot twists than a long-running television soap opera. They run closer to the flesh of human interaction than to war and conquest of new lands.

At the center of this story is the beautiful Byzantine empress Zoë Poledouris.[102] She was a favorite of her uncle Emperor Basil II. The Zoë of this story should not be confused with the earlier clan of Basil I, who was emperor in 867 CE, died in a hunting accident in 886 CE, and left his wife Zoë to rule as the regent for their seven-year-old son, Constantine VII. Constantine VII was the father of uncle Basil II and Zoë's father, Constantine VIII.

Zoë of this story is made immortal, as she appears lost in thoughts, held in the moment by gold tile on the wall of the Hagia Sophia. She may be thinking of her sister and intermittent co-empress, Theodora, whose portrait was never commissioned for the royal church. She may be thinking of her many lovers and several husbands. The face of her husband on the wall of the Hagia Sophia replaced a portrait of an earlier husband. Notice the patched tile work at his throat.

This is the story of Zoë, at the beginning of a new millennium, in the middle of the Constantine dynasty. Her story illuminates what life was like in this period, all too often left dark. When traveling to Istanbul today, Zoë can be visited at the Hagia Sophia, where the visitor can personally interpret what may be behind her enigmatic expression.

Zoë's Formative Years

Zoë was born in 978 CE and lived to 1050 CE. Her formative years run to age fifty. That may seem a long time for a woman to come into her own, although in the age it was not so unusual. Consider that the Oracle of Delphi was chosen

---

[102]   Also known as Porphyrogenita. Many of the names of people and places in Turkey at this time are Greek, since Greeks were the dominant ethnic group of the area. Greeks came from Athens to settle around grain-growing regions of the Black Sea in 600 BCE, but that is another story. See Cruise through History, Itinerary IV. Ports of the Black Sea.

from among candidates who were all fifty-year-old virgins. Fortunately for Zoë, she lived to be seventy-two.

From birth, Zoë was regarded as an empress-in-waiting. Her uncle Basil II had no sons and her father had only two daughters, of which she was the eldest. Her sister Theodora was born in 980.

Uncle Basil was a savvy fellow. He was pleased not to have ambitious young men planning his early demise. He held Zoë and Theodora close to home and in the women's lounge of the palace, where they could not find husbands.

Christian women of Byzantium lived, as did women in Greece and Rome, in the same manner as Jewish women before them and Muslim women after them. They were kept separate from the daily lives of men. The future female empresses lived with the female members of the household, including female slaves, in separate rooms, where they socialized and plotted out social destinies. When women in the Christian era were sent to convents, their lives as nuns were similar to their secular lives, except their outfits and reading choices were narrowly dictated by the church.

In 996, eighteen-year-old Zoë was betrothed to the Holy Roman Emperor Otto III, a German royal. When all was ready, she traveled to her wedding in 1001, across the Via Egnatia in Constantinople and sailed the Adriatic, landing at the port of Bari, where the Via Apia from Rome ends. Before she could travel further, Zoë learned that Otto was dead. She returned to Constantinople and her retook place in the women's' quarters.

Zoë and Theodora remained sequestered until Basil II died childless in 1025. In 1028, Basil's successor and brother, Constantine VIII, facing his own death, considered marriage proposals for his girls. King Henry, the Holy Roman Emperor, and emperor of Italy and Germany, proposed a union between Zoë, aged fifty, and his son Conrad II, aged ten. The union of the couple would rule over all of Christendom except France and Spain.[103]

---

[103] Had Conrad II and Zoë married, ponder whether the Great Schism of 1054, between the pope in Rome and the perfect in Constantinople would have split Christianity into the Eastern Orthodox and Roman Catholic churches.

Constantine VIII preferred the handsome and valiant military commander, Constantine Dalassenos, as a match for Zoë. Zoë may have lobbied for that choice as the two were well acquainted despite the cloister in which Zoë lived. Their mutual admiration continued through Zoë's next two marriages. Unfortunately, Zoë's advisors in court preferred a man with less strength and virtue. They preferred a man they could control.

Zoë was married for the first time at age fifty to Romanos III. He was her third cousin. Romanos was already married, so it was arranged that his wife would renounce their marriage vows and enter a convent. Constantine VIII died three days after the wedding. Zoë was not a happy wife, though she was the empress of Byzantium.

Ruling Byzantium

Zoë did not know how to lead an army. Her strength was in working through the intrigue of government. Her subjects adored her. Romanos did not know how to lead an army either. He had lost many men battling Muslims in the East, which caused him to lose face among his subjects. He blamed generals for losses, making no friends among the military.

Romanos had been a city administrator before becoming emperor. He spent a great deal of money on city structures, none of which have survived. He exempted his new friends among the nobility and church from taxes, which destabilized the economy. Romanos made his biggest mistake when he limited the spending of Zoë and Theodora. Twice Theodora tried to have Romanos killed.

By 1034, Zoë had enough of Romanos. It is believed that he either died while taking a bath, or Zoë poisoned him. Either is plausible. Romanos had no friends in the palace.

One of Zoë's friends in the palace was a young, handsome, peasant Michael. Michael obtained a job as a servant to Zoë through his brother John, who was a government official. It was Michael who helped Romanos into his fatal bath. Michael and Zoë were married the day Romanos died.

TURKEY, ZOE: Back corridors where Zoe had Trysts with lovers

Once Michael became emperor, he spent much less time with Zoë. Michael turned to John to run the government. In a year when crops failed, the brothers raised taxes to fight losing wars at the edge of the Byzantine world. Aleppo fought its way out from the control of Constantinople, which meant the loss of a major shipping port for Byzantium. Then Serbs rebelled against Byzantine rule. The brothers blamed generals for losses.

Michael and John had good reason to be paranoid. Constantine Dalassenos was an open critic of Michael, who he thought was ignorant and vulgar. While Michael was avoiding Zoë, Dalassenos was pleased to take his place. All through Byzantium there were rebellions. Dalassenos knew how to arouse a swarm of angry peasants. He knew how to lead an army.

John lured Dalassenos from his home on the north coast of Turkey, overlooking the Black Sea. Once in Constantinople, Dalassenos was arrested and exiled to an island in the Sea of Marmara. Fearing a return of the popular general, the brothers moved Dalassenos to a prison within the fortification walls of Constantinople.[104] The great walls built by Constantine provided privacy for Constantine Dalassenos and Zoë to spend time together. They had a great deal of time together since Dalassenos was in prison from 1034 to 1041.[105]

Michael IV suffered from epilepsy, aggravated by the stress of leadership. In 1041, he donated funds to all of the monasteries in Byzantium and then chose a retirement home in one of them. Zoë still had fond feelings for Michael. She chose to co-rule with his nephew, who became Michael V. Michael V released Dalassenos from prison and allowed him to become a monk. Michael V, no doubt advised by uncle John, tried to send Zoë off to a convent. Michael even tried to eviscerate the image of Zoë from the Hagia Sophia. Notice the disturbed tiles in the mosaic.

At the assertion of sole leadership, Michael V was greeted by a rock-throwing mob demanding the return of Zoë as empress. When Michael refused to leave the palace, hordes of peasants stormed the place and literally pushed him to a

---

[104] Parts of the fortification walls of Constantine stand today around the city.

[105] The big rumor of 1034 was that Zoë, then aged 56, was trying to conceive with the 64-year-old Dalassenos. More likely, the rumor was a religiously correct sentiment of people accepting the relationship of adored leaders.

monastery. Once there, he was blinded for his audacity. He was emperor for less than a year.

In 1042, Constantine Dalassenos was back home in northern Turkey. He had twice been passed over as a marriage choice for Zoë, although their romance had spanned decades. He was a general of many battles, made more cynical by eight years in prison. Still, when Zoë called him to Constantinople, he came.

At this point in the story, a happy ending was possible. Zoë could have married Dalassenos, making him Constantine IX. Dalassenos never was awarded his Roman numerals. He appeared in court as a harsh, impatient man, accustomed to austerity and disappointment. Zoë was looking for a happier companion for her later but still vibrant years, so she gave the Roman numerals to a different Constantine. Dalassenos left the palace and disappeared from history.

Zoë's interview of a potential marriage partner begs the question of why she would want to marry for a third time at age sixty-four. She held the title of empress as a birthright and had the adoration of her subjects. She did not need to marry to have lovers. Marriage to a lover had not worked out well.

There were two good reasons to remarry and one noble reason. The two good reasons had to do with the distasteful prospect of being co-empress with her sister Theodora, and the energy-draining prospect of clearing the old regime advisors from the palace without a partner. The noble reason suggests Zoë was thinking about the future of the ruling dynasty of Constantine.

As the second sister, Theodora spent much of her time fomenting palace intrigue. Historians record that she regarded herself as their father's favorite daughter. She claimed to have been first offered marriage to Romanos and refused because he was married. She had been accused of plotting an overthrow of the king of Bulgaria, when he was blinded and sent to a monastery.

In 1031, Theodora plotted with a general, Constantine Diogenes, to overthrow Zoë and Romanos III.[106] As a result, Theodora was forced to a convent where she stayed until 1042. When required to leave in order to co-

---

[106] General Constantine Diogenes was not the same Diogenes as the fourth century BCE philosopher, who lived near Sinope on the Black Sea coast, who traveled the world seeking an honest man.

rule with Zoë, Theodora refused to leave the sanctuary. Out of the convent, one of her first acts was to have Michael V blinded. When the sisters held court together in 1042, Zoë's throne was just a few inches forward of Theodora's, to demonstrate seniority. It is hard to believe that anyone would want to have their back to Theodora.

TURKEY, ZOE: Zoe Mosaic in Hagia Sophia

Zoë chose to make Constantine Monomachos the emperor Constantine IX. He was twenty-two years younger than Zoë. He was forty-two and handsome. They had the opportunity to get to know each other intimately years prior when Monomachos was married to his second wife, also a niece of Romanos, Zoë's first husband. Monomachos held a certain attraction for Zoë, as he had conspired against Michael IV. For his efforts, Monomachos spent most of the Michael IV reign as an exile in Lesbos off the western coast of Turkey. In 1042, he was serving as a Byzantine judge.

Greek Orthodox clerics balked at presiding over the marriage, the third each for the wedding couple. They relented at Zoë's financial insistence. When

Constantine IX came to the palace, he was helpful to Zoë in ridding the place of ministers who served Michael IV. She was disappointed to find that palace intrigue increased. The three-way rule of Zoë, Theodora, and Constantine IX was difficult, even without the shadow empress, Constantine's mistress.

When Constantine came to Constantinople, he brought his mistress, Maria, the first cousin of his second wife. She anointed herself a full ruling partner. When someone spread rumors, Theodora perhaps, that Maria was conspiring to kill Theodora and Zoë, a mob threatened Constantine IX, until he dispensed with Maria. Constantine found a new mistress, the quiet, unassuming Irene, from the northwest of Turkey in Georgia.

Constantine IX repeated the actions of his predecessors by waging improvident wars, raising taxes to pay for the war, and buying favor from the church and nobles with the weakened treasury. He began to persecute Catholics in the Armenian, Russian and Georgian churches, who would not adhere to all dogma of his version of the Orthodox Church. Constantine IX weakened Constantinople in the religious and secular domain. He set the stage for the Great Schism.

End of a Dynasty

Zoë did not live to see all the damage done to her world by Constantine IX. She died in 1050, at the age of seventy-two. She is memorialized in gold in the wall of the Hagia Sophia as she looks in the direction of, but not at, Constantine Monomachos. His face was cemented in tile, replacing that of Romanos. Guides to the Hagia Sophia can point to the telling places of replacement tiles.

In 1054, Greek Orthodox and Roman Catholic Church leaders excommunicated each other. The center of the Orthodox Church remained in Constantinople, and the Roman Catholic Church remained in the Vatican, in the center of Rome. By 1055, Constantine IX was dead. He had married his daughter, Anastasia, to a Russian prince in an act of diplomacy, after a failed military action against the Russian king.

Turkey, Zoe: Monomachos crown

The legacy of Constantine Monomachos appears to be that long after his death, the names Anastasia and Monomakh appear in Kiev.[107] His coronation crown is in the Hungarian National Museum. The three co-monarchs are depicted on the crown, along with two dancing girls. It is not known if the girls represent his mistresses.

Theodora finally had the world to herself as sole empress from 1055 to 1056, when she died at the age of seventy-five. During her short reign, Theodora was harsh with nobles. She preferred to rely upon her servants as palace advisors. They always told her what she wanted to hear. She preempted church leaders in appointing clerics. It is not known if she died of natural causes.

Upon the death of Theodora, who left no heir of the Macedonian family line of Constantine, Byzantium cast about for leadership. Instability persisted for

---

107   The Russian double eagle emblem was originally the imperial emblem of Constantine.

Turkey, Zoe: Interior Hagia Sophia Today

twenty-five years, resulting in loss of territory. In 1081, a military commander from a Greek family of Trebizond on the Black Sea coast, Isaac Komnenos, began a family dynasty that lasted for a hundred years.

In 1204, the doge of Venice arrived to plunder Constantinople in the name of a Fourth Crusade. He left the city a charred ruin. In 1453, when the Ottoman sultans arrived in a conquering sweep west, there was little of the age of Constantine to resist them. Large sections of the great city walls of Constantinople fell under Ottoman cannons.

Today the Hagia Sophia, gates of the wall of Constantine, and a few other remnants of Christian Constantinople remain in Istanbul. Notable is the Chora on the outer city wall; a church built as a gift to the city by a wealthy noble. The glory of Constantine was dismantled. Zoë remains the golden woman of an age when Byzantine rulers led the Christian world.

For more reading on Byzantine Rulers, see: Lars Brownworth, Lost to the West, Crown, New York 2009; and Colin Wells, Sailing from Byzantium, Delta, New York, 2007.

TURKEY, CHORA: Donor Presents Church

Chora: Monument to a Man at the Height of an Era

Chora means out in the country. In fields, beyond the city in Turkey known as Byzantium, where Christian martyrs were inauspiciously buried in 298 CE, a little shrine was erected. A few years later the great Roman general Constantine arrived in Byzantium, made being a Christian lawful, and made Byzantium the capital of his Christian empire. The small early Christian structure was enlarged to be a chapel, then a home for men who devoted themselves to god, then a church.

Constantine's city grew to encompass the Chora area. Fields were replaced with houses, then small palaces. City walls were extended outward to include the church. The outsider was now inside. The name of the church remained Chora.

Of the finer homes near Chora, Theodore Metochites owned the largest. Like the Chora, Metochites began his life on the outside of Byzantine society. His father was sentenced to exile before he was born. Based on his personal talent and good timing, he was brought back into the city. Metochites continued to advance in rank, not by the usual means of valor on the battlefield, but by skill in government administration. He became treasurer to the emperor. Then by skill and persistence, he became a most trusted advisor to the emperor, rather like a prime minister, second in command only to the emperor.

The man from outside society adopted the church from outside the city. Metochites used a large part of his fortune to become a benefactor to the Chora. Under his direction, the Chora was repaired, enlarged and decorated with frescoes and mosaics in the style of the Hagia Sophia, grandest of Christian churches. Metochites' personal fortune rivaled that of the emperor, so his church became a monument to reflect his achievement.

From the fourth century to the twelfth century, the Chora had periods of grandeur and periods of neglect. Metochites recognized that his life and the Chora were intertwined. He was insightful. Like the Chora, his life continued to have its ups and downs.

Metochites was pleased when the emperor relied on his advice in the most important matters of the realm. He was surprised to find that one bad recommendation caused him to fall from the top of the royal chain. Metochites returned to his roots as an exile, like his father before him.

This story of Metochites and the Chora has a happy ending. The man who glorified the monument was allowed to return, not as a benefactor, but as a monk. He lived the remainder of his life in that which he restored and embellished.

This story of a man and his monument explains how a grand church became situated in a suburban neighborhood. There is more to enjoy in the Chora than its grandeur. On the walls and ceilings, there is subtext. It is more than the expression of a vain man. It is the story of his life and that of Christian Constantinople at the height of the Christian Byzantine Empire.

The Church Before Metochites

At the entrance to the Black Sea from the Mediterranean, Greeks began a settlement around 600 BCE. The town was destined to be successful. When Greek farmers needed to bring their grain grown around the southern shores of the sea to market in Athens, the port of Byzantium was perfectly situated as a transfer point.

Greek and later Roman gods were good to Byzantium. An incursion from early Christians, who implored townsfolk to become monotheistic, was unwelcome. In the 290s, eighty-four disciples of St. Babylas came to Byzantium from Antioch, the home of St. Luke on the south-central border of Turkey, then part of ancient Syria. Bishop Babylas died in prison, martyred for denying entry to the church to an emperor who had killed his predecessor and not done penance for his sins.[108] Leadership succession by assassination was not unusual in Byzantium, and the preaching of Christians annoyed the emperor. In 298, several Christians in Byzantium were killed, and their bodies disposed of unceremoniously in a field out of town.

TURKEY, CHORA: Chora Church

Local Christians built a small shrine to the martyrs near the field where they were buried. A few decades later, Constantine made Christianity legal, and the shrine was expanded into a modest church.[109] In the fifth century, walls of

---

[108] Emperor Philip, a Roman general, undermined the popular boy-emperor Gordian III, then killed him in 244, when Gordian was nineteen, to take his place rather than be senior co-emperor.   Bishop Babylas of Antioch died while imprisoned in 253, for denying entry to the church to Philip. Babylas was buried near a temple to Apollo. A century later, an emperor who found the Christian burial offensive to Apollo moved Babylas' remains.   Many years later they were moved back near the temple, which morphed to a church. Reburial of relics was not unusual in the era of transition to Christianity. It was not unusual for former pagan temples to be revised as churches.

[109] Constantine issued the Edict of Milan in 313 to end persecution of Christians.

Constantinople were completed by Emperor Theodosius II to include the area of the church. No longer Chora, a country area, the sixth century *Chora* church was venerated as the dwelling place of Christ.

A monastery was added to the Chora in 536. It became a convenient confinement venue for political prisoners, who did not merit public execution. When an earthquake in 557 significantly damaged the buildings, Emperor Justinian thought the complex worthy of extensive repair and additional rooms.[110]

Over the next three hundred years, nothing of historical note occurred in the Chora. Occasionally there were nobles buried in its graveyard, or confined to its monastery. The Chora fell from the view of emperors and slid into benign neglect.[111]

The fortunes of the Chora rose and fell like those of the city. In 843 there was a revival of importance in the church, which benefited all churches with attention to repairs. The ascension of Basil I as emperor in 867, the beginning of a Macedonian dynasty that lasted until 1056, began a Byzantine Renaissance in art and appreciation of the church. Basil, I established a law code, known as Basilica, that governed Byzantium until its fall in 1453.[112]

The Chora was in such a state of ruin by the end of the eleventh century that repair was insufficient. A new building was erected on the grounds of the ancient monastery in 1077. It was partially rebuilt in the twelfth century.

In 1204, the Chora suffered the fate of all Constantinople when the doge of Venice arrived on the Fourth Crusade.[113] Doge Dandolo came from Venice, blind and in his eighties, accompanied by a French contingent, determined to repay Venice for the cost of the crusade from the wealth of

---

[110] Emperor Justinian the Great ruled Byzantium from 527 to 565 CE.

[111] Paul A. Underwood, The Kariye Djami, Routledge, London, 1967, pp. 6-7.

[112] The term basilica predated Basil. The emperor was likely named for the basilica concept originating in Rome, which was the place of civil governance and justice. When Constantine needed a model for a church, he employed that of the Roman Basilica.

[113] See Cruise through History, Itinerary II. Venice – The Well-Traveled Horses of Saint Marks.

Christian Constantinople. The Fourth Crusade was known then and since as the Great Debacle.

Dandolo selected great art from Constantinople to decorate Venice, including the four horses of the Hippodrome. The quadriga has since stood over the entrance to St. Marks Cathedral in Venice, except for a brief visit to France during the reign of Napoleon. By the time Dandolo's fleet left Constantinople, the once-great city was in flames. The city burned to the extent of its walls, leaving the Chora in ruin. The pope in Rome issued an excommunication for Dandolo.

It took a century for Constantinople to recover from the Venetian visit. For fifty years, Venice and Rome controlled Byzantium, and little was done to rebuild Constantinople. In 1261, the personally unpopular, but militarily successful, Michael VIII, retook the city and forced the Latin-Italian rulers to exit. By 1315, the neighborhood surrounding Chora was rebuilt larger and more upscale. Chora church was left waiting for a sponsor to recapture its brighter past.

Metochites Before the Chora

Michael VIII returned Greeks to power in Byzantium. To maintain his power, Michael made a deal with the pope. If it seems a contradiction to force out Latin rulers and then make a deal with the Latin Church, it was. The arrangement cost Michael support of his people. The pope never trusted Michael. Michael had no friends in Italy, or Byzantium.

In 1282, Michael became involved in a scheme, which is known as the infamous Sicilian Vespers.[114] Michael made a devilish deal with the pope in which Michael aided instigation of a revolt in Italy against French occupiers of the Kingdom of Naples, which included Sicily. The goal was to weaken the political standing of Frenchman Charles of Anjou and thwart the Frenchman's

---

[114]   See Cruise through History, Itinerary II. Palermo – The Sicilian Vespers. By the end of the revolt not only was the French army defeated by locals, the clergy suffered significant casualties.

Turkey, Chora: Birth of Jesus

Turkey, Chora: Romans Seeking Jesus

plan to control Italy and capture Constantinople. In exchange for Michael's assistance, the pope was to back Michael as emperor of Byzantium. The pope preferred Spain to control Naples.

The French, distracted by the revolt, were unable to send forces to Constantinople. Threats to Michael VIII from the outside were quelled. His subjects were enraged that Michael would compromise their church in a deal with the pope. He was overthrown by a popular revolt.

In the uprising, nobles of Constantinople supported Emperor Michael to their detriment. The father of Theodore Metochites was one of those nobles. He believed that the two churches, Roman and Orthodox, should be reunified. As a result of his failure to renounce his beliefs, the Metochites family head was labeled a heretic. The family was banished in 1283 to Nicaea, across the channel from Constantinople, and inland from the Sea of Marmara. It was an ancient city with a long Christian heritage. It was also a long way from the urban life of the big city.

Theodore Metochites was born in 1270. Prior to banishment of his family, young Theodore had the benefit of living in a thriving city, where so much was possible. He was educated at home amidst a library of ancient texts. He thrived on learning. In his monastic learning environment, young Metochites developed his own form of writing. He wrote poetry. He was verbose, self-impressed, and fully receptive to the adoration of his mother and house servants, who built his young ego. The lesson gleaned from banishment was that he preferred scholarship to politics.

In 1290, the Byzantine emperor came through Nicaea on a grand tour of his domain. Theodore was chosen to recite the Eulogy of Nicaea from memory. His performance so impressed the emperor that Theodore was invited to return to Constantinople to be part of the imperial court.

Within a year, Metochites was a senator and had a royal appointment as controller of the herds, much like an inventory clerk. By the end of the decade, he had a resume of negotiations and alliances brokered on behalf of the emperor. Metochites had arranged the marriage of the emperor's five-year-old daughter to a Serbian king in an agreement that fixed the line of disputed borders and arranged for a hostage exchange. He was an envoy to Empress

Irene in Greece. By age thirty-six, Metochites was acting as Prime Minister, without the official designation.

In his supreme role, Metochites controlled the treasury and was the bookkeeper to the emperor. He was able to sell favors, titles, and award grants of land to nobles. In the process of doing his job, Metochites became very wealthy. His five sons were married into the royal family and given government positions. One of the sons succeeded Metochites as Grand Logothate, formally prime minister. The wealth of Metochites became second to that of the emperor, as he felt appropriate since he was second in command of Byzantium.

By day Metochites dealt with complex affairs of government. By night he studied astronomy. He wrote commentaries on Homer and Aristotle. Some historians estimate that Metochites wrote nineteen hundred unpublished folios of essays.

The royal family had a palace near the Chora. Metochites also had a palace in the neighborhood. Since the Chora needed a benefactor, and since the royal church was the Hagia Sophia, Metochites decided to be responsible for the Chora. He assumed ktetorship; church caretaker.

TURKEY, CHORA: Dome Frescos

By 1316, the Chora was Metochites' favorite project. Since he was second to the emperor in wealth and power, the Chora emulated the Hagia Sophia in its art. Chora library became unparalleled in the kingdom. The effort to rise the Chora to a royal look-alike took five years to complete.

In 1321, when Theodore Metochites was fifty-one, he was feeling at the top of his world. The Chora was nearing completion. The emperor elevated him to the position of Grand Logothate, making him officially the prime minister.

The man whom Metochites succeeded as Prime Minister, Nikephoras Choumnos was deeply angered by the move. He wrote a pamphlet in which he accused Metochites of being repetitious, obscure, and worst of all insults to Metochites, a bad astronomer. Metochites countered by writing that Choumnos used *excess clarity* in his writing.

By the time the Chora was finished, and Metochites was ready to celebrate his gift, his ascendency came to an end. Byzantium was in decline. Italian merchants were overtaking control of commerce in Constantinople. Borders of the realm were crumbling. Ottoman Turks were moving into edges of Byzantium. The Turks were in control of the east side of the Bosporus.

The emperor transferred governing function to Metochites, while royals attended art and social functions. The monarch was in power for forty years, thirty of those with Metochites running the palace. Shortcomings of the emperor and his son were attributed to Metochites. When the emperor died and his son died shortly thereafter in the 1320s, palace detractors came out in force.

Civil war ensued between a son and grandson of the emperor. Never the soldier, Metochites spent his time hiding in the library at the Chora. He sought to cast himself as a scientist and scholar. Ministers at the palace and senators were not impressed.

Like his father, Metochites backed the wrong aspiring emperor. He was on the losing team in the civil war. The winning team called him an *evil genius* and blamed him for the loss of strength throughout Byzantium. In 1328, Metochites was banished to Thrace in the hinterlands of Greece. Despite bad food and sour wine of which Metochites complained, it was a better sentence than death or blinding. His wealth was confiscated and his palace was destroyed. The new regime did not think any non-royal should accumulate so much wealth. Jealous rivals of Metochites agreed.

By 1330, tempers cooled. Metochites was allowed to return to Constantinople, as long as he was confined in the Chora. The monastery that had been the prison of several confined nobles over the centuries was to Metochites his place of solace. He had made the Chora his monument, and with great irony, his enemies made it his home.

Before he left in exile, Metochites wrote to the monks asking that they take good care of the Chora library. When he returned, the library afforded Metochites all that he could have required in a peaceful retirement from public life. He spent his last days in that library and died in the monastery in 1332, at age sixty-two. His remains were placed in a wall niche of one of the church chambers. Metochites could not have asked for more.

Metochites and the Chora

The first two years of work on the Chora were devoted to structural repair. The drum under the main dome was replaced with one with openings for light. Walls were reinforced with brick and stone, in a pattern that alternated four rows of each. The arches supporting outer walls on the downhill slope were filled in for greater support. Flying buttresses were added, unusual for fourteenth-century architecture, made all the more unusual as they provided no support.

On the north side of the building, a two-story structure was added. The lower level was used to store vestments and the upper level became the large library. A vaulted room was added along the south side. In this room, in a wall niche, the urn of Metochites was placed in repose.

The twelfth-century, painted glass windows, frescos and other decoration that could be salvaged were retained. Marble slabs were cut to line floors and lower walls. New furnishings and vestments were commissioned.

TURKEY, CHORA: Chora Ceiling

Turkey, Chora: Madonna & Child

Artists worked on the frescos and mosaics for three years. Metochites carefully considered every detail. Saints were dressed as Byzantine courtiers, not as ancient Romans. The arrangement of saints and biblical stories in the interior frescos around the small church interior were made to replicate the order of saints and scenes in the Hagia Sophia.

The most self-impressed decision made by Metochites was that art honored the Holy Father and aggrandized the church benefactor. Mosaics portray Old Testament scenes and scenes from the life cycle of Christ. There were no parables and no political statements. Religious scenes touching on internal church conflicts in the schism with Rome were avoided. The Chora was decorated to stand forever as a religious and politically neutral edifice. Everything about the church, from the opulence to the content of the art, was an extension of the personal expression of Metochites, as a proper fourteenth-century dignitary, in Byzantium at its height.

Over the entrance to the Chora, there is an inscription: *chora ton zonton,* that is, dwelling place, land of the living. Once inside there is a hall of saints. Above the saints are scenes from the life of Christ. They include Joseph's dream, the journey of the Magi, the miracle of turning water in wine, the last supper, the crucifixion and the resurrection. Some of the panels are missing today. Most are in spectacular condition, considering their age and intervening events.

In the vault room, other Chora benefactors are included in frescos, such as Isaac Kommenos, the emperor in 1081, who brought a period of peace and stability to Byzantium. On the far wall stand six figures, all church fathers. They include St. Basil, St. Gregory and Cyril of Alexandria. Much of the rest of the room has sustained damage, which obliterated frescos.

Throughout the interior and exterior of the Chora are designs, which some guidebooks suggest are initials of Metochites. Books identify lines and circles like a small "t" over a large "M" to be initials of Theodore Metochites. Guides on site shrug off the idea as fantasy. Visitors can examine the marks and chose what to believe.

There are two panels inside the Chora that unarguably favor Metochites. As a tax collector, he had a desire to portray the position with pride. In one mosaic the Virgin and Joseph are shown enrolling for taxation with the tax officer, who is seated on a throne.

The panel over the entrance to the inner narthex, the central room of prayer, is the one with the portrait of *Ho Ktetor Logothetes tou Genikou Theodore Metochites*, that is, the Founder, Prime Minister Theodore Metochites. In the scene, Metochites is slightly kneeling to Christ, with a small model of the Chora in his hands as a gift to the Father. Metochites wears a large turban, which is a sign of importance. His robes are those of a wealthy man. Metochites is captured in portraiture for posterity in his prime moment, like Constantine and Justinian in the Hagia Sophia.

Epilogue

TURKEY, CHORA: Mosaic

In 1453, the Ottoman Turks conquered Byzantium. All of the courtiers, including the surviving family of Metochites, were out of jobs. In the Chora, Holy Relics of value were salvaged, including an icon of the Virgin painted by St. Luke. The painting was thrown aside and its silver frame retained. The Chora church became a mosque, the Kariye Camii. Over the next two hundred years, mosaics and frescos were covered in plaster. The bell tower was replaced with a minaret.

In 1945, the former church and mosque reopened as a museum, the Kariye Museum. The fourteenth-century marble floors and lower wall remained intact. Other than the belfry, which became a minaret and is now gone, there were few structural changes that could not be undone. An exception was the dome, which was replaced with wood and plaster by the Turks. Plaster over mosaics and frescos was carefully removed. Although some of the art is incomplete, there remains a significant part of the Chora preserved as gifted by Metochites to Constantinople.

TURKEY, CHORA: Chora Neighborhood Today

During his life, Theodore Metochites was called a snob, a false intellectual, a social climber, an evil genius and a traitor. After his death, none of those insults mattered. He is remembered for giving the Chora to Constantinople. That his legacy stands today would please him. When entering the Chora, stop to smile at the man in the picture above the doorway, kneeling before Christ, more opulently attired than his god, handing the Chora to us all.

Further reading on Chora:

Paul Underwood, The Kariye Djami, Routledge, London, 1967.

Robert Outsterhout, The Art of the Kariye Camii, Scala Publishers, London, 2002.

Robert Outsterhout, The Architecture of the Kariye Camii in Istanbul, Dumbarton Oaks Research Library and Collection, Washington, DC, 1987.

Faith Cimok, Chora, A Turizm Yayinlari LTD, Istanbul, 1987. (frequent tour guide reference)

SULTANS OF ISTANBUL
1453 – 1856

In 1453, a clan of people, who seemed to come from out of nowhere, completed their conquest of the Byzantine Empire with the taking of Constantinople. Roman Emperor Constantine's capital of the eastern Roman Empire and center of the Eastern Orthodox Church, from the fourth century, began a new life as not Roman or Greek and not as a Christian center. To understand how this happened, it is necessary to know something about the extraordinary people who created an imposing empire from a modest nomadic encampment.

TURKEY: Hagia Sophia

The Ottomans began as a family clan in central Turkey in the 1300s. In less than a century they became a commanding force in Turkey, the Black Sea region, and around the eastern Mediterranean. They threatened to conquer Western Europe. The Ottoman Turks made Constantinople their first established domicile and their capital.

The Ottomans adopted the Hagia Sophia, made it into a mosque, and became its guardian for the next four hundred years. While in Constantinople, the Ottoman Turks rebuilt the city and endowed it with a new palace and several large and lavish mosques. The Christian city became a city of Islam. The Turks gave the old city a new name, Istanbul.

This is the short story of the rise of the Ottoman Turks from a clan of horsemen on the steppes of Asia to the conquerors of an area that dominated trade in the eastern Mediterranean. It is a story of the conquest of Byzantium that culminated in 1453 with the siege of Constantinople. It is also a story of the rich cultural legacy in Istanbul that stands open to visitors today. The Topkapi Palace, seven great mosques and the sultans who built them contribute to the story of Istanbul.

The Ottomans

The Ottomans were a clan of nomadic Turkmen living in the interior of present-day Turkey. The small band was not associated with any country or kingdom. They recognized loyalty only to their family and their horses.

The Ottomans were not farmers or traders. To them, cities and towns were opportunities for foraging. As expert horsemen and archers, they could take what they liked and move on to new food sources. They conquered the Tartars of the Crimea with their skill in war. An Ottoman could shoot three arrows in a second, backward, while riding his horse forward at full gallop.

These were civilized conquerors, not barbarians. Residents of cities that did not resist their control were spared bloodletting. The Ottomans required food and taxes. They referred daily details of civic management to the locals, as long as they were orderly, peaceful and paid their taxes. In many instances, a town submitted to the Ottomans as a toll the value of three days' work each year, as was expected from a serf, who would otherwise owe the value of three days' work each week to their feudal overlord.

Turkey, Istanbul: Center of Istambul

The Ottoman Turks were Muslim. Prayer several times a day cleared their minds and allowed them a calm retreat from the constant work of survival. In Islam, no priests, or stationary places of worship were necessary. Prayer could be individual or as a group of no certain number.

As the Ottomans took control of more territory, they conquered Christian and Jewish towns. The conquerors were tolerant of other religions. They appreciated that there were other forms of law than theirs. They had no interest in urging conversion. As long as the town remained peaceful and paid taxes when due, all was copacetic.

In 1492, when Spain exiled their Jews, the reigning Ottoman sultan invited the exiles to resettle in the Ottoman Empire. He was surprised at Spanish King

Ferdinand. The sultan is reported to have wondered aloud, why Ferdinand would disadvantage Spain to advantage the Ottoman Empire. The Jews were skilled at making cotton cloth and knew how to calculate interest on investments. They were assets to the Ottoman Empire.[115]

At the beginning of the fourteenth century, the nomadic clan became more than a casual group. When leadership was needed, a man came forward who was as skilled in tactical warfare as he was in finding water for horses. Osman is recognized as the founder of the Ottoman dynasty. He was born around 1280 and became the first sultan in 1300. For twenty-six years, Osman established order for the Ottomans. He stifled opposition from Mongols in the east, Tartars in the north and Byzantines in the west. His progeny conquered all.

One of Osman's most enduring contributions to the group was the establishment of dynastic succession. Tradition was important to the Ottoman Turks. Certain aspects of life were not questioned. Leadership choice was one of them.

By the time Osman's grandson, Sultan Murad I, died in 1389, the Ottoman Empire encompassed an area from Ankara, Turkey on the east, to Sofia, Bulgaria on the west. Their lands went from the Danube to Aegean Sea and east overland. All subjects paid taxes to Istanbul.

Murad I founded an elite fighting corps in 1365, known as the Janissaries. The corps fought with no regard for their personal safety. Kept from marriage, they had no loyalty but to the sultan. Janissaries were well trained, well-armed, and enjoyed a reputation for two hundred years as the feared fighting corps of Europe and the Eastern Mediterranean.[116] The Janissaries were the fighters that defeated the Knights of the Order of St. John in 1523, causing the Knights to move to Malta to regroup. In 1565, Janissaries were in the front lines as they tried to obliterate the Order by a massive assault on Malta.[117]

---

[115] Some Jewish exiles from Spain accepting the sultan's invitation settled in Salonica, a northern Greek town, in which Jews lived in ancient times, and where some became Christian upon hearing the teaching of Christ. The town is now known as Thessalonica.

[116] Some drank alcohol and some were non-practicing Muslims. All held the fatalistic belief that the day of death is preordained. They believed that bravery in battle would not hasten that day.

[117] See Cruise through History this Itinerary – Rhodes and Itinerary V Ports of Arabia to the Atlantic – Malta.

Not all sultans were enlightened leaders who preferred to read ancient literature in their tent in the evenings, with a bowl of figs and some calming music. Murad's son, Bayezit I, was known as Thunderbolt for his rapid action attacks, where carnage was his signature. In 1399, he buried three thousand Christian Armenian soldiers alive, after he slaughtered French and Hungarian crusaders to the Holy Land. He was sultan for fourteen years; the last year spent as a captive of the Tartars whom he ravaged one time too many. They locked Bayezit in a small cage. After a year in captivity, with no rescue rumors to sustain him, Bayezit died by beating his head on the bars of his cage.

Bayezit's progeny were more of the ilk of Murad. His grandson, Murad II, was a strong, calm leader. He was the victorious commander of the Ottomans at the Battle of Varna in 1444.[118] Varna is the Black Sea port for Bulgaria. Opposing Murad II were armies of the kings of Poland, Hungary and Bohemia, the royal princes of Lithuania, Wallachia and Bulgarian Moldavia. Also weighing in on the side of the Christian crusaders were armies of the pope and the Knights Templar. It was a war of the two worlds, Central and Eastern Europe versus the Ottoman Empire.

Although joined European forces at Varna couched their action as a Holy War of the Crusades, against Muslim Ottomans, Murad knew better. Sultans were tolerant of other religions. Ottomans claimed turf because it was there, and conquests increased tax revenue. Conquest, not manufacture or trade, was how Ottomans accumulated fortunes. At stake in the Battle of Varna was not supremacy of one major religion over another. At stake were trade routes to the East.

Murad's victory at Varna left all of Central and Eastern Europe exposed to Ottoman conquest. All land around the Black Sea was in Ottoman control. They controlled all of Greece and lands around the eastern Mediterranean from Turkey to Alexandria. Murad II's son, Mehmet II, also known as Mohammed II, extend the Ottoman Empire west in the next decades to include most of Hungary, including Budapest, and along the southern edge of the Mediterranean to Tripoli. He looked westward to further conquests.

---

[118]   For a story on the Battle of Varna see Cruise through History, Itinerary IV. Ports of the Black Sea – Varna.

As a result of the Ottoman victory at Varna, Genoese, Venetian and Portuguese merchants were required to pay a toll to the Ottomans for their sea cargo transit. Profit margins of European merchants were tightened. The price of goods went up in Europe. For the next fifty years the most vibrant discussions at European and English ports was the desire to find a route to India by sailing west. The quest for a Western route to the East inspired Columbus to cross the Atlantic. Although he did not find the fabled route, his discovery shifted the focus of commerce from the Mediterranean to the Atlantic.[119]

Conquest of Byzantium

Turkey, Istanbul: Blue Mosque

---

[119]   Regardless of the political cast on Columbus, he measured the Atlantic and refocused Mediterranean trade.

Ottomans cut away at the Byzantine Empire for decades. By 1453, the only territory of the once great Byzantine Empire was the immediate area of Constantinople, southern Greece, and some non-contiguous land west of the city on the Black Sea coast.[120] The Renaissance in Italy inspired Byzantine intellectuals, artists, educators and entrepreneurs to leave home for more vibrant venues. By 1453, only about five thousand men within fighting age remained in the city.[121]

By 1452, Byzantine Emperor Constantine XI lived just long enough to regret his leadership. An iron foundry engineer from Transylvania, Orban Urban, designed a really big gun capable of knocking down city walls of stone.[122] He knew he had a marketable item and was looking for a client who could put it into production. He offered the gun, now known as a cannon, to Constantine XI. The last Byzantine Emperor had no funds left in the treasury with which to purchase and produce the guns. He declined the opportune purchase.

Urban took his drawings of the cannon to Mehmet II. The Ottoman sultan was intrigued. He had an immediate need for the guns, and he had the ability to pay Urban's purchase price. Most important, Mehmet had the ability to go into full production of the guns to arm his Janissaries.

Mehmet set up an iron foundry in 1452, near Adrianople, on the far western border of what had been the Byzantine Empire, which was by that time part of the Ottoman Empire. With Urban in charge, within three months, the Ottomans had a supply of cannons. They pulled the big guns on ox-sleds to be within range of Constantinople. The cannons became the new technology of warfare, without which Mehmet II's ability to conquer the capital of the Byzantines would have been frustrated.[123]

In March 1453, Mehmet II began his siege of Constantinople. He first called for the city to surrender. To back up his request, three hundred thousand fighting men accompanied Mehmet. Constantine XI felt duty bound to hold tight the last Christian city in the East.

---

[120]   Colin Wells, Sailing from Byzantium, Delta, 2006, including wonderful maps.
[121]   Jason Goodwin, Lords of the Horizons, Henry Holt, 1998, p. 29.
[122]   Urban lived in the Hungarian Empire, in an area now part of Romania.
[123]   Urban was at the scene of the siege of Constantinople in 1453, training Janissaries in the use of his cannons, until one blew up, ending his life.

Constantine XI was not without resources to protect Constantinople, despite a lack of soldiers in the city. All of non-Ottoman Europe sent soldiers to assist, including Venice and Genoa.[124] A chain was placed across the harbor that was effective to keep out enemy ships. The city walls of Constantine the Great still held firm, improved by Emperor Theodosius a millennium before. The walls had never been breached in a thousand years.

From the beginning of March to the end of May, Mehmet attacked Constantinople. He was not able to breach the walls, enter the harbor, or succeed in obtaining a negotiated surrender. Big guns fired at the walls during the day, which were repaired from within at night. Janissaries swarming the walls were rebuffed. Mehmet was in danger of losing prestige among his people. Byzantium was thought to be a weak opponent. The city should have fallen quickly.

Out of desperation, Mehmet maneuvered his victory. First, he had his Janissaries lug longboats up the eastern side of the Bosporus until they reached the coast above the chains in the harbor. Then the boats were launched into the water, filled with Janissaries, and rowed to the shores of Constantinople. On the western, inland side of the city, at the weakest point in the system of walls, Mehmet had his army drag several cannons into position.

Once more, Mehmet asked the city to surrender. When it did not, shelling by cannon filled the air with smoke.[125] A small breach was opened in the wall, allowing fifty thousand Turkish soldiers to enter the city. Constantine XI was last seen stripping off his royal insignia. He jumped into the fight to stop the breach.

Citizens of Constantinople ran to the Hagia Sophia for safety. Janissaries killed everyone in reach as they followed screaming crowds of mostly women and children into the Hagia Sophia. Inside the church, the death toll was staggering. Bodies were piled high. The Byzantine Empire died that day with Constantine XI at the helm.

---

[124] Kaffa, on the Black Sea, was a Genoese colony. Battle was about trade and profit, not religion.

[125] Cannons could be fired seven times a day. One cannon ball could sink a ship.

The Legacy of Sultans of Istanbul

The conquest of Constantinople offered more than additional taxable land for the Ottomans. It became their capital. The city was in ruin. The population was decimated. Mehmet repopulated the city with slaves gained from conquests around the empire. He repaired the Hagia Sophia and built grand mosques for his people. Instead of a tent, he became comfortable living in a palace. He minted coins using the name Konstantiniyye for his city. New Turkish inhabitants chose a new name. They called it Istanbul.

TURKEY, ISTANBUL: Relax in the Palace Courtyard

Hagia Sophia – Ayasofya

Under Ottoman rule, the Hagia Sophia immediately became a mosque. The church of wisdom became the mosque of faith. It was the only church to become a mosque at the time. Churches in a condition for use remained places of Christian worship. Over time their congregations built new facilities and some abandoned churches became mosques.[126]

---

[126] Lord Kinross, Hagia Sofia, Newsweek, 1972, p. 103.

Sultans believed they consecrated a holy place by entering it. When Mehmet II entered the Hagia Sophia, amidst the carnage, he felt he was in a special holy place. He made it his obligation to be the caretaker of the building that had stood in its form for a millennium. His immediate act of stopping a soldier from removing a piece of the marble floor is well documented. Mehmet II established an ethic of preservation that continued through the Ottoman era in Istanbul until the Hagia Sophia became a museum in the modern era of Turkey.

To make the Hagia Sophia a mosque, the cross on the dome was replaced with a crescent. A wooden and then brick minaret was added. Inside, the throne of the patron of the church and other Christian items were removed. Over the centuries mosaics were covered by plaster. They were not defaced as had occurred in the Christian iconoclast era, seven hundred years earlier.

At the time of the Ottoman conquest, the Hagia Sophia was in sad shape. The massive wooden doors needed replacement. Due to budget constraints, Byzantine emperors allowed deferred maintenance to threaten structural integrity of the church. The sultans repaired, cleaned and maintained the church. Mausoleums and other buildings were added over the centuries to create a complex of rooms, with domed ceilings, which became the style of mosques.

By the mid-nineteenth century, the Ottoman era was winding down. There were scant funds to maintain public buildings. The Hagia Sophia began to show age and effects of a recent earthquake. In 1847, a massive restoration project was undertaken using an Italian architect and $1.5 million in private funds donated by a sheikh.[127]

Topkapi Palace

Mehmet II started work on Topkapi Palace in 1458. He chose a prominent piece of real estate that had been the site of a pre-Byzantine, Greek Acropolis overlooking the Bosporus and Golden Horn. He chose Italian architects, who gave him a series of separate rooms, rather than a single building. Mehmet's palace replicated a tent encampment separated by gardens.

---

[127] Kinross, p. 116.

TURKEY, ISTANBUL: Fountain of Sultan Mahmud I 1740

There are three enclosures of sanctuary in the palace. The first was open to business of the city and the palace. It was a noisy place of government workers and royal slaves. Foreign visitors were received in the first court. In the second court were offices of the sultan's ministers. The area also held archives, which were business records of the empire. Today there are jewels and armaments on display in the former archive halls. In the time of the sultans, the armory display was in the Hagia Irene, the large redbrick church near the entrance garden. Today the Hagia Irene is a museum and concert venue.

The private residence of the sultan was in the innermost third courtyard. Mehmet II's great-grandson, Suleiman the Magnificent, instituted sign language for use in this domain of absolute quiet. No one could sneeze or cough when the sultan was in residence. A large building in this court is the harem. Visitors are usually entertained by the size of the harem. The residents were not all wives of the sultan. Single women of the family and young children were all kept in opulent solitude in the harem.

TURKEY, ISTANBUL: Istambul Harem of Palace and Garden

TURKEY, ISTANBUL: Topaki Palace Entry

Istanbul's Great Mosques

There are many more mosques in Istanbul than those mentioned here. A visitor could make several trips to Istanbul, enjoy several shore excursions to a number of mosques, and still be overwhelmed by the incomplete mosque experience. The mosques highlighted in this brief story are notable for their architecture and art, or the sultan who built them, or both.

Fatih Mosque: The first mosque built by Mehmet II was the Fatih Mosque, also known as the Mosque of the Conqueror. It was built in 1471, on the site of Constantine's Church of the Holy Apostles, after the Christians deemed the original building uninhabitable. Mehmet's tomb was placed in this mosque. The mosque design is based on symmetry and order rather than function. In 1677, the building was heavily damaged in an earthquake. It was repaired in 1776, toward the end of the empire when there were fewer funds for opulent decoration. The structural symmetry is preserved, lacking much of the décor.

Mosque of Beyazid II: Mehmet's son built three public complexes that included mosques, one of which is in Istanbul. The Hagia Sophia inspired the mosque built in 1506, although this mosque is half the size. There is a courtyard that attracts pigeons, giving this mosque the popular name of Pigeon Mosque. The design incorporated a mosque in the center of a complex that included schools, hospitals, asylums and meeting places.

Sultan Selim Mosque: From 1520 to 1522, a mosque was built to honor Selim I, the father of Sultan Suleiman the Great, who died in 1521. The mosque is not a notable architectural achievement. It is known for the tiles crafted in a decorative second glaze technique.

Şehzade Mosque: Construction of the Şehzade Mosque in 1548 began a period of imperial mosques built by the Ottoman architect Sinan, who is regarded as the father of Ottoman architecture. He was a Janissary, trained as an engineer. At the age of fifty, he became an architect. Sinan studied the Hagia Sophia, then built his mosques with larger internal area, filled with light. The Şehzade was his first major project, which so impressed his sponsor, Suleiman the Magnificent, that Sinan quickly had larger commissions.

Suleimaniye: Sinan built his next mosque to be worthy of the sultan for whom it was dedicated, Suleiman the Magnificent. It took from 1550 to 1557, to complete the complex. The sultan and his architect carefully considered every detail.

Numbers were important to the Suleiman. He was the fourth sultan in the dynasty since the conquest of Constantinople, so his mosques had four minarets. Suleiman was the tenth sultan in the dynasty, so there were ten balconies. Ten columns were removed from the Hippodrome and incorporated into his mosque. One hundred and thirty-eight stained glass windows provided greater light to shine on daily prayers than in the Hagia Sophia.

TURKEY, ISTANBUL: Interior Sulyman's Mosque

Blue Mosque: Between 1609 and 1617, a pupil of Sinan built the Blue Mosque, actually named the Mosque of Sultan Ahmet. The blue moniker comes from the floor to ceiling use of blue and white tile. The dome of the large mosque amid half-domed roofs that surround it, make the Blue Mosque as much of a landmark for tourists today as it was for seventeenth and eighteenth-century pilgrims to the Holy Land arriving at Istanbul.

The Blue Mosque sits across a park from the Hagia Sophia. If there is a resemblance between the two, it is understandable. Sinan studied the Hagia Sophia, before he designed mosques.

There are five ornate bronze gates that lead to the courtyard surrounding the Blue Mosque on three sides. There are twenty-six granite columns supporting thirty cupolas lining the way into the mosque. Four massive, fluted columns support the dome.

The mosque presented to Sultan Ahmet had six minarets. Since the mosque at Mecca had six minarets, the sultan quickly commissioned a seventh minaret to be constructed on the Mecca mosque, so that he would not appear to be arrogant.

Yeni Valide, the New Mosque: The New Mosque was last of the great mosques of the Ottoman Empire to be built in Istanbul. Begun in 1598, it was not completed until 1663. The sultan who dedicated the mosque to his mother died before its completion. It was completed seven sultans later with funds from the later sultan's mother. It is known as the Mother's Mosque.

The mosque is now tucked away between buildings that have encroached over the centuries. The mosque and its entry courtyard are not large. What the New Mosque lacks in size it more than compensates for in beauty.

The exterior courtyard and the interior are lavishly tiled in floral and geometric motifs. Inside there are sculpted grills that front the upper balconies. If a walking tour of mosques is part of a port excursion, even a tired traveler will be delighted to be treated to this treasure of Turkish art.

Turkey, Istanbul: Mothers; Mosque of Flowers

Turkey, Istanbul: Sultans' Mothers' Mosque

Turkey, Istanbul: Skyline Istanbul Today

Visiting Istanbul Today

The Ottoman Empire remained in control of Istanbul until the late nineteenth century. As in the restoration of the Hagia Sophia in 1847, in the nineteenth and twentieth century, there were only private funds occasionally offered to maintain buildings the sultans gave to the city. Shortly after Turkey became a republic in the twentieth century, the new president, Mustafa Kemal, better known as Ataturk, made the Hagia Sophia a public museum. The mosaics were uncovered. As a museum, admission can be charged to defray maintenance expenses.

The central city district, which includes the Blue Mosque, the Hagia Sophia, the Hippodrome site and the Topkapi Palace, are tourist favorites. Fortunate is the visitor who wanders beyond the Bazaar to see other mosques and church-to mosque-to museum gems such as the Chora.

When sightseeing exhaustion or art overload takes hold, the fortunate visitor can find a seat overlooking the Bosporus in the café of the Topkapi Palace. It is not necessary to remain quiet here anymore. The sultans are gone. Gone too are Byzantine rulers, who were of a much more boisterous spirit. Looking into the deep blue water, it is hard to imagine sea battles that took place here or the crowd of fifteenth-century merchant ships that sailed past. Voices surrounding guests at small tables in the café today create a multinational fugue, much like those heard in waiting rooms of sultans and Byzantine emperors over the last millennium. Some aspects of Istanbul are timeless.

Istanbul is a monument of history and a vibrant living city. The Byzantines and the Ottomans bequeathed visitors the best examples of their empires at their peak. Cruise visitors are fortunate that so many itineraries include Istanbul.

Swim the Hellespont with Lord Byron

Turkey, Hellespont: Turkish War Memorial in Canakkale where Byron Swam Hellespont

George Gordon Byron, Sixth Lord Byron enjoyed doing the unexpected. Travel inspired his poetry. His bold acts inspired some and horrified others. A handsome man, who appreciated his fine appearance, he defied the physical limitations of a deformed foot by challenging himself to great physical feats.[128] One of his most daring, most memorable, and for travelers, most endearing, was the day he swam the Hellespont.

---

[128] Byron suffered a shortened tendon in his right leg, causing his right foot to turn inward.

The Hellespont, as it was known in antiquity, is the narrow channel that links the Mediterranean to the Black Sea. Today better known as the Dardanelles, the channel that runs south from the Black Sea, through the Sea of Marmara and into the northern Aegean Sea, has been the scene of battles from ancient Troy to the World War I disaster of the Battle of Gallipoli in 1918. Çanakkale is the city at the entrance to the straits today from the south.

It was at this place in the geography of the world, that divides Europe from Asia, that Helle and her twin Phrixus road the golden ram to safe harbor, to escape the fate designed for them by their stepmother. Helle fell from the ram, into the Hellespont, where she drowned. Phrixus landed with the gracious king of Colchis, known today as Georgia, in the Black Sea, to whom he bestowed the ram with golden fleece.[129]

The life of young Lord Byron was not as fortunate as that of mythical Phrixus. His title brought expectations, yet little income. His talent was much observed, yet little compensated. When income did come to Byron, he spent in grand style. Travel was a means of escape. In remote places of the world, little was expected of him. Far from England, Byron could breathe freely and without boundaries. He could dress as a maharaja, without being questioned.

The era of the late eighteenth and early nineteenth century, in which Byron lived, was a time when young people of means left England for a Grand Tour of Europe, and to a lesser extent Asia. For Byron, world travel was more escape than indicia of status. His travel companions were few and memorable.

This short story of Lord Byron puts him in an unexpected venue for those who recognize him in the context of bucolic England. This is an opportunity to expose his wild inner self. The story is also an opportunity to showcase Çanakkale as a welcoming port with its own place in history.

---

[129]   For the story of the Golden Fleece see the stories of Cruise through History © Itinerary IV Ports of the Black Sea.

Life of the Young Lord

In any question of whether breeding or environment impacts character, Byron was twice marked for a short and exciting life.[130] His mother came from a respectable family from Scotland, the Gordons, who seemed to die young, mostly in drowning accidents. His father's family began their history in England when Ralph du Buron came across the Channel with William the Conqueror.

When Henry VIII dissolved the monasteries, he gave the first John Byron an abbey. Queen Elizabeth I knighted the first Lord Byron in 1579. In 1643, King Charles I knighted Lord John Byron of Rochdale, who led Royalist troops into a grand defeat in the Battle of Marston Moor. Sir John was ordered to hold the high ground. Instead, he followed Cromwell's troops into the marsh, where Cromwell's horses became stuck, Sir John's knights became stuck, and from the grasp of victory, Sir John managed a defeat that lost the battle, lost the war and lost the kingdom.

Byron's grandfather, Foul Weather Jack, was a distinguished rear admiral in the Royal Navy, who sailed around the world. His sons, William and Jack, knew how to enjoy themselves. William, the Fifth Lord Byron, desired to leave his son nothing, so he did his best to despoil the estate inheritance of Newstead Abbey. Known as Devil Byron, William was infamous for drunken arguments in which men died. He built a miniature castle on the estate in which he held parties. When he died in 1798, he outlived his son, leaving the estate encumbered in debt, when it was inherited by his nephew Byron as the Sixth Lord.

Byron's father, Mad Jack, lived well from the dowry of Byron's mother. When the money was gone, he left wife and son and went to Paris, where he lived with another woman of means, until her funds were exhausted. Bryon's father died in Paris at age thirty-five. Byron hardly knew his father, or his benefactor uncle.

---

[130] George Gordon Byron was born in 1788 and died in 1824.

Another of Byron's uncles enrolled young Byron in Harrow School, the ideal school for an eighteenth-century aristocrat. At Harrow, Byron was introduced to Virgil and Greek poets. In school, he was teased for his deformity, also for being chubby and poor. As a young man, Byron vowed never to be overweight or underdressed.

To deal with his weight, Byron took up swimming. He swam in long pants to hide his underdeveloped leg. Swimming became a means to relieve anger in a world he thought unfair. Envision him clearing his mind, composing poetry, as he swam long distances.

Byron was never a serious student. By his own admission, he spent his time at Cambridge enjoying intimate relationships and writing poetry. His other pursuit was gambling. While his schoolmates prepared for Oxford, Byron procrastinated until he attended Cambridge by default. Told by his instructors that he was brighter than others, Byron replied, if his mind brought him forward, his leg held him back. When Byron had completed half his coursework, he demanded, and was given, a degree.

The first attempt to publish poetry in 1806, was a disaster for Byron. His collection entitled *Fugitive Pieces* was an autobiographical collection of ladies he had known and a pompous headmaster, with all the names included. The angry reception by those named caused Byron to run around town collecting the copies for the furnace. The collection was republished posthumously, with the names deleted.

The next year Byron published *House of Idleness,* anonymously. The poet described himself as age nineteen, a disadvantaged person, with an illness. The collection garnered no sympathy. It was critically reviewed as school-boy obsessions. Identity of the author was not difficult to discern.

Inherited debt, living beyond his means, gambling debts and lack of income from estates, left Byron a step from the poor house for most of his life. When he turned of age to join Parliament, with the peerage inherited from his uncle, the Sixth Lord Byron had no funds to host a celebration. With no one to sponsor him, Byron put forth his own petition for a peerage. In 1809, when Byron stood in the House of Lords to be sworn to membership, the chamber was almost empty. His poetry had made him few friends.

Travels with Lord Byron

Young aristocrats of means were expected to matriculate from the university and complete their education with a Grand Tour of Europe. When it was time for Byron to travel, the usual itinerary through Europe, to Paris and Rome, was closed to English travelers by the Napoleonic War. Instead, Byron went to Lisbon, where he was captivated by Sintra. From there, he went to the Near East. Along the route of travel, Byron stopped in Cadiz, Gibraltar, Malta and several cities in Greece.

In three years of travel, from 1809 to 1811, Byron traveled to Tripoli, Libya, through Egypt, sailed the Persian Gulf, and went north through Palestine, Turkey, and the Caspian Sea. His was not a typical World Tour. Much of his transportation was on commercial vessels as they presented an inexpensive opportunity.

When in Lisbon, Byron swam across the Tagus River, from the old town of Almada to the Belem Castle. Cruise ships pass along this point when they slip under the Ponte 25 de Abril bridge to dock in Lisbon. The cross-currents are stiff. It took Byron two hours to swim the channel.

Turkey, Hellespont: Byron wrote fondly of Sintra, Portugal

In Cadiz, Byron attended a bullfight, in which British Lord Wellington made a grand entrance, to be acknowledged as a war hero. Byron was not impressed. From Seville, Byron rode horseback to Gibraltar, a three-hundred-mile ride. On a ship bound for Malta, there was a port stop in Cagliari, Sardinia. In Cagliari, the British ambassador to Sardinia invited Byron to join him in his royal box at the opera. Byron was impressed.

TURKEY, HELLESPONT: Tagus in Lisbon

In his travels, Byron went to Missolonghi, Greece. There he had a personal audience with Muhammed Ali Pasha, the Albanian general who was the local ruler of Greece on behalf of the Ottoman Empire. Ali Pasha was a brilliant statesman, strategist and manipulator of circumstances. At the time, Ali Pasha was playing Britain against France as he dangled neutral Turkish options between them.

Byron was taken with Ali Pasha, who shortly self-proclaimed himself ruler of Egypt. War was all around Byron as he traveled through Europe, yet he seemed not to notice war's peripheral effects; the war dead, or the impact on displaced people, until he traveled further through Greece. When he saw first-hand the repression of Greeks under the Ottoman Turks, Byron became an outspoken advocate for Greece.

Later, Bryon returned to Missolonghi. When he did, the place claimed him. It made him a national hero in Greece. All that was years in the future. At the first visit, Byron outfitted himself in a crimson velvet jacket with gold trim and sported daggers and a pistol. He had his portrait painted as an Ottoman lord.

One voyage of Byron's tour was accomplished on a British ship of the East India Company, the HMS *Salsette*. It left Smyrna, on the Turkish coast, where Byron overstayed his welcome in the home of the British counsel. A lovely teak vessel, the *Salsette* moved slowly up the strait from the Aegean to the Sea of Marmara, on its way to Constantinople. At the Dardanelles, the ship made a stop and Byron had the opportunity to explore Troad, the area where Troy was rediscovered.

Bored diving for turtles from the Turkish shore, Byron challenged the lieutenant of the *Salsette* to a race across the Hellespont. Byron lost by a margin of five minutes in the one hour and ten-minute swim from the ice-cold European shore to Asia. The actual distance is one mile. Byron later wrote that the distance was four miles, accounting for strong current and large fish which impeded progress. Byron might have had a better race time, had he not been wearing long pants.

Childe Harold's Pilgrimage

Byron's impressions of places and people gathered on his World Tour became well known, when he composed an epic poem upon return, entitled the *Childe Harold's Pilgrimage*.[131] A childe is a young man, not yet a knight. Byron was a naïve schoolboy at the outset and an opinionated political spokesman by the end of his Tour. He still sought love and beauty in the world around him.

---

[131] Harold was chosen as he was the illegitimate son of Canute, the Viking ancestor of William the Conqueror.

Three years of travel transformed the vain noble to consider circumstances of others.

The first two cantos, sections, of the poem were published in 1812, in an illustrated edition. The first printing sold quickly. There were ten editions published over the next three years. Byron woke one day to find himself famous. His home at Newstead Abbey no longer was papered with foreclosure notices.

By writing of himself and his circumstances, set in foreign venues of mystery, Byron touched an empathetic chord. He created an identity as a flawed hero. His admissions of vanity and need for intimacy were taken as an honest appreciation of the unattainable, even by someone as intellectually capable as Harold. People wanted more. Two more cantos were published by 1818.

Byron saw himself as a royal with the responsibility to be a politician. In 1812, as Britain prepared for war with the United States, King George ordered weavers to use larger frames, which meant more cloth produced for the same fee. Weavers broke their loom frames in protest; an offense punishable by death. Byron gave a speech in support of the weavers, claiming that extreme poverty drove them to break their frames. He asked of the king, why he would treat workers worse than an enemy. Bryon's popularity soared. He was not so well-liked in the House of Lords.

When Byron was in Athens in 1809, he encountered French agents Louis Francois Sebastian Fauvel and Giovanni Battista Lusieri, a landscape painter from Naples. They were making detailed drawings of the Parthenon on the Acropolis, with the plan of aiding French ambassador Comte de Choiseul-Gouffin to dismantle the statuary and cart it off to the Louvre.[132] Their plans were foiled by the British ambassador then in place in Athens.

Ten years later, the new British ambassador was Thomas Bruce, Lord Elgin. He hired Lusieri to remove stones from the Parthenon and place them on ships bound for his home in Scotland. Lusieri and Fauvel competed in bribing the Turks for access to the marbles on the Acropolis.

---

[132] Napoleon was in the habit of collecting cultural objects from places he conquered to install in his new museum in Paris, the Louvre.

Byron disparages Elgin in the *Childe Harold* for casting asunder that which two thousand years of time had not. Byron then wrote the *Curse of Minerva*, a further indictment of Lord Elgin, whom he compared to the barbaric fifth century Hun Alaric. Minerva is the patron saint of Athens.

Byron credits Percy Shelly with pulling him from his self-obsession and encouraging him to keep writing. Bryon met Mary Jane Clairmont, known as Claire, at the Drury Lane Theater and she introduced him to her stepsister Mary and husband, Shelly. The four compatriots often joined by other writers, became exiles in an Italian villa near La Spezia, Villa Diodati, the house where Milton stayed in 1639. Byron enjoyed conversation with Shelly. On rainy nights Mary entertained the group with stories of a man-made monster. She published *Frankenstein* in 1818, the same year Byron published his fourth canto of *Childe Harold*.

Claire and Byron had a child. Byron would not marry Claire, nor acknowledge the child, as Claire was not a royal. Byron maintained his privileged bias, although Shelly, the son of a baronet, had no use for social pretension. Shelly had been expelled from Oxford for writing of atheism and other works that later inspired social ideas of Karl Marx.

Byron was on the beach, with Claire and Mary, when the body of Shelly and two friends who sailed with him were pulled from the sea. They drowned near Livorno on July 8, 1822. The three were cremated on the beach. Byron avoided the burial ceremony by plunging in for a long swim.

In May 1823, Byron was elected to membership of the London Greek Committee. By August, he was in Argostoli, Cephalonia, looking for a meaningful role in the movement for Greek independence from Ottoman control. Byron offered support to fighters in Missolonghi.

The support that was desired was financial. While factions of Greek leaders squabbled among themselves, people were starving. Byron gave liberally from his personal funds to feed people, purchase ammunition, and obtain medicine.[133] He became ill. Doctors bleed him with leeches, a cure at the time for the plague that was rampant in Missolonghi. While attempting to assist

---

[133]   He received a crate of rockets, which turned out to be Bibles.

in mounting an assault on Lepanto, Byron collapsed. He never recovered. He died in a tent, in the midst of a hurricane, on April 19, 1824.

Byron's body was refused burial in Westminster Abbey. In Greece, he was a hero. Friends burned his memoirs. Byron's one acknowledged child, from his brief marriage in 1815, was Augusta Ada Byron. She is the British mathematician credited with recognizing the potential of machine calculations of Charles Babbage's Analytical Engine. The artist fathered the computer scientist.

Çanakkale and the Hellespont Today

Çanakkale is a charming cruise port, least attractive for the large Trojan Horse used in a movie, which is permanently ensconced on an otherwise inviting, open, seaside promenade. The Turkish bazaar is massive, the shopping delightful and the juice bars plentiful. The early twentieth-century section of the port is welcoming, with its small clock tower square and restaurants. Just outside the shopping area is a large park, with installations of art and armaments, leading up to a castle, the Çanakkale Fortress.

TURKEY, HELLESPONT: Swim with Lord Byron

The port is a point of departure for excursions to the site of Troy, the archaeological site, not the movie set. It is also a departure point for Gallipoli and monuments to those who lost their lives in the British led action in 1918. Surveying the battlefield in the bloody aftermath, future Turkish president Kemal Ataturk said, "these are all our children."

Once a year there is a marathon swim across the Hellespont, that ends in Çanakkale. It commemorates the 1810 swimming feat of Byron. Byron is compared to mythical Leander, who swam the Hellespont each evening to his beloved Hero, who held a lantern to guide his path.

Leander was a young man with a certain goal. Byron was a young man, who was only thirty-six when he died while attempting to give his life meaning. Greece achieved its independence. Byron has achieved lasting fame.

TURKEY, HELLESPONT: Çanakkale Today

ISRAEL, JERUSALEM: At sight of holy city Marjorie fell off horse

ISRAEL
FIFTEENTH CENTURY TOURISM TO THE HOLY LAND

Early in the fifteenth century, the premium tourist destination was the Holy Land. There were well-traveled routes, by land and by sea. Tourists of the time complained of crowds at their favorite sites, sparse accommodations, heat, lack of good restaurants and unfamiliar food. Still, guidebooks made the trip appealing.

In medieval times, if a man or woman wanted to step out of village life and seek adventure, but do so within acceptable social rules, the grand tour to Jerusalem, Rome and Santiago de Compostela was the perfect plan. When traveling to the Holy Land, men could travel without their wives. On pilgrimages to the Holy Land, pious women could travel without their husbands.

Travelers from western Europe came overland to the Italian Adriatic coast. From one of several ports on the east coast of Italy, they could purchase a package roundtrip cruise. Once at the port of Jaffa, in Israel, pilgrims could choose from among several shore excursions.

This is the story of two travelers in the late fourteenth and early fifteenth century, on the tri-city, London, Rome Jerusalem, pilgrimage to the Holy Land. One is a man and the other a woman. We know of them because they each kept a diary and wrote travel books, which were published in their day and remain in publication today. Their experiences varied, as did motivations for transitioning from traveler to author. Present-day travelers may be pleased to learn what has and has not changed in over six hundred years of Holy Land Tourism.

The Allure of Fifteenth-Century Tourism

If the human spirit were not so inclined toward travel, homo-sapiens would all be clustered in a few crowded places on earth. The desire to seek out what lies beyond the next hill is motivated by more than the need to find fresh pastures. Without apology or need for justification, people enjoy travel. Fortunately, thousands of years of human movement have resulted in a diversity of cultural experiences available for travelers.

There was something about the late fourteenth and early fifteenth century that sparked a desire in housewives and regular workers to become tourists. In medieval times, one need not be royalty, a soldier, or possess great wealth to embark on a Holy Land tour. Being a tourist then, much as now, meant having a little discretionary time and some uncommitted funds. Tourism meant having the ability to choose a destination just for fun.

Jerusalem was an obvious choice for most favored destination. Unlike Muslim ritual travel to Mecca, travel to Jerusalem is not required to be a devote Christian. This far-away place was well known through Bible stories. Widespread interest in Jerusalem as a tourism destination was understandable.

Travel to the Holy Land was robust in 1099, when crusades became popular. Being a crusader required a substantial upfront investment for horses, weapons and matching outfits. Crusading was dangerous business. Highway bandits were not likely to be a problem for crusaders, who collected more than souvenirs. It was not a vacation with general appeal for peaceful folk.

As the Mongol Empire of Genghis Khan expanded in the mid-1200s, highway passport checkpoints were instigated. Travelers were expected to pay in gold. In 1291, the Holy Land fell to the Moors, who were Arab Muslims, who cared not for Christian tourists. Marco Polo returned home to Venice in 1295. He arrived just in time. By 1322, the roads east were closed.

An ability to travel in the eastern Mediterranean and Holy Land opened after the Mongol Empire began to fall in 1350. About the time travel routes from Italy to Jaffa were reopening, France and England were concluding their Hundred Year's war. British Protestants could freely cross the channel to Catholic France. The educated merchant classes had time, money, and desire to see more of the world. A new century was imminent. It was a wonderful time to be a tourist.

Sir John by Land

ISRAEL, JERUSALEM: Well where Mary encountered Joseph

Sir John Mandeville claimed to be a knight, who traveled through Egypt, the Holy Land, and the Far East. His diary was written in about 1357. It contained notes from thirty-five years of world travel. Copies of the diary exist dated from 1371.[134]

Mandeville wrote of his travels in such detail that he was read and relied upon by Christopher Columbus, Ponce de Leon and Sir Walter Raleigh. They would have been surprised to learn that Sir John Mandeville was not a knight. His name was not John Mandeville. Although he wrote of his travels in French, he was an Englishman from St. Albans, England.

---

[134] The Travels of Sir John Mandeville, Dover, Minneola, NY, 1964, 2006 ed., p. v.

Most surprising would have been the revelation that the author was an armchair traveler. Born in 1322, it was unlikely that he was able to travel to all the places of which he wrote, in such a short time. More likely, the author was an able writer with access to a great library, possibly a monk, with a wonderful imagination and a zeal for travel writing.

The Travels of Sir John Mandeville was a best-selling book in its time. It was translated into English and Latin. By the fifteenth century, the book had been translated into Czech, German, Spanish, Danish and Flemish. When the first printing presses were in operation, there were seventy-two editions. Over three hundred original manuscripts survive, which is about four times as many as the book by Marco Polo. Ponce de Leon was inspired by Mandeville to seek a fountain of youth in the Orient. Columbus went looking for the golden horde of the Great Khan, using Mandeville as a guide.[135]

Israel, Jerusalem: Jaffa Gate into Jerusalem

---

135   The British Museum is in possession of a 1725 edition of Mandeville.

After two hundred years of robust publication, readers began to realize that no one person could have traveled to all the places described in the book. Sales plummeted. It was still a good read. Even if the memoir was a compilation of the experiences of others, there were still fascinating descriptions of many real places.

Sir John Mandeville was likely the *nom de plume* of a clever monk. A telling feature of his memoir is the frequent insertion of moral judgment, or a biblical reference. This is all made delightful reading when the travel itinerary passes through the Holy Land.

Sir John's route to the port of Jaffa ran from England, through Germany and Poland, to Bulgaria. He went down the Danube to Greece and then seaward to Constantinople. From there, he went overland down the Troad, the ancient Greek paths through Western Turkey. At Ephesus, Sir John went to sea through the Greek Islands of Crete and Cyprus, before landing at Jaffa. The traveler then walked inland for a day and a half, to reach Jerusalem.

At each stop, Sir John inserted stories of the major points of interest. The stories relate to lessons in the old and new testaments. He put sights into historical context by much name dropping of biblical persona.

In Constantinople, Sir John went to see the church of *Saint Sophie,* known in reality as the Hagia Sophia. There he pointed out the mosaic of Justinian depicting the gold apple falling from his hand. The traveler is told that this means that emperor Justinian wanted Romania, Asia, Syria and Jerusalem, but all he held was Greece.[136]

Sir John advises his readers that the cross of Christ and a nail from the crucifix are in Constantinople. The cross is made of palm, cedar, cypress and olive. It has Hebrew, Greek and Latin carvings. The cross was hidden in the earth at Mt. Calvary, in Jerusalem, when it was discovered by St. Helen, the mother of Constantine, and brought to Constantinople.[137] Half of the crown of thorns is in Constantinople, and the other half is in Paris.

---

[136]   Mandeville at 7.
[137]   Mandeville also advised his readers that Helen was the daughter of old King Coel (his spelling), in England, the merry old soul. The nursery rhyme originates in

The traveler is warned that Greek Christians in Constantinople are different folk, even if Pope John XXII asked the Eastern Church to conform to western ways. The Eastern Church has no purgatory, usury is no sin, and priests can wed. Eastern priests do not shave their beards. They eat no pork or rabbit. Most of all, they use a Greek alphabet. The passage was a to shock readers.

Sir John left Constantinople following the route of Apostle John. He stopped at the Greek Island of Patmos, where the apostle paused in his travels to write. His next stop was Ephesus, where John died and was buried.

The Mandeville tour runs to the Greek Island of Rhodes and the city of Patere. At this stop, there is the opportunity to see the birthplace of St. Nicholas, before heading to Crete.[138] As a diversion from the biblical itinerary, Sir John wandered to the Isle of Longo, where a witch turned a fair damsel into a dragon. She will breathe fire eternally until a brave knight kisses her.

The last stop before Jaffa for Sir John was Cypress. This is the land of red grapes and white wine. On Cypress exists the Hill of the Holy Cross. Sir John cautions travelers not to be fooled. This is the cross of the good thief next to Christ and not the cross of Christ.

Once on land at Jaffa, Sir John tells his readers to expect a day and a half walk to Jerusalem. Jaffa was named after the son of Noah, before the flood.[139] Near the sea is Palestine, where people transformed sea gravel into glass. Sir John's Palestine was full of people, gay and rich.

On the way to Jerusalem, Sir John came into contact with Bedouins, living in their tents, under harsh conditions. They roasted their food on rocks. He found them to be good fighting men, although "felonious and foul." He admired their linen-wrapped headwear.

Colchester, England, where there is a church to St. Helen.

[138] There really was a St. Nicholas, who lived on the coast of Turkey and whose remains were brought to Bari. In his life, Nicolas was the protector of young children, to whom he gave gifts. He is the patron saint of sailors. See, Cruise through History, Itinerary II. Rome to Venice – Port of Bari.

[139] Sir John also advises travelers that they will find the forty-foot rib of the giant Andromeda.

Sir John reminds travelers that Beersheba is a Christian town founded by Abraham. Twelve miles down the road is Hebron, the principal city of the Philistines. This was the final resting place of persons of the Old Testament: Adam, Abraham, Issac (his spelling), Jacob, and their wives: Eve, Sarah, Rebecca and Leah.[140] Two miles further down the road are the graves of Lot and Abraham's brother. It is as though the Old Testament flows into the new along the walk to Jerusalem.

ISRAEL, JERUSALEM: Bethlehem Shrine

It is five miles from Hebron to Bethlehem, according to Sir John. Christ was born in Bethlehem next to where the choir of the church of roses stood when Saint John visited. It was at this church that a fair maiden stood accused of adultery. She was condemned to die by fire. While surrounded by flames, she proclaimed her innocence to god. The burning flames turned into red roses and the sticks of wood not burning sprouted white roses. White signified her purity and the red rose symbolized her love of God.

---

[140]   Mandeville, at 43.

Sir John tells us that the name Jerusalem comes from the names Jesus and Salem. It was then called Jebusalem. King Solomon called the city Jerosolomye. This was the land of Judea, named for Judas Maccabeus, the king.[141]

The highlight of the journey for Sir John was a visit to the Church of the Holy Sepulcher. Inside the church was the tabernacle of the lord. Sir John describes this as made of gold and inlaid with stones of many colors. So many pilgrims pried away souvenirs of the gold and gems of the tabernacle that a protective wall was built in front of it. Protection from souvenir-taking is true.

The church of the Holy Sepulcher is next to Mount Calvary, where Christ was crucified. It is two hundred paces from the great hospital of Saint John. It is near the site of the temple of Solomon. The one burned by Emperor Titus when he was on a rampage and killed one million Jews.[142]

Titus took the Ark of the Covenant to Rome. At the time it contained the slabs on which were written the Ten Commandments, the staff of Moses, an altar of gold, vessels of gold, twelve precious stones, and seven candlesticks, twelve pots of gold, four gold lions, table silver, and seven barley loaves. Sir John was certain of this.

Next to the church is THE rock. It was while laying on this rock that Jacob saw angels on the ladder. David saw angels that smote the people while resting there. Jesus preached from the same rock, where babies were circumcised and people were blessed with bread and wine.

One hundred and twenty steps from THE rock, Sir John directs the traveler to where Jesus bathed with water from paradise. Close by is the house of King Herod, where he slew his wives, children and mother. It is one hundred and twenty more steps to Mount Zion. There is a chapel there where Christ celebrated the last supper. Next to the chapel is where Jesus was baptized and gave the blind their sight. Nearby is the garden of Gethsemane, where Jesus was arrested by Romans.

Outside the walls of Jerusalem is Jericho. It is two miles further to Jordan, according to Sir John. This is the location of the Dead Sea, where a feather will sink, and people can float. Sodom and Gomorrah and Aldena are under the

---

[141] Mandeville, at 49.
[142] Without counting paces, Mandeville's proximity description is close to accurate.

sea. Also, under the sea are Zeboin and Zoar, but not before Lot slept with his daughters to replenish the world after his wife turned to salt.

Once Sir John Mandeville finished his travelogue of the Holy Land, he went on to tell where people or at least parts of the people went. The twelve tribes of Israel went to Samaria, where Saint John the Baptist was buried between the prophets Elijah and Abdon. John was burned, leaving his head in a church wall. Emperor Theodosius I pulled the head from the wall and took it to Constantinople. The back of the head was left behind, while the forehead went to Rome and is at the Church of Saint Sylvester. Saint John's lower jaw went to Genoa, and other parts reside in French churches. On this point, Sir John is not too far off the truth.

Before wrapping up the travelogue, Sir John recounted the birth and death places of the saints, as signposted along roads. He advised that a traveler could take a five-day camel excursion from Jerusalem to Damascus to stand on the spot where Caen slew Abel. He had exceptional insight.

Returning from Damascus to Constantinople by land, the traveler would pass through Antioch, Oman and the Port of Nicaea. The return would be overland past Cappadocia and the Sinope Castle on the banks of the Black Sea. Of course, there was a sea route, as Sir John had gone that way too.

Lady Margery by Sea

Margery Kempe was born in 1373, in Norfolk, England. Her father was the mayor of her town. Despite being raised in an affluent family, Margery remained illiterate throughout her life. She married John Kempe when she was twenty-two. By the time she was forty, the couple had fourteen children. Margery had enough of domestic life, left the marital bed, and went shopping. To pay for purchases, she started businesses. She proved to be a savvy business-woman as a brewer and then a miller, earning more than her husband. However, being illiterate put Margery at a disadvantage. Even though business was robust, cash flow fell, while her business managers hid profits.[143]

---

[143] Louis Callis, Memories of a Medieval Woman: The Life and Times of Margery Kempe, Harper and Row, New York, 1964. Margery dictated her memoirs late in life. She was candid about her travels, even aspects of her behavior that were unflattering.

ISRAEL, JERUSALEM: Pilgrims at Nazareth at the site of the manger
in which Christ was born

Margery needed another plan to get out of the house. She offered herself to a young man at church. He ran from her. Neighbors started talking about her. Margery responded that she was not crazy; she was divinely inspired. She had seen god during her last childbirth. After all, it was 1413. The king was burning heretics at the stake. She would wear a hair shirt, go to mass every Sunday and be devotedly religious. No one could judge her.

Becoming a nun was not an option. Nuns lived truly pious lives and worked hard. They wore awful outfits. There was no caché in being part of the organized church. People were shocked at the way popes raised cash by selling indulgences. Instead, people looked inward to their private devotions. Margery decided to become a missionary. Missionaries lived well, supported by sponsors. In a missionaries' life, Margery could travel and feel special.

Margery began to sing out at church louder than anyone. She loudly proclaimed her visions. God spoke to her. He told Margery to go to Jerusalem. She convinced herself that she was another Saint Bridget.[144]

Margery needed only clerical affirmation of her calling and a wealthy patron to pay for the trip. She thought a wealthy friend would pay for the trip if she could convince the woman to see a certain priest. The woman preferred her own priest. Margery wailed about her visions. The woman told Margery not to visit again. Margery wrote an angry letter to the woman, then accosted the woman's priest.

One day in 1413, a piece of church structure fell on Margery. To the amazement of the parish, Margery was not injured. This was the miracle she had been wanting. Margery played on the event as she traveled around the country enjoying minor celebrity.

Margery's father died that year. With some of her inheritance, she paid her husband's debts and bought her freedom. Margery still needed clerical acknowledgment of her status to be considered a saintly missionary to Jerusalem, rather than a mere tourist. The step to missionary status required an audience with no one less than the archbishop of Canterbury.

At Canterbury, Margery went into the church and immediately fell into dramatic fits. She went into deep contemplation. The big city monks were not impressed. They almost carried her out into the street. They did, however, give Margery a modest audience. She was given dispensation to separate from her husband so that she could travel as a missionary.

Margery returned home victorious. She could travel alone, without the permission of her husband. She could wear white and go to Rome, or Santiago d' Compostela in Spain.[145]

Of all the pilgrimage tours of the fifteenth century, the *Jerusalem Journey* was the most popular. There were risks. Still, the far-away destination had such

---

[144]   Saint Bridget was canonized in 1391. She saw visions like Margery and railed against abuses in the church.

[145]   See Cruise through History, Itinerary I. London to Rome - Port La Coruna, The Way of Saint James.

prominence that Margery felt it would adequately elevate her status back home. She planned to return home by way of Rome and Santiago d' Compostela to complete her Grand Tour.

Margery arranged to travel with a tour group. They planned to leave England, headed for Venice. There they could buy a three-week package tour, from Venice to Jaffa, the port for Jerusalem.

There were more risks to personal safety traveling across Europe than on the Venice to Venice portion of the trip. Venetian sea captains competed for lucrative pilgrim trade. They carried soldiers on ships as guardians to protect passengers from pirates and occasional brawls among the crew. Once in Jaffa, the two-day camel ride to the holy cities and back, plus time at the main sites, was carefully controlled, exploited and safeguarded by Muslim resident tour guides. Holy Land tourism was an important business in the fifteenth century. Keeping travelers safe was good business.

Margery's upcoming trip was announced in church. John stayed home with the children. Margery's maid agreed to come with her.

Margery showed up in a grey robe, with a large cross on her chest and a broad-brimmed hat. She was dramatically overdressed. The travel group decided immediately that they did not like her.

The Holy Land travelers sailed down the North Sea, then down the Rhine River in Germany. By the time they all reached Switzerland, the group voted to part with Margery. Her fellow pilgrims had begged her once too often to be quiet during prayers. Margery's maid was allowed to remain with the group and she joyously agreed.

Margery found a non-English speaking group of travelers who allowed her to join them. Since they could not understand her, they ignored her overzealous antics. By the following night Margery was warm and snug in a Swiss mountain cabin, when her former group trudged into the inn. Reluctantly, they allowed her to rejoin them.

When the pilgrims reached Venice, there was a war in progress. The Italian wars of the time were not bloody. Rather the two sides hired surrogates to rough each other up a bit. Still, the war had the effect of stalling traffic at the docks.

Margery used her free time to walk through Venice. Around her, there were hawkers selling relics, such as pieces of the skull of a saint. There were well-dressed women shopping for lovely bakery items and fresh fruit. There were also elegant villas and art in Venice, none of which made a memorable impression on Margery.

The travel group spent three months in Venice waiting to board ships. During this time Venetian inn and shop keepers absorbed much of their travel funds. It was as if all the merchants of Venice had a grand scheme to profit from travelers. Finally, ship captains started to vie for passengers.

For an 8£ fare, passengers received room, round trip sailing, board, entrance fees, and tour guide services. The room consisted of sleeping space on a lower deck, marked off in chalk. The traveler provided their own bedding. The board was a salad, dressed with olive oil, heavenly to the Italians, but not to the liking of English tastes.

Israel, Jerusalem: Old Jaffa

It was a month sailing from Venice to Jaffa. The route took the ship down the Dalmatians past the islands of Crete, Rhodes and Cyprus. Arriving at the port of Jaffa, the travelers had reason to be enthusiastic. Jaffa did not offer much to see, although the beach held memories. This was the place where Jonah left the whale and Saint Peter went fishing.

Tents appeared onshore to register visitors. The crew lined up and held out their mugs for tips. The city of Jaffa looked deserted, so the travelers stayed in caves, huddled around their belongings, awaiting their land tour guides.

It was a two-day mule ride to Jerusalem. The trail snaked through mountains, where robbers lurked. At long last, the travelers scaled Mount Gibeon to look down upon the Holy City. Margery became so excited that she fell off her mule.

Margery carried with her the diary of John Polaner, another traveler of the time. In Polaner's journal, the number of steps to each site in the Holy City was detailed. Margery wanted to take the journal literally. She wanted to sit every place the Virgin Mary sat and stand each place she stood. At each shrine to Christianity Margery swooned.

ISRAEL, JERUSALEM: Margery was locked in the Church of the Holy Sepulchre for the night

As it was for Sir John Mandeville, so it was for Margery; the highpoint of the trip came upon entering the Church of the Holy Sepulcher. The Moors held the keys to the church. Before the doors could be opened, tourists were admonished not to chip away souvenirs from the church.

Once doors to the Church of the Holy Sepulcher were opened, priests jockeyed for the best places inside to say mass for their flock. Margery's group prepared for their twenty-four-hour vigil locked inside the church. Margery was in her element. She held her arms out to form a cross with her body as she moved around the church, convulsing at appropriate intervals.

By the time Margery and her travel group returned to Venice, her fellow travelers were anxious to part company with her. She traveled alone from Venice until she met another group that was duly impressed with her imminent candidacy for sainthood. Among her new friends, Margery entered Rome.

Margery entered Rome in 1414, a low point in the history of the city. It was sparsely populated. The Coliseum and other Roman ruins were being looted for building materials. Still, tourism was a big business. Tours guides for the city were plentiful.

In 1414, the Catholic church was in flux. There was an Italian pope in Rome and a French pope in Avignon. The Italian pope was Pope John XXIII, a former pirate from Naples. Margery recollected, in her journal that Pope John was from a good family. Then one day, an owl landed on Pope John's head as he was saying mass. This was an evil omen. He was run out of Rome soon after that, just as the king of Naples arrived in town.

The abundance of classical antiquity outside her door mattered little to Margery, as did the political problems of Rome and the church. Margery was consumed with her mission to enter as many churches as she could, then to lie prostrate at each alter. At Saint Peter's Basilica, Margery sought out an English-speaking priest to hear her confession. The priest became concerned with Margery's loud bellows during mass. He offered her a private communion. Margery was pleased with special treatment.

Margery identified with Swedish Saint Bridget. Bridget left her husband after giving birth to her eighth child. That Bridget had a mission on behalf of the church, the likes of which Margery lacked, did not deter Margery's self-comparison. Margery scurried through Rome looking for people who may have personally known Saint Bridget. Margery's newfound fellow travelers mimicked her and then threw her out of their hostel.

By Easter of 1415, Margery was headed home to England. She had given away her last personal possessions at Christmas, to show her piety. Having accrued no followers as a burgeoning saint, Margery ran out of energy. She was also out of resources. Fortunately, a priest arrived from England with funds from her husband, John.

Instead of booking passage to England, Margery donned a new costume with a scallop shell badge and tried to book passage to Santiago de Compostela, in Spain. Before her new shipmates could throw her overboard, Henry V of England commanded that all British ships return to England to aide his mounting assault on Normandy, set for 1417. Margery had no choice but to return home.

Back in Leicester, Margery caused quite a stir with her white costume and self-proclaimed saint status. She was put on trial as a heretic, but was acquitted as a mere screamer. When her husband John, then aged sixty, fell down the stairs, Margery became his caretaker. It improved her community standing. Unable to complete the Holy Land trilogy and go to Spain, Margery later went instead to Aachen, Germany, the home of Charlemagne.

Still illiterate, in 1438, Margery enlisted the aid of a priest to take down her dictated journal. She spoke as though delivering a sermon. The depictions of fellow travelers, as well as Margery, were vivid and candid. The book was completed in three weeks. The edited and hand-printed book looked like a hymnal, which aided its popularity. Margery was able to capitalize on her travels, even though she never attained sainthood. She died in 1448, at the age of seventy-five.

Epilogue

Present-day travelers to the Holy Land still encounter heat and crowds. The sites popular in the days of Sir John and Lady Margery are just as popular today. Ships arrive in Holy Land ports from numerous embarkation sites in Italy, Greece and the western Mediterranean. Today tourists travel from Jaffa to Jerusalem by bus over modern highways, instead of by mule. The holy sites are just as compelling today as they were for tourists who came east, in a time before Columbus sailing to the west.

Israel, Jerusalem: Jaffa retreat for travelers

ISRAEL, JERUSALEM: Streets of Eternal Holy City

Heart of the Heart of Jerusalem

There is no city in the world today as sacred to Jews, Christians and Muslims as Jerusalem. Viewed from a distance, the city of limestone appears as a city built of gold on top of a hill. It has been so for thousands of years. Within Jerusalem's walls occurred events of the Old Testament and the beginning of the New. While centers of pantheism grew in Athens and Rome, Jerusalem is and has always been the center of monotheism. Jerusalem is built of the Rocks of Ages; the stones at the heart of the world.

It was in Jerusalem that David united quarreling tribes under the Law of Moses and became king of Israel. It was in a garden nearby that Jesus met with his disciples before he was crucified on a hill close to the City of David. It was to Jerusalem that Mohamed sped on his midnight ride to receive the word of Allah, bringing peace to warring tribes.

Jerusalem is strikingly small considering it looms so large as the epicenter of the three major monotheistic religions. It was within the city walls that Cain slew Abel and Noah prayed before the great flood. It is the place of the Calvary of Christ. It is the first city in the Quran. As cities of religious importance, Jericho is older, Mecca is larger, and Rome is more powerful. Jerusalem stands above all others as the eternal city of pilgrimage.

Pilgrims have been making spiritual journeys to Jerusalem for almost three thousand years. Jews are commanded in the Torah to appear before the Lord in Jerusalem three times a year: during Passover, the remembrance of deliverance from Egypt; Shavuot, the time of the wheat harvest; and Sukkot, the seven days of the harvest festival. They have been doing so since at least 832 BCE when the Temple of Solomon was the destination.

Israel, Jerusalem: Walled City of Jerusalem

Christian pilgrims, following in the steps of Jesus, began arriving in Jerusalem in the third century of the Christian era. One of the earliest recorded pilgrimage guides chronicled a fourth-century pilgrim from Bordeaux, who traveled between 333 and 334 CE. Jerusalem is the third most holy city of the Quran, which placed the city as a point of pilgrimage, in addition to mandated journeys to Mecca. Although the times of sacred pilgrimage differ between religions, the site is the same. Travel to Jerusalem is a year around spiritual destination.

As other cities of sacred pilgrimage have risen and fallen, Jerusalem has stood constant. In early Christendom, pilgrims traveled to Constantinople, Ravenna and Jerusalem. In the ninth century, Santiago de Compostela came into vogue, as Ravenna receded. After the fall of Constantinople to the Muslim Suleiman the Magnificent in 1453, and the resurgence of Rome upon the return of popes from Avignon; Rome, Jerusalem and Santiago became top destinations for Christian pilgrims. They remain so today.

Despite differences in cosmology, and political differences of organized religion, the situs of sacred pilgrimage within Jerusalem for Jews, Christians and Muslims is a small area, of a continuous historic site, within the walls of a city where every inch is imbued with significance. This is the heart of the Holy City of Jerusalem. For Muslims, it is the Dome of the Rock, within the grounds of Al-Aqsa-Mosque. For Christians, it is the Calvary, the site of the Crucifixion and tomb of Jesus, beneath the Church of the Holy Sepulcher. For Jews, hemmed in by Muslim and Christian domains, and having lost control of the site of Solomon's temple, it is the remaining wall of the temple, to which they have access, the Western Wall of Jewish Jerusalem.

As a cruise destination city, reached from the ports of Jaffa, or Ashdod, Jerusalem is so rich in historic places and sites of monumental significance that it is impossible to dwell on them completely in several shore visits. It is not feasible to be comprehensive of historic explanation in a short story. With all due deference to the enormity of the task and the religious significance of the sites, even a well-focused story must be superficial. This is the short story of the Heart of the Heart of Jerusalem, built of the Rocks of Ages, comprised of the Dome of the Rock, the Church of the Holy Sepulcher, and the Western Wall.

Dome of the Rock

If there is one place within the heart of Jerusalem where the three religions converge, it would be within the few square feet, at the top of the rock, inside the mosque that comprises the Dome of the Rock. It was this spot that King David purchased from a farmer, who used it as his wheat threshing floor. David used the spot on which to build an altar to God, as a place to celebrate the renewal of life. His son evolved the alter to an opulent temple; the unmistakable center of Jewish holiness. Reduced again to bare rock by Romans, it became a place of Christ's teaching. Muslims revere the same rock as the place where the Prophet Mohamed stepped up to heaven and returned. It is the Muslim threshold to paradise. The world holds several holy rocks, yet no piece of unworked stone is imbued with so much meaning by so many adherents to several religions.

Emotional attachment to the small area of rock behind the screen, under the Dome, emanates from blended memories of real and imagined events. Regardless, the integrity of memory and abstract attribution of place are not questioned in matters of faith. Stories are for dispersal to the adherents of religion, which gives meaning to their sense of humanity, whether or not the fixed point of the cosmos can be archaeologically proven.

The rock is attributed to be the place of birth of Adam and King David's sin. Some see the footprints of Christ in the stone. Mohamed's steed, Barak, took him heavenward from this spot. All three Abrahamic religions look to this place as the spot where Abraham offered to sacrifice his son to god. The history of this tiny piece of real estate is the bedrock story of Jerusalem.

There are differing details in the Torah, Quran and Bible of events in ancient Jerusalem. There is general agreement that the tribes of Israel became united under David, son-in-law to the first Hebrew king Saul, sometime in the tenth century BCE. David used cunning to breach the defenses of those holding control of a city on Mount Moriah, which became known from the time of David's conquest as Jerusalem.[146] David's palace was erected on the ten-acre site, within Jerusalem, now known as the City of David.[147]

David purchased the peak of Mount Moriah from Araunah, a Jebusite farmer, for whom it was a wheat threshing floor. At this high point, David built an altar. It became the most coveted and contested piece of rock in the history of man. This is Temple Mount, known as Mount Zion until the name Zion transferred to the Western Hill of Jerusalem.

David's son and successor, King Solomon, evolved the alter into a temple of majesty. Employing Phoenician artisans, the First Temple of Solomon was thirty feet wide, ninety feet long and forty-five feet high, decorated with gold, ivory and bronze. The thirty feet square, inner chamber of the temple, the Holy of Holies, held the Ark of the Covenant, in which the tablets of Moses lay protected. Missing from the temple, typical in pagan temples, was an actual deity.

---

[146] The residents of Jebus, conquered by David, known as Jebusites, simply, the people of Jebus, may have been Hittites or Amorites. They were a tribe of Canaan, not a Hebrew tribe.

[147] The City of David is an archaeological site, deserving of its own story.

ISRAEL, JERUSALEM: Golden Dome of the Great Mosque
above the Golden Limestone Heart of the Old City of Jerusalem

ISRAEL, JERUSALEM: Dome of the Rock Mosque Entrance

Solomon began the use of a temple as a house of the word of the lord, that is, a place to pray and store the accouterments of religious practice. The First Temple was such a successful symbol of Judaism, that when the Israelites divided again, upon the death of Solomon, the Temple remained a unifying point for religious observance.

The First Temple was a site of holy pilgrimage from 832 to 422 BCE, until Babylonian king Nebuchadnezzar II laid siege to Jerusalem, taking the city and burning the temple.[148] A Second Temple was built upon the Jews' return to Jerusalem. It was five times the size of the First Temple. The governor of Jerusalem at the time, Zerubbabel, led by example, donating personal funds to rebuild. Missing from the First Temple was the Ark of the Covenant, a silver chest containing vestments of the high priests, the ashes of Moses, anointing oil and the sacred fire. Thus, began legends of the lost Ark of the Covenant and stories of its possible location.

Under the Temple Mount were stone quarries, sometimes referred to as Solomon's Stables. Explanations for removal of the Ark from the Temple have included a secret trap door, which allowed the Ark to be lowered into the quarry, from which it could be carried to safety through a string of connected cave passages. Exploration of the caves has resulted in findings that these passages extend to Jericho, thirteen miles from Jerusalem.[149]

During the Second Temple period, in the breakup of the empire of Alexander the Great, one of his generals took control of Jerusalem. These Greeks had no desire to maintain religious toleration. In 164 BCE, Jews, led by the Maccabee father and five sons, drove out occupiers and sanctified the Temple. The miracle of continuity of the eternal light in the Temple is celebrated as Hanukkah today. The Maccabees reinforced their domain by adding the fortress wall around Temple Mount.

The Second Temple stood five hundred years until Roman king Herod tore it down to build a pagan temple. His other contributions were the Antonia Fortress, around the upper city and the retaining wall around Temple Mount,

---

[148]   These dates are contested, as are many dates in ancient ecclesiastical history.

[149]   British explorer James Barclay is credited with rediscovery of the caves in 1854. No Ark was found.

which includes the Western Wall. The next Roman emperor of note was Titus, who came to Jerusalem to destroy the capital of the Jews. His victory arch in Rome, near the Coliseum, displays plundering the Temple by Roman legions.

ISRAEL, JERUSALEM: Roman era stone street in the Old City

One of the last pagan Roman emperors, Hadrian, built a temple to Venus on Temple Mount in the late third century CE. The first Christian emperor of Rome, Constantine, removed the pagan temple in 335 and consecrated Jerusalem in memory of Christ. Temple Mount was preempted by the Church of the Holy Sepulcher.

For three hundred years, Temple Mount was a ruin. Hebrew prophecy includes a Third Temple to be built. It will greet the Messiah, sometime in the Jewish year 6,000, which is 2240 CE.

Muslim Caliph Omar arrived in 638 CE, finding the Temple Mount a refuse heap. He cleared the area and built a shrine to the ascension of Mohammed to heaven, from which he returned with the word of god. The first Dome of the Rock Mosque was built between 687 and 695, largely the effort of Caliph Abd el-Malik. It was financed by taxes levied on Egyptians for seven years. The Caliph intended Jerusalem to become an alternative to pilgrimage to Mecca.

The Dome of the Rock was built in the Muslim tradition of perfect proportion. It exists today as it was built, making it the oldest building in Jerusalem and one of the oldest mosques in the world. It was built to enshrine Haram al-Sharif, the Noble Sanctuary. Inside a screen was placed around the Rock, making it viewable only by the faithful.

Near to Temple Mount, with its own bright dome, sits the Church of the Holy Sepulcher. El-Malik wanted no structure to surpass the majesty of his mosque. He employed Byzantine artisans to create a dome, held seventy feet aloft and mounted on a circle of arched windows, inlaid with gold mosaics. So over-subscribed were funds assigned to the mosque project, that the dome was covered with excess contributed gold.

Inside the Dome of the Rock, there was incense and light to encourage all the senses into daily prayer. The Dome of the Rock did not replace Mecca and Medina, where Mohammed was born and died, as a primary place of pilgrimage. The mosque did join churches and synagogues of Jerusalem of the eighth through tenth centuries, to maintain the city as an important pilgrimage site for Jews, Christians and Muslims. The city prospered as a result, becoming a major trade fair venue of the early medieval era.

ISRAEL, JERUSALEM: The Aedicule under the Dome of the
Church of the Holy Sepulchre

Christian knights of the First Crusade entered Jerusalem in 1099, briefly abating Muslim control of the city. Jews, Christians and Muslims, who had lived in peaceful coexistence for centuries, were slaughtered in the looting by fortune-seeking crusaders. The knights hoisted a cross to the top of the Dome of the Rock, recast the imprints of Mohammed as footprints of Christ and rewrote history in Jerusalem to begin and end with the Christian era.[150]

The knights revered equally the Church of the Holy Sepulcher and the Dome of the Rock, transfigured to a church. Christian tourists delighted in chipping bits of the rock to take home as a souvenir. Fences were placed around fragile places in both buildings, while visitors of all faiths were allowed access. Dome of the Rock became the mother church of the Knights Templar. The knights carved steps into the face of the rock under the Dome.

---

[150] Disgruntled more militant Muslim sects were unified in their reaction to the knights, resulting in reversion to jihad as warfare, when jihad as holy war had been a campaign of conversion, not actual bloodshed.

In 1187, the Muslim Caliph Saladin amassed an army that brought the crusading knights to their knees. To make a point of his disdain for the holy ruse of the crusades, Saladin ensured that in retaking Jerusalem there was no looting, or harming of civilians. He had the Dome of the Rock reguilded. Forty years later, Emperor Frederick II, who abstained from the Second Crusade, sat down with Saladin's successor, using negotiation to open Jerusalem to Christian control for a century.[151] Seven centuries after that, Jerusalem was a Muslim city, controlled by the Ottoman Turks, who had swept through the Middle East. City walls of Jerusalem seen today, date to 1538, the time of Ottoman Suleiman the Magnificent.

Israel, Jerusalem: Excavation of the southwest retaining wall

---

[151] Frederick II became King of Jerusalem after he negotiated Third Crusade, while he was under excommunication by the pope for having sat out the Second Crusade. See more on Frederick in Cruise through History, Itinerary II. Port of Bari - Stupor Mundi, Emperor of the World.

At the beginning of the nineteenth century, Napoleon's armies swept through Europe and into the Holy Land.[152] In Jerusalem, French poet François René Chateaubriand found the Dome of the Rock clad only in lead. His resignation from the French army to take a Grand Tour, including the Holy Land, inspired young people of means to repeat the trip, renewing interest in pilgrimage to Jerusalem and concern for the preservation of holy sites.

In 1898, Dome of the Rock was refurbished by Ottoman Turkish Sultan Abdul-Hamid II, who placed a crescent on top. It was a time when Ottoman fortunes were falling. By the twentieth century, Arab nationalism and desire for a Jewish state were on the rise. In the present division of control in Jerusalem, the Dome of the Rock is in the Muslim sector. Jews are not allowed access to the Rock, and Christian access is restricted. The Dome of the Rock is preserved as a historical icon, while religious practice on Temple Mount is held in the Al-Aqsa-Mosque. Of the seventeen original gates to Temple Mount, eleven remain open and six are sealed.

Israel, Jerusalem: Garden of Gethsemane

---

[152] In Egypt, Napoleon recovered the Rosetta Stone.

ISRAEL, JERUSALEM: Station of the Ctoss III and IV

Church of the Holy Sepulcher

A short distance west of Temple Mount is the Rock of Calvary; the hill of the Crucifixion of Christ and his entombment in the cave below. The story of the Church of the Holy Sepulcher begins with the veneration of Golgotha, the spot on the rock of the Crucifixion.

In 325 CE, Roman Emperor Constantine came to Jerusalem with his mother, Helen. While he directed the transition of Hadrian's Temple of Venus to a church, his eighty-year-old mother climbed around the Rock of Calvary. She is credited with discovering Christ's burial tomb.

Immediately, Constantine directed that a church be built to encase the site. The hillside was dug away until only the cavern remained. The stone around the Golgotha was removed until only the spindle of the rock remained. The tiny church was itself was encased with a dome fifty years later. For fifteen centuries, denominations of Christians added to the church.

The compact, yet complex, structure of the Church of the Holy Sepulcher is due in part to its history of control, damage by fire and earthquake, and varied opinions on preservation and restoration. Many Christian groups, including the Knights Templar, added their vision of reverence to the holiest church. The city grew to encase the church.

A fire damaged the Church in 614, at which time the True Cross was taken by Persians, then in control of Jerusalem. It was restored in 630 by the Byzantine Emperor, then damaged in the next century by an earthquake. Fires in the Church were recurring events over the centuries.

When the Muslims took Jerusalem in the seventh century, they chose to protect and preserve the Church, rather than turn it into a mosque. At the beginning of the eleventh century, the caliph ordered the destruction of all churches in Palestine and Egypt, shocking Christians throughout Europe. They urged the

ISRAEL, JERUSALEM: Golgotha

ISRAEL, JERUSALEM: Close up detail of Aedicule

pope to authorize a crusade to recapture the Holy Land while blaming Jews for the destruction. Contested control and blame have been recurring themes.

Pope Urban II launched the First Crusade to the Holy Land in 1099. He later regretted his action. Knights Templar and Knights of St. John held Jerusalem for eighty-eight years. Temple Mount became a temple to St. Helena, the mother of Constantine. Various chapels of the Church of the Holy Sepulcher were united in motley fashion into a single church, with a bell tower. The tower was later lowered to height, not to exceed the city minarets.

ISRAEL, JERUSALEM: Visiting the Church of the Holy Sepulchre

In 1555, Franciscans arrived to renovate the Church of the Holy Sepulcher and add a chamber to the Aedicule, all of which was badly in need of repair. They tangled with Eastern Orthodox priests, who had their own vision for maintaining the Church. Acrimony escalated for more than two hundred years, until Ottoman rulers in charge of Jerusalem stepped up in 1757, to mediate the dispute by giving control jointly to six Christian orders: Roman Catholic,

Israel, Jerusalem: Immovable Ladder

Greek Orthodox, Armenian Orthodox, Coptic Christian, Syrian Orthodox, and Ethiopian Orthodox. The Immovable Ladder remains as a testament to the inability of the six to agree on mundane matters. Imagine trying to change a lightbulb!

The 1808 fire, in which the dome of the Church of the Holy Sepulcher collapsed, only added to partisan rancor during repairs. Finally, in 1853, the Ottoman sultan issued a decree of Status Quo. Every detail of the Church was to remain as it was, unless and until an agreement of joint caretaker Christian orders. The Immovable Ladder went from saga to institution.

Not one of the joint controlees has control of the front door of the church. Wisely, in 1192, after retaking control from the Knights, Saladin assigned a Muslim family to be an eternal keeper of the keys to the church. Today the Wajech Nusesibeh family claims to have been doorkeepers since 638.[153] They continue the responsibility by tradition.

---

[153] Door keeping responsibility was suspended for eighty-eight years, during the time of the Knights.

In 2016, the floor of the Aedicule, in place since church restoration by the Franciscans in 1555, was removed, to confirm the existence of the burial bed of Jesus. Researchers and church officials satisfied that the burial chamber dated to the first century CE, saw the tomb resealed. The rest is left to faith.

Western Wall

ISRAEL, JERUSALEM: Western Wall

The western retaining wall of the First Temple platform stands as the often-called Wailing Wall. Wailing reference emanates from when Constantine entered Jerusalem in 324. Jews were excluded from Jerusalem for the next three hundred years, except during certain ceremonial times, when entry was allowed to weep at holy sites. The wailing connotation is an insult.

Jews were similarly restricted from the Western Wall during the British era, a period from 1920 to 1967. In the 1948 Arab-Israeli War, the Jewish State of Israel held West Jerusalem, not to include the Old City and Western Wall, which were within Jordanian control. Jews were excluded from the Old City. The Six-Day War in 1967, reset access to and control of areas throughout Israel, adding East Jerusalem, inclusive of the Western Wall, to the Jewish state.

The Six-Day War marked the first time since 70 CE that Jews could freely approach the Western Wall.[154] It was a crescendo emotional moment in the history of a city often amid emotional cross-hairs. The war ended with an accord, wherein Arab factions would no longer defend the city, and the Jewish state agreed not to claim the Dome of the Rock. The war resolved ambiguity building from the 1947 United Nations-brokered *Two-State Solution* to Arab-Jewish hostilities, upon withdrawal of the British.

Over three millennia, at various times, Jews and Muslims have been the majority of Jerusalem's population. The City of David was imposed upon a pagan landscape, before the time of Christianity and Islam. Romans controlled a city of pagans and Jews, which became under Roman Emperor Constantine, a mix of Jews, pagans and Christians. By the end of the first millennium of the current era, Jerusalem had socially divided into neighborhoods of Jews, Muslims, Christians and Armenian Christians. Those quarters exist today, formalized in 1948.

Today, the Dome of the Rock is in the Muslim Quarter, the Church of the Holy Sepulcher is in the Christian Quarter, and the Western Wall is in the Jewish Quarter. The remaining quarter is the Armenian Christian Quarter, home to significant Armenian religious sites. Today, the Christian population of Jerusalem is small. The population is two-thirds Jewish and one-third Muslim. Jerusalem is the capital of the political state of Israel.

The Western Wall, viewed from the lower plaza today, is the segment of the historic wall within the Jewish Quarter. The actual extent of the wall continues into the Muslim Quarter, where it is engulfed in buildings. Visible at the

---

[154] In the Jewish-Roman War of 70 CE, Roman General Vespasian lay siege, then burned the city

lower level of the Wall are stone blocks, most of which weigh two to eight tons, put in place under the direction of Herod two thousand years ago. Of a total height of one hundred and five feet, only sixty-two feet of wall is above ground today.

ISRAEL, JERUSALEM: Massive stone of Western Wall

The Western Wall Plaza was made possible in 1967, by removing the ancient Moroccan Quarter, where homes were densely built, and animals grazed near the wall. During periods when Jews had not been physically restricted from access to the wall, the area was not conducive to reflective prayer, nor was there space for congregating at the Wall. The 1853 *Status Quo* decree effect on the Wall meant that no chairs could be used where there had been no chairs prior to 1853.

There are people who maintain that the Western Wall is indeed a surviving wall of the First Temple of Solomon. Others accept the wall as the retaining wall of the temple platform, the closest edifice to the temple itself, with an east-facing trajectory toward the original Holy of Holies, the room of the Ark of the Covenant. Regardless of individual views, the plaza is regarded as a place of prayer. It is an area of reverence in which appropriate conduct may be expected.

A practice of leaving prayers on scraps of paper placed in crevices of the Wall began in the eighteenth century. It is preferable to touching the Wall. Taking chips from the Wall is illegal.

Visiting Jerusalem Today

Omar, the first great leader of the Ottoman Turks, was believed to have chosen Muslim as a religion with which to inspire his people into a unified identity because no building was required. A devout Muslim requires only a small space on the ground on which to demonstrate devotion several times a day. Jews and Christians hold the majesty of the divine in their hearts, irrespective of a great building in which to congregate. The act of pilgrimage in the three religions is a time of reflection, not dependent upon the destination. Yet, pilgrims of all three religions continue to converge on Jerusalem as the brightest star in the cosmos. Its magnetism is as much tangible as it is spiritual. It is the prime destination of the ages. The Heart of the Heart so preserved will persevere.

Israel, Jerusalem: Golden Gate

Haifa: Ancient and Modern

The port of Haifa, the third-largest city in Israel, is a gateway to the interior, with its rich history of northern Israel and a modern, secular, city looking out to the world. Romans, crusaders and Ottoman Turks landed on the beaches of Haifa Bay, from which they traveled up the beach to Acre and down to Caesarea. Traveling inland to Nazareth and the Sea of Galilee, the conquering arrivals encountered locals including Jewish tribes and Jesus and his Disciples. The area became the epicenter of the history of the monotheistic western world.

Ancient cities of northern Israel include Haifa, a modern port today; Acre, the bastion of the Knights of St. John, now known as Akko; Caesarea, named for Augustus Caesar by Herod; and Nazareth, where footsteps of Jesus begin. Roman ruler Herod was a builder of great edifices, seen in Caesarea and Tiberias, on the shore of the Sea of Galilee. Jesus walked to Galilee, the home of Apostles Peter, Andrew, James and John. Along his path, Jesus built a following and performed miracles. The footpaths of Jesus and the Roman roads were traveled by Jews from Caesarea to Jerusalem, in their revolt against Roman rule.

The Old and New Testaments are filled with stories of northern Israel. These stories drew the first Christian Roman Emperor, Constantine, to commemorate sites with churches. Churches established by Helen, Constantine's mother and greatest influence, are found across the landscape. Over time and changes in

Israel, Haifa: Walls of Jerico

control of the ancient cities, many of the visual vestiges of cities have been lost. Some are merely archaeological sites. Still, the landscape is memorable. Looking out from Haifa to Mt. Carmel and Mt. Tabor, which look over the Sea of Galilee, the view today is much as it was in the time of Jesus.

This story is told in two parts: the story of ancient times of Jewish life and early Christianity, intersected by Romans, Crusaders and Ottoman Turks; and the modern city of Haifa, which has had a significant ongoing role in history from the twentieth century forward. It is a story illustrated by visible remnants of history across a landscape of cities and by the recent additions of those who have built the modern state of Israel.

The characters in this story include Herod, the great builder, the Knights of St. John Hospitaller, protectors of pilgrims to the Holy Land, and Helen, protector of the story of Jesus. Rather than a travelogue of area cities, their stories are set as venues in time. Great historical events are rarely bounded by place. This story follows the lines of history.

As a cautionary note: It is not possible to walk in the footsteps of Jesus and tell of the perseverance of Jews in Israel, including the birth of the modern state, inclusive of all significant details, in a short story. Just as cruise port destinations are brief and travelers must regrettably be selective in their choice of excursion, so too this story is brief.

In the Beginning …

Early evidence of man living together and cultivating crops was in Israel. *Galilee Man,* a skull discovered in 1925, in a cave near Galilee, is 300,000 years old. Semitic languages, which include ancient Hebrew, Aramaic and Arabic, appeared more than two thousand five hundred years ago.

The Biblical Land of Canaan stretched along the eastern Mediterranean from Turkey, through Israel, to Egypt. Among people of the area were Phoenicians, Philistines, Israelites and several smaller groups. This Ancient Near East of the fourteenth century BCE was sought for control by Egyptians, Hittites and Assyrians. It is an area of archaeological study today.

Israel, Haifa: Capernaum Synagogue where Jesus preached

The ancient Hebrews, united under the god of Israel, began with the twelve tribes; the twelve sons of Jacob, the grandson of Abraham.[155] Famine pushed them to Egypt. Moses brought them out of bondage in Egypt to Israel, with the Torah and tablets of the Ten Commandments. The tribes united under the first king, Saul. The son-in-law of Saul is David, who established his city in Jerusalem. His son Solomon built the First Temple.

Upon the death of King Solomon in 930 BCE, ten northern Jewish tribes split from two in the south, forming a Kingdom of Israel in the north and Kingdom of Judah in the south. Biblical and historical sources disagree on the reason for and the gravity of the divide. It may have been a disagreement over leadership or taxation. The division was not unyielding. The north and south had squabbles, coming together against common threats, such as Damascus. Intermarriage brought the tribes together for a century.

---

[155]   The twelve sons were: Reuben, Simeon, Levi, Judah, Dan, Naphtali, Gad, Asher, Issachar, Zebulun, Joseph and Benjamin.

For twenty years, from 740 BCE, Assyrian kings waged war on the Northern Kingdom of Israel. Eventually, people were resettled as slaves in Assyrian land, the area between the Tigris and Euphrates Rivers, north of Babylon. They are the Ten Lost Tribes of Israel.

Depopulated land of the north came under Babylonian rule. Judea was a vassal state. The dynasty of Babylonian King Nebuchadnezzar II was overthrown by the Persian king, Cyrus the Great in 537 BCE. He was called great, as he allowed Jews religious toleration.

In the third century BCE, Alexander the Great swept eastward from Greece to conquer Asia, up to India. Upon his death, the kingdom was divided, putting Israel under former Alexander generals. Between 140 and 37 BCE, Judea was independent, with its capital in Jerusalem. Romans arrived in 37 BCE, installing Herod as king of the vassal state of Israel.

Herod, the Great Builder

Israel, Haifa: Masada & Fortress of Herod

Israel, Haifa: Dead Sea and Golan Heights beyond

Herod was a Jew, whose family had high-ranking positions in Roman Judea. His brother was governor of Jerusalem. In the continuing turbulent power struggles, which characterized the times, Herod went to Rome, sought the support of Roman Senator Mark Anthony, and returned to Judea as the Roman-supported client-king of Judea, a Roman territory.

Never the heroic figure, due to his political maneuvering, a succession of five wives and his brutality, Herod is derided in the Book of Mathew for the slaughter of the babes of Bethlehem, fearing the birth of a king of the Jews as told by the Magi. Always ambitious, Herod built great edifices. In Jerusalem, he is credited with reconstruction of the Second Temple, its retaining wall and the Antonia Fortress, the walls of which still stand.

In Masada, Herod built two palaces and enlarged the fortress. He built at least four other fortresses; such was his concern for insurrection. Jericho, possibly the oldest city in the world, was given to Cleopatra as a gift by Mark Anthony. Herod wintered there.

Herod's signature building achievement was the port city of Caesarea. From 29 to 13 BCE, the old Phoenician port received the attention of the most advanced building technologies. Walls began underwater to secure the harbor. An aqueduct and amphitheater were built, which stand today. Herod positioned his palace to look out over the harbor.

In the tradition of the times, the sons of Herod divided his domain, although they vied for total control. Herod Antipas held the north, establishing his capital at Tiberias on the Sea of Galilee, in honor of his Roman emperor, Tiberius. It became a grand city. The hot springs in Tiberias were as popular in ancient times as they are today.

Life in Judea came to an end for the Jews in the first and second century CE. The brutality of Roman rulers erupted into the First Jewish Revolt of 66 CE, which began in Caesarea. With military precision, Roman soldiers decimated the population and leveled cities. The culminating battle was at Masada in 73 CE. There, the entire population perished, rather than submit to the Romans. Herod's hilltop fortress was leveled. The Second Jewish Revolt ended in 135 CE with the Romans exiling the entire Jewish population from Judea. Thus, began and chapter in the Jewish Diaspora.[156]

Walking in the Footsteps of Jesus

Touring ancient cities of Galilee is the place to walk in the footsteps of Jesus. Mary of Nazareth gave birth to Jesus in Bethlehem, then returned to Nazareth, where her child was raised. It was in a small town near Nazareth that Jesus performed the miracle of turning water into wine, enabling the proper celebration of a local wedding.

Walking along the shores of the Sea of Galilee, Jesus came to Capernaum. There he met fishermen, who would become his disciples, the Fishers of Men, including Simon Peter. People came from Capernaum to nearby Tabgha, where Jesus fed his growing flock with the miracle of the multiplication of the loaves and fishes on the shores of Galilee.

---

[156] Emperor Hadrian rebuilt Jerusalem as a Roman city, which Jews could not enter. He sold survivors into slavery in Rome. Jews fled to Egypt, Syria, across North Africa and eventually into Europe. Not all Jews left Judea. Those who remained preserved oral history into the Talmud.

ISRAEL, HAIFA: Chapel at Nazareth

St. Helen, the mother of Constantine the great Byzantine emperor, founder of Constantinople, the seat of the Greek Orthodox Church and first Christian Roman church leader, was beatified for her efforts in fourth century Judea to commemorate sites of importance in the life of Jesus by instigating the establishment of churches. The Church of the Multiplication of the Loaves and the Fishes, built-in 1982, sits on the site of an early Byzantine basilica, built on the actual site of the miracle of Christ. The Church of the Primacy of St. Peter, also in Tabgha, was begun in the time of St. Helen. It is built on or near the site where Jesus appeared to the apostles after the Resurrection.

On the shores of the Galilee, between Tabgha and Capernaum, Jesus is believed to have stood on a hill and delivered the Sermon on the Mount. The place is revered today as the Mount of the Beatitudes. On the site of a fourth-century church, marking the place of the sermon is the 1938 Church of the Beatitudes, commissioned by the Italian government.

ISRAEL, HAIFA: Church of the Mount of the Beatitudes

It would be a mistake to believe that Judaism disappeared from Judea with the expulsion of Jews by the Romans and their exclusion from Jerusalem. Capernaum is also the site of a fourth-century synagogue. In remote cities of the Galilee, Jewish scholars gathered and committed oral cultural and religious history to written record in the Talmud.

Contesting the Legacy

The seventh century was a tumultuous time in the Holy Land. Early in the century, Persians arrived and persecuted Christians. Byzantines arrived in 638 to drive off the Persians.

It was in the seventh century that the Prophet Muhammed was spreading the word of the Quran. Six years after the Prophet's death in 632, his disciple Omar led an army into the Holy Land. Muslims revered Jerusalem as the place where the Prophet ascended into heaven to receive the Quran. The

ISRAEL, HAIFA: St. Peter's Church of the Fishes

Temple Mount, the place of the First and Second Temple of Solomon, had been abandoned by Christians in favor of the Church of the Holy Sepulcher on the site of the Crucifixion and Entombment of Christ. On the Jewish temple site, Muslims erected Dome of the Rock. It was a mosque intended to outshine the dome of the church.

All was peaceful in the Holy Land, while Arab Muslim leaders in Jerusalem allowed Jews and Christians access to the city. Then, at the beginning of the eleventh century, peaceful coexistence of the three monotheistic religions ended. At the beginning of the century, Muslims began to persecute non-Muslims. The Church of the Holy Sepulcher was destroyed. By 1071, non-Muslims were excluded from Jerusalem.

In response to outcries from Christian Europe, the pope launched the First Crusade to liberate the Holy Land. In 1099, after a five-week siege of Jerusalem, Vatican sponsored knights ruled the land. They remained in Israel for one hundred and ninety-two years, until overthrown by Muslim Turks.

An order of military knights, headquartered on Temple Mount, became known as Knights Templar. They wore tunics with red crosses on a white background. Another order of knights prioritized their mission as caretakers of pilgrims to the Holy Land. To distinguish themselves from military knights, they wore tunics with white crosses on a red background. These were the Knights of St. John, Hospitaller. Both Orders built castles and restored churches in Jerusalem and throughout Israel. Several remain today.

Crusaders landed in northern Israel on the shores of Caesarea and Acre, now Akko. They went inland, to sites in Nazareth, Tiberias, and Galilee, where pilgrims had been walking in the footsteps of Jesus for seven hundred years. The final defeat of crusading Knights came in Acre in 1291 under victorious Muslim leadership.

In Caesarea, Knights sought to protect their supply lines to the sea by building a fortress at the port built by Herod. Further protection was gained by building a wall at the entrance to the harbor area. They repaired Byzantine walls around the old city.

Nazareth was a special place of reverence for the crusaders, as the boyhood home of Jesus. They developed city attractions as pilgrim destinations. The city economy prospered.

In Nazareth, crusaders erected the Church of the Annunciation in 1102, over the site of a fourth-century church and grotto. The church was destroyed by Muslims in 1260, during battles to retake control of Israel. The Greek Orthodox church on the site today was built in 1769.[157]

During the crusader era, Tiberias was the capital of northern Israel, under a French knight, maintained as a vassal of the Knights of Jerusalem. Jerusalem and Tiberias had their own bishopric. Tiny St. Peter's Church, commemorated the area in which Peter fished when he met Jesus. In 1187, Knights lost control of Tiberias, and the church became a mosque. Remains of a monastery sit within the Knight's fortress on the water.

---

[157] The crusaders removed Greek Orthodox Priests from residence in the church, replacing them with Roman Catholic Priests. In the 1969 restoration, the church returned to Greek Orthodox.

Israel, Haifa: Church of Nazareth Today

Like most of the churches seen in northern Israel today, the Church of the Transfiguration on Mount Tabor, completed in 1924, was built on the site of earlier churches from the time of St. Helen, in the mid-fourth century and rebuilt by twelfth-century crusaders. The Transfiguration of Christ, to a man revered above Moses and Elijah, the two main Jewish prophets, occurred on, or near, this site on Mount Tabor near Nazareth.

Acre is a seaport that has a timeline reaching into deep antiquity. Sitting on the northern edge of Israel, it was home to Phoenicians and Canaanites. Greeks arrived in Acre, led by Alexander the Great and Egyptians came to the port led by the last Ptolemy Pharaoh, Cleopatra. The highpoint of city history is tied to the Knights of St. John. For the Knights, Acre was their key city and their last bastion in defense of the Holy Land in Jerusalem.

In 1104, Acre was conquered by Baldwin II, King of Jerusalem, a French crusading fortune seeker and independently-minded secular governor.[158] Genoese assistance enabled Baldwin to oust Muslims, who were supported by Egyptians. Baldwin granted land to the Knights of St. John, who used Acre as a pilgrimage stopover point on the way to Jerusalem. Under the leadership of Baldwin, with assistance from the Knights, Acre went from a sparsely populated minor port to a robust city, with a population rivaling Jerusalem. Prosperity came to the city as a major trade center in the Mediterranean.

The Knights of St. John built a church to St. John in Acre. They expanded city infrastructure, building streets, drainage systems, and palaces. From the crypt of the church, there were underground passageways which connected to the Knights' quarters. Pilgrims lodging with the Knights would have felt safe.[159] Marco Polo was one of their guests.

In 1187, Muslims took control of the Holy Land, including Acre. Acre was far too lucrative a port for the Knights to accept their loss. Having been removed from their position in Jerusalem, the Knights of St. John focused on the recapture of Acre. Four years later, with reinforcements from the Third Crusade, Acre was again a city of the Knights.

Knights held Acre for a century, until 1291, when forces of Caliph Saladin overwhelmed the stronghold of well-stocked halls of the Knights. Under siege, unable to reach reinforcements from the sea, Acre fell to Ottoman Turks. It remained an Ottoman Turkish city until the British period in the nineteenth century. In the fight for a Jewish homeland in the twentieth century, halls of the Knights of St. John became a prison, holding Jewish soldiers.

---

[158] Baldwin was a handsome, affable fellow, loved by his followers and feared by his opponents, Christian and Muslim. He is deserving of his own story for his exploits in France, on the crusader trail, in his conquest of Caesarea and in becoming King of Jerusalem, as successor to his brother. Upon the death of his wife, loss of income left him needing other means to support his crusader expenses. His political and bigamous marriages caused a rift with the Catholic church.

[159] Knights processed sugar used in confections to delight their guests.

20ᵗʰ Century Haifa

Haifa is now a city that lays across Mount Carmel, like a white-studded carpet of buildings, punctuated by colorful Baha'i Temple gardens. Shores of the Bay of Haifa have been sparsely occupied over several millennia by settlements of fishermen. Several times the tiny settlements were passed over for Acre, the growing seaport and habitation area.

Haifa's time as a prominent city began in the twentieth century. Late in the nineteenth century, German migrants to Haifa began an organized modernization of city infrastructure. A power station was built and factories opened. Jews were attracted by the improved city to move to Haifa from Romania, Morocco and Turkey. Haifa's prosperity eclipsed Acre by the early twentieth century.

Nineteenth-century prophet of the Bahá'í faith, Báb, Sayyed 'Ali Muhammad Shirāzi, was executed in Azerbaijan, then part of Iran, and entombed in Acre. Acre remains the major holy site of the Bahá'í faith. In 1909, the remains of Báb were moved to Haifa, where the large Bahá'í complex and gardens were built. Haifa is now the second city of the faith.

The decline of the Ottoman Empire, by the end of the nineteenth century, gave cause for the League of Nations to create caretaker governments in some areas by mandate. Control of Haifa by the British began in 1918. Under League mandate, British oversight of Palestine continued for thirty years, through the Second World War, until the creation of the Jewish state of Israel by the United Nations in 1948. Britain imparted to Israel generally, and to Haifa directly, administrative and infrastructure capability to grow into a major industrial port. From Haifa, crude oil from the Middle-East is exported to the world. Muslims, Jews and Christians contribute to city growth.

Between the United Nations announcement of intent in 1947 and the establishment of the Jewish State in 1948, civil war broke out in streets of Haifa. As the Jewish population of Haifa grew post-statehood, tensions continued. Growth of the city, general, non-sectarian availability of jobs, and ownership in the new prosperity, abated some tensions. Haifa has established itself as a secular city, where the Carmelit railway runs on Saturday. Still, tensions remain, divided by religion.

Desert wadis (ravines), in the valleys of Haifa, run down to the beaches. Bat Galim is a neighborhood on the Mediterranean coast that has a beach popular with locals. A railway and cable cars connect nightlife in Bat Galim with neighborhoods high on Mount Carmel.

Cruise visitors to Haifa will benefit from the development of the old passenger port into a new cruise port terminal adjoining restaurants, shops, and other attractions. Former Navy Base areas will become public beaches and a promenade. As the third city of Israel, with Jerusalem as the capital and historical center, and Tel-Aviv as the industrial and business center, with its proximity to the port of Ashdod, Haifa aims to claim a title as the tourism destination point of cruise travelers, seeking proximate access to the northern Israel historic and religious sites.

Haifa looks to a promising future of being a destination cruise port, with plenty of attractions awaiting travelers within the city. It can also look to the past and the role Haifa has played as a gateway to the historical cities of interior northern Israel. Haifa offers cruise travelers access to ancient and modern Israel.

ISRAEL, HAIFA: River Jordan Baptism

Israel, Acre: Vaulted Dining Hall of the Knights of Saint John of Jerusalem

Acre – From Bastion of Holy Land Knights to City of Coexistence

The city of Acre welcomes visitors today with a cute video of an animated horse. This is recent history. Acre, on the edge of Palestine and the Muslim world, has through history thrust Arab people; Muslim, Jewish, Christian, Druze, and Baha'i, into brutal conflict. Usually, cities of international trade develop a multi-faceted population that is stabilizing, although envied and sometimes conquered. The history of Acre is anything but sanguine.

Acre played an important role as a military port for Christian Knights and Muslim Ottoman Turks. Rather than foster economic growth of the city, the port functioned as strategic means to supply forces. Acre was the staging ground for some of the most brutal battles of the Biblical, Medieval and transitionary periods into the modern century.

In Biblical times, when Israelites ruled the land, residents of ancient Akko, as Acre was known, sided with Phoenician enemies of Israel. Akko was the land of Canaan. In 165 BCE, when Judas Maccabeus drove the enemies of Israel to the sea, he deposited them at Akko.

Romans controlled Acre, they knew as Ptolemais, while Cleopatra and Caesar were dreaming of merging empires of Rome and Egypt. Roman control bridged the period from pagan to Christian times. Arab inhabitants of Acre, Christians or not, were within the Byzantine Empire, with its capital at Constantinople. Centuries before the Byzantine Empire fell to the Ottoman Empire in 1453; Acre was already an Ottoman fortified city from which to attack the Byzantines.

In the effort to contain the westward spread of Muslim empires, popes sent forth crusades from Rome. The Vatican sanctioned forces, the Knights Templar and the Knights of St. John Hospitaller, came to liberate the Holy Land in the name of Christianity. Acre was the first, and the last, stronghold of the knights in their battles with Muslim forces from 1104 to 1291.

The Ottoman Empire began to crumble in the late nineteenth century. By the end of World War I, the Ottoman Empire was one of several empires to end their time on the center stage of world dominance.[160] Palestine, the land of the Jews, since Biblical times, and the land of Muslim Arabs since the seventh century, remained a point of contention in building twentieth-century nations.

Britain oversaw a mandate period of attempted government in Palestine, which showed its failings in Acre. In Acre, where the predominant population in 1922 was Arab Muslim, creation of Israel as a Jewish state was met with violence. Historic forts became prisons.

Against a lengthy history of dissension and war, Acre continues to grow as a model for achieving peace. Rather than invite visitors to carefully preserved historic sites, where they may tread pensively through divided neighborhoods, Acre has taken its most revolutionary step toward overcoming its legacy as a venue of violence. This story of Acre ends by showcasing efforts being made today, by Jews and Muslims of Acre, toward building lasting coexistence.

Knights, Crusades and Ottoman Conquest of the Holy Land

Delving into the history of medieval times in Acre requires some understanding of the complex relationships of various power-brokers of the era. Not all Arabs were Muslim, and not all Muslims were Arab. There were evolving alignments among and between descendants of the Prophet and his generals and Persian, Kurdish and Arab Sunni and Shi'ite Muslims. The Knights Templar and Knights of St. John gave their allegiance to the Catholic Pope and not to the Byzantine Emperor of Eastern Orthodoxy in Constantinople. The Great

---

[160] The Austro-Hungarian Empire and the reign of the Romanovs also ended by 1918.

Schism cut ties between the two leaders of Christendom in 1054, about the time large mosques were built in Acre.[161]

Israel, Acre: Citadel of the Knights

During battles between Crusaders, sent by the Pope, or by Orthodox Byzantine Emperors, or during battles with either Saladin, the Sunni-Kurd Sultan of Egypt and Syria, his predecessors, or successors in power, Jews were present in Acre. Their numbers were not large, nor were they armed combatants in the ebb and flow of powerful lords, seeking control of commerce at the port. When the Ottoman Turks took control, their ecumenical style of governance included employees of the Sultan based on skill. Several Jews held responsible positions under the Ottomans.

In the first sweep of generals of the Prophet, as they traveled across the Near East, bringing converts to Islam, Acre soon became a Muslim controlled port. By 861, Acre was a premier naval port of the Abbasid Caliphate. Abbas

---

[161] The leader of the Eastern Orthodox Church in Constantinople declared independence from the Vatican in 1054.

was the uncle of the Prophet Muhammad. The third generation of Abbasid Caliphs founded mosques, including large mosques seen in Acre today.[162]

Trouble in the Holy Land, of which Acre is a gateway, ensued in 1085, when Turks captured Nicaea, a town of Christians and one of significance, as the birthplace of Constantine's Nicaean Code of Christian worship. The Emperor of Byzantium appealed to the Pope for assistance. Pope Urban II responded in 1095, calling for the First Crusade to defend Christianity.[163]

Knights responding to call of the pope were usually second sons of wealthy noblemen. They could raise funds to build armies on behalf of the pope. It was an honor to lead the pope's army.

One of the knights responding to the pope was thirty-five-year-old Godfrey of Bouillon, heir to most of Belgium and the Netherlands, plus land in Germany. He liquidated his assets and amassed an army of forty thousand. In Constantinople, Godfrey was joined by more crusader armies. Byzantine Emperor Alexius I had a substantial force joined to push the Turks out of Nicaea and secure, for a time, Constantinople, capital of Byzantium.

Using the threat of a superior force, Alexius made a deal with the Turks to leave Nicaea to him. Crusading knights were not part of the negotiation. Godfrey and the knights decided to press on to Jerusalem, without Alexius. The army of the Pope and forces of Byzantium separated.

In Jerusalem, the knights faced a different foe. Jerusalem was controlled by Fatimid Muslims, a group descendant from the sister of the Prophet, Fatima, a group initially led by her husband. Crusaders set up a siege of the city. By 1099, Godfrey and his knights were in control of Jerusalem. The army of the pope captured sites of the Holy Sepulcher and ruled Jerusalem as a Christian city.

---

[162] The Abbasid Caliphate were Sunni Islam, whose capital was in Baghdad toward the end of the eighth century. The Caliph controlled north Africa from Tunis east; a strip of northern Egypt; the whole Arab peninsula; and lands east of Turkey, including Persia and Syria. In 1258, the Abbasids were pushed west from Persia by the Khan Mongols. Thereafter, the Abbasid Caliphate moved the capital to Cairo and predominated in Arab territory.

[163] The Pope had hopes that the effort might unite Christians under the Vatican.

Godfrey refused to be called the king of Jerusalem, as he regarded Christ as the only king. When Godfrey died in 1100, and his brother Baldwin succeeded him, Baldwin preferred the title of king. One of the first acts of Baldwin I was to place a siege around Acre, then controlled by Muslims.

It took four years for Baldwin I to secure Acre for his knights. The town was important as a transportation hub in the eastern Mediterranean. Income from commodities transactions greatly increased income of the knights. Protecting the port required an army of knights and a fortress for their housing, storage of goods, and an arsenal. During the reign of Baldwin I, from 1100 to 1118, the population of Acre swelled to 25,000. Only Jerusalem was larger in the knights' domain.

Baldwin II inherited an established kingdom. Loyal to the Pope in Rome, the kingdom of Jerusalem was not a vassal state of the pope. Baldwin II kept a contingent of knights housed on Temple Mount in Jerusalem. Founded in 1119 as a military order, the group became known as the Knights of the Temple Mount, or later, simply the Knights Templar.

Israel, Acre: Knights' last stand in Acre

Not content with the kingdom of Jerusalem, Baldwin II wished to attack Damascus, a trade center with far more wealth than Acre. To accomplish his ambitions, Baldwin II offered his daughter in marriage to the wealthy count of Anjou, France, Fulk V. As a wedding present, Baldwin II gave Acre and the trade center of Tyre to the couple. Fulk V brought more soldiers to the field.

Baldwin II never conquered Damascus. He left a wealthy estate to Fulk V, his daughter Melisende and their son Baldwin. In a bit of family intrigue, Melisende ruled as a much-loved queen-regent for her son, the future Baldwin III. Fulk tried to assert himself and marginalize Melisende. Court insiders rallied around Melisende, and Fulk soon died in a hunting accident.

In 1144, rival Muslim tribes seized crusader territory in an area of Syria today. The pope called for a second crusade to regain the land. A council was held in Acre to decide a battle strategy. Attending the conference were King Louis VII of France and his queen, Eleanor of Aquitaine. Eleanor and Melisende preferred to take control of the territory by attacking Aleppo since Jerusalem had a treaty with Damascus. The knights chose to attack Damascus. The attack was not successful, forever damaged relations between the two trading cities, and when Jerusalem was under siege by Saladin decades later, Damascus did not send aid.

Melisende was so appreciated as a ruler, that when Baldwin III came of age, the royal council denied him a sole coronation. Mother and son ruled jointly. He invaded Jerusalem, causing a civil war. Melisende negotiated a peace, by conceding most of the domain. In 1158, when Baldwin III was twenty-eight, he married a Byzantine princess. His wedding gift to her was Acre.

Melisende died in 1161, Baldwin III was poisoned in 1163, and his brother Amalric became king. Amalric's contribution to discord in the region was to join with the Byzantine Empire in attacking Egypt. In so doing, the young Egyptian military leader Salah ad-Din, or Saladin, established his priority for taking Jerusalem when he later rose to found the next dynasty of Ayyubid leaders.[164]

---

[164] Saladin rose from his Kurdish origin to head the powerful Ayyubid dynasty. He vanquished Fatimah Muslims, and took control of Egypt and Syria.

Saladin brought his military to Acre in 1187, easily taking the city. The man who rose to retake Acre and Jerusalem was Guy of Lusignan, prince of a small domain in west-central France. Guy's brother distinguished himself in Cyprus, so Guy went to Jerusalem in his knightly quest.

Guy quickly married Sibylla, Queen of Jerusalem, giving him legitimacy as the king of Jerusalem in the period of reconquest. When Guy besieged Saladin in Acre, Saladin sent in his overwhelming forces to besiege the besiegers. Guy was caught in the middle of a hopeless situation. His plight spurred the pope to call for a Third Crusade to the Holy Land.

Answering the call to save Jerusalem for Christianity were King Richard I of England and King Philip II of France. These were the glory days of knights in shining armor. To die in defense of the Holy Land was an honor. To return safely home was heroic.

Israel, Acre: Knights' Escape Tunnel

Christian knights were successful in retaking Acre. Their attempt on Jerusalem failed. Guy claimed his kingship of Jerusalem until 1192, when he moved on to Cyprus. The knights made Acre their Holy Land capital for the next century.[165]

Buildings dating to the period of the knights seen today were built after 1193, when the knights retook Acre and failed to take Jerusalem. Building fortifications within the city and connecting the city to a secure port was the focus of their activity and expenditure. Access created at this time from the castle to the port, through a connecting tunnel, exists today.

By 1291, the port of Acre was within city walls. There were twelve towers along the wall, each named for the benefactor king or country of the tower, or section of wall. The German Teutonic knights built a tower, as did the English knights of St. Thomas. The Knights Templar operated the tower nearest the sea, and the Knights Hospitaller took responsibility for the central tower. Each of the knight organizations had a building in the city. They jointly armed the castle, seen today, just inside the Gate of St. Anthony. It is still an imposing structure today.

Knights funded their efforts by taking enemy ships, defined as those, not of a Christian empire. Remnants of their inner harbor can be seen today. Nearest the harbor were enclaves of Genoans, Pisans and Venetians, representing the main Italian power cities of international commerce from the ninth to the sixteenth century. During residence of the knights, Acre was a major port.

In 1291, a powerful group known as the Mamluks[166] rose to take over the Ayyubid empire. The Mamluk siege of Acre was an all-out battle not only for control of the Holy Land, to the victor also went control of the eastern Mediterranean. Mamluk forces brought to the siege were 200,000 strong, pitted against fifteen thousand knights. The Siege of Acre was a bloody affair.

---

[165] There were three additional crusades to the Holy Land. The Fourth crusade in 1204, never went beyond sacking and burning Christian Constantinople. The Fifth and Sixth Crusades were unsuccessful attempts to capture Jerusalem in 1221 and 1228.

[166] Sometimes spelled as Mamelukes. The word means slave. The soldiers began as slave or mercenary soldiers.

After expulsion from the Holy Land in 1291, the Knights of St. John were homeless. They eventually found a new capital city for their enterprise in Rhodes. That is another story.[167]

The Mamluks were mercenary soldiers, not administrators of a vast domain. They were overcome by the Ottoman dynasty, which took control of the eastern Mediterranean from Egypt to Greece. The Mediterranean became known as an Ottoman Lake, until the Napoleonic Wars of the nineteenth century and world wars of the twentieth century. In 1799, Ottoman Turks, assisted by the British, repulsed Napoleon in his unsuccessful siege of Acre. After World War I, and the demise of the Ottoman Empire, British officials administered the city.

Twentieth Century Discord

Acre began the twentieth century as a city in flux. Jewish leaders of a movement to oust the British were incarcerated in the old fort at Acre. It became a prison, in which several leaders of the Zionist underground organization, Irgun, were executed.[168] Prisoners, Jewish and Muslim, were freed in May 1947, in a prison break accomplished by Irgun.

In 1947, the United Nations devised a partition plan for Israel. The plan created the Jewish State of Israel in 1948. In the partition plan, Acre was held out of the Jewish state to become part of a possible Arab state. Those plans were put on hold when Israel's Arab neighbors began a war.

In over five hundred years of Mamluk then Ottoman rule, Acre was predominantly an Arab and Muslim city. Major mosques of significance were built in the city. Several historic mosques can be seen today. The population of over seventeen thousand was predominately Muslim in 1948.

Acre was drawn into the Arab-Israeli War. When Israel prevailed in the war, Acre was subsumed into the state of Israel. Over thirteen thousand inhabitants

---

[167] Knights Templar went their own way, on a somewhat surreptitious path, while the Teutonic Knights next appear in history in Germany and the Baltic.

[168] Irgun was a group formed from the Hagenah Zionist forces.

Israel, Acre: Mosque of Old Acre

of the city relocated. Those who remained formed the core of the old city, known by its historical name of Akko. Surrounding neighborhoods of Acre were populated by Jews, Christians and Baha'i residents.

Today, the greater area of Acre is a city of over forty-six thousand residents. Of those, one third are Muslim, and two-thirds are predominately Jewish. The population includes Arabs from the desert who have moved into the city and Jews of Europe and Russia, who have moved to Israel.

Building a City of Coexistence

The long history of Acre as a geographically desirable port city has also placed it in the center of controversy. In the last millennium, there have been few centuries of peace in the city. The knights used Acre as their stronghold from which to mount an assault on Jerusalem. In the Partition Era of Israel statehood, Acre was a Muslim/Arab center of assaults on Jewish enclaves.

Residents of Acre today: Jewish, Muslim, Christian and Baha'i, realize that violence only begets more violence. War is an expression of frustration. War does not resolve human issues.

Working together, residents of Acre have devised a model city of coexistence. Where religion separates people by tradition and culture, the city of Acre has multiple programs, where all religions have a common responsibility to promote a secular understanding of a civic environment that is multi-cultural tolerant. Peaceful interaction is a work in progress toward acceptance of differences. Violence has been replaced in Acre with an effort toward understanding. It is a work in progress.

The Sir Charles Clore Jewish-Arab Community Center and Mohammed Faheli founded Jewish-Arab Association, are examples of community-building across religious lines. Theatre and the arts are used as a means of personal expression to build understanding. Inter-denomination youth programs and summer camps teach tolerance rather than violence as a means of intercultural interaction.

Visiting Acre Today

Visitors to Acre today, arriving in October, may attend the Akko Festival of Alternative Israeli Theatre, performed and staged by Jewish and Arab producers and actors. Children from city youth programs assist visitors to understand their city, as the children look beyond cultural borders.

Under Acre's central city plaza, archaeologists have excavated and partially reconstructed a three millennia-old settlement, dating to the Canaanites. In the welcome center, visitors are treated to an animated vision of Roman-era Acre. Guided tours walk through streets of crusader and Ottoman buildings of the old city. The castle of the knights is a museum, an event space, and an extension of present-day Acre. The city has five-hundred-year-old dwellings incorporated into eight-hundred-year old city walls. The eighteenth-century White Mosque, or known by its historical name of Al-Jazzar Mosque, sits within a residential neighborhood as it has for two hundred years. The ancient port of Acre is an archaeological site and a parking lot.

Acre is a city of history. It is also a living city. If the programs which bring together residents of diverse cosmology and united geography will endure, Acre will be a model city, not only as a World Heritage Site city, but also as a world model of coexistence, tolerance and peace.

Israel, Acre: Spice Market

INDEX

A